His Royal Seduction

MELANIE MILBURNE

KATE WALKER

ELIZABETH POWER

MILLS & BOON

Published in Great Britain 2015
by Mills & Boon, an imprint of Harlequin (UK) Limited,
Eton House, 18-24 Paradise Road, Richmond, Surrey, TW9 1SR

HIS REVENGE SEDUCTION © 2015 Harlequin Books S.A.

The Mélendez Forgotten Marriage, The Konstantos Marriage Demand and *For Revenge or Redemption?* were first published in Great Britain by Harlequin (UK) Limited.

The Mélendez Forgotten Marriage © 2010 Melanie Milburne
The Konstantos Marriage Demand © 2009 Kate Walker
For Revenge or Redemption? © 2010 Elizabeth Power

ISBN: 978-0-263-25200-2
eBook ISBN: 978-1-474-00379-7

05-0215

THE MÉLENDEZ FORGOTTEN MARRIAGE

BY
MELANIE MILBURNE

Melanie Milburne says: "I am married to a surgeon, Steve, and have two gorgeous sons, Paul and Phil. I live in Hobart, Tasmania, where I enjoy an active life as a long-distance runner and a nationally ranked top ten Master's swimmer. I also have a Master's Degree in Education, but my children totally turned me off the idea of teaching! When not running or swimming I write, and when I'm not doing all of the above I'm reading. And if someone could invent a way for me to read during a four-kilometre swim I'd be even happier!"

To Gaile Donoghue,
a loyal and trusted friend for more years
than I can count. Thank you for your love and support.

Also, special thanks to Rebecca Fleming
and her grandmother, who were so helpful with
translating some words for me into Spanish. Thanks!

CHAPTER ONE

EVEN before Emelia opened her eyes she knew she was in hospital. At the blurred edges of her consciousness she vaguely registered the sound of shoes squeaking on polished linoleum and the swish of curtains and voices, both male and female, speaking in low hushed tones.

She half-opened her eyes. The light was bright, making her pupils shrink painfully. She squeezed her eyes shut and, after a moment or two, blinked again and, narrowing her still flinching gaze, looked at the nurse who was standing at the end of the bed with a chart in her hands.

'W-what happened?' Emelia asked, trying to lift herself upright in the bed. 'What am I doing here? What's going on?'

The nurse clipped the folder on the end of the bed before coming to lay a gentle hand on Emelia's shoulder to ease her back down. 'Mrs Mélendez, please don't upset yourself. You're in hospital. You had a car accident a week ago. You've been in a coma.'

Emelia felt her heart give a jerky beat in her chest like a kick. She frowned and then wished she hadn't as it made her head ache unbearably. She put a hand up to her forehead, her fingers encountering a thickly wadded bandage positioned there.

Hospital? Accident? Coma?

The words were foreign to her, but the most foreign of all was how the nurse had addressed her. 'W-what did you call me?' she asked, staring at the nurse with her heart still thudding out of time.

The nurse glanced over her shoulder as if looking for backup. 'Erm…I think I'd better get the doctor to explain,' she said and quickly bustled away.

Emelia felt as if she were trying to find her way through a thick fog while blindfolded. *Accident? What accident?* She looked down at her sheet and hospital blanket-covered body. Although she ached all over, she seemed to be in all one piece. No plaster casts were on any of her limbs so she obviously hadn't broken any bones. The worst pain was from her head, although she felt horrendously nauseous, but she assumed that was from the pain medication she had been given. She could see the drip leading from a vein in the back of her left hand where it was lying on the top of the bed. She quickly looked away as her stomach gave a rolling turn.

What had the nurse called her again… Mrs Mel… something or other? Her heart gave another little stutter. *Married?* Of course she wasn't married! There must be some mistake, a mix-up in the paperwork or something. They'd obviously got her name wrong. Her name was Emelia Louise Shelverton. She had moved abroad from Australia a couple of months ago. She lived in London, in Notting Hill. She worked part-time as a singer in The Silver Room at one of the top hotels a couple of blocks from Mayfair while she looked for a more permanent position as a music teacher.

Married? What a laugh. She wasn't even dating anyone.

'Ah, so you are finally awake.' A man who was clearly one of the senior doctors swished the curtains around Emelia's bed closed. 'That is very good news indeed. We've been quite worried about you, young lady.'

Emelia glanced at his name tag through eyes that were still slightly blurry. 'Dr…um…Pratchett? What am I doing in hospital? I don't know what's going on. I think there's been some sort of mistake. The nurse called me Mrs something or other but I'm not married.'

The doctor gave her a formal trust-me-I'm-a-doctor smile. 'You have suffered a head injury, Emelia,' he said. 'This has obviously caused you to have some memory loss. We don't know how extensive it is until we conduct further tests. I will have the staff psychologist assess you presently. We may also need to rescan you under MRI.'

Emelia put her hand to her head again, her brows coming together in a tight frown. 'I…I have amnesia?'

The doctor nodded. 'It seems so. Do you know what day it is?'

Emelia thought for a moment but knew she was only guessing when she offered, 'Friday?'

'It is Monday,' Dr Pratchett said. 'September tenth.'

Emelia drew in an uneven breath. 'What year is it?' she asked in a frightened whisper.

The doctor told her and she blinked at him in horror. 'That can't be right,' she said. 'I can't have forgotten two years of my life. That's ridiculous!'

Dr Pratchett placed his hand over hers where it was lying on the bed clutching the sheet in her fingers. 'Try to keep calm, Emelia,' he said soothingly. 'This is, of course, a very frightening and confusing time for you. You have been in a coma for several days so things will seem a little strange at first. But in time you may well remember everything. It just takes a little time. You need to take things very slowly at first. Baby steps, my dear. Baby steps.'

Emelia pulled her hand out from beneath the doctor's, holding it up like an exhibit at an investigation. 'Look,' she said, pushing her chin up. 'No rings. I told you—there's been some sort of mix-up. I'm not married.'

'You are very definitely Mrs Emelia Louise Mélendez,' the doctor assured her with authority. 'That is the name the police found on your driver's licence. Your husband is waiting outside to see you. He flew over from Spain as soon as he was informed of your accident. He has positively identified you as his wife. He has barely left your bedside the whole time you have been unconscious. He just stepped out a moment ago to take a phone call.'

Emelia's mouth fell open so wide she felt her chin drop almost to her chest. She felt her heart boom like a cannon exploding in her chest.

Her husband?

Her *Spanish* husband?

She didn't even know his Christian name. How could it be possible for her to forget something as important as that? Where had they met? When had they got married? Had they? How many times…?

Her stomach gave a funny little quiver… It wasn't possible…*was it*? How could she have lived with and loved a man and not remember him? Her skin broke out in a sweat, her palms hot and moist with uncertainty and fear. Was she dreaming? Surely she must be dreaming. *Think. Think. Think.*

What was the last thing she had been doing? She scrunched her eyes closed and forced herself to concentrate but her head pounded sickeningly as she tried to recall the last few days. It was all a blur, a foggy indistinct blur that made little, if any, sense.

When Emelia opened her eyes the doctor had already moved through a gap in the curtains and a short time later they twitched aside again, the rattle of the rings holding the curtain on the rail sounding too loud inside her head.

She felt her breath stall in her throat.

A tall raven-haired stranger with coal-black deep set eyes stood at the end of the bed. There was nothing that was even vaguely familiar about him. She studied his face for endless seconds, her bruised brain struggling to place him. She didn't recognise any one of his dark, classically handsome features. Not his tanned, intelligent-looking forehead or his dark thick brows over amazingly bottomless eyes or that not short, not long raven-black hair that looked as if it had last been groomed with his fingers. She didn't recognise that prominent blade of a nose, and neither did she recognise that heavily shadowed jaw that looked as if it had an uncompromising set to it, and nor that mouth... Her belly gave another involuntary movement, like a mouse trying to scuttle over a highly polished floor. His mouth was sculptured; the top lip would have been described as slightly cruel if it hadn't been for the sensual fullness of his lower one. That was a mouth that knew how to kiss and to kiss to conquer, she thought, as her belly gave another little jiggle. She sent the tip of her tongue out to the sand dune of her lips. Had *she* been conquered by that mouth? If so, why couldn't she remember it?

'Emelia.'

Emelia felt her spine prickle at the way he said her name. His Spanish accent gave the four syllables an exotic allure, making every part of her acutely aware of him, even if she didn't know who the hell he was.

'Um… Hi…' What else was she supposed to say? *Hello, darling, how nice to see you again?*

She cleared her throat, her fingers beginning to pluck at the hem of the sheet pulled across her middle. 'Sorry…I'm a little confused right now…'

'It's quite all right.' He came to the side of her bed in a couple of strides, his tall presence all the more looming as he stood within touching distance, looking down at her with those inscrutable black eyes.

Emelia caught a whiff of his aftershave. It wasn't strong, but then he looked as if he hadn't shaved for a couple of days. There was a masculine urgency about the black stubble peppering his jaw, making her think of the potent male hormones surging through his body. She shakily breathed in another waft of his aftershave. The light fragrance had citrus undertones that smelt vaguely familiar. Her forehead creased as she tried to concentrate… Lemons…sun-warmed lemons…a hint of lime or was it lemon grass?

'The doctor said I can take you home as soon as you are well enough to travel,' the man said.

Emelia felt the skin on her back tingle all over again at the sound of his voice. It had such a sexy timbre, deep and low and unmistakably sensual. She could imagine him speaking in his native tongue; the musical cadences of Spanish had always delighted her. But there was something about his demeanour that alerted her to an undercurrent of tension. There was something about the unreachable depths of his eyes. There was something about the way he hadn't yet touched her. Not that she wanted him to…or did she?

She glanced at his long fingered tanned hands. They were hanging loosely by his sides—or was that a tight clench of his fingers he had just surreptitiously released?

Her eyes slowly moved up to meet his. Her chest tightened and her breathing halted. Was that anger she could see in that tiny flicker of a nerve pulsing by the side of his mouth?

No, of course it couldn't be anger. He was upset, that was what it was. He was obviously shocked to see her like this. What husband wouldn't be, especially if his own wife didn't even know who he was?

She moistened her lips again, trying to find a way out of the confusing labyrinthine maze of her mind. 'I'm sorry…you must think I'm terrible…but I don't even know…I mean…I…I…I don't remember your name…'

His top lip lifted in a movement that should have been a wry smile but somehow Emelia suspected it wasn't. 'I do not think you are terrible, Emelia,' he said. 'You have amnesia, sí? There is much you do not remember, but in time hopefully it will all come back to you. The doctor seems to think your memory loss will not be permanent.'

Emelia swallowed. What if it was? She had read a story a couple of years ago about a young woman who had lost her memory after a horrific attack. Her whole life had changed as a result. She hadn't even recognised her parents. Her brother and two sisters were total strangers to her.

'Perhaps I should introduce myself,' the man said, breaking through her tortured reverie. 'My name is Javier Mélendez. I am your husband. We have been married for almost two years.'

Emelia felt the cacophonous boom of her heart again. It felt as if her chest wall was going to blow open with the sheer force of it. She struggled to contain her composure, her fingers now clutching at the sheet of the bed either side of her body as if to anchor herself. 'M-married?' she choked. 'Truly? This is not a joke or something? We are legally married?'

He gave a single nod. 'It is our anniversary at the end of next month.'

Emelia had no hope of disguising her shock. She opened and closed her mouth, trying to get her voice to work. Her brain was flying off in all directions, confused, frightened, lost. How could this be? How could this man be her husband? How could her mind let her down in such a way? How could she forget her own wedding day? What cruel stroke of fate had erased it from her memory? She let out a breath that rattled through her lungs. 'Um…where did we meet?' she asked.

'We met at The Silver Room in London,' he said. 'You were playing one of my favourite songs as I walked in.'

Emelia ran her tongue over her lips again as part of the fog cleared in her head. 'I…I remember The Silver Room…' She put her hand to her aching eyes. 'I can picture it. The chandeliers…the piano…'

'Do you remember your employer?' Javier asked.

Emelia looked up at him again but his eyes were like glittering diamonds: hard and impenetrable.

'Peter Marshall…' she said after a moment, her spirits instantly lifting as the memories flooded back. At least she hadn't lost too much of her past, she thought in cautious relief. 'He manages the hotel. He's from Australia like me. I've known him since childhood. We went to neighbouring private schools. He gave me the job in the piano bar. He's been helping me find work as a private music teacher…'

Something flickered in his gaze, a quick lightning flash of something she couldn't quite identify. 'Do you remember why you came to London in the first place?' he asked in a voice that was toneless, showing no hint of emotion.

Emelia looked down at her hands for a moment. 'Yes…yes I do…' she said, returning her gaze to his. 'My father and I had a falling out. A big one. We have a rather difficult relationship, or at least we have had since my mother died. He married within a couple of months of her death. His new wife…the latest one? We didn't get on. Actually, I haven't got on with any of his wives. There have been four so far…' She lowered her gaze and sighed. 'It's complicated…'

'Yes,' he said. 'It always is.'

She brought her gaze back to his, searching his features for a moment. 'I guess if we're married I must have told you about it many times. How stubborn my father is.'

'Yes, you have,' he said, 'many times.'

Emelia pressed her fingers to the corners of her eyes, her frown still tight. 'Why can't I remember you?' she asked. 'I *should* be able to remember you.' *I need to be able to remember you, otherwise I will be living with a total stranger,* she thought in rising alarm.

His dark eyes gave nothing away. 'The doctor said you should not rush things, *querida*,' he said. 'You will remember when the time is right. It might take a few days or maybe even a few weeks.'

Emelia swallowed a tight knot of panic. 'But what if I don't?' she asked in a broken whisper. 'What if I never remember the last two years of my life?'

One of his broad shoulders rose and fell in a dismissive shrug that Emelia somehow felt wasn't quite representative of how he felt. 'Do not concern yourself with things that are out of your control,' he said. 'Perhaps when you are back at home at my villa in Seville you will remember bits and pieces.'

He waited a beat before continuing. 'You loved the villa. You said when I first took you there it was the most beautiful place you had ever seen.'

Emelia tried to picture it but her mind continued to be a blank. 'What was I doing in London?' she asked as soon as the thought popped into her head. 'You weren't with me in the car, were you?'

That lightning-quick movement came and went in his gaze again; it was like the hand of an illusionist making something disappear before the audience could see how it was done. 'No, I was not,' he said. 'You were with your—' he paused for a moment '—with Peter Marshall.'

Emelia felt a hand grab at her insides and twist them cruelly. 'Peter was with me?' Her heart gave a lurch against her breastbone. 'Was he injured? Is he all right? Can I see him? Where is he? How is he?'

The ensuing silence after her rapid fire of panicked questions seemed to contain a deep and low back beat, a slow steady rhythm that seemed to be building and building, leading Emelia inexorably to a disharmonious chord she didn't want to hear.

'I am sorry to be the one to inform you of this, but Marshall did not survive the accident,' Javier said again without any trace of emotion in his voice.

Emelia blinked at him in stunned shock. *Peter was dead?* Her mind couldn't process the information. It kept shrinking back from it, like a battered dog cowering out of reach of the next anticipated blow. *'No…'* The word came out hoarsely in a voice she didn't recognise as her own. 'No, that can't be. He can't be dead. He *can't* be… We had such plans…'

Javier's expression didn't change. Not even a flicker of a muscle in his jaw revealed an iota of what he was feeling. It was as if he were reading from a script for a role he had no intention of playing. His words were wooden, cool. 'He is dead, Emelia. The doctors couldn't save him.'

Emelia felt tears burst from her eyes, hot scalding tears that ran unchecked down her cheeks. 'But I loved him so much…' Her voice was barely audible. 'We've known each other for years. We grew up in the same suburb. He was such a supportive friend to me…' A thought hit her like a glancing blow and her eyes widened in horror. 'Oh, God…' she gulped. 'Who was driving? Did I kill him? Oh, God, God, God—'

He touched her then. His hand came down over hers on the bed just like the doctor's had done earlier, but his touch felt nothing like the cool, smooth professional hand of the *medico*'s. Javier's touch was like a scorching brand, a blistering heat that scored her flesh to the fragile bones of her hand as he pinned it beneath the strength of his. 'No, you did not kill him,' he said flatly. 'You were not driving. He was. He was speeding.'

Her relief was a minute consolation given the loss of a dear friend. *Peter was dead?* The three words whirled around and around in her head but she wouldn't allow them to settle. Maybe she was dreaming. Maybe this was nothing but a horrible nightmare. Maybe she would wake up any second and find herself lying in her sunny shoebox flat in Notting Hill, looking forward to meeting up with Peter later to discuss the programme for that night's performance, just as she did every night before taking her place at the grand piano.

Emelia looked down at her hand beneath the tanned weight of Javier Mélendez's. There was something about his touch that triggered something deep inside her body. Her blood recognised him even if her mind did not. She felt the flicker of it as it began to race in her veins, the rapid escalation of her pulse making her heart pound at the thought of him touching her elsewhere. *Had* he touched her elsewhere? Well, of course he must have if they were married…

She gave her head a little shake but it felt as if a jar of marbles had spilled inside. She groaned and put her free hand to her temple, confusion, despair, grief and disbelief all jostling for position.

Javier squeezed her hand with the gentlest of pressure but even so she felt the latent strength leashed there. 'I realise all this must be a terrible shock. There was no easy way of telling you.'

Emelia blinked away her tears, her throat feeling so dry she could barely swallow the fist-sized wad of sadness there. As if he had read her mind, he released her hand and pulled the bed table closer, before pouring her a glass of water and handing it to her.

'Here,' he said, holding the glass for her as if she were a small child. 'Drink this. It will make you feel better.'

Emelia was convinced nothing was ever going to make her feel better. How was a sip of water going to bring back her oldest friend? She frowned as she pushed the glass away once she had taken a token sip. 'I don't understand…' She raised her eyes to Javier's ink-black gaze. 'Why was I in London if I am supposedly married and living with you in…in Seville, did you say?'

His eyes moved away from hers as he set the water glass back on the table. 'Seville, yes,' he said. 'A few kilometres out. That is where I…where we live.'

Emelia heard the way he corrected himself and wondered if that was some sort of clue. She looked at his left hand and saw the gold band of a wedding ring nestled amongst the sprinkling of dark hairs of his long tanned finger. She felt another roller coaster dip inside her stomach and doing her best to ignore it, looked back up at him. 'If we are married as you say, then where are my rings?' she asked.

He reached inside his trouser pocket and took out two rings. She held her breath as he picked up her hand, slipping each of the rings on with ease. She looked at the brilliance of the princess cut diamond engagement ring and the matching wedding band with its glittering array of sparkling diamonds set right around the band. Surely something so beautiful, so incredibly expensive would trigger some sort of memory in her brain?

Nothing.

Nada.

Emelia raised her eyes back to his. 'So…I was in London…alone?'

His eyes were like shuttered windows. 'I was away on business in Moscow,' he said. 'I travel there a lot. You had travelled to London to…to shop.'

There it was again, she thought. A slight pause before he chose his words. 'Why didn't I go to Moscow with you?' she asked, frowning.

It was a moment before he answered. Emelia couldn't help feeling he was holding something back from her, something important.

'You did not always travel with me on my trips, particularly the foreign ones,' he finally answered. 'You preferred to spend time at home or in London. The shops were more familiar and you didn't have to worry about the language.'

Emelia bit her lip, her fingers plucking again at the sheet covering her. 'That's strange…I hate shopping. I can never find the right size and I don't like being pressured by the sales assistants.'

He didn't answer. He just stood there looking down at her with that expressionless face, making Emelia feel as if she had stepped into someone else's life, not her own. If she was deeply in love with him she would have gone with him, surely? What sort of wife was she to go off shopping—an activity she normally loathed—in another country instead of being by his side? It certainly didn't sound very devoted of her. More disturbing, it sounded a little bit like something her mother would have done while she was still alive.

After a long moment she forced herself to meet his gaze once more. 'Um…I know this might seem a strange question but—' she quickly licked her lips for courage before she continued '—were we…happily married?'

The question seemed to hang suspended in the air for a very long time.

Emelia's head began to ache unbearably as she tried to read his expression, to see if any slight movement of his lips, eyes or forehead would provide some clue to the state of the relationship they apparently shared.

Finally his lips stretched into a brief on-off smile that didn't involve his eyes. 'But of course, *cariño*,' he said. 'Why would we not be happy? We were only married for not quite two years, *sí*? That is not long enough to become bored or tired of each other.'

Emelia was so confused, so very bewildered. It was totally surreal to be lying here without any knowledge of her relationship with him. Surely this was the stuff of movies and fiction. Did this really happen to ordinary people like her? She began to fidget with the sheet again, desperate to be alone so she could think. 'I'm sorry but I'm very tired…'

He stepped back from the bed. 'It's all right,' he said. 'I have business to see to, in any case. I will leave you to rest.'

He was almost through the curtains when she found her voice again. 'Um…Javier?'

His long back seemed to stiffen momentarily before he turned to look at her. 'Yes, Emelia?'

Emelia searched his features once more, desperate to find some hook on which to hang her new, totally unfamiliar life. 'I'm sorry…so very sorry for not recognising you…' She bit her lip again, releasing it to add, 'If it was me in your place, I know I would be devastatingly hurt.'

His dark eyes seared hers for a beat or two before they fell away as he turned to leave. 'Forget about it, *querida*,' he said.

It was only after the curtains had whispered against each other as they closed did Emelia realise the irony of his parting words.

CHAPTER TWO

'WELL, today's the big day,' the cheery nurse on duty said brightly as she swished back the curtains of the private room windows where Emelia had spent the last few days after being moved out of the High Dependency Unit. 'You're finally going home with that gorgeous husband of yours. I tell you, my girl, I wouldn't mind changes places with you, that I wouldn't,' she added with a grin as she plucked the pillows off the bed in preparation for a linen change. 'If his looks weren't enough compensation, just think—I wouldn't have to work again, married to all that money.'

Emelia gave the nurse a tight smile as she tried to ignore the way her stomach nosedived at the mention of the tall, dark, brooding stranger who had faithfully visited her each day, saying little, smiling even less, touching her only if necessary, as if somehow sensing she wasn't ready for a return to their previous intimacy. To limit her interaction with him, she had mostly feigned sleep, but she knew once she went home with him she would have to face the reality of their relationship.

She had seen how the nurses practically swooned

when he came onto the ward each day. And this one called Bridget was not the only one to gently tease her about not recognising him. Everyone seemed reasonably confident her memory loss would be temporary, but Emelia couldn't help worrying about the missing pieces and how they would impact on her once she left the relative sanctuary of the hospital.

She had spoken to the staff psychologist about her misgivings and what she perceived was Javier's tension around her. Dr Carey had described how some partners found it hard to accept they were not recognised by the one they loved and that it would take a lot of time and patience on both sides to restore the relationship to what it had been before the accident. There could be anger and resentment and a host of other feelings that would have to be dealt with in time.

The psychologist had advised Emelia to take time to get to know her husband all over again. 'Things will be more natural between you once you are in familiar surroundings,' Dr Carey had assured her. 'Busy hospitals are not the most conducive environment to re-establish intimacy.'

Emelia thought about her future as she waited for Javier to collect her. She sat on the edge of the bed, trying not to think about the possibility of never remembering the last two years of her life. She had no memory of her first meeting with Javier, no memory of their first kiss, let alone their wedding day and what had followed. He had said she loved his villa but she couldn't even imagine what it looked like. She was being taken to live in a foreign country with a man who was a stranger to her in every way.

She ran her hands down her tanned and toned thighs.

She couldn't help noticing how slim she was now. Surely she hadn't lost that much weight during her coma? She had only been unconscious a week. She had struggled on and off with her weight for most of her life and yet now she was almost reed-thin. Her legs and arms were toned and her stomach had lost its annoying little pouch. It was flat and ridged with muscle she hadn't known she possessed.

Was this how Javier liked her to look? Had she adopted a gym bunny lifestyle to keep him attracted to her? How soon had she succumbed to his attentions? Had she made him wait or had she capitulated as soon as he had shown his interest in her? What had he seen in her? She knew she was blessed with reasonable looks but somehow, with his arrestingly handsome features and aristocratic bearing, he seemed the type who would prefer supermodel glamour and sophistication.

The police had come in earlier and interviewed her but she had not been able to tell them anything at all about the accident. It too was all a blank, a black hole in her memory that no attempt on her part could fill.

One of the constables had brought Emelia her handbag, retrieved from the accident, but even searching through it she felt as if it belonged to someone else. There was the usual collection of lip gloss and pens and tissues and gum, a frighteningly expensive atomizer of perfume and a sophisticated mobile phone that hadn't survived the impact. The screen was cracked and it refused to turn on.

She took out a packet of contraceptive pills and stared at the name on the box: *Emelia Mélendez*. There were only a couple of pills left in the press out card. She fingered the foil rectangle for a minute and then, without another thought, tossed it along with the packet in the rubbish bag taped to the edge of her bedside table.

Emelia placed her hand on her chest near her heart, trying to ease the pain of never seeing Peter again. That was a part of her life that was finished. She hadn't even been given the chance to say goodbye.

Javier schooled his features into blankness as he entered the private suite. '*Cariño,*' he said, 'I see you are all packed and ready to leave.'

He saw the flicker of uncertainty in her grey-blue gaze before she lowered it. 'There wasn't much to pack,' she said, slipping off the bed to stand upright.

He put out a hand to steady her but she moved out of his reach, as if his touch repelled her. He set his jaw, fighting back his fury. She didn't used to flinch from his touch. She used to be hungry for it. He thought of all the times he had taken her, quickly, passionately, slowly, sensually. She hadn't recoiled from his love-making until Marshall had come back on the scene. Javier's gut roiled with the thought of what she had got up to while his back was turned. How convenient for her to forget her perfidy now when the stakes had changed. The way she had received the news of Marshall's death confirmed her depth of feeling for him. She hadn't forgotten her lover and yet she had for-gotten him—her legal husband.

Javier clenched his fingers around the handle of the small bag containing Emelia's belongings. A tiny flick knife of guilt nicked at him deep inside. He had to admit there were some things he hoped she wouldn't remember about their last heated argument. He had lost control in a way that deeply ashamed him. Had his actions during that ugly scene driven her into her lover's arms? Or had she been planning to run away with Marshall in any case?

What if she *never* remembered him?

No. He was not going to think about that possibility, in spite of what the doctors and the psychologist had said. He lived for the day when she would look at him with full recognition in her grey-blue eyes. For the day she would smile at him and offer her soft, full bee-stung mouth for him to kiss; she would give him her body to pleasure and be pleasured until every last memory of her dead lover was obliterated.

And then and only then he would have his revenge.

'My car is waiting outside,' Javier said. 'I have a private jet waiting for our departure.'

She gave him one of her bewildered looks. 'You… you have a private jet?'

'*Sí*,' he answered. 'You are married to a very rich man, *mi amor*, or have you forgotten that too?'

She bit into her bottom lip, her gaze falling away from his as she continued walking by his side. 'Dr Carey, the psychologist, told me some husbands find it very hard to accept their wives don't remember them,' she said. 'I know this must be hard for you. I know you must feel angry and upset.'

You have no idea how angry, Javier thought as he led the way out of the hospital. Anger was like a turbulent flood inside him. His blood was surging with it, bulging in his veins like red-hot lava until he felt he was going to explode with it. How could he conceal the hatred he felt for her at her betrayal? The papers were full of it again this morning, as they had been for the past week.

Every headline seemed to say the same: the speculation about her affair with Marshall, their clandestine dirty little affair that had ended in tragedy. Javier knew he would have to work harder at controlling his emotions. This was not the time to avenge the past. What was the point? Emelia apparently had no recollection of it.

He cupped her elbow with the palm of his hand as he guided her into the waiting limousine. 'I am sorry, *querida*,' he said. 'I am still getting over the shock of almost losing you. Forgive me. I will try and be more considerate.'

She looked at him once he took the seat beside her, her eyes like luminescent pools. 'It's OK,' she said in a whisper-soft voice. 'I'm finding it hard too. I feel like I am living in someone else's body, living someone else's life.'

'It is your life,' Javier said. 'It is the one you chose for yourself.'

She frowned as she absently stroked her fingers over the butter-soft leather of the seat between them. 'How long did we date before we got married?'

'Not long.'

She turned her head to look at him. 'How long?'

'Six weeks.'

Her eyes went wide, like pond water spreading after a flood. 'I can't believe I got married so quickly,' she said, as if talking to herself. She shook her head but then winced as if it had hurt her. She lowered her gaze and tucked a strand of her honey-blonde hair back behind her ear, her tongue sweeping out over her lips, the action igniting a fire in his groin despite all of his attempts to ignore her physical allure. Sitting this close, he could smell the sweet vanilla fragrance of her skin. If he closed his eyes he could picture her writhing beneath him as he pounded into her, his body rocking with hers until they both exploded. He clenched his jaw and turned to look out of the window at the rain lashing down outside.

'Was it a white wedding?' she asked after a little silence.

Javier turned and looked at her. 'Yes, it was. There were over four hundred people there. It was called the wedding of the year. Perhaps if you see the photographs it will trigger something in your memory.'

'Perhaps…' She looked away and began chewing on her bottom lip, her brow furrowing once more.

Javier watched her in silence, mulling over what to tell her and what to leave well alone. The doctor had advised against pressuring her to remember. She was disoriented and still suffering from the blow of losing her lover. Apart from that first show of grief, she hadn't mentioned Peter Marshall again, but every now and then he saw the way her eyes would tear up and a stake would go through his heart all over again.

She suddenly turned and met his gaze. 'Do you have family?' she asked. 'Brothers or sisters and parents?'

'My mother died when I was very young,' he said. 'My father remarried after some years. I have a half-sister called Izabella.' He paused before adding, 'My father left Izabella's mother and after the divorce remarried once again. As predicted by just about everyone who knew him, it didn't work out and he was in the process of divorcing his third wife when he died.'

'I'm sorry for your loss,' she said quietly. 'Did I ever meet him?'

Javier stretched his lips into an embittered smile.

'No. My father and I were estranged at the time. I hadn't spoken to him for ten years.'

Her expression was empathetic. 'How very sad. How did the estrangement come about?'

He drew in a breath and released it slowly. 'My father was a stubborn man. He was hard in business and even harder in his personal life. It's why each of his marriages turned into war zones. He liked control. It irked him that I wanted to take charge of my own life. We exchanged a few heated words and that was it. We never spoke to each other again.'

Emelia studied his stony expression, wondering how far the apple had fallen from the tree. 'Were you alike in looks?' she asked.

His eyes met hers, so dark and mysterious, making her stomach give a little unexpected flutter. 'We shared the same colouring but had little else in common,' he said. 'I was closer to my mother.'

'How old were you when she died?' Emelia asked.

His eyes moved away from hers, his voice when he spoke flat and emotionless. 'I was four, almost five years old.'

Emelia felt her insides clench at the thought of him as a dark-haired, dark-eyed little boy losing his mother so young. She knew the devastation so well. She had been in her early teens when her mother had died, but still it had hit hard. Her adolescence, from fourteen years old, had been so lonely. While not particularly close to either of her high-flying parents, there had been so many times over the years when Emelia had wished she could have had just one more day with her mother. 'Are you close to your half-sister?' she asked.

His lips moved in a brief, indulgent-looking smile

which immediately softened his features, bringing warmth into his eyes. 'Yes, strangely enough. She's a lot younger, of course. She's only just out of her teens but, since my father died, I've taken a more active role in her life. She lives in Paris with her mother but she comes to stay quite regularly.'

'So…I've met her, then?' Emelia asked, trying to ignore the way her stomach shifted in response to his warmer expression.

His eyes came back to hers, studying her for a pulsing moment. 'Yes,' he said. 'You've met her numerous times.'

Emelia moistened her lips, something she seemed to do a lot around him. 'Do we…get on?' she asked, choosing her words carefully.

His unreadable gaze bored into hers. 'Unfortunately, you were not the best of friends. I think it was perhaps because Izabella was used to having my undivided attention. She saw you as a threat, as competition.'

She frowned as she thought about what he had said about his sister. The girl sounded like a spoilt brat, too used to having her own way. No wonder they hadn't got on. 'You said Izabella was used to having you to herself. But surely you'd had women in your life before…before me?'

'But of course.'

Emelia felt a quick dart of jealousy spike her at the arrogant confidence of his statement. Just how many women *had* there been? Not counting him, for she could not recall sleeping with him, she had only had one lover. She had been far too young and had only gone out with the man to annoy her father during one of her teenage fits of rebellion. It was not a period of her life she was particularly proud of and the loss of self-esteem she had experienced during that difficult time had made it hard for her to date with any confidence subsequently.

Her belly gave another little quiver as she thought about what Javier might have taught her in the last two years. Had he tutored her in the carnal delights he seemed to have enjoyed so freely?

His dark eyes began to glint as if he could read her mind. 'We were good together, Emelia,' he said. 'Very, very good.'

She swallowed tightly. 'Um…I…it's…I don't think I'm ready to rush into…you know…picking up where we left off, so to speak.'

He elevated one of his dark brows. 'No?'

Emelia pressed her trembling thighs together, the heat that had pooled between them both surprising and shocking her. 'The doctor said not to rush things. He said I should take things very slowly.'

The little gleam in his eyes was still there as he held her gaze. 'It would not do to go against doctor's orders, now, would it?'

She couldn't stop herself from looking at his mouth. The sensual curve of his lips made her heart start to race. How many times had that mouth sealed hers? Was he a hard kisser or soft? Fast and furious with passion or slow and bone-meltingly commanding? The base of her spine gave a shivery tremor, the sensation moving all the way up to nestle in the fine hairs on the back of her neck.

Her thoughts went racing off again.

Had he kissed her *there*? Had he stroked his long tanned fingers over the nape of her neck? Had he dipped his tongue into the shell of her ear?

Her heart rammed against her ribcage.

Had he gone lower to the secret heart of her? Had he explored her in intimate detail, making her flesh quiver and spasm in delight? What positions had they made love in? Which was their favourite? Had she taken him in her mouth; had she…? Oh, God, *had* she…?

She sneaked a quick glance at him, her face flaming when she encountered his unknowable eyes.

He lifted his hand and with a barely there touch tracked the tip of one of his fingers over the curve of her warm cheek. 'You don't remember anything, do you, *querida*?' he asked in a husky tone.

Emelia pressed her lips together in an effort to stop them from prickling with sensation, with an aching burning need. 'No…no… I'm sorry…'

He gave her a crooked smile that didn't quite make the full distance to his eyes. 'It is no matter. We can take our time and do it all again, step by step. It will be like the first time again, *sí*?'

Emelia felt her heart start to flap as if it had suddenly grown wings. 'I wasn't very experienced…I remember that. I'd only had one lover.'

'You were a fast learner.' His eyes dipped to her mouth, lingering there for a moment before coming back to her eyes. 'Very, very fast.'

She swallowed again to clear the tightness of her throat. 'You must find this rather…unsettling to be married to someone who doesn't even remember how you kiss.'

His fingers went to her chin, propping her face up so she had to lock gazes with him. 'You know, I could clear up that little mystery for you right here and now.'

She tried to pull back but he must have anticipated

it as his fingers subtly tightened. 'I…I wasn't suggesting…' she began.

'No, but I was.'

Emelia felt her skin pop up in goosebumps as he angled his head and slowly brought his mouth within touching distance of hers. She felt the warm breeze of his breath waft over her lips, a feather-light caress that made her mouth tingle with anticipation for more. She waited, her eyes half closed, her heart thudding in expectation as each second passed, throbbing with tension.

His fingers left her chin to splay across her cheeks, his thumbs moving back and forth in a mesmerising motion, his eyes heavy-lidded as they focused on her mouth. She sent her tongue out to moisten her lips, her heart giving another tripping beat as his mouth came just that little bit closer…

'It might complicate things for you if I kiss you right now,' he said in a rumbling deep tone. 'It wouldn't do to compromise your recovery, now would it, *cariño*?'

'Um…I…I…It's probably not a good idea right now…'

He gave a low deep chuckle and released her, sitting back in his seat with indolent grace. 'No,' he said. 'I thought not. But it can wait. For a while.'

Emelia sat in silence, trying to imagine what it was like for him. Of course he would find this situation unbearably frustrating. He was a full-blooded healthy male in the prime of his life. And for the last two years he had been used to having her as his willing wife. Now she was like a stranger to him and him to her. Would her reticence propel him into another woman's arms? The thought was strangely disturbing. Why would the thought of him seeking pleasure in another woman's arms make her feel so on edge and irritable? It wasn't as if she had any memory of their time together.

Emelia looked down at the rings on her finger. It was strange but the weight of them was not as unfamiliar as the man who had placed them there. She turned them around; they were loose on her but she had lost even more weight from being in hospital. She hadn't noticed it earlier but she had a slight tan mark where the rings had been, which put to rest any lingering doubts about the veracity of their marriage. She glanced at him and found him watching her with a brooding set to his features. 'Is everything all right?' she asked.

'Of course,' he said. 'I just hope the flight will not be too tiring for you.'

He leaned forward to say something to the driver. Emelia felt the brush of his thigh against hers and her heart stopped and started at the thought of how many times those long strong legs had been entwined with hers in passion. He had held off from kissing her but how long before he decided to resume their physical relationship in full? She squeezed her thighs together again, wondering if she could feel where he had been; might it have been only just over a week ago?

They boarded the private jet after going through customs. She couldn't remember flying on a private Gulfstream jet before. She couldn't recall even seeing one other than in a magazine. Even her father, as wealthy as he was, always used a commercial plane, albeit business or first class. Had travelling in such opulent luxury and wearing diamonds that were priceless become commonplace to her in the last two years?

Even though Emelia could see her married name on

her passport, it still seemed as if someone had stolen her identity. The stamps on her passport made no sense to her. She had been to Paris, Rome, Prague, Monte Carlo and Zurich and London numerous times yet she remembered nothing of those trips.

The jet was luxuriously appointed, showcasing the wealth Javier had alluded to earlier. He was clearly a man who had made his way in the world in a big way. The staff members were all very respectful and, unlike some of the wealthy men Emelia had met amongst her father's set, Javier treated them with equal respect. He addressed each of them by name and asked after their partners and family as if they were as important to him as his own.

'Would you like today's papers?' one of the flight attendants asked once they were settled in their seats.

'Not today, thank you, Anya,' Javier said with a ghost of a rueful smile.

Emelia suppressed a little frown of annoyance. She would have liked to have read up on the news. After all, it was a different world she lived in now. She had two years' worth of news and gossip to catch up on. And then another thought came to her. Maybe there was something about the accident in the papers, some clue as to what had caused it. Peter, as the manager of a trendy hotel, well frequented by the jet-setting crowd of London, had been a popular public figure. Surely she had a right to know what had led up to the tragic accident that had taken her friend from her.

'Don't pout, *querida*,' Javier said when he caught the tail end of her look. 'I am trying to protect you.'

Emelia frowned at him. 'From what?' she asked.

He gave her one of his unreadable looks. 'I think you

should know there has been some speculation about your accident,' he said.

Her frown deepened. 'What sort of speculation?'

'The usual gossip and innuendo the press like to stir up from time to time,' he said. 'You are the wife of a high profile businessman, Emelia. You might not remember it, but you were regularly hounded by the press for any hint of a scandal. It's what sells papers and magazines, even if the stuff they print isn't always true.'

Emelia chewed on the end of one of her neatly manicured nails. *She* was the focus of the press? How could that be possible? She lived a fairly boring life, or at least she thought she had until after she had woken up from her coma. She had long ago given up her dreams of being a concert pianist and was now concentrating on a career in teaching. But the sort of fame or infamy Javier was talking about had definitely not been a part of her plan.

She dropped her finger from her mouth. 'What are the papers saying about the accident?' she asked.

His dark eyes hardened as they held hers. 'They are saying you were running away with Peter Marshall.'

Emelia opened her eyes wide. 'Running away? As in…as in leaving you?'

'It is just gossip, Emelia,' he said. 'Such things have been said before and no doubt they will be said again. I have to defend myself against similar claims all the time.'

She pressed her lips together. 'I might not be able to remember the last two years of my life but I can assure you I'm not the sort of person to run away with another man whilst married to another,' she said. 'Surely you don't believe any of that stuff?'

He gave her a slight movement of his lips, not exactly a smile, more of a grimace of resignation. 'It is the life we live, *querida*. All high profile people and celebrities are exposed to it. It's the tall poppy syndrome. I did warn you when we met how it would be. I have had to live with it for many years—lies, conjecture, gossip, innuendo. It is the price one pays for being successful.'

Emelia gnawed on her fingernail again as the jet took off from the runway. She didn't like the thought of people deliberately besmirching her name and reputation. She wasn't a cheater. She believed in absolute faithfulness. She had seen first-hand the damage wrought when a partner strayed, as her father had played around on each of his wives, causing so much hurt and distress and the betrayal of trust.

'Do not trouble yourself about it for now,' Javier said into the silence. 'I wouldn't have mentioned the press except they might be waiting for us when we arrive in Spain. I have made arrangements with my security team to provide a decoy but, just in case, do not respond to any of the press's questions, even if they are blatantly untrue or deliberately provocative. Do you understand?'

Emelia felt another frown tug at her brow. 'If they are as intrusive and persistent as you say, I can't evade the press for ever, though, can I?' she asked.

His eyes were determined as they tethered hers. 'For the time being, Emelia, you will do as I say. I am your husband. Please try to remember that, if nothing else.'

Emelia felt a tiny worm of anger spiral its way up her spine. She squared her shoulders, sending him a defiant glare. 'I don't know what you expected in a wife when you married me, but I am not a doormat and I don't intend to be one, with or without the possession of my memory.'

A muscle clenched like a fist in his jaw, and his eyes became so dark she couldn't make out where his pupils began and ended. 'Do not pick fights you have no hope of winning, Emelia,' he said in a clipped tone. 'You are vulnerable and weak from your injury. I don't want you to be put under any more pressure than is necessary. I am merely following the doctor's orders. It would help if you would do so too.'

She folded her arms tightly beneath her breasts. 'Do not speak to me as if I am a child. I know I am a little lost at present, but it doesn't mean I've completely lost my mind or my will.'

Something about his expression told Emelia he was fighting down his temper with an effort. His mouth was flat and white-tipped and his hands resting on his thighs were digging into the fabric of his trousers until his knuckles became white through his tan.

It seemed a decade until he spoke.

'I am sorry, *cariño*,' he said in a low, deep tone. 'Forgive me. I am forgetting what an ordeal you have been through. This is not the time to be arguing like an old married couple.'

Emelia shifted her lips from side to side for a moment, finally blowing out her cheeks on a sigh. 'I'm sorry too,' she said. 'I guess I'm just not myself right now.'

'No,' he said with an attempt at a smile. 'You are certainly not.'

She closed her eyes and, even though she had intended to feign sleep, in the end she must have dozed off as when she opened her eyes Javier was bringing his airbed seat upright and suggested she do the same, offering her his assistance as she did so.

Within a short time they were ushered through customs and into a waiting vehicle with luckily no sign of the press Javier had warned her about.

The Spanish driver exchanged a few words with Javier which Emelia listened to with a little jolt of surprise. She could speak and understand Spanish? She hadn't spoken it before coming to London. Had she learned in the last couple of years? Why, if she could remember his language, could she not remember the man who had taught it to her? She listened to the brief exchange and, for some reason she couldn't quite explain, she didn't let on that she understood what was being said.

'*Ella se acuerda algo?*' the driver asked. *Does she remember anything?*

'*No, ninguno,*' Javier responded heavily. Not a thing.

During the drive to the villa Emelia looked out at the passing scenery, hoping for a trigger for her memory, but it was like looking at a place for the first time. She felt Javier's gaze resting on her from time to time, as if he too was hoping for a breakthrough. The pressure to remember was all the more burdensome with the undercurrent of tension she could feel running beneath the surface of their tentative relationship. She kept reassuring herself it was as the doctors had said: that Javier would find it difficult to accept she couldn't remember him, but somehow she felt there was more to it than that. Even the driver's occasional glances at her made her feel as if she were under a microscope. Was it always going to be like this? How would she bear it?

When the car purred through a set of huge wrought iron gates, Emelia felt her breath hitch in her throat. The villa that came into view as they traversed the tree-lined driveway was nothing if not breathtaking. Built on four levels with expansive gardens all around, it truly was everything a rich man's castle should be: private, imposing, luxurious and no expense spared on keeping it that way. Even from the car, Emelia could see a team of gardeners at work in the grounds and, as soon as the driver opened the car door for her and Javier, the massive front doors of the villa opened and a woman dressed in a black and white uniform waited at the top of the steps to greet them.

'*Bienvenido a casa, señor.*' The woman turned and gave Emelia a haughty look, acknowledging her through tight lips. '*Señora. Bienvenido a casa.*'

'Thank you,' Emelia said with a strained smile. 'It is nice to be…er…home.'

'*Querida.*' Javier put his hand in the small of Emelia's back. 'This is Aldana,' he said. 'She keeps the villa running smoothly for us. Don't worry. I have explained to all of the staff that you will not remember any of them.'

'I'm so sorry,' Emelia said to Aldana. 'I hope you are not offended.'

Aldana folded her arms across her generous bosom, her dark sparrow-like eyes assessing Emelia in one sweeping up and down look. 'It is no matter,' she said.

'I will take Emelia upstairs, Aldana,' Javier said and, switching to Spanish, asked, 'Did you do as I asked when I phoned?'

Aldana gave a nod. '*Sí, señor.* All is back where you wanted it.'

Emelia continued to pretend she hadn't understood what was being said but she couldn't help wondering what exactly Javier had asked the housekeeper to do.

Her lower back was still burning where his hand was resting. She could feel each and every long finger against her flesh; even the barrier of her lightweight clothes was unable to dull the electric sensation of his touch. Her body tingled from head to foot every time she thought of those hands moving over her, stroking her, caressing her, touching her as any normal loving husband touched a wife he loved and desired.

When he led her towards the sweeping grand staircase she felt the wings of panic start to flap inside her with each step that took her upwards with him.

Even though he was nothing but a stranger to her would he expect her to share his bedroom?

His bathroom?

Or, even more terrifying…his bed?

CHAPTER THREE

'TRY not to be too upset by Aldana's coldness,' Javier said as they came to the first landing. 'It means nothing. She will get over it in a day or so. She was like that the first time I brought you home with me after we were married. She thought I was making the biggest mistake of my life, not just by marrying a foreigner, but by marrying within weeks of meeting you.'

Emelia suppressed a frown as she continued with him up the stairs. She had seen undiluted hatred in the housekeeper's eyes. How long had that been going on? Surely not for the whole time they had been married? How had she coped with such hostility? It surely wouldn't have made for a very happy home with a household of staff sending dagger looks at every opportunity.

She put her hand on the banister to steady herself after the climb. Her legs felt weak and her chest tight, as if she had run a marathon at high altitude.

'Are you all right?' he asked, taking her free hand in his.

She gave him a weak smile. 'Just a little light-headed… It'll pass in a moment.'

Emelia felt his fingers tighten momentarily on hers, the itchy little tingles his touch evoked making her feel even more dazed than the effort of climbing the staircase. His eyes were locked on hers, penetrating, searing, all-seeing, but showing nothing in return. 'Did your housekeeper eventually come to approve of your choice of wife?' she asked.

He released her hand, his eyes moving away from hers. 'I do not need the approval of my housekeeper, Emelia,' he said. 'We are married and that is that. It is no one's business but our own.'

Emelia's teeth sank into her bottom lip as she trudged up the rest of the stairs. She looked for signs of her previous life in the villa but there was nothing to show her she had lived here for close to two years. The walls were hung with priceless works of art; as far as she could see, there were no photographs of their life together. The décor was formal, not relaxed and welcoming. It spoke of wealth and prestige, not family life and friendliness. She could see nothing of herself in the villa, no expression of her personality and taste, and wondered why.

Javier opened a door further along the hall that led into a master bedroom of massive proportions. 'This was our room,' he said.

Emelia wasn't sure if he spoke in the past tense to communicate he would no longer be sharing it with her and she was too embarrassed to ask him to clarify. 'It's very big…'

'Do you recognise anything?' he asked as he followed her into the suite.

Emelia looked at the huge bed and tried to imagine herself lying there with Javier's long strong body beside her. Her stomach did a little flip-flop movement and she shifted her gaze to the bedside tables instead. On one side there was a wedding photograph and she walked over and slowly picked it up, holding her breath as she looked at the picture of herself smiling with Javier standing by her side.

She wrinkled her brow in concentration. Surely there was somewhere in her mind where she could locate that memory. The dress she was wearing was a dream of a wedding gown, voluminous and delicately se-quinned all over with crystals. She could only imagine how much it must have cost. The veil was at least five metres long and had a tiara headpiece, making her look like a princess. The bouquet of orange blossom she carried and the perfection of her hair and make-up spoke of a wedding day that had been meticulously planned. It looked like some of the society weddings she had been forced to attend back at home with her father. All show and fuss to impress others, crowds of people who in a year or so would not even remember the bride's and groom's names. She loathed that sort of scene and had always sworn she would not be a part of it when or if she married. But, as far as she could tell from the photograph in her hands, she had gone for shallow and showy after all.

She shifted her concentration to Javier's image. He was dressed in a dark suit and a white shirt and silver and black striped tie that highlighted his colouring and his tall commanding air. His smile was not as wide as Emelia's; it seemed a little forced, in fact. She wondered if she had noticed it on the day and been worried about it or whether she had been too caught up in being the centre of attention.

Emelia looked up from the photograph she was holding to see Javier's watchful gaze centred on her. 'I'm sorry…' She placed it back on the bedside table with a hand that was not quite steady. 'I can't remember anything. It's as if it happened to someone else.'

His dark gaze dropped to the image of them in their wedding finery. 'Sometimes when I look at that photograph, I think the very same thing,' he said, the slant of his mouth cryptic.

Emelia studied him for a moment in silence. Was he implying he had come to regret their hasty marriage? What had led him to offer her marriage in the first place? So many men these days shied away from the formal tie of matrimony, choosing the less binding arrangement of living together or, even more casually, moving between two separate abodes, thus maintaining a higher level of independence.

Had those first two years of marriage taken the shine off the passion that had apparently brought them together? Relationships required a lot of hard work; she knew that from watching her father ruin one relationship after another with no attempt on his part to learn from his previous mistakes. Had Javier fallen out of love with her? He certainly didn't look like a man in love. She had seen desire in his eyes, but as for the warmth of lifelong love…well, would she recognise it even if she saw it?

Javier caught her staring at him and raised one brow. 'Is something wrong, Emelia?'

She moistened her lips, trying not to be put off by the dark intensity of his gaze as it held hers. 'Um…I was wondering why you wanted to get married so quickly. Most of the men I know would have taken years to propose marriage. Why did you decide we should get married so quickly?'

There was a movement deep within his eyes, like a rapid-fire shuffle of a deck of cards. 'Why do you think?' he said evenly. 'Do you think you were not in the least agreeable to being married to me? I can assure you I did not have to resort to force. You accepted my proposal quite willingly.'

Emelia gave a little shrug, trying not to be put off by the black marble of his gaze as it held hers. 'I don't know…I guess it's just that I don't remember being on the hunt for a husband or anything. I'm only twenty-five—'

'Twenty-seven,' he corrected her.

Emelia chewed at her lip. 'Ri-ght…twenty-seven…' She lowered her gaze and frowned.

He tipped up her face with one finger beneath her chin. 'I wanted you from the moment I saw you sitting at that piano,' he said. 'It was an instant attraction. You felt it too. There seemed no point in delaying what we both wanted.'

Emelia looked into the blackness of his eyes and felt the tug of attraction deep and low in her body. Was this how it had been? The magnetic pull of desire, an unstoppable force that consumed every bit of common sense she possessed? She felt the burn of his touch; the nerve endings beneath her skin were jumping and dancing where his fingertip rested. 'How soon did we—' she swallowed tightly '—sleep together?'

He brushed the pad of his thumb across her bottom lip. 'How soon do you think?' he asked in a low, smoky tone.

Emelia felt the deep thud of her heart as his strong

thighs brushed against hers. 'I…I'm not the type to jump into bed with someone on the first date.'

His dark eyes glinted. 'You sound rather certain about that.'

Her eyes widened in shock. 'Surely I didn't…?'

He dropped his hand from her face. 'No, you didn't,' he said. 'I was impressed by your standards, actually. You were the first woman I had ever dated who said no.'

Emelia gave herself a mental pat on the back. He would be a hard one to say no to, she imagined. 'Did that make me a challenge you wanted to conquer?' she asked.

He gave her an enigmatic smile. 'Not for the reasons you think.'

Her gaze went to the wedding photograph again. 'I don't suppose we waited until the wedding night.'

'No.'

Emelia wondered how one short word could have such a powerful effect on her. Her skin lifted all over at the thought of him possessing her. Her breasts prickled with sensation, her belly flapped like washing on a line in a hurricane and her heart raced. But all she had was her imagination. Her mind was empty, a total blank. She felt cheated. She felt lost and afraid she might never be able to reclaim what should have been some of the most memorable days of her life. She gave a little sigh and faced him again. 'The funny thing is there are some people—like my father, for instance—who would give anything to forget their wedding days. But I can't recall a thing…n-not a thing…' Her voice cracked and she placed her head in her hands, embarrassed at losing control of her emotions in front of him.

He placed a gentle hand on her shoulder. 'Don't cry, *querida*,' he said.

His low soothing tone was her undoing. She choked on another sob and stumbled forward into the rock-hard wall of his chest. Her arms automatically wound around his lean waist, her face pressing into his shirt front, breathing in his warm male scent. Her body seemed to fit against him as if fashioned exactly to his specifications. She felt the strong cradle of his pelvis supporting hers, his muscled thighs holding her trembling ones steady. Her body tingled with awareness as she felt the swelling of his groin against her. How many times had he held her like this? She felt the flutter of her pulse in response, the tight ache between her thighs that felt both strange and familiar.

One of his hands went to the back of her head and began stroking her in a gentle, rhythmic motion, his voice when he spoke reverberating against her ear, reminding her of the deep bass of organ pipes being softly played in a cavernous cathedral. 'Shh, *mi amor*. Do not upset yourself. Do not cry. It can't change anything.'

Emelia tried to control her trembling bottom lip as she eased back to look up at him. 'I want to remember. I want to remember everything. What girl can't remember her wedding day? How can I live my life with whole chunks of it missing?'

Javier brushed her hair back from her face, his dark steady eyes holding her tear-washed ones. 'There are no doubt other things you have forgotten that are worth forgetting. What about that, eh? That is a positive, *sí*?'

He took out a handkerchief and used a folded corner of it to mop up the tears that had trailed down her cheeks. Emelia found it a tender gesture that seemed at odds with his earlier aloofness. Was he finally coming to terms with her inability to remember him?

'What things would I want to forget?' she asked with a puzzled frown.

His eyes shifted away from hers. He refolded the handkerchief and put it in his trouser pocket. 'No marriage is perfect,' he said, 'especially a relatively new one. We had the occasional argument, some of them rather heated at times. Perhaps it is a good thing you can't remember them.'

Emelia tried to read his expression but, apart from a small rueful grimace about his mouth, there was little she could go on. 'What sort of things did we argue about?' she asked.

He gave a one shoulder shrug. 'The usual things. Most of the time little things that got blown all out of proportion.'

She angled her head at him questioningly. 'Who was the first to say sorry?'

There was a slight pause before he answered. 'I am not good at admitting it when I am in the wrong. I guess I take after my father more than I would like in that regard.'

'We all have our pride,' Emelia conceded.

'Yes.' He gave her another brief rueful twist of his mouth. 'Indeed.'

He moved over to a large walk-in wardrobe and opened the sliding doors. 'Your things are in here. You might feel more at home once you are surrounded by your own possessions. The travelling bag you had with you in London was destroyed in the accident.'

Emelia looked at the rows and rows of elegant clothes and shelves of shoes and matching bags. Again, it was like looking into someone else's life. Did *she* wear all these close-fitting designer dresses and sky-high heels? Her eyes went to the other side of the wardrobe where the racks and shelves were empty. She turned and looked at Javier. 'Where are your things?' she asked.

His eyes became shuttered. 'I had Aldana move them into one of the spare rooms for the time being.'

Emelia felt a confusing mixture of relief and disappointment. The relief she could easily explain. The disappointment was a complete mystery to her. 'So—' she quickly ran her tongue over her lips '—so you're not expecting me to…to sleep with you…um…like right away?'

He hooked one dark brow upwards. 'I thought you said you don't usually sleep with perfect strangers?'

She frowned at his tone, not sure if he was teasing her. 'Technically, you're not a stranger, though, are you?' she said. 'I might not remember you, but there's enough evidence around to confirm we are married.'

A glint appeared in his dark-as-night gaze as it held hers. 'Are you inviting me to sleep with you, Emelia?'

Emelia felt her belly fold over itself. 'Er…no…not yet…I mean…no. No. It wouldn't be right for me or even fair to you.'

He came up close, lifting a portion of her hair, slowly twirling it around his finger until she felt the subtle tension on her scalp as he tethered her to him. 'We could do it to see if it unlocks your memory,' he said in a voice that sounded rough and sexy. 'How about it, *querida*? Who knows? Perhaps it is just your mind that has forgotten me. Maybe your body will remember everything.'

Emelia could barely breathe. His chest was brushing against her breasts; she could feel the friction of his shirt through her clothes. Her nipples had sprung to attention, aching and tight, looking for more erotic stimulation. A warm sensation was pooling between her thighs, a pulsing feeling that was part ache, part pleasure, making her want to move forwards to press herself against the hardness she knew instinctively would be there. Her mouth was dry and she sent the point of her tongue out to moisten it, her heart slipping sideways when she saw the way his eyes dropped to follow its passage across her lips.

The pad of his thumb pressed against her bottom lip, setting off livewires of feeling beneath her sensitive skin. 'Such a beautiful mouth,' he said in that low sexy baritone. 'How many times have I kissed it, hmm? How many times has it kissed me?' He pressed himself just that little bit closer, pelvis to pelvis, the swell of his maleness heating her like a hot probe. 'What a pity you can't remember all the delicious things that soft full mouth of yours has done to me in the past.'

Emelia swallowed tightly, the sensation between her thighs turning red hot. She could imagine what she had done; she could see it in his eyes. The erotic pleasure he had experienced with her seemed to be gleaming there to taunt her into recalling every shockingly intimate moment.

His thumb caressed her bottom lip again, pushing against it, watching as it bounced back to fullness as it refilled with blood.

Emelia couldn't take her eyes off his mouth; the enigmatic tilt of it fascinated her. The way he half-smiled, as if he was enjoying the edge he had over her in knowing every sensual pleasure they had shared while she remained in ignorance. Her spine loosened with each stroke of his thumb, the tingling sensation travelling from her lips to every secret place.

'Do you want me to tell you some of the things you did with me, Emelia?' he asked in a gravel-rough tone that made the hairs on the back of her neck lift one by one.

She stood silently staring up at him, like a small nocturnal animal caught in the high beam of headlights: exposed, vulnerable, blinded by feelings she wasn't sure belonged to her. 'I...I'm not sure it would be a good idea to force me to...to remember...' she faltered.

He smiled a lazy smile that made her spine loosen even further. His palm cupped her cheek, holding it gently, each long finger imprinted on her flesh. 'You were shy to begin with, *cariño*,' he said. 'But then perhaps you were shy with your other lovers, *sí*?'

Emelia frowned. 'But I have only had one lover. I must have told you about it, surely? It happened when I was singing in a band in Melbourne. I was too young and didn't realise what I was getting into with someone so much older and experienced. I should have known better, but I was in that rebellious stage a lot of teenagers go through.'

His hand moved from her cheek to rest on her shoulder, his eyes still holding hers like a searchlight. 'You told me some things about it, yes,' he said. 'But then perhaps there are other things you didn't tell me. Things you preferred to keep a secret from me even during our marriage.'

Her frown deepened across her forehead. 'Like what?'

He gave her an inscrutable look and dropped his hand from her shoulder. 'Who knows?' he said. 'You can't remember, or so you say.'

The ensuing silence seemed to ring with the suspicion of his statement.

Emelia sat on the bed in case her legs gave way. 'You think I'm *pretending*?' she asked in an incredulous choked whisper. 'Is that what you think? That I'm making my memory loss up?'

His eyes bored into hers, his mouth pulled tight until his lips were almost flattened. 'You remember nothing of me and yet you grieve like a heartbroken widow over the loss of Marshall.'

She pushed herself upright with her arms. 'Have I not got the right to grieve the loss of a beloved friend?'

His jaw tightened as he held her stare for stare. 'I am your husband, Emelia,' he bit out. 'Your life is with me, not with a dead man.'

She glared back at him furiously. 'You can't force me to stay with you. I might never remember you. What will you do then?'

'Oh, you will remember, Emelia,' he said through clenched teeth, each bitten out word highlighting his accent. 'Make no mistake. You will remember everything.'

Emelia felt a rumble of fear deep and low in her belly. 'I don't know you. I don't even know myself, or at least that's what it feels like it,' she said. 'I don't know who I've become over the past two years. Do you have any idea what it's like for me to step back into the life that was supposedly mine when I don't recognise a thing about it or me?'

He let out a harsh breath. 'Leave it. This is not the time to discuss it.'

'No I can't leave it,' she said. 'You don't seem to trust me. What sort of marriage did we have?'

His eyes were fathomless black pools as they held hers. 'I said I don't wish to discuss this,' he said. 'You need to rest. You are pale and look as if a breath of wind would knock you down.'

'What would you care?' she asked with a churlish look.

'I am not going to continue with this conversation,' he said with an implacable set to his mouth. 'I will leave you to rest. Dinner will be served at eight-thirty. I would suggest you stay close to the villa until you become more familiar with your surroundings. You could easily get lost.'

Emelia sank back down on the mattress once the door had closed on his exit. She put a shaky hand up to her temple, wishing she could unlock the vault of memories that held the secrets of the past two years. What sort of wife was she that her husband didn't seem to trust her? And why did he look at her as if he was torn between pulling her into his arms and showing her the door?

After changing into riding gear, Javier strode down to the stables and, politely declining the offer from his stable-hand, Pedro, quickly saddled his Andalusian stallion, Gitano, and rode out of the villa courtyard. The horse's hooves rattled against the cobblestones but, once the stallion was on the grass of the fields leading to the woods, Javier let him have his head. The feel of the powerful muscles of his horse beneath him was just the shot of adrenalin he needed to distract himself from being with Emelia again.

Holding her in his arms when she had cried had been like torture. He couldn't remember a time when she had shown such emotion before. She was usually so cool and in control of herself. It had stirred things in him to fever pitch to have her so close. Her body had felt so warm and soft against his, so achingly familiar. He could so easily have pushed her down on the bed and reclaimed her as his. His body had throbbed to possess her. It disgusted him that he was so weak. Had he learned nothing? Women were not to be trusted, especially women like his runaway wife.

He had noted every nuance of her face on the journey home to Spain. If she truly had forgotten how wealthy he was, she was in no doubt of it now. Even if she did recall what a sham their marriage had become, she was unlikely to admit it now. Why would she? He could give her everything money could buy. Her lover was dead. She had no one else to turn to, nowhere else to go. She was back in his life due to a quirk of fate. There was no way now that he could toss her out as he had sworn he would do when he'd found out about her affair. The public would not look upon him kindly for divorcing his amnesiac wife. But there could be benefits in keeping her close to his side, he conceded. He still wanted her. That much had not changed, even though it annoyed him that he could not dismiss his attraction for her as easily as he wanted to. It had been there right from the beginning; the electric pulse of wanting that fizzled between them whenever they were within touching distance. She might not recognise him mentally but he felt sure her body was responding to him the way it always had. It would not take him long to have her writhing and twisting beneath him; all memory of her lover would be replaced with new memories of him and him alone.

He would cut her from his life when he was sure she was back on her feet. Their marriage would have ful-filled its purpose by then, in any case. Their divorce would be swift and final. All contact with her would cease from that point. He had no intention of keeping her with him indefinitely, not after the scandal she had caused him. The public would forget in time as new scandals were uncovered, but he could not.

He *would* not.

The horse's hooves thundered over the fields, the wind rushing through Javier's hair as he rode at break-neck speed. He pulled the stallion to a halt at the top of the hill, surveying the expanse of his estate below. The grey-green of the olive groves and the fertile fields of citrus and almonds reminded him of all he had worked so hard and long for. For all the sacrifices he had made to keep this property within his hands. His father's gambling and risky business deals had cost Javier dearly. He'd had to compromise himself in ways he had never dreamed possible. But what was done was done and it could not be undone. It eased his conscience only slightly that he hadn't done it for himself. Izabella had a right to her inheritance, and he had made sure it was not going to be whittled away by his father's home-wrecking widow.

The stallion tossed his head and snorted, his hooves drumming in the dust with impatience. Javier stroked the stallion's silky powerful neck, speaking low and soothingly in Spanish. The horse rose on his hindquar-ters, his front hooves pawing at the air. Javier laughed as he thought of his wayward wife and how fate had handed her back to him to do with her as he wished. He turned the horse and galloped him back down through the forest to the plains below, the thrill of the ride nothing to what waited for him at the end of it.

Emelia ignored the comfort of the big bed and, after a refreshing shower and change of clothes, went on a solitary tour of the villa in the hope of triggering something in her brain. Most of the rooms were too formal for her taste. They were almost austere, with their priceless works of art and uncomfortable-looking antiquated furniture. She couldn't help wondering why she hadn't gone about redecorating the place. Money was certainly no object, but perhaps she'd felt intimidated by the age and history of the villa. It was certainly very old. Every wall of the place seemed to have a portrait of an ancestor on it, each pair of eyes following her in what she felt to be an accusatory silence. She found it hard to imagine a small child feeling at home here. Was this the place where Javier had grown up? There was so much she didn't know about him, or at least no longer knew.

She breathed out a sigh as she opened yet another door. This one led into a library-cum-study. Three walls of floor to ceiling bookshelves and a leather-topped desk dominated the space, but she could see a collection of photo frames beside the laptop computer on the desk, which drew her like a magnet. The floorboards creaked beneath the old rugs as she walked to the desk, the hairs on the back of her neck lifting like antennae.

'Don't be stupid,' she scolded herself. 'There's no such thing as ghosts.' But, even so, when she looked at the photographs she felt as if she were encountering something supernatural—the ghost of who she had been for the past two years.

She picked up the first frame and studied it for a

moment. It was a photo of her lying on a blanket in an olive grove, the sun coming down at an angle, highlighting her honey-blonde hair and grey-blue eyes. She was smiling coquettishly at the camera, flirting with whoever was behind the camera lens.

She put the frame down and picked up the next one, her heart giving a little skip when she saw Javier with his arms wrapped around her from behind, his tall frame slightly stooped as his chin rested on the top of her head, his smile wide and proud as he faced the camera. She could almost feel his hard body pressing into her back, the swell of his arousal, the pulse and thrum of his blood…

The door of the study suddenly opened and Emelia dropped the frame, the glass shattering on the floor at her feet. She stood frozen for a moment as Javier stepped into the room, closing the door with a click that sounded like a prison cell being locked.

'Don't touch it,' he commanded when she began to bend at the knees. 'You might cut yourself.'

'I'm sorry…' Emelia said, glancing down at the floor before meeting his gaze. 'You frightened me.'

His black eyes didn't waver as they held hers. 'I can assure you that was not my intention.'

Emelia swallowed as he approached the desk. He was wearing a white casual polo shirt and beige jodhpurs and long black leather riding boots, looking every inch the brooding hero of a Regency novel. He smelt of the outdoors with a hint of horse and hay and something that was essentially male, essentially *him*. He filled her nostrils with it, making her feel as if she was being cast under an intoxicating spell. His tall authoritarian presence, that aura of command he wore like an extra layer of skin, that air of arrogance and assured-ness that was so at odds with her insecurities and doubts and memory blanks. 'I…I was trying to see if anything in here jogged my memory,' she tried her best to explain.

He hooked a brow upwards. 'And did it?'

She bit her lower lip, glancing at the shattered glass on the floor, which seemed to sever them as a couple. Was it symbolic in some way? A shard of glass was lying across their smiling faces, almost cutting them in two. She brought her gaze back to his. 'No…' She let out a sigh. 'I don't remember when that photo was taken or where.'

He bent down and carefully removed the remaining pieces of glass from the photo frame before placing it back on the desk. 'It was taken a few days after we got home from our honeymoon. I took you for a picnic to one of the olive groves on the estate. The other photo with us together was taken in Rome.'

Emelia ran her tongue over her dry lips before asking, 'Where did we go for our honeymoon?'

He was standing close, too close. She felt the alarm bells of her senses start to ring when he stepped even closer. The wall of bookshelves was at her back, each ancient tome threatening to come down and smother her. His dark eyes meshed with hers, holding them en-tranced. She felt her heart give a knock against her breastbone in anticipation of that sensuous mouth coming down to hers. She suddenly realised how much she wanted that mouth to soften against hers, to kiss her tenderly, lingeringly, to explore every corner of her mouth in intimate detail.

He placed his hand under the curtain of her hair, his

fingers warm and dry against the sensitive skin of her neck. 'Where do you think we went?' he asked.

Emelia's teeth sank into her bottom lip, her brain working overtime. 'Um…Paris?'

His hand stilled and one of his dark brows lifted. 'Was that a guess or do you remember something?' he asked.

'I've always dreamed of honeymooning in Paris,' she said. 'It's supposed to be the most romantic city in the world. And I saw the stamp on my passport so I suppose it wasn't such a wild guess.'

He continued to hold her gaze for endless moments, his fingers moving in a rhythmic motion at her nape. 'Your dream came true, Emelia,' he said. 'I gave you a honeymoon to surpass all honeymoons.'

She sucked half of her bottom lip into her mouth, releasing it to say, 'I'm sorry. You must be thinking what a shocking waste of money it was now that I can't even recall a second of it.'

He gave a couldn't-care-less shrug. 'We can have a second honeymoon, *sí*? One that you will never forget.'

Emelia's eyes went to his mouth of their own volition. He was smiling that sexy half-smile again, the one that made her blood race through her veins. What was it about this man that made her so breathless with excitement? It was as if he only had to look at her and she was a trembling mass of needs and wants. She felt the tingling of her skin as he touched her with those long fingers. The fingers that had clearly touched her in places she wasn't sure she wanted to think about. He knew her so well and yet he was still a stranger to her.

A second honeymoon?

Her belly turned over itself. How could she sleep

with a man she didn't know? It would be nothing but physical attraction, an animal instinct, an impulse she had never felt compelled to respond to before.

Or had she?

How did she know what their history was? She could only go on what he had told her. She hadn't thought herself the type to fall in love so rapidly, to marry someone within weeks of meeting them. But then maybe she hadn't fallen in love with him. Maybe she had fallen in lust. She shied away from the thought but it kept creeping back to taunt her. He was so dangerously attractive. She could feel the pull of his magnetism even now, the thrill of him touching her, the stroke of his fingers so drugging she could feel herself capitulating second by second. His eyes were dark pools of mystery, luring her in, making her drown in their enigmatic depths. She felt her eyelids come down to half mast, her breathing becoming choppy as his hand stilled at the back of her neck, pressing her forwards with a gentle but determined action as his mouth came within a breath of hers.

'D-don't…' Her voice came out hoarse, uncertain and not at all convincing.

His hand still cupped the nape of her neck, warm and strong, supportive and yet determined. 'Don't what?' he asked in a low deep burr.

She swallowed. 'You know what…'

'Is it not right for a husband to kiss his wife?' he asked.

'But I…I don't feel like your wife,' Emelia said breathlessly.

There was a three beat pause as his dark eyes locked on hers.

'Then it is about time you did,' he said and, swooping down, covered her mouth with his.

CHAPTER FOUR

EMELIA's heart almost stopped when his mouth touched down on hers. The raw male scent of him was intoxicating, dangerous, and that alone would have had her senses spinning, but the pressure of his lips upon hers drew from her a response she wasn't entirely sure she should be giving. He cradled her head in his hands, giving her no room to pull away even if she had the wherewithal to do so. The contact of his mouth on hers was explorative at first, light, tentative almost, but then, with just one very masculine stroke of his tongue, everything changed.

Her lips opened to him as if of their own volition, instinctively, welcoming him inside the moist cave of her mouth. Her tongue met his briefly, flirting around it, dancing with it until finally mating with it at its command. He subdued her with the power of each stroke and thrust of his tongue, teasing her into submission, relishing the victory by crushing his mouth to hers with increasing pressure. Emelia felt the surge of his body against her, his arousal so thick and hard it made her realise how much history existed between them, a history she had yet to discover. Her body, however, seemed familiar with it. It was reacting with fervour to every movement of his mouth on hers, her arms automatically going around his neck, holding him to her as if she had done it many times before, her pelvis seeking the hardened throb of his, her inner core melting with longing. Her breasts bloomed with pleasure against the contact with his hard chest, her nipples tightening to buds, aching to feel the slippery warmth of his mouth and tongue.

His mouth moved from hers on a searing pathway down the side of her neck, slowly, sensuously bringing every nerve to gasping, startled life. Goosebumps rose all over her skin as he discovered the delicate scaffold of her collarbone, his tongue dipping into the tiny dish of her tender flesh. His lips feathered against her skin as he spoke in a low sexy tone. 'You taste of vanilla.'

Emelia felt electric jolts shoot up and down her legs at the thought of where that mouth and tongue had been on her body. She could almost feel its pathway now, the way her secret feminine flesh was pulsing, as if in anticipation of him claiming it. She clutched at his head with her fingers, feeling the thick strands of his dark hair move like silk beneath her fingertips.

'I want you.' He mouthed the words against her neck, making her nerves leap and dance again. 'God, but I want you.'

'W-we can't…' Emelia gasped as his mouth showered kisses all over her face: over her eyelids, over her cheeks, her nose and so temptingly close to her tingling, swollen lips.

'What's to stop us?' he said in a husky tone as he pressed a hot moist kiss to her trembling mouth. 'We are married, are we not?'

Emelia was too drunk on his kiss to answer. His tongue went in search of hers again, mating with it in an erotic tango that left her gasping with need. His kiss was hungry, demanding, leaving her in no doubt of where it was leading. It was a pre-sex kiss, blatant in its intent, shockingly intimate as his hands moved from cradling her head, sliding down her bare arms to encircle her wrists. The latent strength of him sent a shiver of reaction through her. He was so strong; she was so weak, but not just in physical strength. Her will-power seemed to have totally evaporated. She was molten wax in his arms, fitting to his hard form as if she had known no other place.

He released her hands and moved his up under her top, sliding his warm palms over her belly and her ribcage. Her heart gave a lurching movement as his fingers splayed over her possessively. Emelia thought she would die if he didn't touch her breasts and she moved against him, silently pleading for him to pleasure her.

His hand cupped her and she let out a tiny whimper of pleasure, for even through the fine lace of her bra she could feel the tantalising heat of his touch. 'You want more, *querida*?' he asked softly, seductively.

Emelia gasped as he pushed aside the cobweb of lace, his fingers skating over her burgeoning flesh. His thumb lingered over her engorged nipple, moving back and forth, hot little rubs that lifted every hair on her scalp.

'You want this, *sí*?' he said and bent his mouth to her breast and suckled softly at first and then harder.

Emelia's fingers clutched at his hair, trying to anchor herself as delicious sensations washed through her. 'Oh… Oh, God…' she whimpered.

'You like this too,' he said and swept his tongue down the outer curve of her breast, licking like a jungle cat, the sexy rasp of his tongue melting every vertebrae of her spine into trembling submission.

'And this,' he added, pressing her back against the desk, his thighs parting hers with shockingly primal intention.

Emelia's passion-glazed eyes flew open and her hands thrust against his chest. 'N-no…' she said but it came out so hoarsely she had to repeat it. 'No…no, I can't.'

One of his dark brows hooked upwards, his body still poised against hers. 'No?'

She shook her head, her teeth sinking into her lower lip as her eyes momentarily fell away from his.

He let out a theatrical sigh and straightened, pulling her upright against him, his hands settling on her waist, his powerful body, hot, aroused and hard, just a breath's distance away. 'That wasn't what you used to say,' he said with a taunting gleam in his dark eyes. 'This was one of your favourite places for a quick—'

Emelia pushed two of her fingertips against his mouth, blocking off the coarse word she was almost certain he intended to use. 'Please…don't…' she said hollowly.

He peeled her fingers away from his mouth, kissing the tips one by one, his bottomless eyes holding hers. 'Don't you want to be reminded of how sensually adventurous you were, Emelia?' he asked.

Her throat rose and fell over a tight swallow. 'No… no, I don't.'

He pressed a soft kiss to the middle of her palm and then dipped his tongue right into the middle of it, hotly, moistly, his eyes still locked with hers. 'I taught you everything you know,' he went on. 'You were so eager to learn. A straight A student, in fact.'

She closed her eyes tight. 'Stop it. Stop doing this.'

'Open your eyes, Emelia,' he commanded.

She scrunched them even tighter. 'No.'

His hands went to her waist, holding her against his rock-hard arousal. 'This is what you do to me, *querida*,' he said in a sexy growl.

Emelia wrenched out of his hold with a strength she had no conscious knowledge of possessing. Her chest heaved with the effort as she stood, trembling and shaken, a few feet away. She folded her arms across her chest, fighting for breath, fighting for control, fighting for some self-respect, which seemed to have gone AWOL some minutes ago.

Javier gave her an indolent smile. 'What are you frightened of, *mi amor*?' he asked.

'I don't know you,' Emelia said.

'But you want me, all the same.'

'I'm not myself right now.' She tightened her arms beneath her breasts. 'I don't know what I want.'

'Your body remembers me, Emelia. It wants me. You can't deny it.'

Emelia moved even further away because she had a sneaking suspicion what he said was true. Every sense was alive to him, to his presence and to his touch. She could still taste him in her mouth, the musky male heat of him lingering there like a fine wine on her palate. Was he an addiction she had developed over the last two years? How could any woman resist such incredible potency? He oozed sensual heat through the pores of his skin. She felt the waves of attraction tighten the air she breathed in. Every part of her body he had touched was still tingling with the need for more. His incendiary suggestion was still ringing in her ears, making her mind race with erotic scenarios: of her spread before him like a feast; her legs open to his powerful thrusting body, her senses in a vortex of sensation, her back arching in pleasure, her mouth falling open in sharp, high cries of ecstasy.

He came to where she was standing, her back pressed against the bookshelves, his eyes smouldering so darkly they seemed to strip her bare. 'Maybe it was a mistake for me to move out of our room,' he said. 'Perhaps I should insist on you sleeping with me, even though you can't remember me.'

Emelia's back felt as if it was being bitten into by the shelves. 'You c-can't mean that,' she said croakily.

He tipped up her chin, holding her frightened gaze with the powerful beam of his. 'Making love with me might trigger something in your brain. It might be the part of the missing puzzle, *sí*?'

His disturbing presence was triggering all sorts of things in her body, let alone her brain, Emelia thought in rising panic. She placed her hands on his chest with the intention of pushing him away again, but the feel of his hard muscles under her palms sent off a little flashbulb in her head. It was a tiny spark of memory, a pinpoint of light in the darkness. She splayed her fingers experimentally and, as if of their own accord, her fingertips began moving over his hard flat nipples, over his perfectly sculptured pectoral muscles and up to his neck, where she could see a pulse beating like a hammer beneath his skin. She moved her fingertips to the raspy skin of his lean jaw, the prickle of his stubble sending tantalising little tingles right up her arms.

'What is it?' he asked, holding her hand against his face with the broad span of his. 'Have you remembered something?'

She frowned as she fought to retrieve the fleeting image. It was like the shadow of a ghost, barely visible, but she could sense its presence. 'I don't know…' She bit down on her lip, pulling her hand out from under his. 'I thought for a minute…but I just don't know…'

He picked up her hand again and held it against his mouth, his lips feathering against her curled up fingers as he spoke. 'Touch me again, *cariño*,' he commanded softly. 'Touch is an important part of memory. Taste and smell, too.'

Emelia uncurled her fingers and carefully traced the outline of his lips, her fingertip grazing against his stubble again. She felt transfixed by the shape of his mouth, the way his top lip was carved almost harshly and yet his lower one was so generous and sensual. He drew her fingertip into his mouth and sucked on it. It was such an intimate thing to do, flagrantly sexual, especially when his eyes captured hers and glinted at her meaningfully. She pulled out of his hold once more, gathering herself with an effort. 'I'm sorry,' she said crisply. 'I don't remember anything.'

His expression gave little away but Emelia sensed a thread of anger stringing his words together as he spoke. 'I will leave you to rest before dinner. Leave this.' He indicated the broken glass on the floor. 'I will get Aldana to clean it up later. If you need anything just press nine on the telephone by the bed upstairs. It is a direct line to Aldana's quarters. She will bring you some tea or coffee or a cool drink if you should require it.'

She watched as he strode out of the library, the squeak of the expensive leather of his riding boots the only sound in the silence.

Emelia woke from a nap feeling totally disoriented, her heart beating like the wings of a frightened bird as she sat upright on the big bed. She put a hand to her throat, trying to control her breathing to bring down her panic to a manageable level. She dragged herself off the bed and stumbled into the en suite bathroom. Seeing her reflection was like looking at another version of herself, a more sophisticated and yet unhappier version. She put a fingertip to each of her sharp cheekbones. Her mouth was pulled down at the corners as if smiling had become a chore. Her eyes looked tired but also a little haunted, as if they were keeping secrets they didn't really want to keep.

She washed her face with cold water and then turned and looked longingly at the huge spa bath next to the double shower cubicle. She had at least an hour before dinner and the thought of sinking into a huge bath tub full of fragrant bubbles was too much for her to resist.

The water lapped at her aching limbs as she lowered herself into the bath, the scent of honeysuckle filling the air, reminding her of the hot summers and long lazy days of her childhood back in Australia. She closed her eyes and laid her head back, her body relaxing for the first time since she had woken from the coma.

Even in her languid repose, it was hard not to think of Peter. The thought of him lying in a cold dark grave was surreal when it seemed only a few days ago they were having coffee together at the end of her session at The Silver Room. The police had told her it had been a high speed accident but the knowledge hadn't sat well with her. Peter had lost a close mate in a car accident when he was a teenager. His intractable stance on reckless and dangerous driving was one of the things she had admired about him—one of the many things. During their youth, he had hinted more than once that he wanted more than a platonic friendship from her but she had let him down as gently as she could. While they had been close friends and had many interests in common, she had never envisaged him as an intimate partner. She had always looked on him as a brother. There was no chemistry, or at least not from her point of view. She knew it was different for men, and Peter had not been an exception. She had seen his head turned by many beautiful women who came into his hotel bar. She knew men's desires were more often than not fuelled by their vision. Sex was a physical drive that could just as easily be performed with a perfect stranger.

Emelia felt her belly give a distinct wobble when she thought of the stranger who was her husband. She saw raw unbridled desire in Javier's eyes; it smouldered there like hot coals every time he looked at her. He had openly declared how much he wanted her. She had heard the erotic promise in the words. It was not a matter of *if* but *when*.

He knew it.

She knew it.

Emelia looked down at her breasts, her rosy nipples just peeping out of the water amidst the bubbles, a riot of sensations rippling through her as she thought of how he had caressed her earlier. He had touched her with such possessive familiarity. Was that why she had responded so instinctively? She felt her insides give another fluttery movement as she thought about him possessing her totally. Would she remember him in the throes of making love as he suggested? She reared back from her thoughts like a horse shying at a jump. It was too soon to be taking that step. She couldn't possibly give herself to a man she didn't know.

But you're married to him, a little voice reminded her.

And you're attracted to him, another voice piped up.

Emelia slipped under the water to escape her traitorous thoughts, holding her breath for as long as she dared…

Javier tapped on the bathroom door but there was no answer. It was quiet. Too quiet. There was not even the sound of running or splashing water.

He opened the door and when he saw Emelia's slim body lying submerged in the bath he felt a hand clutch at his insides.

'Emelia!' He rushed to the tub and grabbed her under the armpits, hauling her upright as water splashed everywhere.

She gave a gasping cry of shock, her wet hair like seaweed all over her face. 'What do you think you're doing?' she spluttered.

Javier waited until his heart had returned to his chest from where it had leapt into his throat. 'I thought you were unconscious,' he explained in a voice that sounded as ragged as he felt. 'I thought you might have hit your head again or something.'

She flashed him a livid glare as she hastily crossed

her arms over her breasts. 'You could have knocked before you came barging in.'

'I did knock.' He stepped out of the puddle of water he was standing in, glancing ruefully at his sodden trousers and shoes. 'You didn't answer.'

Her knees bent upwards, shielding her chest even further. 'You had no right to come in without my permission,' she said.

He sent one of his brows up in a mocking slant. 'That little knock on the head has turned you into a prude, eh, Emelia? I remember a time not so long ago when you made room for me in there.' He bent down and scooped up a handful of bubbles, holding them just above her bent knees. 'Do you want to know what we got up to?'

She stiffened as if the water had turned to ice around her. 'Get out,' she said in a clipped voice.

Javier let the bubbles fall from his hand, his eyes unwavering on hers. He felt her tension, the way she gave a tiny, almost imperceptible flinch as each cluster of bubbles slid down from her kneecaps and down her thighs to slowly dissipate as they landed on the surface of the water. As each throbbing second passed he could hear the soft popping sound of the lather gradually losing its vigour. Within minutes the soapy shield she was hiding behind would be gone.

In spite of her betrayal, he felt his body surge with excitement. Hot rushing blood filled his groin, the ache for release so quick, so urgent it made him realise how hard it was going to be to keep his distance from her. But then wanting her had always been his problem, his one true vulnerability.

From that first moment he had heard her clever little fingers playing those lilting cadences when he'd walked into The Silver Room, he had felt something deep inside shift into place. She had looked up from the piano, her fingers stumbling over a note as their eyes had locked. He had smiled at her with his eyes—that was all it had taken—and she had been his.

He looked down at her now, wondering if she had any idea of the war going on inside him. She was cautious around him, understandable given she no longer recognised him, but he felt the sexual undertow of her gaze every time it meshed with his. It would not take him long to have her back in his bed and threshing in his arms as she used to do. But would that finally dissolve the anger and hatred he felt whenever he thought of her with the man she had run away to be with?

'It is not the behaviour of a devoted wife to order her husband out of his own bathroom,' Javier said, breaking the taut silence.

'I…I don't care,' she said, her teeth chattering slightly.

He plucked a bath sheet off the warming rail and held it just out of her reach. 'You'd better get out. You're starting to get cold.'

Her grey-blue eyes battled with his. 'I'm not getting out until you leave.'

He settled his tall frame into a trenchant stance. 'I am not leaving until you get out.'

She clenched her teeth, her voice coming out as a hiss, reminding him of a snarling cat. 'Why are you doing this? Why are you being such a beast?'

'What is all the fuss about, *querida*?' he asked evenly. 'I have seen you naked countless times.'

Her throat rose and fell. 'It's different now… You know that…'

He came closer with the towel, unfolding it for her to step into. 'Come on, Emelia. You are shivering.'

She flattened her mouth and, giving him another livid glare, stood and grasped for the towel, covering herself haphazardly, but not before he feasted his eyes on her slim feminine form. There were catwalk models who had less going for them, Javier thought. With her coltish long legs and beautifully toned arms and those small high breasts with their delectable rosy nipples, it was all he could do not to pull her out of the slippery tub and crush his body to hers. How many times had he tasted the sweet honey of her feminine body? How many times had he plunged into her, his cataclysmic release unlike any he had ever experienced with anyone else? As much as it felt like a dagger in his gut, he wondered how it had been with her lover. Had she gone down on him with the same fervour? Had she whispered words of love to him in the afterglow of lovemaking? Javier felt his top lip curl as he watched her try to cover herself more effectively. 'You are wasting your time, Emelia,' he said. 'I know every inch of your body and you know every inch of mine.'

Her eyes shifted away from his, her throat doing that nervous up and down thing again. 'I would like some privacy,' she said, wiping her brow with the back of her hand. 'I…I'm not feeling well.'

Javier's brows shot together. 'Why didn't you tell me?' he asked. 'What is wrong? A headache? The doctor said headaches are common after—'

'It's not a bad one, just an ache behind one eye.' She brushed at her damp brow once more, this time with a corner of the towel. 'It's making me feel a little nauseous. Perhaps it's the change of climate. It's a lot hotter here than in England.'

'You were only in London a week,' he pointed out. 'Hardly time to be reacclimatising, don't you think?'

Her gaze returned to his, two small frown lines sectioning her forehead. 'Oh…yes…yes, of course…I forgot.' She pressed her lips together and looked away.

Javier saw the shadow of grief pass through her eyes before she averted her gaze. He fought down his anger, reminding himself she was with him now. His rival was dead. It was just Emelia and him now, to get on with their lives as best they could. 'Dinner is not long away,' he said. 'I will need to get changed. Do you want me to escort you downstairs or do you think you will find your way?'

She clutched at the towel as she looked at him with her guarded gaze. 'I'll find my own way…thank you.'

He gave a brisk nod and left the bathroom.

Emelia opened the wardrobe and, searching through the array of clothes, selected a simple black dress and heels to match. As she dressed she couldn't quite suppress the feeling that she was dressing in someone else's clothes. The dress was made by a French designer and must have cost a fortune; the shoes, too, were a brand celebrities and Hollywood stars regularly wore. She used the cosmetics in the drawer in the en suite bathroom, but only lightly and, after drying her hair with a blow-dryer, she left it lying about her shoulders.

As she came down the grand staircase she heard Javier's voice from the study. He was speaking in Spanish and sounded angry. Emelia knew it was probably beneath her to eavesdrop but, even so, she couldn't resist pausing outside the closed study door. Of course hearing only one side of a conversation was not all that revealing and, although she understood very basic Spanish, he spoke so rapidly she found it hard to follow everything he said. One or two sentences did stand out, however.

'There is not going to be a divorce.'

Emelia's eyes widened as she listened even harder, wincing as one or two expletives were uttered before his next statement.

'The money is not yours and never has been and, as long as I live, it never will be.'

The phone slammed down and, before Emelia could move even a couple of paces down the hall, Javier came storming out of the study. He pulled up short as if someone had jerked him back by the back of his jacket when he saw her standing there with guilt written all over her face.

'How long have you been standing out here?' He almost barked the words at her.

Emelia took a layer of her lip gloss off with the nervous dart of her tongue. 'I…I was just walking past. I heard you raise your voice.'

His expression was thunderous but Emelia had a feeling the anger was not directed at her. He raked a hand through his hair and released a heavy sigh, as if deliberately trying to suppress his fury. 'Just as well you don't remember any Spanish,' he said. 'I don't usually swear in the presence of women, but my father's third wife is nothing but a gold-digging, trouble-making tramp.'

Emelia wondered if she should tell him she could speak and understand a little of his language, but in that nanosecond of hesitation she decided against it. Wouldn't it seem strange that she couldn't remember him and yet she could remember every word of Spanish she had learned over the past two years? After all, he had already implied she might be pretending. Why he would think that was beyond her, although, given the conversation she had just overheard, it made her wonder if their marriage had been as happy as he had intimated. She had just heard him say there was not going to be a divorce. Did that mean there had been recent speculation about their marriage ending? Javier had mentioned how the press had made some scurrilous comments about her relationship with Peter Marshall. There would be few men who would cope well with their private life being splashed all over the papers and gossip magazines, but Javier struck her as a particularly proud and intensely private man. There was so much she didn't know and she didn't feel comfortable asking in case the answers he gave were not the ones she wanted to hear.

'It must be very difficult for you, under the circumstances,' she offered.

He gave her a long look and sighed again, taking her elbow to lead the way to the dining room. 'My father was a fool leaving Izabella's mother for Claudine Marsden. That woman is a home wrecker. Why he couldn't see it is beyond me.'

'Some men are like that,' she said. 'My father is the same.'

He glanced down at her as they came to the dining room door. 'Did your father contact you while you were in hospital?' he asked.

Emelia's mouth tightened. 'No, why should he? As far as he is concerned, I am as good as dead to him. He told me he never wanted to see me again. I have no reason to suspect he didn't mean it.'

Javier pressed his lips together, a frown creasing his

forehead as he led her to the table. 'People say all sorts of things in the heat of the moment.' He paused before adding, 'I should have phoned him. I didn't think of it, I'm afraid. There was so much going on at the time. He should have been notified about the accident.'

'Did I at some point give you his contact details?' Emelia asked.

'No, but it wouldn't have been all that hard to track him down,' he said. 'Would you like me to make contact now, just to let him know you are all right?'

Emelia thought about her father with his new wife, who was only three years older than her. After their last insult-throwing argument, she couldn't see him flying all the way to Spain with flowers and a get well card in hand. He was probably sunning himself at his luxurious Sunshine Coast mansion with his child bride waiting on him hand and foot. 'No, don't bother,' she said, trying to remove the bitterness from her tone. 'He's probably got much more important things to see to.'

Javier gave her a thoughtful look as he drew out her chair.

Emelia took the seat, waiting until he sat down opposite to say, 'Our backgrounds—apart from the level of wealth—are very similar, aren't they? Your father was estranged from you and mine from me. Is that something that drew us together when we first met?'

His dark eyes held hers for a moment before he answered. 'It was one of many things.'

'What were some of the other things?' she asked.

He poured wine for each of them, his mouth tilting slightly. 'Lust, lust and more lust,' he said.

Emelia pursed her lips, hating that she was blushing,

hating him for watching with such mocking amusement. 'I can assure you I would never fall in lust with someone,' she said. 'I would only ever love someone I admired as a man, for his qualities as a person, not his possessions or social standing. And I most certainly wouldn't marry a man on physical attraction alone.'

His mocking smile was still in place. 'So you must have loved me, eh, Emelia?' He flicked his napkin across his lap, his eyes still tethering hers. 'The thing is, will you remember to love me again?'

CHAPTER FIVE

EMELIA placed her own napkin over her lap, all the time avoiding those black-as-pitch eyes. The hairs on the back of her neck were tingling and her stomach was rolling like a ball going down a very steep hill. Had she felt like this during their marriage? Had her skin felt prickly and sensitive just with his gaze on her, let alone his touch? She desperately wanted to remember everything about him, everything about them—their relationship, the love they supposedly had shared.

Or had they?

The thought slipped into her mind, unfurling like a curl of smoke beneath a closed door. Did he love her the way she had evidently loved him? It was so difficult to know what he felt; he kept himself to himself most of the time. She understood his reluctance to reveal his feelings, given her loss of memory. He might resent looking a fool if she never regained her memory of him. In any case, the doctors had warned him not to pressure her. Was that why he was acting like the perfect stranger, polite but aloof, with just occasional glimpses of his personality? There was so much she didn't know about him, things she would need to know in order to navigate her way through the complex labyrinth her mind had become. With an effort she raised her eyes back to his. 'I feel such a fool for not asking you this earlier, but what is it you do for a living?'

'I buy and sell businesses,' he said. 'I own and head an international company. We do work all over the world. That was why I have been in Moscow a lot lately. I have a big deal I am working on. It requires a lot of intense negotiation.'

Emelia sat quietly absorbing that information, hoping it would trigger something in her brain. She looked at his hands as they poured wine into both of their glasses. She could imagine him being a formidable opponent in business, his quick mind and sharp intelligence setting him apart from his rivals. 'What sort of businesses do you buy?' she asked.

'Ailing ones,' he said. 'I buy them and reinvent them and sell them for a profit.' He hitched one shoulder indifferently. 'It's a living.'

Emelia picked up her crystal wine glass. 'Apparently quite a good one.' She took a tentative sip and put the glass back down. 'Was your father in the same field of work?'

'No, he was in retail,' he said. 'Electrical, mostly. He had several outlets in Spain. He expected me to go into the business with him but I never wanted that for myself. Selling refrigerators and televisions and toasters never appealed to me. I wanted more of a challenge.'

'Is that what caused the rift between you?'

'That and other things,' he said, frowning slightly as he returned his glass to the table.

Aldana came in with their starters and, while she was serving them, Emelia thought about Javier's background. There was no shortage of wealth; the private jet, the villa and grounds and the staff to maintain it must cost a fortune. Had he inherited it from his father or accumulated it himself? He must be very good at what he did. No one could buy a company without a huge amount of money behind them. And if he was buying and selling more than one and all over the world, he must be far more successful than she had thought. She decided to check out his profile on the Internet later, to see a little more into the man she was married to.

'*Gracias*, Aldana,' Javier said as the housekeeper left with a sour look in Emelia's direction, which she was sure he didn't see. Emelia wondered if she should comment on it but then decided against it. Maybe Javier would think she was making trouble. Aldana seemed very much a part of the woodwork of the villa. But it worried Emelia that the housekeeper had not warmed to her over the last two years. She was not used to people disliking her on sight. It made her feel as if she didn't know herself any more. Who was she now? Why had the housekeeper taken such an active dislike to her?

A moment or two of silence passed.

'Is the wine not to your liking?' Javier asked. 'It used to be one of your favourites.'

Emelia wrinkled her nose. 'Sorry, I guess my palate has changed or something. I'll stick to water. I need the fluids, in any case.'

'Would you like me to call a doctor?' he asked. 'You might have picked up a bug in the hospital.'

'No, I'm fine.' She twisted her mouth wryly. 'To tell you the truth, I'm a little sick of doctors. I just want to get well again.'

He gave her a tight smile. 'Of course.'

Emelia picked at her main course after Aldana had brought it in, but with little appetite. The tight band of tension around her forehead she had been trying so hard to ignore was making her feel ill again. All she could think of was retreating to the sanctuary of bed.

'You're really not feeling well, are you?' Javier asked once the housekeeper had cleared the plates.

Emelia gave him an apologetic grimace. 'I'm sorry. My headache's been getting worse all evening.'

He rose from the table and gently helped her out of her chair. 'Come on,' he said. 'I'll take you upstairs and help you get settled. Are you sure about the doctor? What if I just make a call to ask his opinion?'

'No, please don't bother. Dr Pratchett told me headaches are common sometimes up to weeks after a head injury. I just need a painkiller and sleep.'

Javier left the bedroom while Emelia changed into nightwear and after a few minutes he came back in with a glass of water and a couple of painkillers. Once she had taken them, he took the glass and set it down on the bedside table. 'I have to fly back to Moscow tomorrow,' he said, sitting on the edge of the bed next to her. 'I just got a phone call while I was downstairs. I am sorry about the short notice but, with the accident and everything, I had to cut short my business there.'

'I'm sorry to have been such a bother—'

He placed a hand over hers, silencing her. 'I have given Aldana and the others instructions to keep a watch over you. I will only be away two days, three at the most.'

'I'm perfectly able to look after myself.' She pulled her hand out from under his and crossed her arms over her chest. 'I don't need to be watched over like a small child.'

'Emelia, there are journalists lurking about looking for a story,' he said. 'If you set foot outside the villa grounds you will be under siege. You are not well enough to fend off their intrusive questions. You will end up even more confused and disoriented.'

Her grey-blue eyes narrowed slightly. 'Are these precautions for me or for you?'

He squared his shoulders. 'What exactly are you implying?'

She bit down on her bottom lip so hard it went white. 'I don't know what's going on,' she said. 'I don't know what's what any more. You say we were happily married, but you don't seem to like me, let alone love me.'

Javier placed his hand on the curve of her cheek, turning her head to face him. 'This is not the time to be talking about my feelings,' he said. 'This is the time for you to concentrate on getting well again. That's why I want you to stay within the confines of the villa grounds.'

'What did I used to do to occupy myself when you went away on business?' she asked.

Javier would have dearly liked to ask her the same thing. How long had her affair gone on, for instance? How many times had she met her lover while he was abroad on business? How many of her 'shopping trips' to London been a cover for other activities? 'You used the gym in the building near the pool and you occasionally practised the piano.'

She frowned as she looked down at her manicured hands with their elegant French-polished nails. When had she stopped biting her nails? And how on earth did she play the piano with them so long? She looked up at him after a moment. 'So I wasn't teaching?'

'No. You said you were no longer interested in teaching children,' he said. 'You said it didn't suit your lifestyle any more.'

She was still frowning. '*I* said that?'

Javier studied her for a moment. 'You said a lot of things, Emelia.'

'What other things did I say?' she asked.

'You didn't want children, for one thing,' he said. 'You were adamant about it.'

Her eyes widened. 'Not want children?'

He nodded. 'You didn't want to be tied down.'

She put a hand to her head, as if to check it was still there. 'I can't believe I didn't want kids. That seems so…so selfish.' She looked at him again. 'Did *you* want children?'

'No, absolutely not,' he said. 'Children need a lot of attention. They can be a strain on a strong marriage, let alone one that is suffering some teething problems.'

Her forehead creased again. 'So we were having some problems?'

Javier carefully considered how to answer. 'Very few relationships don't go through some sort of adjustment period. It was hard for both of us initially. I travel a great deal and you were new to my country and my language. In any case, it wasn't always convenient to take you with me because I like to concentrate on business when I am away. On the few occasions you did come with me, you were bored sitting around waiting for me. Some meetings go on and on until things are sorted out to everyone's satisfaction.'

'So I decided to stay at home and play the corporate wife role…' She chewed her lip again, as if the concept was totally foreign to her.

'Emelia.' He took her hand in his again, stroking the back of it with his thumb. 'It was the way things were between us. It was what we both wanted. You seemed happy with the arrangement when I asked you to marry me. You understood the rules. You were happy to play the game. You slipped into the role as if you were born to it.'

She looked at their joined hands, a sigh escaping from her lips. 'When I was a little girl I used to wish I could see into the future.' She looked back up into his gaze. 'But now I wish I could see into the past.'

He let her hand go and stood up from the bed. 'Sometimes the past is better left alone,' he said. 'It can't be changed.'

She pulled the sheet up to her chest, her forehead still creased in a frown. 'Will I see you before you leave tomorrow?' she asked.

He shook his head. 'I am leaving first thing.' He bent down and brushed his mouth against hers. *'Buenas noches.'*

'Buenas noches.' Her voice was a soft whisper that feathered its way down his spine as he left the room.

Aldana was in the kitchen when Emelia came downstairs the next morning. The atmosphere was distinctly chilly but she decided to ignore it. Ignore the bad, praise the good seemed the best way to handle a difficult person, she thought.

'Good morning, Aldana,' she said with a bright smile that she hoped didn't look too forced. 'It's a beautiful day, isn't it?'

The housekeeper sent her a reproachful look. 'I suppose as usual you will turn your nose up at the food I have set out for you?'

Emelia's smile fell away. 'Um…actually, I am quite hungry this morning,' she said. 'But you shouldn't have gone to any trouble.'

Aldana made a snorting noise and turned her attention to the bread she was making. 'I am paid to go to trouble,' she said. 'But it is a waste of my time and good food when people refuse to eat it.'

'I'm sorry if I've offended you in the past,' Emelia said after a tense silence. 'Would it help if I sat down with you and planned the week's menus? It would save you a lot of trouble and there would be less waste.'

Aldana dusted her hands on her apron in a dismissive fashion. 'You are not the right wife for Señor Mélendez,' she said. 'You do not love him as he deserves to be loved. You just love what he can give you.'

Emelia tried to disguise her shock at the housekeeper's blunt assessment by keeping her voice cool and controlled. 'You are entitled to your opinion but my relationship with my husband is no one's business but my own.'

Aldana gave another snort and turned her back to open the oven, signalling the end of the conversation.

Emelia decided to carry on as if things were normal, even though it troubled her deeply that the housekeeper thought her so unsuitable a wife for Javier. She had always imagined she would make a wonderful wife. After all, she had learned what not to do by watching first her parents' disastrous and volatile marriage, and then her father's subsequent ones after her mother had died. She had determined from a young age to marry for love and love only. Money and prestige would hold no sway with her. But now she wondered how closely she had clung to her ideals.

She ate a healthy breakfast of fruit and yogurt and toast and carried a cup of tea out to a sun-drenched terrace overlooking the villa's gardens.

The scenery was breathtaking and the fresh smell of recently cut grass teased her nostrils. Neatly trimmed box hedges created the more formal aspect of the garden, but beyond she could see colourful herbaceous borders and interesting pathways that led to various fountains or statues.

After she carried her cup back into the kitchen, Emelia went on a tour of the garden. The sun was warm but not overly so and a light breeze carried the delicate scent of late blooming roses to her. She stopped and picked one and, breathing in its fragrance, wondered how many times she had done exactly this. She poked the stem of the rose behind her ear and carried on, stopping at one of the fountains to watch the birds splashing and ruffling their feathers in the water.

The sound of a horse whinnying turned her head. In the distance Emelia could see a youth leading a magnificent looking stallion to what appeared to be a riding arena near the stables a little way from the villa. She walked back through the garden and made her way to where the youth was now lunging the horse on a lead rope. He was a powerful-looking animal with a proud head and flaring nostrils, his tail arched in defiance as his hooves pounded through the sand of the arena.

Emelia stood on the second rail of the fence so she could see over, watching as the stallion went through his paces. Without thinking, she spoke in Spanish to the youth. 'He's very temperamental, isn't he?'

'*Sí, señora,*' the youth answered. 'Your mare is much better mannered.'

Emelia looked at him blankly. 'I have a horse of my own?'

The youth looked at her as if she was *loca* but then he must have recalled what he had been told about her accident. '*Sí, señora,*' he said with a white toothed smile. 'She is in the stable. I exercised her earlier this morning.'

'Could I ride her, please?' Emelia asked.

He gave her a surprised look. 'You want to *ride* her?'

She nodded. 'Of course I do.'

'But you have never wanted to ride her before,' he said with a puzzled frown. 'You refused to even look at her.'

Emelia laughed off the suggestion. 'That's crazy. I love to ride. I had my own horse when my mother was alive. I used to spend every weekend and holidays at Pony Club or on riding camps.'

Pedro shrugged his shoulders as if he wasn't sure what to make of her as he made his way to the stables.

Emelia jumped down from the railing and followed him. 'I'm sorry but I've forgotten your name,' she said.

'Pedro,' he said. 'I look after the horses for Señor Mélendez. I have been working for him for two years now. The same time you have been married, *sí*?'

Emelia gave him a small smile, not sure how much he knew of her situation. The stallion snorted and pawed the ground and she stepped up to him and stroked his proud forehead. 'You are being a great big show-off, do you know that?' she crooned softly.

The stallion snorted again but then began to rub his head against her chest, almost pushing her over.

Pedro's look was still quizzical. 'He likes you, Señora Mélendez. But you used to be frightened of him. He is big and proud and has a mind of his own. He is…how you say…a softie inside.'

Emelia wondered if Pedro was talking about the horse or her husband. Probably both, she imagined. She breathed in the sweet smell of horse and hay and felt a flicker of something in her memory. She put a hand to her head, frowning as she tried to retrieve it before it disappeared.

'*Señora?*' Pedro's voice was concerned as he pulled the horse back from her. 'Are you all right? Did Gitano hurt you?'

'No, of course not,' Emelia said. 'I was just trying to remember something but it's gone now.'

Pedro led the stallion back to his stall and a short time later led out a pretty little mare. She had the same proud bearing as Gitano but her temperament was clearly very different. She whinnied when she caught sight of Emelia and her big soft round eyes shone with delight.

Emelia put her arms around the horse's neck, breathing in her sweet scent, closing her eyes as she searched her memory. A scene filtered through the fog in her head. It was a similar day to today, sunny with a light breeze. She was being led blindfolded down to the stables; she could even feel the nerves she had felt buzzing in the pit of her stomach. She could feel warm strong hands guiding her, a tall lean body brushing her from behind, the sharp citrus of his aftershave striking another chord of memory in her brain…

'Señora Mélendez?' Pedro's voice slammed the door on her memory. 'Are you all right?'

Emelia opened her eyes and, disguising her frustration, sent him a crooked smile. 'I'm fine,' she said.

'Callida looks very well. You must be doing a wonderful job of looking after her.'

'Señora,' Pedro said with rounded eyes, 'you remember her name, *sí*? Callida. Señor Mélendez bought her for you as a surprise for your birthday last month.'

Emelia stared at the youth for a moment, her brain whirling. 'I…I don't know how I remembered her name. It was just there in my head,' she said.

Pedro smiled a wide smile. 'It is good you are home. You will remember everything in time, *sí*?'

Emelia returned his smile but a little more cautiously. If only she had his confidence. But it did seem strange that Callida's name had been there on her tongue without her thinking about it; strange too that her Spanish had come to her equally as automatically. What else was lying inside her head, just waiting for the right trigger to unlock it?

Callida nudged against her, blowing at her through her velvet nostrils. Emelia tickled the horse's forelock. 'Can you saddle her for me?' she asked Pedro.

The lad's smile was quickly exchanged for a grave look. 'Señor Mélendez…I am not sure he would want you to ride. You have a head injury, *sí*? Not good to ride so soon.'

Emelia felt her neck and shoulders straighten in rebellion. 'I am perfectly well,' she said. 'And I would like to take Callida out to see if it helps me remember anything else. I need some exercise, in any case. I can't sit around all day doing nothing until my…hus…until Señor Mélendez returns.'

Pedro shifted his weight from foot to foot, his hands on Callida's leading rein fidgeting with agitation. 'I have been given instructions. I could lose my job.'

Emelia took the leading rein from him. 'I will explain to Señor Mélendez that I insisted. Don't worry. I won't let him fire you.'

The lad looked uncertain but Emelia had already made up her mind and led the mare to the stables. Pedro followed and, wordlessly and with tight lips, saddled the horse, handing Emelia a riding helmet once he had finished.

Emelia put it on and, giving him a smile, swung up into the saddle and rode out of the stable courtyard, relishing the sense of freedom it afforded her. She rode through the fields to the woods beyond, at a gentle walk at first and then, as her confidence grew, she squeezed Callida's sides to get her to trot. It wasn't long before she urged the horse into a canter, the rhythm so easy to ride to she felt as if she had been riding her for ever. How strange that Pedro had said she had refused to ride the horse Javier had bought for her. The horse was well bred and would have cost a mint. Why had she rejected such a beautiful precious gift?

After a while Emelia came to an olive grove and another flicker of memory was triggered in her brain. She slipped out of the saddle and led the horse to the spot where she thought the photograph she had seen in Javier's study was taken. Callida nudged against her and Emelia absently stroked the mare's neck as she looked at the soft green grass where she had lain with Javier. Had they made love under the shade of the olive trees? she wondered. Her skin tingled, the hairs on the back of her neck rising as she pictured them there, limbs entangled intimately, Javier's leanly muscled body pinning hers beneath the potent power of his.

She thought back to their conversation about the

terms of their marriage. The rules she had accepted supposedly without question. No children to tie either of them down. When had she decided she didn't want children? Had she said it just to keep Javier happy? He struck her as a man who valued and enjoyed his freedom. In many ways he seemed to still live the life of a playboy: regular international travel on private jets, a disposable income, no ties or responsibilities other than a relatively new wife who apparently didn't travel with him with any regularity. Children would definitely require a commitment from him he might not feel ready to agree to at this stage of his life.

Emelia, on the other hand, had always loved children; it was one of the reasons she had wanted to teach instead of perform. She loved their innocence and their wonder at the world and had always dreamed of having a family of her own some day. Growing up as an only child with numerous stepmothers entering and exiting her life had made her determined to marry a man who would be a wonderful husband and father, a man who was faithful and steadfast, nothing at all like her restless father. Why then had she married a man who didn't want the same things she did? Surely she hadn't slept with him for any other reason than love. She had vowed ever since her disastrous affair of the past that she would never make that mistake again. But, thinking about the current of electricity that had flared between her and Javier from the first moment he had stepped up to her bedside in the hospital, Emelia had to wonder if she had fallen victim to the power of sexual attraction after all. If only Peter was still alive so she could ask him to fill in the gaps for her.

She had made a couple of girlfriends at the hotel but

none of them were particularly close. Besides, they had been on temporary visas and would have moved on by now. It seemed the only way to find out her past was piece by piece, like putting a complicated jigsaw puzzle back together without the original picture as a guide.

Emelia rode back to the villa and handed Callida over to Pedro, who had very obviously been hovering about, waiting for her return. He took the mare with visible relief and reluctantly agreed on having the horse ready for another ride at the same time tomorrow.

When Emelia came downstairs after a shower she was informed by Aldana she had a visitor.

'She is waiting in *la sala*,' the housekeeper said with a frosty look.

'*Gracias*, Aldana,' Emelia said. 'But who is it? Someone I should know?'

Aldana pursed her lips but, before she could respond, female footsteps click-clacked from behind Emelia and a young voice called out, 'So you are back.'

Emelia turned to see a young female version of Javier stalking haughtily towards her. The young woman's dark-as-night eyes were flashing, her mouth was a thin line of disapproval and her long raven hair practically bristled with anger. 'Izabella?'

The young woman's eyes narrowed to paper-thin slits. 'So you remember me, do you? How very interesting.'

Emelia took a steadying breath. 'It was a guess, but apparently a very good one.'

Izabella planted her hands on her boyishly slim hips, sending Emelia another wish-you-were-dead glare. 'You shouldn't be here. You have no right to be here after what you did.'

Emelia marshalled her defences, keeping her tone civil but determined. 'I'm not sure what I am supposedly guilty of doing. Perhaps you could enlighten me.'

Izabella tossed her glossy dark head. 'Don't play the innocent with me. It might have worked with my brother but it won't work with me. I know what you are up to.'

Emelia was conscious of the housekeeper listening to every word. 'Would you like to come into *la sala* and discuss this further?' she asked.

Izabella gave another flash of her midnight eyes. 'I don't care who hears what I have to say.'

'Does your brother know you are here?' Emelia asked after a tense pause.

The young woman's haughty stance slipped a notch. 'He is not my keeper,' she said, making a moue of her mouth.

'That's not what he told me,' Emelia returned.

Izabella gave her head another toss as she folded her arms across her chest. 'He wouldn't have taken you back, you know. He only did it because he had no choice. The press would have crucified him if he'd divorced you so soon after the accident.'

Emelia felt as if a heavy weight had landed on her chest. She felt faint and had to struggle to remain steady on her feet. She would have excused herself but her desire to know more about her forgotten marriage overruled any concern for her well-being. 'Wh-what are you saying?'

'He was going to divorce you,' Izabella said with an aristocratic hoist of her chin. 'He had already contacted his lawyer.'

Emelia moistened her lips. 'On…on what grounds?'

Izabella's gaze was pure venom. 'Adultery.' She almost spat the word at Emelia. 'You ran away to be with your lover.'

Emelia stood in a frozen silence as she mentally replayed every conversation she'd had with Javier since she had woken in the hospital. While he hadn't accused her of anything openly, he had alluded to what the press had made of her relationship with Peter. He had also expressed his bitterness at her remembering Peter while not remembering him, which she had thought was a reasonable reaction under the circumstances. But if Javier truly believed her to have been unfaithful, what was he waiting for? Why not divorce her and be done with it? Did he really care what the press would make of it? What did he hope to gain by taking her back as if nothing had happened? It didn't make sense, not unless he loved her and was prepared to leave the past in the past, but somehow she didn't think that was the case. He desired her. She was acutely aware of the heat of his gaze every time it rested on her, indeed as aware of her own response to him. She was not immune to him, in spite of her memory loss. One kiss had shown how vulnerable she was to him.

'But it's not true,' she said after a moment. 'I didn't commit adultery.'

Izabella rolled her eyes. 'Of course you would say that. Your lover is dead, so what else could you do? You had to come back to Javier. He is rich and you had nowhere else to go. Even your own father would not take you back. You are nothing but a gold-digger.'

Emelia felt ill but worked hard to hold her composure. 'Look, Izabella, I realise you must be upset if you have heard rumours such as the outrageous one you just relayed to me, but I can assure you I have never been unfaithful to your brother. It's just not something I would do. I know it in my heart.'

Izabella gave her a challenging glare. 'How would you know? You say you don't remember anything from the past two years. How do you know *what* you did?'

It was a very good point, Emelia had to admit. But, deep down, she knew she would never have betrayed her marriage vows. How she was going to prove it was something she had yet to work out. Her reputation had been ruined by scandalous reports in the media. Who would believe her, even if she could remember what had happened that fateful day?

'Did you ever love my brother?' Izabella asked.

The question momentarily knocked Emelia off course. She looked at the young woman blankly, knowing as each pulsing second passed another layer of blame was being shovelled on top of her. 'I…I don't feel it is anyone's business but Javier's and mine,' she said.

Izabella gave a scathing snort. 'You never loved him. What you love is what he can give you—the lifestyle, the clothes, the jewellery. It's all you have ever wanted from him.'

'That is not true.' *Please don't let it be true*, Emelia thought.

'He is not going to remain faithful to you, you know. Why should he when you played up behind his back?'

Emelia felt a stake go through her middle. It surprised her how much Izabella's coolly delivered statement hurt her. Her mind filled with images of Javier with other women, his body locked with theirs, giving and receiving pleasure. Perhaps even now he was entertaining himself with some gorgeous creature in

Moscow. She shook her head, trying to get the torturous images to disappear. 'No,' she said in a rasping whisper. 'No…'

'He should never have married you,' Izabella said. 'Everyone told him it would end in disaster.'

Emelia lifted her aching head to meet Izabella's gaze. 'Why did he marry me, then?'

'Because he needed to be married to gain access to our father's estate,' Izabella said.

Emelia felt her heart give another sickening lurch. 'He married me to…to get *money*?'

'You surely don't think he loved you, do you?' Izabella threw her a disdainful look. 'He wanted you and what he wants he usually gets. You were a convenient wife. A trophy he wanted by his side. But that is all you are to him. He does not love you.'

'Did I *know* this?' Emelia asked in a hoarse whisper.

Izabella's expression lost some of its hauteur. 'I am not sure…' She bit down on her bottom lip in a way that seemed to strip years off her. 'Perhaps not. Maybe I shouldn't have said anything…'

Emelia reached for something to hold onto to steady herself. 'I can't believe I agreed to such an emotionless arrangement…' She looked at the young girl with an anguished expression on her face. 'I always wanted to marry for love. Are you sure I was not in love with Javier?'

Izabella looked troubled. 'If you were, you never said anything to me. You kept your feelings to yourself, although it was pretty obvious you were attracted to him. But then he's attractive to a lot of women.'

Emelia didn't want to think about that. It was just too painful. 'I'm sorry if I've given you the wrong impression,' she said after a moment. 'Javier told me you and I haven't had the easiest of relationships. I hope I haven't done anything to upset you. I have never had a sister before. I've always wanted one, especially after my mother died. It would have been nice to have someone to talk to about girl stuff.'

Izabella's dark brown eyes softened a fraction. 'Javier is the best brother a girl could have but there are times when I would rather share what is going on in my life with another woman. My mother is OK but she just worries if I talk to her about boys. She always thinks I am going to get pregnant or something.'

Emelia smiled. 'I guess it's what mothers do best—worry.'

Izabella's mouth tilted in a wary smile. 'You seem so different,' she said. 'Almost like a completely different person.'

'To tell you the truth, Izabella, I feel like a completely different person from the one everyone expects me to be,' Emelia confessed. 'I look at the clothes in my wardrobe and I can't believe I have ever worn them. They seem so…so…I don't know…not me. And when I was down at the stables Pedro told me I had refused to ride the horse Javier bought me last month for my birthday. I don't understand it. Why would I not ride that beautiful horse?'

'Ever since your birthday you seemed a little unsettled,' Izabella said. 'When you had the accident we all assumed it was because you were in love with another man. Now, I wonder if it wasn't because you were becoming a little tired of your life here. There is only so much time you can spend in the shops or the gym.'

Emelia felt her face heat up with colour. 'Yes, well,

that's another thing I don't get. I *hate* the gym. I can think of nothing worse than an elliptical trainer or a stationary bike and weight machines.'

'You worked out religiously,' Izabella said. 'You lost pounds and pounds within weeks of meeting Javier. And you are always dieting whenever Javier's away.'

Emelia thought back to her hearty breakfast that morning. 'No wonder I've been such a pain to be around,' she said with a wry grimace. 'I'm hopeless at diets. I have no self control. I get bitchy when I deprive myself.'

Izabella grinned. 'I do too.'

There was a little pause.

'You won't tell Javier I was so horrible to you, will you?' Izabella said with a worried look. 'He will be angry with me for upsetting you. I should have thought... You have just had a terrible accident. I am sorry about your friend. You must be very sad.'

'I am coping with it,' Emelia said. 'But I wish I knew what really happened that day.'

Izabella bit her lip again. 'Maybe you were leaving Javier because you didn't want to continue with the marriage as it was. The press would have latched on to it pretty quickly and made it out to be something it wasn't. Javier was furious. He was determined to divorce you but then he got news of the accident.' Her slim throat rose and fell. 'He was devastated when he heard you might not make it. He tried to hide it but I could tell he was terrified you would die.'

Emelia frowned as she tried to make sense of it all. If Javier didn't want her in his life permanently, why suffer her presence just because of her memory loss? Given what he believed of her, what hope did she have of restoring his trust in her? Had he known her so little that he had readily believed the specious rumours of the press? What sort of marriage had they had that it would crumble so quickly? Surely over the almost two years they had been together a level of trust had been established? She felt sure she would not have settled for anything else. It was so frustrating to have no way of finding out the truth. Her mind was like the missing black box of a crashed aircraft. Within it were all the clues to what had happened and until it was found she would have to try and piece together what she could to make sense of it all. Her head ached from the pressure of trying to remember. Her eyes felt as if they had been stabbed with roofing nails, pain pulsed from her temples like hammer blows.

Izabella touched Emelia on the arm. 'You are very pale,' she said. 'Is there anything I can ask Aldana to get for you?'

'I don't think Aldana will appreciate having to act as nursemaid to me,' Emelia said, putting a hand to her throbbing temple. 'She doesn't seem to like me very much.'

'She has never liked you but it's probably not your fault,' Izabella said. 'Her daughter once had a fling with Javier. It wasn't serious but, ever since, Aldana has been convinced no one but her daughter was good enough for Javier. I think you tried hard at first to get along but after a while you gave up.'

It explained a lot, Emelia thought. She couldn't imagine being deliberately rude to the household staff under any circumstances. But perhaps she had lost patience with Aldana, as Izabella had suggested, and consequently acted like the spoilt, overly indulged trophy wife everyone assumed her to be. 'I am so glad you came here today,' she said. 'I hope we can be friends.'

'I would like that very much,' Izabella said and, looking sheepish, added, 'I haven't always treated you very well. You were so beautiful and accomplished, so talented at playing the piano. I was such a cow to you, I guess because I was jealous. I probably contributed to your unhappiness with Javier.'

'I am sure you had no part to play in that at all,' Emelia said. 'I should have been more mature and understanding.'

'Please, you must promise not to tell Javier I was rude to you before,' Izabella said. 'I am so ashamed of myself.'

'You have no need to be,' Emelia said. 'Anyway, you were only acting out of your concern for him.'

Izabella's gaze melted. 'Yes, he's a wonderful brother. He would do anything for me. I am very lucky to have him.'

'He's lucky to have you,' Emelia said, thinking of all of her years alone, without anyone to stand up for her. It seemed nothing had changed: this recent scandal demonstrated how truly alone she was. No one had challenged the rumours. No one had defended her.

Izabella suddenly cocked her head. 'Your memory must be coming back, Emelia,' she said with an engaging grin.

Emelia shook her head. 'No, I've tried and tried but I can't remember much at all.'

'Except Spanish.'

Emelia felt her heart knock against her ribcage. She

hadn't realised until that point that every word she had exchanged with Izabella had been in Spanish.

Every single word.

CHAPTER SIX

IZABELLA had arranged to join some friends in Valencia the following day before she flew back to Paris so Emelia was left to her own devices. After a shower and breakfast, she wandered out into the gardens, stopping every now and again to pick a rose until, after half an hour, her arms were nearly full. She went back to the villa and laid them down on one of the large kitchen benches, breathing in the delicate fragrance as she searched for some vases.

Aldana appeared just as Emelia was carrying a vase full of blooms into *la sala*. 'What are you doing?' she asked, frowning formidably.

'I picked some roses,' Emelia said. 'I thought they would look nice in some of the rooms to brighten them up a bit. I hope you don't mind.'

Aldana took the vase out of Emelia's grasp. 'Señor Mélendez does not like roses in the house,' she said in a clipped tone.

Emelia felt her shoulders slump. 'Oh…sorry, I didn't realise…'

The housekeeper shot her another hateful glare as she carried the roses out of the room. The look seemed to suggest that, in Aldana's opinion, Emelia had never known her husband's likes and dislikes like a proper loving wife should do.

Emelia let out a sigh once she was alone. There was a baby grand piano at one end of *la sala*, positioned out of the direct sunlight from the windows. She went over to it and sat down and after a moment she opened the lid and ran her fingers over the keys, trying to remember what song she had played the night she had met Javier, but it was like trying to play a new piece without the musical score. She played several pieces, hoping that one would unlock her mind, but none did. She closed the lid in frustration and left the room to make her way down to the stables.

Pedro had Callida saddled for her when she arrived but he looked disgruntled. 'Señor Mélendez will not be happy about this,' he said. 'He told all the staff to watch out for you, to make sure you do not come to any harm while he is away.'

'Señor Mélendez is several thousand kilometres away,' Emelia said as she swung up into the saddle. 'While the cat's away this little mouse is going to do what she wants.'

Pedro stepped back from the horse with a disapproving frown. 'He sometimes comes back early from his trips abroad,' he said. 'He expects his staff to act the same whether he is here or not. He trusts us.'

But not me, Emelia thought resentfully as she rode off. No doubt he had only put his staff on watch over her to see that she didn't stray too far from the boundaries of the villa. His solicitous care had nothing to do with any deep feelings on his part. He wanted to keep her a virtual prisoner until the press interest died down. After that, who knew what he planned to do? All she knew was his plans would probably not include her being in his life for the long term.

As enjoyable as the ride was, it didn't unearth any clues to her past. She came back to the stables an hour and a half later, fighting off a weighty despondency. The olive grove today had simply been an olive grove. No further memories surfaced. Nothing struck a chord of familiarity.

Disappointment and frustration continued to sour her mood as she walked back to the villa through the gardens. She felt hot and sticky so when she came across a secluded section of the garden where an infinity pool was situated, she decided to take advantage of the sparkling blue water and the warmth of the afternoon.

Rummaging through the walk-in wardrobe in search of swimwear was another revelation to her. Naturally modest, she found it hard to believe she wore any of the skimpy bikinis she found in one of the drawers. There were pink ones and red ones and yellow ones and ones with polka dots, a black one with silver diamantés and a white one with gold circles in between the triangles of fabric that would barely cover her breasts, let alone her lower body. In the end she chose the red one as it was the least revealing, although once she had it on and checked her appearance in the full length mirrors she was glad Javier was not expected home. She might as well have been naked.

The water was warmed by the sun but still refreshing enough to make Emelia swim length after length without exhaustion. She wondered how many times she had done this, stroking her way through the water, perhaps with Javier swimming alongside her, or his long legs tangling with hers as he kissed or caressed her. In spite of the warmth of the pool and the sun, Emelia felt her skin lift in little goosebumps the more she let her mind wander about what had occurred in the past.

As she surfaced at the end of the pool she saw a long pair of trouser-clad legs, the large male feet encased in expensive-looking leather shoes. Her heart gave a stop-start as her eyes moved upwards to meet the coal-black gaze of Javier.

'I thought I might find you here,' he said.

Emelia pushed her hair out of her face, conscious of her barely clad breasts just at the water's level. 'I didn't realise you would be back. I thought you were coming home tomorrow.'

He tugged at his tie as his gaze held hers. 'I managed to get through the work and flew back ahead of schedule.'

Emelia swallowed as she saw him toss his tie to one of the sun loungers. His fingers began undoing the buttons of his business shirt, one by one, each opening revealing a little more of his muscular chest. 'Um… what are you doing?' she said.

'I thought I might join you,' he said, shrugging himself out of his shirt, tossing it in the same direction as his tie, his dark eyes still tethering hers.

She watched in a spellbound stasis as his hands went to his belt, slipping it through the waistband of his trousers, casting it on top of his shirt and tie. The sound of his zip going down jolted her out of her trance. 'Y-you're surely not going to swim without bathers…are you?'

A corner of his mouth lifted. 'Do you have any objection, *querida*?' he asked.

Emelia could think of several but she couldn't seem to get her voice to work. She stood in the water as he heeled himself out of his shoes and purposefully pulled off his socks. Her heart started thumping irregularly as he stepped out of his trousers, leaving him in close-fitting black briefs that left almost nothing to her imagination. She felt a stirring deep and low in her belly. He was so potently male, so powerfully built, lean but muscular at the same time, hair in all the right places, marking him as different from her as could be. His skin was a deep olive, tanned by the sun, each rippling ridge of his abdomen like coils of steel. Her fingertips suddenly itched to explore every hard contour of him, to feel the satin quality of his skin and unleash the latent power of his body. She wondered if her attraction was a new thing or an old thing. Was her body remembering what her mind could or would not? How else could she explain this unbelievable tension she felt when he was near her? She had never felt like this with anyone before. It was as if he awakened everything that was female in her body, making her long to discover the power of the passion his glittering dark gaze promised.

Being at the shallower end, he didn't dive into the water; instead, he slipped in with an agility that made Emelia aware of every plane of his body as the water his entry displaced washed against her. It was as if he had touched her; the water felt just like an intimate caress: smooth, gentle, cajoling, tempting. Her eyes were still locked with his; she couldn't seem to move out of the magnetic range of his dark-as-night eyes. They burned, they seared and they smouldered as he closed the distance between their bodies, stopping just in front of her, not quite touching but close enough for her to feel the pull of his body through the weight of the water.

'Why so shy?' he asked.

Emelia licked a droplet of water off her lips. 'Um…I know this is probably something you…I mean we have done lots of times but I…I…feel too exposed.'

His lips slanted in a smile. 'You got rid of your timidity a long time ago, Emelia. We skinny-dipped together all the time.'

She felt the pit of her stomach tilt. 'But surely someone could have seen us?'

He gave a little couldn't-care-less shrug. 'The pool area is private. In any case, what would it matter if someone had seen us? We are married and this is private property. It is not as if we were doing anything wrong.'

Emelia chewed at her lip, wishing she could download all her memories so she wasn't feeling so lost and uncertain. While she had been dressing in the bikini earlier she had seen from her lightly tanned skin that she had been in the sun and not always with all her clothes on. She had not been the type to sunbathe topless in the past, but then two whole years of her life were missing. Who knew what she had grown comfortable with over that time? It made her feel all the more on edge around Javier. He knew far more about her than she knew about him. And yet she could sense in her body a growing recognition that flickered a little more each time they were together.

'Aldana told me you had a visitor while I was away,' Javier said.

Emelia kept her expression masked. 'Yes. Izabella called in. She's gone to stay with friends in Valencia before she goes back to Paris.'

'Did you recognise her?'

She shook her head. 'No, but I soon figured out who she was. She is very like you. It is obvious you are related. You have the same hair and eyes.'

'I hope you refrained from getting into an argument with her,' he said, still holding her gaze. 'I would not want either of you upset.'

'No, we didn't argue,' Emelia said. 'I found her to be friendly and pleasant and not in the least hostile. She's a very beautiful and poised young woman. You must be very proud of her.'

He frowned as he studied her through narrowed eyes. 'What did you talk about?'

'The usual girl stuff,' she said. 'We have a lot in common, actually.'

'She is a little headstrong at times,' he admitted. 'But then she is still young.'

Emelia went to move to the steps leading out of the pool but he placed a hand on her arm, stopping her from moving away from him. 'Where are you going?' he asked.

'I'm getting cold,' she said. 'I want to have a shower.'

He cupped both of her shoulders with his hands. 'No kiss for my return?'

Emelia felt her eyes widen and her stomach did another flip turn. 'It's not as if things are the same...as before,' she said. 'I need more time.'

Something moved at the back of his eyes. 'I think the sooner we slip back into our previous routine the better,' he said. 'I am convinced it will help you remember.'

'You're assuming I will remember,' she said. 'I had no such assurance from any of the doctors or therapists at the hospital.'

His hands tightened as soon as he felt her try to escape again. 'It doesn't matter if you remember or not. It doesn't change the fact that we are married.'

Emelia straightened her spine in defiance but, by doing so, it brought her pelvis into direct contact with his. The hot hard heat of him was like being zapped with a thousand volts of electricity. She felt the tingles shoot through her from head to foot. His eyes dropped to the startled *'O'* of her mouth and then, as if in slow motion, gradually lowered his head until his lips sealed hers.

It was a slow burn of a kiss, heating her to her core as each pulsing second passed. His tongue probed the seam of her mouth for entry and she gave it on a whimper of pleasure. The rasp of his tongue as it mated with hers sent a cascading shiver down the backs of her legs and up again, right to the back of her neck. She felt her toes curl on the tiled floor of the pool as his kiss deepened. His arms had gone from the tops of her shoulders down the slim length of her arms to settle about her waist, holding her against his pelvis, leaving her acutely aware of his rock-hard arousal. Her body responded automatically, the ache between her thighs becoming more insistent the firmer he held her against him. She moved against him, a slight nudge at first and then a blatant rub to feel the pleasure his body offered.

He slowly but surely walked her backwards, his thighs brushing hers with each step, his mouth still locked on her mouth, his body jammed tight against her. His hands moved up from her waist to deftly untie the strings of her bikini. It fell away, leaving her breasts free for his touch. She drew in a sharp breath as his hands cupped her, his thumb gently stroking over each nipple, making her flesh cry out for more. His mouth left hers and went on a leisurely mission, exploring every dip and curve on the way down to her breasts: the sensitive pleasure spots behind each of her earlobes, the hollows above her collarbone and the super-reactive skin of her neck. She tilted her head to one side as he nibbled and nipped in turn, her belly turning over in delight as he finally made his way to her breasts. He left her nipples alone this time and concentrated instead on the sensitive under curves of each breast, first with his fingers and then with the heat and fire of his mouth. She arched up against him, wanting more, wanting it all, wanting to feel whatever he had made her feel in the past.

His mouth came back to her searching, hungry one, his hands going to the strings holding her bikini bottom in place. Emelia's hands moved from around his neck to the small of his back, delighting in the way he groaned deeply as he surged against her. Casting inhibition aside, she peeled away his briefs, freeing him into her hands. She felt a hitch in her breath as she shaped his steely length, the throb of his blood pounding against her fingers. He was so thick with desire it made her own blood race at the thought of him moving inside her.

He tore his mouth off hers, looking down at her with eyes glittering with desire. 'You have certainly not forgotten how to drive me wild with wanting you,' he said. 'How about it, *querida*? Shall we finish this here and now, or wait for later?'

Emelia felt the cold slap of shock bring her back to reality. What was she doing allowing him such liberties and outside where anyone could see if they put their mind to it? And what was she doing touching him as if she wanted him to finish what he had started? What was wrong with her? Surely she had not become such a

slave of the flesh? She had always abhorred such irresponsible behaviour amongst her peers; the casual
approach to sex was something she had never gone in
for. She put up her chin, working hard to maintain her
composure when she was stark naked. 'What makes you
so sure I would give my consent, here or anywhere?'

His smile was on the edge of mocking. 'Because I
know you, Emelia. I know how you respond to me. A
couple of minutes more and you would have been
begging for it.'

There was nothing figurative about the slap Emelia
landed on the side of Javier's face. It jerked his head
back, made his nostrils flare and his mouth tighten to a
flat line of tension. 'You know, you really shouldn't
have done that,' he said with a coolness she was sure he
was nowhere near feeling.

Emelia refused to wilt under his hard black gaze.
'You insulted me. You practically called me a wanton
tramp.'

One of his hands rubbed at the red hand-sized mark
on his jaw. 'So if someone allegedly insults you it's OK
to use violence?' he asked.

She bit the inside of her mouth, suddenly ashamed
of how she had reacted, but there was no way she was
going to apologise to him. She turned and searched for
her bikini, struggling to put it back on while still in the
water. She was conscious of Javier's eyes following her
every movement and her resentment and anger
hardened like a golf ball-sized lump in the middle of her
chest. Once she was covered, she stomped up the pool
steps, snatching up her towel on the way past the sun
lounger where she had left it.

* * *

The moment Emelia came out of the en suite bathroom after a lengthy shower she knew something was amiss. Her eyes went to the bed where a black leather brief-case was lying at the foot of it. She heard the sound of someone moving about in the walk-in wardrobe and, clutching her bathrobe a little tighter, spun around to find Aldana coming out with some spare coat hangers.

'What's going on?' Emelía asked in Spanish.

The housekeeper gave her a pursed-lipped look. 'Señor Mélendez instructed me to hang his clothes.'

Emelia's eyes widened in alarm. 'What? In…in *here*?'

Aldana gave a shrug as she walked past. 'It is none of my business what he wants or why. I just do as I am told. He wanted me to bring his things back in here where they belong.'

The housekeeper left before Emelia could respond and within seconds Javier strode in. She turned on him, her eyes flashing with fury. *'Qué diablos está pasando?'* she asked. 'What the hell is going on?'

He stood very still for a moment before responding in Spanish. 'I could ask you the very same thing. What the hell *is* going on? Especially as it seems at least some part of your memory has returned without you telling me.'

Emelia felt her cheeks fill with colour. 'I…I was going to tell you…'

'When did it happen?' he asked.

She could barely hold his gaze as she confessed. 'I found myself understanding it and speaking it from the start. I don't know why. It was just…there.'

'How convenient.'

Emelia's hands tightened where they clutched the

neckline of her bathrobe. 'I know what you're thinking but it's not true. I don't remember anything else. I swear to you.'

He gave her a cynical smile that contained no trace of amusement. 'I met Pedro the stable boy on my way in earlier,' he said. 'He was full of excitement over how you remembered your mare's name without any prompting from him.'

Emelia pressed her lips together. 'I forgot I remembered…' It sounded as stupid as she felt and she lowered her gaze from the hard probe of his, hating herself for blushing.

'He also told me you have finally ridden your horse,' he said.

'I can't explain why I never rode Callida before.' She looked up at him again. 'You must have been very annoyed with me after spending so much money on such a beautiful animal.'

He held her gaze for a long moment. 'It wasn't the first present you rejected of late,' he said. 'It seemed over the last few weeks nothing I did for you or bought for you could please you.'

Emelia wondered if she had been hankering after more from him than what money could buy. It seemed much more in line with her true character. She had been given expensive gifts for most of her life but they hadn't made her feel any more secure.

Javier used two fingers to lift her chin, searing her gaze with his. 'I want you to tell me the moment you remember anything else, do you understand? I don't care what time of day it is or if I am away or here. Just tell me.'

She let out an uneven breath as she stepped out from

under his hold. 'You can't force me to remember you, Javier. It doesn't happen like that. I read up about it. Sometimes the memories are blocked because of trauma, either physical or emotional or maybe even both.'

A muscle worked in his jaw, the silence stretching and stretching like a threadbare piece of elastic.

'So what you are saying is you might be subconsciously blocking all memory of our life together?' he finally said.

Emelia released her bottom lip from the savaging of her teeth. 'I'm not sure if that's what has happened or not,' she said. 'Was there something that happened that might have caused me to do that? Something deeply upsetting, I mean.'

The silence stretched again, even further this time.

'I was away the day you left for London,' Javier said heavily. He waited a beat before continuing. 'I had only just come back from Moscow when we had an argument. I flew straight back afterwards.'

Emelia felt a frown tugging at her forehead. 'What did we argue about?'

His eyes met hers briefly before moving away to focus on a point beyond her left shoulder. 'The papers had printed some rubbish about me being involved with someone in Russia, a nightclub singer.'

Emelia felt a fist wrap itself around her heart. 'Was it…was it true?'

His dark eyes flashed with irritation as they came back to hers. 'Of course it wasn't true. I have to deal with those rumours all the time. I thought you were OK about it. We'd talked about it early in our marriage. We used to laugh about some of the stuff that was printed.

I warned you what it would be like, that there would be constant rumours, often set off by business rivals.'

He stopped to scrape a hand through his hair. 'But this time for some reason you refused to accept my explanation. You got it in your head that I was playing up behind your back. It seemed nothing I said would change your mind.'

'So we had an argument…'

'Yes,' he said. 'I'm afraid it was a bit of an ugly scene.'

Emelia raised her brows questioningly. 'How ugly?'

He let out a long tense breath. 'There was a lot of shouting and name calling. We were both angry and upset. I should have cut the argument short but I was annoyed because you seemed determined to want our marriage to be something it was never intended to be.'

Emelia sent him a let's-see-if-you-can-deny-this look. 'So apparently I wasn't too happy you had married me to gain access to your father's estate, right?'

His dark gaze turned flinty. 'That was one of the things we argued about, yes. While I was away, my father's mistress had rung you and filled your head with that and other such nonsense to get back at me. But the truth is my reasons for marrying you had very little to do with my father's will.'

She rolled her eyes in disbelief. 'Oh, come now, Javier. You talk of our marriage as some sort of business proposal, rules and regulations and me suddenly stepping outside of them. What the hell was the point of being married if not because we loved each other?'

'Love was not part of the deal,' he said, shocking Emelia into silence. 'I wanted a wife. Some of the business people I deal with are old-fashioned and conservative in their views. They feel more comfortable dealing with a man in a seemingly stable relationship. I know it sounds a little cold-blooded but you were quite happy to take on the corporate wife role. We were ideally matched physically. It was all I wanted from you and you from me.'

She stood looking at him with her emotions reeling. How could she have agreed to such a marriage? A relationship based on sex and nothing else? Had she turned into a clone of her father's set, in spite of her determination not to? She had become a trophy wife, an exotic bird in a gilded cage. Indulged and pampered until her mind went numb.

Javier let out another breath and sent his hand through his hair again. 'Emelia…' He hesitated for a moment before he continued. 'You might not remember it but we made love during that last argument.'

Emelia felt her brows lift again but remained silent.

His gaze remained steady on hers. 'In hindsight, it was perhaps not the best way to leave things between us. There was so much left unresolved. I have had cause to wonder if that is why you rushed off to London the way you did.'

Emelia searched her mind for some trace of that scene but nothing came to her. 'Did I explain why I left? In a note or something?'

'Yes,' he said.

Hope flickered in her chest. 'Can I see it?'

'I tore it into shreds,' he said, his mouth tightening at the memory. 'I got home from Moscow two days after you left. That is another thing I am not particularly proud of. I should have come straight to London as soon as I knew you were there. I was packing a bag when I got the call about the accident.'

'What did I say in the note?' Emelia asked.

He looked at her silently for several moments. 'You said you were leaving me, that you no longer wanted to continue with our marriage. You wanted out.'

Emelia rubbed at her forehead, as if that would unlock the memories stored inside her head. OK, so she had been leaving him. That much was pretty certain. Was it because she had become tired of their shallow relationship, as Izabella had suggested? Emelia knew she must have been very unhappy to have come to that decision. Unhappy or desperate. 'The rumours…' she said. 'You mentioned a few days ago there was some speculation about my relationship with Peter Marshall. Did you afford me the same level of trust you expected of me, in similar if not the same circumstances?'

He visibly tensed; all of his muscles seemed to contract as if sprayed with fast setting glue. 'I am the first to admit that I was jealous of your relationship with him,' he said, biting each word out from between his clenched teeth. 'He seemed at great pains whenever I was around to show me just how close you were. He was always touching you, slinging an arm around your waist or shoulders. It made me want to lash out.'

Emelia frowned at his vehement confession. 'Peter was a touchy-feely sort of person. It was just his way. I am sure I would have told you that right from the start.'

His eyes flashed with heat. 'You did, but it still annoyed the hell out of me.'

He was jealous. He hated admitting it, Emelia was sure, but he was positively vibrating with it. She could see it in the way he held himself, his hands clenching and unclenching as if he wanted to hit something.

He paced the room a couple of times before he came back to stand in front of her. 'If I was wrong about your relationship with Marshall then I am sorry,' he said. 'All the evidence pointed to you being guilty of an affair, but in hindsight there are probably numerous explanations for why you were in that car with him.'

Emelia felt a weight come off her shoulders. 'You truly believe I wasn't unfaithful?'

He held her look for endless seconds. 'Let's just let it go,' he said on a long breath. 'I don't want to be reminded of the mistakes I have made in the past. We have to concentrate on the here and now. I want to see you get well again. I feel it is my fault you were almost killed. I cannot forgive myself for driving you away in such an emotionally charged state. I should have insisted we sit down and sort things out like two rational adults. Instead, I let business take precedence, hoping things would settle down by the time I got back.'

Emelia stood looking at him in silence. His gruff admission of guilt stirred her deep inside. She could tell it was unfamiliar territory for him. He didn't seem the type to readily admit when he was in the wrong.

She breathed in the clean male scent of him as he stood so broodingly before her. He had showered and changed into a polo shirt and casual trousers. His hair was still damp, ink-black and curling at the ends where it needed a trim. She wanted to run her hands through it the way she used to do… She jolted as if he had struck her, staring up at him, her heart beating like a hyperactive hammer.

'What's wrong?' he asked, taking her by the shoulders.

She looked up into his face, frowning as she tried to focus on the sliver of memory that had made its way through. As if by their own volition, her hands went to his hair, her fingers playing with the silky strands in slow, measured strokes. She saw his throat move up and down and, glancing at his mouth, she felt another tiny flicker of recognition. Her right hand went to his lips, her fingers tracing over the tense line, again and again until it finally softened, the slight rasp of his evening shadow as she stroked the leanness of his jaw, the only sound, apart from their breathing, in the silence.

'Emelia—' his voice was low and deep and scratchy '—what have you remembered?'

She looked into his dark eyes. 'Your hair…I remembered running my fingers through it…lots and lots of times… It's longer now, isn't it?'

'Yes, I've been too busy to get it cut.' His grip on her shoulders tightened and his eyes were intense as they held hers. 'Can you remember anything else?' he asked.

'I'm not sure…' Emelia tried to focus again. 'It was just a fleeting thing. Like a flashback or something.'

His hands slipped down from her shoulders to encircle her wrists, his thumbs absently stroking her. 'Don't force it. It will come when it wants to. We have to be patient.' He let out a rough sounding sigh and added ruefully, '*I* have to be patient.'

Emelia felt the drugging warmth of his touch on the undersides of her wrists. Her blood leapt in her veins and she wondered if he could feel the way he affected her. Her belly was turning into a warm pool of longing, her legs unsteady as his eyes came to hers, holding them for a pulsing moment.

Time seemed to slow and then stand impossibly still.

Without a word, he lifted one of his hands to the curve of her cheek, cupping her face gently, his thumb moving back and forth in a mesmerising touch that seemed to stroke away every single reason why she should ease back out of his embrace. Instead, she found herself stepping closer, her body touching his from chest to thigh, feeling the stirring of his body against her, the hot hard heat of him lighting a fire that she now realised had smouldered within her from the moment she had woken up in the hospital and encountered his dark unreadable gaze.

'Emelia.'

The way he said her name was her undoing. Low and deep, an urgency in the uttering of the syllables, a need that she could feel resonating in her own body, like a tuning fork being struck too hard, humming, vibrating and quivering with want.

She lifted her mouth to the slow descent of his, her arms snaking around his middle, her breasts pressed up against his hard chest, a feeling, as his lips sealed hers and his hands cradled her head, that she had finally come home...

CHAPTER SEVEN

EMELIA sighed with pleasure as Javier's mouth urged hers into a heated response. Desire was like a punch, hitting her hard as his tongue deftly searched for hers. He found it, toyed with it, stroking and stabbing, calling it into a dance that mimicked what was to come. Her body felt as if spot fires had been set all through it, the blood raced and thundered in her veins as his kiss grew all the more insistent, all the more hotly sensual. The delicate network of nerves in her core twanged with need, her breasts tightened and tingled where they were pressed against him, and her mouth was slippery and wet and hot with greedy want as it fed off his.

His hands moved from cupping her face to pressing against the small of her back, bringing her hard against him. Emelia felt the outline of his erection; it stirred something deep and primal in her. Her thighs trembled as she felt the slickness of need anointing her. She sent her hands on their own journey of discovery: the hard planes of his back and shoulders, the taut trimness of his waist, the leanness of his hips and the heat and throbbing of his blood rising so proud and insistent from between his legs.

He groaned against her mouth, something unintelligible, a mixture of Spanish, English and desperation as her fingers freed him from his clothing. He stepped out of the pool of his trousers, his shoes thudding to the floor as he succumbed to her touch. She felt another punch of lust in her belly. She wondered if this was how it had been from the start of their relationship. Physical attraction that was unstoppable, not underpinned with feelings other than primal lust.

Javier shrugged himself out of his shirt, tossing it aside before he started to work on hers. He pulled her top away from one of her shoulders, his hot mouth caressing the smooth flesh he had uncovered. Emelia gave herself up to the heady feel of his lips and teeth, her legs quivering with expectation as he continued the sensual journey, removing her clothes and replacing them with his mouth until she was standing in nothing but her lacy knickers.

His eyes were almost completely black as he stood looking at her, his hands on her hips, his touch sending livewires of need to her core.

Emelia's fingers splayed over his chest, the hard smooth muscles delighting her, the thunder of his heartbeat against her palm. She pressed a hot wet kiss to his throat, moving down, through the rough dark hair that narrowed from his chest to his groin. She went to her knees in front of him and he sprang up against her, hard, hot and swollen. She breathed over him, the air from her mouth making him tense all over. She touched him with the tip of her tongue, a light experimental taste that had him gripping her by the shoulders, his fingers digging in almost painfully as he anchored himself. She stroked her tongue along the satin length of him, feeling each pulsing ridge of his flesh, delighting in the way his breathing intervals shortened, the way the muscles of his abdomen clenched and his fingers dug even deeper into the flesh of her shoulders.

Before she could complete her sensual mission he hauled her back up to her feet, his eyes almost feverish with desire as they locked on hers. 'Enough of that for now,' he said. 'I won't last.'

Emelia could feel the pressure building inside him and wanted to feel it inside her, to feel him stretching her, filling her, possessing her totally, irrevocably.

His mouth came back to hers, hungrily, feeding off her with a new desperation as his body pulsed with urgency against hers. His hand cupped her feminine mound, a possessive touch that made every hair on her scalp lift in anticipation. The lacy barrier of her knickers only intensified the scalding heat of his touch. She arched up against him, an unspoken need crying out from every pore of her flesh.

He moved her to the bed, guiding her, pushing her, urging her with his mouth still seared to hers, his tongue enslaving hers.

Emelia gasped as he peeled her knickers away, the brush of lace against her thighs nothing to what it felt like to have his mouth do the same. His hot breath whispered down her thighs and up again and then against her feminine folds, his fingers gently separating her, his tongue tasting her like an exotic elixir. She whimpered as the sensations rippled through her, everything in her fizzled and sparked with feeling. She writhed under his erotic touch, panting against the building crescendo. Her fingers dug into the cover on the bed, her heart racing as he continued his shockingly intimate caress until she finally exploded. It was a hundred sensations at once: a cataclysmic eruption, a tidal wave, a landslide, every nerve twitching in the aftermath, her chest rising and falling as her breathing fought to return to normal. She felt limbless, floating on a cloud of release, wondering how many times he had done this to her. How could she have forgotten such rapture?

But it was not over.

Javier moved up over her, his strong thighs gently nudging hers apart, his erection brushing against her swollen flesh. His expression was contorted with concentration, a fierce determination to keep control. She felt it in the way he held himself as if he was worried he would hurt her in his own quest for release. She reassured him by stroking his back, urging him to complete the union, positioning her body to receive him, aching to feel that musky male thickness inside her.

He groaned as he surged into her slick warmth, the skin of his back lifting under her fingertips. She felt him check himself but she was having none of it. She urged him on again, lifting her hips to meet the downward thrust of his, the pumping action of his body sending waves of shivering delight through her. His breathing quickened, his body rocking with increasing speed, carrying her along with him on the racing breakneck tide. She felt the stabbing heat of him, the primal rush of her senses pulling her into another vortex. She arched some more, the tight ache beginning all over again as he thrust all the harder and faster. She panted beneath the sweat-slicked heat of him, the hairs on his chest tickling her breasts, her molten core tingling for that final trigger that would send her to paradise once more.

He slid one of his hands down between their rocking

bodies, his fingers finding the swollen-with-need pearl of her body, the stroking motion tipping her over the edge into oblivion.

As she was swirling back from the abyss of pleasure she felt him work himself to orgasm, the way he thrust on, his breathing ragged and heavy, his primal-sounding grunts as he finally let go making her shiver all over in response.

The silence was heavy and scented with sex.

Emelia opened her eyes after timeless minutes to see Javier propped up on his elbows, looking down at her with those unreadable black eyes. She felt shy all of a sudden. She had not thought her body capable of such feeling, of such powerful mind-blowing responses. He had stirred her so deeply, and not just physically. It was more than that, so much more. She felt a feather brush over her heart. She felt a fluttering feeling in her stomach, like the wings of a small bird. She tried to hold on to the image that had appeared like a ghost inside her mind, but it vaporised into nothingness before she could make sense of it.

Javier brushed a damp strand of her hair back from her face. 'You have a faraway look on your face,' he said.

Emelia blinked herself back to the present. 'I thought I remembered something else but it's gone.'

As if sensing her frustration, he bent his head and kissed her forehead softly. 'As long as you don't forget this,' he said, kissing both of her eyebrows in turn. 'And this.' He kissed the end of her nose. 'And this.' He kissed the corner of her mouth and she turned her head so her lips met his.

The heat leapt from his mouth to hers, the lightning

flash of his tongue meeting hers causing an instant conflagration of the senses. Emelia felt the stiffening of his
body where it was still encased in hers, the rapid rise
of her pulse in time with his as he started moving within
her. She ran her fingers through his hair, down over his
shoulders, his back and then grasped the firm flesh of
his buttocks, relishing the tension she could feel
building in his body.

'It is always this way between us,' he growled against
her mouth. 'Once is never enough. I want you like I
want no other woman. This need, it never goes away.'

Emelia felt a spurt of feminine pride that she had
captivated his desire in such a way. 'I want you too,' she
said, giving herself up to his passionately determined
kiss.

He left her mouth to suckle on her breasts, a light
teasing movement of his lips that left her breathless for
more. He kissed the sensitive underside of each breast
before coming back to her mouth, crushing it beneath
his as his need for release built.

This time his lovemaking was fast and furious, as if
all the frustration at her not remembering could only be
expressed through the passionate connection of their
bodies. He rolled her over until she was on top, his
hands cupping her breasts as his dark eyes held hers.
'You like it like this, *querida*,' he said in a deep gravelly
voice. 'Make yourself come against me. Let me watch
you.'

Shyness gripped her but the sensual challenge was
too tempting to ignore. She could feel him against her
most sensitive point when she shifted slightly. It was
like a match to a flame to feel him hard and thick against
her, the friction so delicious she was gasping out loud

as she rode him unashamedly. She came apart within seconds, her cries of ecstasy ringing in the silence, her breathing choppy and her heart rate uneven.

He used her last few contractions to bring himself to completion, his eyes now screwed shut, his face contorted with the exquisite pleasure he was feeling. Emelia felt him empty himself, each rocking pulse of his body triggering aftershocks in hers.

She slumped down over him, more out of shyness than exhaustion, although her limbs felt leaden after so much pleasure. She felt his fingers absently stroking over each knob of her spine, lingering over her lower vertebrae, his touch still lighting fires beneath her skin.

When he spoke his voice reverberated against her chest. 'Did that trigger anything in your memory?'

Emelia opened her eyes and, raising her head, looked down at him. Her heart squeezed in her chest as if a hand were closing into a fist around it. His dark eyes were like liquid, melted by passion, warm and softer than she had ever seen them. A feeling rushed up from deep inside her, an overwhelming sense of rightness. It was like a door creaking open in her head. Memories started filing through, like soldiers called to action. It was blurry at first, but then it cleared as she put the pieces together in her mind.

She remembered their first meeting. She remembered the way he had met her gaze across the room and how her fingers had stumbled on the piece she was playing. She had quickly looked away, embarrassed, feeling gauche and unsophisticated as she continued playing through her repertoire. She had never before reacted like that to any man who had come in. It had been an almost visceral thing. His presence seemed to reach out across the space that divided them and touch her.

She remembered how he had come over to the piano when she was packing up and asked her to join him for a drink. An hour later he had offered to drive her home, an offer she politely declined. He came the next night and the next, sitting listening to her play, slowly sipping at his drink, watching her until she finished. And each night he would offer to drive her home. By the third night she agreed. She remembered how she fell in love with him after their first kiss. She remembered how it felt to feel his arms go around her and draw her close to his body, the way her body felt in response, the way her heart beat until it felt as if it was going to work its way out of her chest.

She remembered the first time they made love. It was a month after they had met. He had been so gentle and patient, schooling her into the delights of her own body and the heat and potency of his. She could feel herself blushing just thinking about where they had gone from there. How eager she had been to learn, how willing she had been to be everything he wanted in a partner and then as his wife.

In spite of her initial reservations, she had moulded herself into the role, trying so hard to fit into his lifestyle, fashioning herself into the sort of trophy wife she assumed he wanted: a rail-thin clothes horse, a glamour girl always with a glass of champagne in one hand and a brilliant smile pasted on her perfectly made-up face. She had ignored the doubts that kept lurking in the shadows of her mind. Doubts about the way he refused to discuss his feelings, doubts about his adamantine stance about not having children, doubts about having signed the prenuptial document he'd insisted she sign, doubts about the intimidation she felt when alone at the villa with just his staff for company when he was away on business, which he seemed to be so often.

She had begun to feel she didn't really belong in his life and that the fiery attraction that had brought them together initially was not going to be enough to sustain them in the long term. She had always known he desired her; it was the one thing she could count on. He never seemed to tire of making love with her. It had thrilled her at first but after a while she had begun to crave more from him than sex. She had fooled herself she would be able to change him, to teach him how to love her the way she loved him.

And then, in spite of what she had told him, she had begun to dream of having a baby. She silently craved to build a family with him, to put down the roots that had been denied her throughout her childhood. But she had never been brave enough to bring up the subject. She had obediently taken her contraceptive pills and done her best to ignore the screeching clamour of her biological clock until that fateful day when she had finally had enough. Finding out about his father's will, on top of the press photo of him with the Russian singer, had tipped her over the edge. She had left him in the hope he would come after her and beg her to return. She had hoped he would insist on changing the rules of their marriage so they could have a proper fulfilling life together.

But of course he hadn't. A man as proud as Javier would not beg anyone to come back to him. Look at what had happened between him and his father. A decade had gone past and he hadn't budged.

'Emelia?' Javier's deep voice broke through her thoughts. 'What's going on?'

She met his concerned gaze. 'I remember…'

He sat upright, tumbling her onto her back, his fingers grasping her by both arms. 'What? Everything?' he asked.

She shook her head. 'Bits and pieces. Like when and how we met. Some of our time together. Most of our time together.'

One of his hands moved in a slow stroking motion up and down her arm. 'So I was right,' he said. 'Your body recognised me from the first. Your mind just had to catch up.'

She touched his lips with her fingers, tracing over their contours. 'How could I have forgotten you? I can't believe I didn't remember you. Were you very angry about that?'

Javier captured one of her fingers with his mouth, sucking on it erotically, all the while holding her gaze. He released her finger and said, 'I have to admit I was angry, especially when you hadn't forgotten Marshall.'

Her eyes dropped from his, a frown pulling at her forehead. 'I can't explain that. I'm sorry.'

'It is not important now,' he said. 'We have to move on.'

'Javier?' Her soft voice was like a feather brushing along his lower spine.

Javier looked down at her tussled hair and slim naked body. His groin tightened as he thought of having her back in his life permanently. His plans to divorce her seemed so ridiculous now. He had acted stupidly, blindly and in anger. His pride had taken a hit from what had been reported in the press about her and Marshall and he had let it block out his reason. He wanted her too much to let her go. He didn't like admitting it. He would rather die than admit it. She was the one woman who had brought him to his knees. He had nearly gone out of his head when he found she had left him. He had not realised how much he wanted and needed her until she had gone.

A part of him blamed himself. He had been so pre-occupied with the Moscow takeover. It was the deal of a lifetime. The negotiations had been tricky from the get-go but he had always believed he could pull it off. His goal had been to add that Russian bank to his empire and he had done it. It was the ultimate prize, the bench-mark business deal. But he just hadn't realised it would come at such a personal cost.

He brushed some damp tendrils of hair back off her face. 'Tired, *cariño*?'

She shook her head, her grey-blue eyes like shimmering pools. 'Not at all.' She stretched her slim body against him just like a sinuous cat and smiled. 'Not one little bit.'

His blood rocketed through his veins and he pressed her back down and covered her mouth with his, kissing her hungrily, delighting in the way she responded just as greedily. His tongue played with hers, stroking and sweeping until she succumbed with a whimpering sigh of pleasure. His hands moved over her breasts, the already erect nipples a dark cherry-red. He closed his mouth over each of them, flicking them with the point of his tongue, before sucking deeply. Her fingers scored through his hair, her body bucking under him as she opened for him.

He knew he was rushing things but he was aching

and heavy with longing. She was already slick with his seed from before, hot, wet and wanting him just as much as he wanted her. It sounded prehistoric but he wanted to stake his claim again and again, to mark his territory in the most primal way of all. Her body wrapped around him tightly as he thrust into her, the walls of her inner core rippling against him. He had to fight to stay in control, each thrusting movement sending gushing waves of need right through him. She squirmed beneath him, searching for that extra friction to send her to paradise. He made her wait; he wanted to make her beg. It seemed fitting since he had suffered so much because of her leaving him, for putting him through such a tormented hell.

'I want…' she panted beneath him. 'I want you to… Oh, please, Javier…'

He smiled over her mouth as he took it in another scorching kiss, his hands sliding between her thighs, teasing her with almost-there caresses.

She whimpered again and grasped at his hand, pushing it against her pearly need. 'Please,' she begged him passionately.

Javier flicked his fingers against her, just the way she liked. He knew her body like a maestro knew his instrument. She felt so silky and feminine, the scent of her driving him mad with the need to let go. He waited until she had started to orgasm, the spasms of her body gripping him until he had no choice but to explode. He pumped into her harder and harder, forcing the images of her alleged affair that had tortured him out of his head. He felt her flinch, he even felt her fingers grasping at his shoulders but he carried on relentlessly, until finally he spilled himself with a shout of triumph.

He rolled onto his back, his chest rising and falling as he tried to steady his breathing. He turned his head as he felt the mattress shift. Emelia had rolled away with her back to him, huddled into a ball. He reached out and stroked a finger down her spine. 'Emelia?'

She flinched and moved further away from him, mumbling something he didn't quite catch.

Javier sat upright and, taking her nearest shoulder, turned her onto her back. 'What's wrong?' he asked.

Her eyes flashed at him like lightning. 'I think you know what's wrong.'

'I'm not a mind reader, Emelia. If you have something to say, then, for God's sake, say it.'

She continued to glare at him but then her eyes began to swim with tears. 'Don't ever make love to me as if I was your mistress,' she said, her voice cracking over the words. 'I am your wife.'

Javier felt a knife of guilt go between his ribs. 'I got carried away,' he said. 'I'm sorry. You said you liked it like that in the past.'

She gave him a cutting look. 'Did you ever think I might have been saying that just to please you?'

He sent his fingers through his hair before he reluctantly faced her. 'I am not sure of what you want any more, Emelia,' he said. 'It's like I have a different wife from the one I had only a month or so ago. It's going to take some time to adjust.'

She looked at him through watery eyes. 'Was our relationship about anything but sex?' she asked.

He got off the bed as if she had pushed him. 'Now that some of your memory has returned you should know how much I detest these sorts of discussions,' he said with a harsh note of annoyance. 'I laid out the terms of our marriage and you agreed to them. Now you want to change things.'

She pulled the bedcovers over her. 'Why don't you just answer the question? Did you ever feel anything for me other than desire? Did you love me, even just a little?'

Javier tried to stare her down but she held firm. He let out a savage breath. 'My father told me he loved me but it didn't mean a thing. It was conditional, if anything. He wanted me to be a puppet. As soon as I wanted to choose my own path, his love was cut off.'

'That was wrong of him,' she said. 'Parents should never withhold their love, not for any reason.'

He made a scoffing sound in his throat. 'My father loved his wives, all four of them, and they apparently loved him back, but look where that ended—an early death and two, almost three, very expensive divorces.'

Her brow wrinkled with a frown. 'So what you're saying is you don't believe love can ever last?'

'It's not a reliable emotion, Emelia. It changes all the time.'

'I'm not sure what you're saying in relation to us…'

'The things that make a relationship work are common ground and chemistry,' Javier said. 'A bit of mutual respect doesn't go amiss either.'

Her expression was crestfallen and he felt every kind of heel as a result. Was he incapable of loving or just resistant to being that vulnerable to another person? He couldn't answer with any certainty.

'Don't push me on this, Emelia,' he said into the silence. 'Our relationship has been through so much of late. This is not the time to be saying things neither of us are certain is true.'

'But I know I love you,' she said. 'I know it with absolute certainty. I loved you from the first moment I met you. I didn't tell you because I knew you didn't want to hear it. But I need to tell you now. I can't hold it in any longer.'

He pinned her with his gaze. 'You speak of loving me and yet you were leaving me, Emelia, or have you not remembered that part? You had given up on our relationship. You wouldn't be here now if you hadn't been injured and lost your memory. You would be back in Australia. You were in that car with Marshall because he was driving you to the airport.'

Her teeth sank into her bottom lip until it went white.

'Why don't we wait until all the pieces are in place before you start planning the future?' he said when she didn't speak. 'Unless we deal with the past, we might not even have a future.'

'You…you want a divorce?' Her voice sounded like a wounded child's.

'I don't believe we should stay shackled together if one or both of us is unhappy,' he said. 'We'll give it a month or two and reassess. It is early days. You've only just come out of hospital after a near-fatal accident. You're damned lucky to be alive.'

Her mouth went into a pout. 'No doubt it would have been much better for you if I had been killed.'

Javier ground his teeth as he thought about that moment when Aldana had informed him there was a call from the police in London. His heart had nearly stopped until he had been assured she hadn't been fatally wounded. 'My mother died when she was three years younger than you are,' he said. 'She didn't see my first day at school. She didn't hear the first words I learned to read. I didn't get the chance to tell her how much I loved her or if I did I was too young to remember doing it. Don't you dare tell me I would rather have you dead and buried. No one deserves to have their life cut short through the stupidity of other's actions.'

She sent him a defiant glare. 'Maybe it suits you to have me alive so you can pay me back for daring to leave you. I bet I'm the first woman who ever has.'

Javier drew in a sharp breath. 'You're the one who moved the goalposts, not me.'

'I can't be the sort of wife you want,' she said, her eyes shining with tears. 'I can't do it any more. I'm not that sort of person, Javier. I want more from life than money and sex and endless hours in the gym or the beauty salon. I want to be loved for who I am, not for what I look like.'

He snatched up his trousers and zipped himself into them. 'I care about you, Emelia. Believe me, you would not be here now if I didn't.'

'Is that supposed to make me feel better?' she asked. 'You *care* about me. For God's sake, Javier, you make me sound like some sort of pet.'

He sent her a frustrated look as he grasped the door handle. 'We will talk about this later,' he said. 'You are not yourself right now.'

'You're damn right I'm not,' she said. 'But that's the heart of the problem. I have never been myself the whole time we've been married. I am a fake wife, Javier, a complete and utter fraud. How long do you expect such a marriage to last?'

He set his mouth. 'It will last until I say it's over.' And then he opened the door and strode out, snapping the door shut behind him.

CHAPTER EIGHT

EMELIA went to bed totally wrung out after her conversation with Javier. She lay awake for hours, hoping he might come in and join her but he apparently wanted to keep his distance. She spent a restless night, agonising over everything, ruminating over all the stupid decisions she had made, all the crazy choices to be with him in spite of how little he was capable of giving her emotionally. No wonder she had grown tired of their arrangement. She was amazed it had lasted as long as it had. She had compromised herself in every way possible. With the wisdom of hindsight, she knew that if she'd had better self-esteem she would never have agreed to such a marriage. But, plagued with insecurities stemming from childhood, she had been knocked off her feet with his passionate attention. His ruthless determination to have her in his bed had curdled her common sense. She had acted on impulse, not sensibly.

When she woke the next morning after snatches of troubled sleep she felt the beginnings of a vicious headache. The light spilling in from the gap in the curtains was like steel skewers driving through her skull. She groaned and buried her head under the pillow, nausea rolling in her stomach like an out of control boulder.

The sound of the door opening set a shockwave of pain through her head and she groaned again, but this time it came out more like a whimper.

'Mi amor?' Javier strode quickly towards the bed. 'Are you unwell?'

Emelia slowly turned her head to face him, her eyes half-open. 'I have the most awful headache…'

He placed a cool dry hand on her forehead, making her want to cry like a small child at the tender gesture. 'You're hot but I don't think you're feverish,' he said. 'I'll check your temperature and then call for the doctor.'

Right at that moment Emelia didn't care if he called for the undertaker. She was consumed with the relentless, torturous pain. The nausea intensified and, before he could come back with a thermometer, she stumbled into the en suite bathroom and dispensed with the meagre contents of her stomach in wretched heaves that burned her throat.

Javier came in behind her. 'Ah, *querida*,' he said soothingly. 'Poor baby. You really are sick.' He dampened a face cloth and gently lifted her hair off the back of her neck and pressed the coolness of the cloth there.

Emelia brushed her teeth once the nausea had abated. She slowly turned, embarrassed at her loss of dignity. She felt so weak and being in Javier's strong, commanding presence only seemed to intensify her feelings of feeble vulnerability. She could not remember a time when she had been sick in front of him before. He was always so robustly healthy and energetic, which had made her feel as if he would be revolted by any sign of weakness or fragility. In the past she had hidden any of her various and mostly minor ailments, putting on a brave face and carrying on her role of the always perfect, always biddable wife.

'The doctor is on her way,' he said, supporting her by the elbow. 'Why don't you get back into bed and close your eyes for a bit?'

'I'm sorry about this…' she said once she was back in bed. 'I thought I was getting better.'

'I am sure you are but perhaps yesterday was too much for you,' he said. He brushed the hair back from her face, his expression more than a little rueful. 'I'm sorry for upsetting you. I keep forgetting you're not well enough to go head to head with me.'

'I am fine…really…'

He grimaced and added, 'I shouldn't have made love with you. Perhaps it was too soon.'

Emelia wasn't sure what to say so stayed silent. It seemed safer than admitting how much she had wanted him to make love to her.

There was the sound of someone arriving downstairs and Javier rose from the bed. 'That sounds like the doctor,' he said. 'I'll be right back.'

Within a couple of minutes a female doctor came in, who had clearly been briefed by Javier, and she briskly introduced herself and proceeded to examine Emelia, checking both of her pupils along with her blood pressure.

'Have you had migraines in the past?' Eva Garcia asked as she put the portable blood pressure machine back in her bag before taking out a painkiller vial and needle for injection.

'Not that I can remember,' Emelia said. 'But I've had a few headaches since I had the accident a couple of weeks ago.'

'Your husband tells me you've recovered a bit of your memory,' Eva said, preparing Emelia's arm for the injection. 'That was yesterday, correct?'

'Yes…'

'You need to take things more slowly,' Dr Garcia said. 'I'm going to take some bloods just to make sure there's nothing else going on.'

Emelia felt a hand of panic clutch at her throat, imagining an intracranial haemorrhage or the onset of a stroke from a clot breaking loose. 'What else could be going on?' she asked hollowly.

The doctor took out a tourniquet and syringe set. 'You could be low on iron or have some underlying issue to do with your head injury.' She expertly took the blood and pressed down on the puncture site, her eyes meeting Emelia's. 'What about your periods? Are they regular?'

Emelia was suddenly glad Javier had left the room as soon as he had brought the doctor in. 'Um…I really can't remember…'

'So you haven't had one since the accident?'

Emelia bit her lip. 'No…'

'Don't worry,' the doctor said. 'After the ordeal you've been through, your system is probably going to take some time to settle down. Stress, trauma, especially physical as in your case, would be enough to temporarily shut down the menstrual cycle. Are you taking any form of oral contraception?'

'My prescription has run out,' Emelia said. 'I wasn't sure whether to go back on it or not. I thought I should wait until…until I knew more about…things…'

'I'll write you one up, just in case.' The doctor took out her prescription pad and Emelia told her the brand name and dose.

Within another minute or two the doctor was being seen out and Javier came back in. 'How are you feeling now? Headache still bad?'

'The doctor gave me an injection,' she said. 'It's starting to work. I'm already feeling a bit sleepy.'

He stroked a hand over her forehead. 'I'll bring something for you to drink. Do you fancy anything to eat?'

Emelia winced at the thought of food. 'No. Please, no food.'

His hand lingered for a moment on her cheek before he left her, closing the door so softly Emelia hardly heard it as her eyelids fluttered down over her eyes…

When she woke it was well into the evening. She gingerly got out of bed and dragged herself into the shower. As she came out of the bathroom, wrapped in nothing but a towel, the bedroom door opened and Javier came in.

'Feeling better?' he asked.

'A lot.' Emelia tried to smile but it didn't quite work. 'Thank you.'

'Do you feel up to having some dinner?' he asked. 'Aldana's prepared something for us.'

'I'll just get dressed,' she said, feeling shy, as if she was on her first date with him.

She could see he was trying hard to put her at ease. He had been so gentle earlier, so concerned for her welfare she wondered if he loved her just a tiny bit after all. She chided herself for dreaming of what he couldn't or wouldn't give. As much as she loved him, she couldn't afford to waste any more of her life waiting for him to change. If he didn't want the same things in life she did, then she would have to have the courage to move on without him, for his sake as well as her own. She hated to think of never seeing his face again or, worse, imagining him with some other woman. How would she endure it?

'Take your time,' he said, gently flicking her cheek with the end of his finger. 'I have some business proposals to read through.'

She touched her face when he left, wishing for the moon that was so far out of reach it was heartbreaking.

Javier came back to find Emelia dressed in a simple black dress that skimmed her slim form, highlighting the gentle swell of her breasts and the long trim legs encased—unusually for her—in ballet flats. Her hair had been blow-dried but, rather than styling it, she had pulled it back into a simple ponytail. She had the barest minimum of make-up on, just a brush of mascara which intensified the grey-blue of her eyes, and a pink shade of lip gloss which drew attention to her soft full mouth with its rounded upper lip. He felt the heat of arousal surge into his groin as he remembered how that mouth felt around him. She was the most naturally sensual woman he had ever met and yet at times, especially right now, he seriously wondered if she was aware of it.

'You are looking very beautiful this evening, *querida*,' he said.

She smoothed her hands down over the flatness of her stomach as if she was conscious of the close-fitting nature of the dress. 'Thank you,' she murmured and shifted her gaze from his to pick up a light wrap she had laid on the end of the bed.

He escorted her down the stairs, holding her hand in his, noting how her fingers trembled slightly as they approached the formal dining room.

Aldana brought in the meal and Javier watched as Emelia kept her gaze down, as if she was frightened of saying or doing the wrong thing. He was the first to recognise that Aldana was a difficult person, but she was dependent on the income he gave her after her husband had gambled away everything they had owned. Javier didn't want to dispense with her services just because of a personality clash with his wife, but he could see Emelia was on edge and he had cause to wonder if things were worse when he wasn't around to keep an eye on things.

After watching Emelia pick at her food for several minutes, he dabbed his napkin at the edges of his mouth and laid it back over his lap. 'Emelia,' he said, 'I know, like many women, you are keen to keep slim, but I have never agreed with you starving yourself. In my opinion, you were perfectly fine the way you were when I first met you. There is no need to deny yourself what you want. Your health is much more important.'

She looked up at him with a sheepish expression. 'I haven't been to the gym once since I've been home. I can't believe I did it before. Izabella said I was obsessive about it. I normally have no self-discipline. I much prefer incidental exercise, like walking or swimming.'

'And sex?' he asked with a teasing smile.

Her face coloured and she lowered her gaze to her plate. 'Is that all you think about?' she asked in a tight little voice.

'It's what we both used to think about,' he said. 'You are the most sensually aware woman I have ever been with.'

Her grey-blue eyes flashed back to his. 'And I bet there have been hundreds.'

He took a moment to respond. 'You knew about my lifestyle when we met. I have made it no secret that I lived a fast-paced life.'

'Which is no doubt why you wanted a shallow smokescreen marriage to impress your business contacts,' she put in. 'I can't believe I agreed to it. I never wanted to turn out like my poor mother, preening herself constantly in case her wayward husband strayed to someone slimmer or better looking or better groomed or better dressed.'

Javier frowned at the sudden vehemence of her words. Her face was pinched and her mouth tight and her shoulders tense. Without her veneer of sophistication, she looked young and vulnerable, and yet she looked far more beautiful than he had ever seen her. 'I didn't realise you felt like that,' he said after a little pause. 'You always seemed so confident. I didn't know you felt so unsure of yourself.'

Her throat moved up and down, as if she regretted revealing her insecurities to him. 'I haven't been honest with you,' she said. 'I mean right from the start. I should have told you but I was frightened you would walk away, that I would appear too needy or something. I guess back then I wanted you on any terms. I was prepared to suspend everything I wanted in life to be with you.'

He reached out a hand and picked up one of hers, entwining his fingers with her soft trembling ones. 'I don't want to lose you, *querida*,' he said. 'But I can only give you what I can give you. It might not be enough.'

She pressed her lips together, he assumed to stop herself from crying, but even so her eyes moistened. 'I want to be loved, Javier,' she said softly. 'I want to be loved the way my mother craved to be loved but never got to be loved. I want to wake up each morning knowing the man I love is right there by my side, supporting me, loving me, cherishing me.' She drew in an uneven breath and added in an even softer voice, 'And I want a baby.'

Javier felt a shockwave go through his chest. He recalled his lonely childhood: the ache of sudden loss, the devastation of being cast aside by his father after his mother had died. He could not face the responsibility of being a parent. He would mess it up, for sure. Even people from secure backgrounds occasionally ran into trouble with their kids. What chance would *he* have? He would end up ruining a child's potential, crippling them emotionally, stunting their development or making them hate him as much as he had ended up hating his own father for his inadequacies.

He couldn't risk it.

He *would not* risk it.

'That is not negotiable,' he found himself saying in a cold hard voice that he could scarcely believe was coming from his throat. 'There is no way I want children. I told you that right from the start and you were in total agreement.'

She looked at him with anguished eyes that scored his soul. 'I only accepted those terms because I was blindsided by love. I still love you, Javier, more than ever, but I don't want to miss out on having children.'

Javier pushed out his chair and got to his feet. 'You can't spring this sort of stuff on me, Emelia,' he said. 'Less than a month ago everything was fine between us. It was fine for almost two years. You did your thing. I did mine.' He pointed his finger at her. 'You are the one who suddenly changed things.'

Emelia put up her chin. 'I'm tired of doing things your way. I'm tired of seeing your picture splashed over every international paper with yet another wannabe model or starlet. Surely you have more control over who you are seen with?'

He clamped down on his jaw. 'The person I should be seen with is my wife,' he said. 'But she is always too busy shopping in another country or having her hair or nails done.'

Emelia flinched at his stinging words. But perhaps the sliver of truth in them was what hurt the most. She had been caught up in the world of being his wife instead of being his companion and soulmate. There was a big difference and it was a shame it had taken this long for her to see it. 'I'm sorry,' she said. 'I thought I was doing what you wanted.'

There was a stiff silence.

'Forget I said that,' Javier said. 'I didn't exactly make it easy on you on the few occasions you came with me. I am perhaps too task-oriented. I tend to focus on the big picture and lose sight of the details.'

'We've both made mistakes,' she said. 'I guess we just have to try not to make them again.'

He pushed his hand through his hair. 'I want this to work, Emelia,' he said. 'I want us to be happy, like we were before.'

'Javier, you were happy but I wasn't, not really,' she

said. 'My accident has shown me what a lie I've been living. The woman you want in your life is not the one I am now. I have never been that person.'

He came over and took her hands in his, pulling her to her feet. 'You *were* happy, Emelia,' he said, squeezing her hands for effect. 'I gave you everything money could buy. You wanted for nothing. I made sure of it.'

Emelia tried to pull away but he held firm. 'You're not listening to me, Javier. We can't go back to what we were before. *I* can't go back.'

'Let's see about that, shall we?' he said and brought his mouth down hard on hers.

At first Emelia made a token resistance but her heart wasn't in it. She wanted him any way she could get him, even if it was in anger or to prove a point. At least he was showing some emotion, even if it was not the one she most wanted him to demonstrate. She kissed him back with the same heat and fire, her tongue tangling with his in a sensual battle of wills.

He pressed her back against the nearest wall, pulling down the zip at the back of her dress, letting it fall into a black puddle at her feet, his mouth still locked on hers. She clawed at his waistband, her fingers releasing his belt in a quest to uncover him.

He tore his mouth off hers. 'Not here,' he said. 'Aldana might come in to clear the table. Let's take this upstairs.'

Emelia had her chance then to call an end to this madness but still she let her heart rule her head. Later, she barely recalled how they got upstairs; she seemed to remember the journey was interspersed with hot drugging kisses that ramped up her need of him unbearably.

By the time they got to the bedroom she was almost delirious with desire. He came down heavily on top of her on the bed, his weight pinning her, his mouth crushing hers in a red-hot kiss that made her toes curl.

He removed her bra and cupped her breasts possessively, subjecting them to the fiery brand of his mouth. He went lower, over the plane of her belly, lingering over the dish of her belly button before he parted her thighs. She gulped in a breath as he stroked her with his tongue, the raw intimacy as he tasted her making her spine unhinge. She felt the tension building and building to snapping point, the waves of pleasure coming towards her from a distance and then suddenly they swamped her, tossing her around and around in a wild sea of sensual pleasure that superseded anything she had felt before.

Then he drove into her roughly at first and then checked himself, murmuring something that sounded like an apology before he continued in a rhythmic motion that triggered all of her senses into another climb to the summit of release. His thrusts came closer together, a little deeper each time, his breathing intervals shortening as he approached the ultimate moment.

Emelia felt her body preparing for another freefall into pleasure. She pushed her hips up to intensify the feeling his body provoked as it rubbed against her point of pleasure, her breathing becoming increasingly ragged as she felt the tremors begin. This time when her orgasm started she pushed against him as if trying to expel him from her body, the action triggering her G spot, sending her into an earth-shattering release that rippled through her for endless seconds.

Javier came with an explosive rush, his deep grunt

of ecstasy sending shivers of delight down Emelia's spine. This was the only time she felt he allowed himself to be vulnerable. She clung to him as he emptied himself, the shudders of his body as it pinned her to the bed reverberating through her. She kept her arms wrapped around him, hoping he wouldn't roll away and spoil the moment.

'Am I too heavy for you?' he asked against the soft skin of her neck.

'No,' she said as she ran her fingers up and down his back.

He lifted himself on his elbows, looking down at her for a lengthy moment. 'I didn't hurt you, did I?'

She shook her head. 'No.'

His eyes travelled to her mouth, watching as she moistened it with her tongue. 'Still unhappy?' he asked.

Emelia searched his features for any sign of mockery but she couldn't find anything to suggest he was taunting her. But then he was a master at inscrutability when he chose to be. Even his dark eyes gave nothing away. 'There are times when I am not sure what I feel,' she said, taking the middle ground.

His mouth tilted in a rueful smile. 'I suppose I deserve that.'

Emelia let a silence underline his almost apology.

After another moment or two he lifted himself off her, offering her a hand to get up. 'Want to have a shower with me?'

The invitation she could see in the dark glitter of his eyes stirred her senses into a heated frenzy. How could he do this to her so soon after such mind-blowing satiation? Just one look and he had her quivering with need all over again. Wordlessly, she took his hand, allowing him to lead her into the en suite bathroom, standing to one side as he turned on the shower lever that was set at a controlled temperature.

He stepped under the spray and pulled her in under it with him. The fine needles of hot water cascaded over them as he brought his mouth to hers. It was a softer kiss this time, a leisurely exploration of her mouth that lured her into a sensual whirlpool. His tongue swept over hers, stroking and gliding with growing urgency, his erection hot and heavy against her belly. She slid down the shower stall and took him in her hands, exploring him with sensuous movements that brought his breathing to a stumbling halt. 'Careful, *cariño*,' he said. 'I might not be able to hold back.'

'I don't care,' she said recklessly.

She gave him a sultry look from beneath her lashes before taking him in her mouth in one slick movement that provoked a rough expletive from him. She smiled around his throbbing heat, her tongue gliding wetly along his length. She tasted his essence, inciting her to draw more of him into her mouth. His hands shot out to the glass walls of the shower to anchor himself, his thighs set apart, his chest rising and falling as he struggled to control his breathing. 'You don't have to do this,' he said, but the subtext, she knew, was really: *please don't stop doing this*.

'I like doing this to you,' she said. 'You do it to me so it's only fair I get to do the same to you.'

He swallowed tightly, his jaw clenching as he watched her return to his swollen length. Emelia felt the tension in the satin-covered steel of his body. He was drawing closer and closer to the point of no return and it excited her to think she could have such a powerful hold over him.

He jerked and then shuddered into her mouth, spilling his hot life force, his flesh lifting in goose-bumps in spite of the warmth of the shower.

Emelia glided back up his body, rinsing her mouth under the shower spray before meeting his dark lustrous eyes. He didn't say anything. He just looked at her with dark intensity, his hands reaching for the soap and working up a lather. She quivered with anticipation as he started soaping her, firstly her neck and shoulders, and then her breasts, the length of her spine and then her belly. He used circular movements that set all her nerves into a frantic dance, his touch so smooth and sensual she felt every bone inside her frame melt.

His hand cupped her feminine mound, seeking the swollen nub of her desire. She felt her breathing come to a stumbling halt as he bent down before her as she had done to him. His tongue separated her, teasing her, a soft flicker at first and then increasing the pace until she was gasping her way through an orgasm that shook her like a rag doll.

She collapsed against him as he rose to hold her, his arms coming around her as she rested her head against his chest. His heart was drumming under her cheek, one of his hands coming up to stroke her wet hair. He rested his chin on the top of her head and for a moment she wondered if he was going to tell her he loved her after all, that he wanted the same things she wanted.

But of course he didn't. Instead, he turned off the water and silently reached for a bath towel, wrapping her in it as one would a small child.

Emelia stepped out of the shower cubicle and did her best to squash her disappointment. Was this intense physical attraction the only thing she could cling to in order to keep him by her side? How long would it last? What if he tired of her and went to someone else to fulfil his needs? The thought of it was like an arrow through her heart. She hated even thinking about all the partners he had had before her. He never spoke of them and she never asked, but she knew there had been many women who had come and gone from his bed.

Javier turned her face to look at him. 'What is that frown for?' he asked.

She gave him a half-smile. 'Nothing…I was just thinking.'

His hand moved to cradle her cheek. 'About what?'

She pressed her lips together momentarily. 'I don't know…just where this will lead, I guess.'

His hand dropped from her face. 'Life doesn't always fit into nice neat little boxes, Emelia,' he said. 'And it doesn't always give us everything we want.'

'What do you want from life?' she asked.

He paused in the process of drying himself to look at her. 'The same things most people want—success, a sense of purpose, fulfilment.'

'What about love?'

He tossed the damp towel on the bed. 'I don't delude myself that it's a given in life. Love comes and it goes. It's not something I have ever relied on.'

Emelia mentally kicked herself for setting herself up for more hurt. If he loved her, he would have told her by now. He'd had almost twenty-three months of marriage to do so, irrespective of what had occurred over the past couple of weeks.

'Come to bed, *querida*,' he said. 'You look like a child that has been kept up way past its bedtime.'

She crawled into bed, not for a moment thinking she

would be able to sleep after spending so much of the day in a drug-induced slumber, but somehow when Javier pulled her into his body she closed her eyes and, limb by limb, her body gradually relaxed until, with a soft sigh, she drifted off…

Javier lay with her in his arms, his fingers laced through the silky strands of her hair, breathing in its clean, newly washed fragrance. In sleep she looked so young and vulnerable. Her soft full mouth was slightly open and one of her hands was lying against his chest, right where his heart was beating.

He'd thought he had the future all mapped out but now he was not so sure. Things were changing almost daily. The more time he spent with her, the more he wanted to believe they could be in this for the long haul.

He tried to picture a child they might make together: a dark-haired little boy or perhaps a little girl with grey-blue eyes and hair just as silken and golden as her mother. But the image faded, as if there was no room in his head for it.

Perhaps it was fate. He wasn't meant to be a father. It wasn't that he didn't like children. One of his business colleagues had recently become a father and Javier had looked at the photos with a strange sense of loss. His lonely childhood had marked him for life. He couldn't imagine himself as a parent. He didn't think he would know what to do. He hated the thought of potentially damaging a child's self-esteem by saying or doing the wrong thing. Children seemed to him to be so vulnerable. *He* had been so vulnerable.

He had never forgotten the day his mother had died. She had been there one minute, soft and scented and nurturing, and the next her body was in a shiny black coffin covered with red roses. He still hated the sight of red roses, any roses, in fact. They made his stomach churn. Within a year he had been sent off to boarding school in England as his father couldn't handle his ongoing grief. Javier had taught himself not to love anything or anyone in case it was ripped away from him without warning.

The thing that worried him the most was that it might be too late to change.

CHAPTER NINE

EMELIA woke up in bed alone and when she came downstairs Aldana informed her that Javier had left to see to some business in Malaga and would be back later that evening. She handed her a note with pursed lips. Emelia thanked her politely and, taking a cup of tea with her, went out to the sunny terrace overlooking the gardens.

The note was simple and written in Javier's distinctive handwriting, the strong dark strokes reminding her of his aura of command and control. It read:

Didn't want to wake you. See you tonight. J.

Emelia felt disappointed she hadn't woken before he'd left. There was so much she still wanted to say to him. She felt he had sideswiped her yet again by enslaving her senses. It was always the way he dealt with conflict, by reminding her of how much she needed him. It made her less and less confident of him shifting to accommodate her needs. He still had control, as he had always done. Nothing had changed, except the depth to which she could be hurt all over again.

The phone rang a little later in the morning and Aldana came out to the pool where Emelia was doing some laps and handed her the cordless receiver. 'It is the doctor,' she said, leaving the receiver on the table next to the sun lounger.

Emelia got out of the pool and quickly dried her hands on her towel before she picked up the phone. 'Hello? This is Emelia Mélendez speaking.'

'Señora Mélendez, I have some results for you from the blood tests I took,' Eva Garcia said.

Emelia felt her stomach shuffle like the rapidly thumbed pages of a book. 'Y-yes?'

'You are pregnant.'

Emelia's fingers clenched the phone in her hand until her knuckles became white, her heart thumping like a swinging hammer against her breastbone. 'I…I am?'

'Yes,' Dr Garcia said. 'Of course I am not sure how far along. It can't be too many weeks, otherwise I am sure the doctors who examined you after your accident would have noticed. You had an abdominal CT scan at some stage, didn't you?'

'Yes,' she said, still reeling from the shock announcement. 'It was done to check for internal bleeding but it was all clear. But how can I be pregnant? I was taking the Pill, or at least I assume I was. I don't really remember that clearly.'

'Perhaps you missed a dose here and there,' Dr Garcia suggested. 'It is very easy to forget and with these low dose brands it can create a small window of fertility. If you can remember when your last menstrual period was, I can calculate how far along you might be.'

Emelia thought for a moment. 'I think it might have been about three or four weeks before the accident. I remember I got a stomach virus right after. I couldn't keep anything down for forty-eight hours.'

'That would have been enough to render the Pill ineffective,' Dr Garcia said. 'But if, as you say, your last period was well over a month ago, you had probably fallen pregnant before you went to London. It is still very early days, but that doesn't mean you are not having all the symptoms. Some women are more sensitive to the hormonal changes than others.'

Emelia wondered how much her headaches and nausea were the result of the accident or of the early stages of pregnancy. She wondered too if her decision to leave Javier had been an irrational one brought on by the surge of hormones in her body. She could recall being more emotional than usual, her frustration at his absence escalating to blowout point when he'd come back just as the newspaper article had appeared, showing him with the nightclub singer. She was almost thankful she couldn't remember that 'ugly scene' as he called it. She was almost certain she would have been as wanton and needy as ever. It would not have helped her cause, saying with one breath she wanted out and begging him to pleasure her with the next.

'Well, then,' the doctor continued in a businesslike manner, 'I'd like you to start some pregnancy vitamins and we can make an appointment now if you like so we can organise that ultrasound.'

Emelia ended the call a minute or two later, her head spinning so much she had to sit down on the sun lounger.

Pregnant.

She placed a hand on her smooth flat abdomen. It

seemed impossible to think a tiny life was growing inside there. What would Javier say? she wondered sickly. Would he think she had 'accidentally' fallen pregnant? He was so cynical, she couldn't see how else he would react. But she didn't for a moment believe she had done it on purpose. Yes, she had become increasingly unhappy about taking the Pill, but she would not have deliberately missed a dose. She had wanted Javier to commit to bringing a child into their relationship. Foisting one on him was not something she had thought fair. It was a joint decision that she had longed he would one day be ready to make, but now it seemed neither of them had made the decision—fate, chance or destiny had made it for them.

She spent the rest of the day in an emotional turmoil as she prepared herself for facing Javier. She would have to tell him. She couldn't possibly keep it from him. He had a right to know he was to become a father, even if it was the last thing he wanted to be.

She heard him arrive at eight in the evening. Each of his footfalls felt like hammer blows to her heart as he made his way into *la sala* where she was waiting. She stood as he came in, her hands in a tight knot in front of her stomach.

'Sorry I'm late,' he said, coming over to her. He brushed his knuckles down the curve of her cheek. 'You look pale, *querida*. You haven't been overdoing it, I hope.'

She gave him a nervous movement of her lips that sufficed for a smile. 'No, I spent most of the day by the pool. It was hot again today.'

He pressed a soft kiss to her bare shoulder. 'Mmm, you are a little pink here and there.' He met her eyes again. 'You shouldn't lie out there without protection. Did you put on sunscreen?'

Emelia lowered her gaze from his. 'I did have some on but it must have worn off while I was in the water.'

He tipped up her face, studying her with increasing intensity. 'Is something wrong?' he asked. 'You seem a little on edge.'

She took a breath but it caught on something in her chest. 'Javier…I have something to tell you…'

A frown pulled at his brow. 'You've remembered something else?'

She bit the inside of her mouth. 'No, it's not that. I…I got a call from the doctor.'

His eyes narrowed slightly and his voice sounded strangely hollow. 'There's nothing seriously wrong, is there?'

Emelia gave him a strained look. 'I guess it depends on how you look at it.'

'Whatever it is, we will deal with it,' he said. 'We'll get the best doctors and specialists. They can do just about anything these days with conditions that had no cure in the past.'

She couldn't quite remove the wryness from her tone. 'This isn't a condition you can exactly cure, or at least not for a few months.'

'Are you going to tell me or am I supposed to guess?' he asked after a slight pause.

Emelia could feel his suspicion growing. She could see it in his dark eyes, the way they had narrowed even further, his frown deepening. She took another uneven breath. 'Javier, I'm pregnant.'

The words fell into the silence like a grenade in a glasshouse.

She saw the flash of shock in his face. His eyes flared and he even seemed to jolt backwards as if the words had almost rocked him off his feet.

'Pregnant?' His voice came out hoarsely. 'How can you possibly be pregnant? You've been on the Pill for the whole time we've been together.' He cocked his head accusingly. 'Haven't you?'

Emelia wrung her hands, deciding there was no point in pretending she was invincible any longer. 'I was sick about a month or so ago. I didn't tell you. I had some sort of stomach upset. I think that would have been enough to cancel out the Pill.'

His rough expletive made Emelia flinch. He turned away from her and rubbed a hand over his face. Then he paced the floor a couple of times, back and forth like a caged lion, his jaw pushed all the way forward with tension.

'Don't dare to mention a termination,' she said. 'I won't agree to it and you can't force me.'

He stopped pacing to look at her. 'I do have some measure of humanity about me, Emelia. This is not the child's fault.'

She gave him an accusing glare. 'Are you saying it's *my* fault?'

He raked his hair with his fingers. 'You should have told me you weren't well. What were you thinking?'

'Being sick doesn't come with the job description of corporate trophy wife,' she threw back. 'I'm supposed to be glamorous and perfectly groomed and ready for you at the click of your fingers, remember?'

He stood staring at her, as if seeing her for the first time. 'You think that is what I always expected of you?'

'Wasn't it?' she asked with an embittered look.

He swallowed tightly and sent his hand back through his hair. 'You have it so wrong, Emelia.'

'I know you probably won't believe me, but this is not something I planned,' she said. 'Not like this. I wanted to have a baby but I wanted us to both want it.'

He was so silent she started to feel uncomfortable, wondering if his mind was taking him back to what the press had speciously claimed about her relationship with Peter Marshall.

'This baby is yours, Javier,' she said, holding his gaze. 'You have to believe me on this. There has been no one but you.'

'No one else is going to believe that,' he said, pacing again.

Emelia flattened her mouth. 'So that's what's important to you, is it? What other people think? You didn't seem to mind what people thought when that nightclub singer draped herself all over you.'

He frowned darkly as he turned back to face her. 'Emelia, this is not helping. We have to deal with this.'

'*You* have to deal with it,' she said. 'I have already dealt with it. I want this baby more than anything. It's a miracle to me that it's happened.'

'How many weeks are you?'

'I'm not sure,' she said. 'The doctor thinks only a month, if that.'

He gave a humourless laugh, shaking his head in disbelief. '*Dios mio*, what a mess.'

'This is a child we are talking about,' Emelia said, feeling a little too close to tears than she would have liked. 'I don't consider him or her to be a mess or a problem that has to be solved. I want this baby. I will love it, no matter how or why or when it was conceived.'

Javier saw the shimmering moisture in her eyes and felt a hand grab at his insides. Her hormones were no doubt all over the place and he wasn't helping things by reacting on impulse instead of thinking before he spoke. No wonder she had been so het up about his regular trips to Moscow, especially when that ridiculous article came out on his return. 'Emelia, we'll deal with it,' he said. 'I will support you. You have no need to worry about that. You and the baby will want for nothing.'

She looked at him with wariness in her grey-blue gaze. 'I'm not sure I want my child to grow up with a parental relationship that is not loving and secure.'

He came over and unpeeled her hands from around her body, holding them in the firm grasp of his. 'There are not many things you can bank on in life, Emelia. But I can guarantee you this—whatever happens between us will not affect our child. I won't allow it. We will have to put our issues aside. They can never have priority over the well-being of our child.'

Her expression was still guarded. 'You're not ruling out divorce at some stage, though, are you?'

He drew in a breath, holding it for a beat or two before releasing it. 'There is no reason why a divorce cannot be an amicable arrangement,' he said. 'If we feel the attraction that brought us together is over, I see no reason not to move on with our lives as long as it doesn't cause upset to our child.'

She pulled out of his hold and hugged herself again. 'We clearly don't share the same views on marriage,' she said. 'I've always believed it should be for life. I know things can go wrong but that's true of every relationship, not just a marital one. Surely two sensible adults who respect each other can work their way through a rough patch instead of bailing out in defeat.'

'I find it intriguing that you are suddenly an expert on marriage when you were the one to leave the marital home, not me,' Javier said. 'You pulled the plug, remember?'

Her mouth was pulled so tight it went white at the edges. 'That is so like you, to put the blame back on my shoulders, absolving yourself of any culpability. You drove me from you, Javier. You had no time for me. I was just a toy you picked up and put down at your leisure. I had no assurances from you. I didn't know from one day to the next whether you would be called away on business. Business always came first with you. I gave up everything to be with you, and yet you didn't give me anything in return.'

'I beg to differ, *cariño*,' he said. 'I spent a fortune on clothes and jewellery for you. Every trip I returned from, I gave you a present of some sort. I know many women who would give anything to be in your position.'

She glared at him hotly. 'You just don't get it, do you? I don't want expensive jewellery and designer clothes. I hate those clothes and ridiculous shoes upstairs. They make me feel like a tart. I've never wanted any of that from you.'

'Then, for God's sake, what do you want?' he asked, goaded into raising his voice.

She looked at him bleakly. 'I just want to be loved,' she said so softly he had to strain his ears to hear it. 'I have dreamed of it for so long. My father couldn't do it without conditions. I thought when I met you it would be different, but it wasn't. You want something I can't give you, Javier. I can't be a trophy wife. I can't be a shell of a person. I have to love with my whole being. I gave you my heart and soul and you've crushed it beneath the heel of your cynicism.'

Javier watched as she turned and left the room. She didn't slam the door, as many women would have done. She closed it with a soft little click that ricocheted through him like a gunshot.

CHAPTER TEN

ALMOST a week went past and Emelia saw very little of Javier over that time. He hadn't even come to bed each night until the early hours of the morning, which made her wonder if he was avoiding talking to her. He seemed to be throwing himself into his work until he fell into bed exhausted. Even in sleep she could see the lines of strain around his mouth, and on the rare occasions when his eyes met hers during waking hours they had a haunted shadowed look.

Aldana had come across Emelia being sick a couple of mornings ago as she'd come into the master suite to change the bedlinen. The housekeeper's dark gaze seemed to put two and two together for she said, 'Is that why you came back to Señor Mélendez—because you need a father for your bastard child?'

Emelia straightened her shoulders and met the housekeeper's derisive gaze head on. 'I have tried my best to get on with you. I know you don't think I am good enough for Javier. But if you wish to keep your job, Aldana, I think you should in future keep your opinions to yourself.'

Aldana mumbled something under her breath as she

bundled the rest of the linen in her arms on her way out of the bedroom.

Emelia had put the incident out of her mind but when Javier came home from a trip to Cadiz on Friday evening she could tell something was wrong. She came into the sitting room to see him with a glass of spirits in his hand and it apparently wasn't his first. His mouth was drawn and his eyes were even more shadowed than days before. She could see the tension in his body, his shoulders were slightly hunched and his tie was askew and his shirt crumpled.

'Did you have a hard day?' she asked.

'You could say that.' He took another deep swallow of his drink. 'How about you?'

She sat on the edge of one of the sofas. 'It was OK, I guess. I went for a long ride on Callida.'

'Is that wise?' he asked, frowning at her. 'What if you fell off?'

'I didn't fall off and I will only ride until the doctor says it's time to stop.'

There was a long silence.

'Is something wrong, Javier?' she asked.

He gave her a brooding look. 'Have you spoken to anyone about your pregnancy? I mean outside the villa. A friend or acquaintance or anyone?'

She frowned at him. 'No, of course not. Who would I speak to? I've been stuck here for days on end with nothing better to do than lounge about the pool or ride around in circles while you're off doing God knows what without telling me when you'll be back.'

He moved across to the coffee table and picked up a collection of newspapers. He spread them out before her, his expression dark with fury. 'Have a look at these,' he said. 'You don't need to read them all. Each one of them says the same. *Mélendez Reunion—Love-Child Scandal.*'

Emelia felt her heart slip sideways in her chest. She clutched at her throat as she looked down at the damning words. 'I don't…I don't understand…' She looked up at him in bewilderment. 'How would anyone find out I was pregnant? The doctor wouldn't have said anything. It would be a breach of patient confidentiality.'

In one sweep of his hand he shoved the papers off onto the floor. 'This is exactly what I wanted to avoid,' he said, scowling in anger.

Emelia moistened her bone-dry lips. 'I exchanged a few words with Aldana the other day,' she said. 'I was going to mention it to you but you were late getting back.'

His gaze cut to hers. 'What did you say?'

'It was more what she said to me,' she said. 'She was in our room changing the bed when she heard me being sick. When I came out she accused me of only coming back to you because…because I needed a father for my child.'

His brow was like a map of lines. 'What did you say to her in response?'

Emelia elevated her chin. 'I told her she should keep her opinions to herself if she wanted to continue working here.'

A dark cloud drifted over his features. 'I see.'

'She's never liked me, Javier,' she said. 'You know yourself she's never really accepted me as your wife. She won't let me do anything or touch anything or bring anything into this stupid over-decorated, too formal mausoleum. I've tried to be polite to her but I can't allow her to say such an insulting thing to me.'

'I understand completely,' he said. 'I will have a word with her.'

'You don't have to fire her on my account,' she said, looking down at her hands. 'It might not have been her, in any case…I mean, leaking the news of my pregnancy to the press.'

Javier came over to her and placed one of his hands on her shoulder. 'You are prepared to give her the benefit of the doubt when everything points to her being guilty?'

She looked up at him. 'But of course. She's never spoken to the press before. She loves working for you. It's her whole life, managing the villa. I don't think she would deliberately jeopardise that.'

He placed his fingers beneath her chin, his thumb moving over the fullness of her bottom lip. 'You are far too trusting, *querida*,' he said. 'People often have nefarious motives for what they do, even the people you care about.'

'That stuff in the paper…' She glanced down at the scattered mess on the floor. 'Is there nothing we can do?'

He pulled her gently to her feet, holding her about the waist. 'Don't worry about it,' he said. 'It will blow over eventually.'

She looked into his eyes. 'Javier… You really believe this baby is yours, don't you?'

Javier realised she was asking much more than that. She was asking for a commitment from him that he had never wanted to give before. He wasn't sure he wanted to give it even now. How could he be sure he wouldn't turn out like his father? But what he had begun to realise over the past few days was that being a father was not just a biological contribution. It was a contract of love and commitment with no conditions attached. His father had not been capable of going that step further. He had impregnated his mother but once she had died he had not fulfilled his responsibilities as a father. He had shunted Javier off to teachers and nannies while he'd got on with his life. This baby Emelia was carrying deserved to be loved and cherished and he was going to make sure it lacked for nothing. 'The baby is ours,' he said watching as her eyes shone with tears. 'I am proud to be its father.'

'I love you,' she said as she wrapped her arms around him tightly.

He rested his chin on the top of her head and held her close. 'I'm very glad that is one thing you remembered,' he said.

She looked up from his chest and smiled. 'I would have fallen in love with you all over again if I hadn't.'

'You think so?'

'I know so,' she said and reached up to meet his descending mouth.

Paris was enjoying an Indian summer and each day seemed brighter and warmer than the previous one. The first week they had spent wandering around the Louvre and Notre Dame, stopping for coffee in one of the numerous cafés. They had mostly been able to avoid the paparazzi, although one particularly determined journalist had followed them all the way up the Eiffel Tower steps for an impromptu interview. Javier had been extremely protective of Emelia, holding her close against his body as he'd curtly told the reporter to leave them alone. It had made Emelia glow inside to think of him standing up for her like that. It made her wonder if he was in love with her after all. She sometimes caught him looking at her with a thoughtful expression on his face, as if he was seeing her with new eyes.

The hotel Javier had booked them into was luxurious and private and close to all the sights. He even organised a private tour of the Palace of Versailles, outside of Paris, which meant she didn't have to be jostled by crowds of tourists.

They were walking past the fountain towards the woodland area when Emelia felt the first cramp. She had been feeling a little out of sorts since the night before but had put it down to the rich meal they had eaten in one of Paris's premier restaurants.

Javier noticed her slight stumble and put his arm around her waist. 'Steady there, *cariño*,' he said. 'You don't want to take a fall.'

She smiled weakly and settled against his hold, walking a few more paces when another pain gripped her like a large fish hook. She placed a hand against her abdomen, her skin breaking out in clamminess.

'Emelia?' Javier stopped and gripped her by both arms. 'What's wrong?'

She bit down on her lip as another cramp clawed at her. 'I think something's wrong…I'm having cramps. Oh, God…' Her legs began to fold but he caught her just in time.

He scooped her up in his arms and walked briskly to the nearest guide, who promptly called an ambulance.

Emelia remembered the pain and the ashen features of Javier as she was loaded into the back of the ambulance and then nothing…

* * *

When she woke the first thing Emelia saw was Javier sitting asleep in the chair beside her bed. He jolted awake as if he had sensed her looking at him. Relief flooded his features as he grasped her hand and entwined his fingers with hers. 'You gave me such a fright, *querida*. I thought I was going to lose you all over again. You have taken ten years off my life, I am sure.'

Emelia dreaded asking, but did so all the same. 'The baby?'

He shook his head. 'I'm sorry, *mi amor*. They couldn't prevent the miscarriage but you are safe, that is the main thing.'

Emelia felt her hopes plummet. The main thing was he was off the hook, surely? No more baby. No more commitment. No more pretending to be happy about being a father. 'How far along was I?' she asked in an expressionless tone.

'Not long, just a month, I think I heard one of the doctors say.'

Emelia studied his expression without saying anything.

He shifted in his seat, his eyes going to their joined hands. 'I know what you are thinking, Emelia,' he said gruffly. 'And I know I deserve it for how I reacted to the news of the pregnancy. I didn't exactly embrace the idea with any enthusiasm.'

'I'd like to be alone for a while,' she said.

He looked at her again. 'But we need to talk about the future.'

She pulled her hand away and stuffed it under the sheets. 'I don't want to talk right now.'

He slowly rose to his feet as if his bones ached like those of an old man. 'I'll be waiting outside.'

Emelia held off the tears until he had left but once

the door closed on the private room she let them fall. So he wanted to talk about the future, did he? What future was that? She had been lulled into thinking they could make a go of their marriage but he had not once told her he loved her. He always held something of himself back. She was never going to be able to penetrate the fortress of his heart. Not now, not without the baby she had longed for, the baby she had hoped would be the key to showing him the meaning of love. She had seen the flicker of relief in his eyes. No pregnancy meant he could continue with his life the way he always had—free and unfettered. Well, he was going to be much more free and unfettered than he bargained for, she decided.

'How is she?' Javier asked the doctor on duty when he came back from the bathroom.

'She doesn't want to see anyone right now,' the doctor said. 'She is still feeling rather low. It's quite normal, of course. The disruption of hormones takes its toll. She can go on some antidepressants if she doesn't improve.'

'When can I take her home?'

'She lost a lot of blood,' the doctor said. 'She's had a transfusion so we'd like her to stay in for a few days to build up her strength. She has been through rather a lot just lately, I see from the notes.'

'Yes,' Javier said, feeling guilt like a scratchy yoke about his shoulders. 'Yes, she has.'

'Just be patient,' the doctor advised. 'There's no reason why she can't conceive again. These things happen. Sometimes it's just nature's way of saying the time is not right.'

Javier sighed as the doctor moved on down the

corridor. He had never thought there would be a right time, and yet the right time had come and gone and he had not even realised it.

The nurse handed Emelia her discharge form with a disapproving frown. 'The doctor is not happy about you wanting to leave so soon, especially without your husband with you. Can't you wait until he gets here? He's probably stuck in traffic. There was an accident in one of the tunnels this morning.'

Emelia straightened her shoulders. 'I have been here for four days as it is. I am sick of being fussed over. I am sick of hospitals. I want to get on with my life.'

'But your husband—'

'Will understand completely when he hears I have left,' Emelia said with a jut of her chin as she picked up her bag. 'You can tell him goodbye for me.'

Emelia slipped out of the hospital, keeping her head down in case anyone recognised her. The press had been lurking about, or so one of the cleaning staff had informed her. That had made her decision a lot easier to make. She was tired of living in a fish bowl. She was tired of being someone she wasn't, someone she had never been and never could be. The accident had been devastating but it hadn't been the catalyst everyone assumed it had been. She had already made up her mind that she could no longer live the life Javier had planned for them both. It didn't matter what his reasons were for marrying her, the fact remained that he didn't love her. He wasn't capable of loving anyone. And, while she loved him and would love him for the rest of her life, she could not continue living in hope that he would change.

A taxi pulled into the entrance of the hospital and,

once its occupants had settled up, Emelia got in and directed the driver to the airport. She had already booked the flight via the high tech mobile phone Javier had brought in for her. It was another one of his expensive presents, one of many he had brought in over the last few days: a pair of diamond earrings and a matching pendant, a bottle of perfume, a designer watch that looked more like a bracelet than a timepiece, and some slips of lace that were supposed to be underwear. She had received them all with a tight little smile, her heart breaking into little pieces for the one gift he withheld— his love.

The flight was on time, which meant Emelia could finally let out her breath once she was strapped into the seat, ready for take-off. She checked the watch Javier had given her, her fingers tracing over the tiny sparkling diamonds embedded around the face as she thought about him arriving right about now on the ward. He would be demanding to know where she was, where she had gone and who she had gone with. She could almost see his thunderous expression, his tightly clenched hands and the deep lines scoring his forehead. But, for some reason, instead of making her smile in satisfaction, she buried her head in her hands and wept.

CHAPTER ELEVEN

EMELIA had spent the afternoon on the beach. The walk back to her father's palatial holiday house at Sunshine Beach in Queensland was her daily exercise. It still felt strange to be on speaking terms with her father after all this time. But his recent health scare had made him take stock of his life and he had gone out of his way since she had returned to make up for the past. He had given her the house to use for as long as she wanted. He flew up on occasional weekends when he could get away from work and she enjoyed their developing relationship, even though they didn't always see eye to eye on everything. Emelia had even made a fragile sort of peace with his young wife who, she realised, really did love her father in spite of his many faults. In many ways Krystal reminded her of herself when she had met and married Javier. Krystal was a little naïve and star-struck by the world her husband lived in and did everything she could to please him. It made Emelia cringe to witness it, but she knew there was nothing she could say.

The one thing Emelia and her father crossed swords over was Javier. Her father thought she shouldn't have run away without speaking to him. In Michael Shelverton's opinion, sending Javier divorce papers three weeks after she had left was a coward's way out. He felt she should have at least given him a hearing.

Emelia was glad she had done things the way she had. She wanted a clean break to allow herself time to heal. But after a month she still had trouble sleeping in spite of the hours of walking and swimming she did each day to bring on the mindless exhaustion she craved.

She had covered her tracks as best she could to avoid Javier finding her. She'd gone back to her maiden name and only answered the phone if she recognised the number on the caller ID device. She had also organised with her father to have all mail go via his post office box address and he then forwarded it on to her.

She tried not to think about Javier but it was impossible to rid her memory of his touch. Her body ached for him night after night and sometimes when she was half-asleep she found herself reaching into the empty space beside her in the bed in the vain hope of finding him there.

Emelia came up the path to the front door of the house with keys in hand, but stopped dead when a tall figure rose from the wrought iron seat on the deck.

'Hello, Emelia,' Javier said.

She set her mouth and moved past him to open the door. 'You had better leave before I call the police,' she said, stabbing the keys into the lock.

He stepped closer. 'We need to talk.'

She tried not to shrink away from his towering presence. 'You can say whatever you want to say via my lawyer.'

'That is not the way I do things, Emelia, or at least not this time around. I made that mistake before. I won't be making it again. This time it is face to face until we work this out.'

Emelia tried to block him from following her inside but he put one foot inside the door. 'If you don't want to be visiting a podiatrist for the rest of your life, I suggest you take your foot out the doorway.'

He took hold of the door, his eyes challenging hers in a heated duel she knew she would never win. 'We can discuss this out here or we can discuss it inside,' he said in an implacable tone. 'I am not leaving until this is sorted out, one way or the other.'

Emelia let the door go and stalked inside. She tossed her beach bag on the floor of the marbled foyer and, hands on hips, faced him. 'How did you find me?' she asked.

'Your father gave me the address.'

Her eyes flared with outrage. *'My father?'* She clenched her hands into fists. 'Why, that double-crossing, lying cheat. I knew I shouldn't have fallen for that stupid father-daughter reunion thing. I should have known he would take sides with you. What a jerk.'

'He loves you, Emelia,' Javier said. 'He's always loved you but he's not good at showing it, much less saying it.'

Her hands went to her hips again. 'So now you're the big expert on relationships,' she said. 'Well, bully for you.'

'He wants you to be happy.'

'I'm perfectly happy.' She put up her chin. 'In fact, I've never been happier.'

'You look tired and far too thin.'

She rolled her eyes. 'You're not looking so hot yourself, big guy.'

'That's because I can't sleep without you.'

Something flickered in her eyes. 'I'm sure you will find someone to take my place, if you haven't already.'

He shook his head at her. 'You don't get it, do you?'

She stood her ground, reminding him of a small terrier in a stand-off with a Rottweiler. 'What am I supposed to get? I understand why you married me, Javier. I've always understood. I was an idiot to agree to it, but that's what people who are blinded by love do, stupid, stupid things. But things are different now. I left you before but the accident put things on hold. This time I am determined to go through with it. It's over, Javier. Our marriage is over.'

Javier swallowed the restriction in his throat. 'I don't want a divorce.'

She visibly stiffened. 'What did you say?'

'You heard me, *querida.*'

She screwed up her face in a scowl. 'Don't call me that.'

'*Mi amor.*'

Her eyes flashed at him angrily. 'That's an even bigger lie. I am not your love. I have never been and never will be. I can handle it, you know. I get it, *finally.* Some men just can't love another person. They hate being vulnerable. It's the way they are wired. It can't be changed.'

'On the contrary, I think it can be changed,' Javier said. '*I* have changed. I am prepared to let myself be vulnerable. I love you so much but I refused to admit it before in case it was snatched away from me. I have been lying to myself for all this time. Well, maybe not lying—more protecting myself, just as you described. I have always held something back in case I was let down.'

She stood so still and so silent, as if she had stopped breathing.

He took a breath and continued. 'I think I have always loved you, the *real* you, Emelia. You don't have to be stick-thin and done up like a supermodel to make my heart leap in my throat. You do that just by waking up beside me with pillow creases on your cheeks and blurry eyes and fighting off a cold.'

Emelia swallowed. Was she dreaming? Was she hearing what she wanted to hear instead of what he was actually saying? That happened sometimes. She had heard of it. She had done it herself, talked herself into thinking she had heard things, just because she hoped and hoped and hoped someone would say them…

'I have shut off my emotions for most of my life,' he said. 'Saying *I love you* is something I saw as a weakness. I guess I have seen any vulnerability as a weakness. That is probably why you felt you couldn't tell me when you weren't feeling well. I blame myself for that. I should have known. I should have looked out for you. Even Izabella has pointed it out to me, how closed off I am.'

'I'm not sure what this has to do with me now…' she said uncertainly.

'It has everything to do with you, *cariño*,' he said softly. 'I have loved you from the first moment you smiled at me. I can even remember the day. It was our first date. Do you remember it? Please tell me you haven't forgotten it. I would hate for you not to remember the one moment that has defined my life from then on.'

Emelia gave a small nod, her breath still locked in her throat. 'I remember.'

'You looked at me across the table at that restaurant and smiled at something I said. It was like an arrow had pierced my heart, just like Cupid's bow. I didn't know what had hit me. I hated feeling so out of control.'

She summoned up a frown, not quite willing to let go just yet. 'Your father's will,' she said. 'You can't deny that it had something to do with why we married in such a rush. You should have told me about it from the start. Finding out the way I did really hurt me. I felt so used.'

He pushed his hand through his hair. 'I didn't even know about my father's will until I had been seeing you for over a month. I had never considered myself the marrying kind. I had seen the way my father had ruined three women's lives. I didn't want to do that. I guess that's why he wrote his will that way. It was just the sort of sick joke he would have liked—to force me to do something I didn't want to do. Prior to being involved with you, I had always kept all of my relationships on a casual basis.'

His expression twisted with remorse as he continued. 'I should have told you everything about that damned will. Instead, I let Claudine get her claws in. The thing is, I didn't want my father's money for myself. I wanted Izabella to have what was rightly hers and I didn't want to lose you. Marriage seemed a good way of keeping both things secure.'

She still looked at him doubtfully. 'I don't think I can cope with living at the villa any longer. I know it's beautiful and grand and all that but it's way too formal for me. I feel like I am going to get roused on for bumping into things or if something breaks.'

He came over to where she was standing, stopping just in front of her. 'The villa needs to be a home instead of a showpiece,' he said. 'I can see that now. No wonder you never felt at ease there. That is another thing I should have realised. It needs a woman's touch—your touch—to make it the home it should always have been. Aldana has decided to retire. I have been a fool not to realise how difficult she made things for you. She didn't speak to the press—apparently, that was one of the junior gardeners—but she told me about the roses. She feels very remorseful about how she treated you. I should have told you myself why I hate having them in the house.'

She looked at him with a searching gaze. 'Did I know that before the accident?'

He brushed his fingertips over the gentle slope of her cheek. 'No,' he said. 'That was another vulnerability I didn't allow you to see. They remind me of my mother's funeral. Red ones are the worst. I can't bear the sight of them. I would have had every rose bush at the villa dug up and burned by now but my mother had planted them herself.'

Emelia felt the ice around her heart begin to crack. 'I didn't really want to leave you, Javier. I just felt I had no choice. And then the accident...' She gulped and continued hollowly, 'Maybe Peter would still be alive if it hadn't been for me.'

He gripped her hands. 'No, you must not think like that. I have heard from the police since you left. The accident was no accident. Peter's lover was being stalked by her ex. He was following you and Peter, mistakenly believing you to be her. He ran Peter off the road. Charges are in the process of being laid. You were not at fault.'

She put a hand to her head and frowned as the memory returned. 'I remember Vanessa. She was the best thing that had ever happened to Peter. They were so in love.'

He gave her a pained look. 'I know. I am ashamed of how I reacted to that ridiculous press story. I should have trusted you. You've had to endure similar rubbish and yet you've always trusted me.'

'Until that last time,' she said. 'The Russian singer.'

'Yes, well, that was perfectly understandable,' he said. 'You were in the early stages of pregnancy. I had never made you feel all that secure in our marriage. I was always flying off to sign up some big business deal. But all that has to change—if you'll only give me a chance.' He tightened his hold of her hands. 'Say you'll come back to me, Emelia. Come back to me and be my wife. Be the mother of my children.'

Emelia blinked back tears. 'We lost our little baby…'

He pulled her into his chest. 'I know,' he said, softly planting a kiss on the top of her head, her seawater-damp and salty hair tickling his nose. 'I blame myself for that. If you hadn't been so worried about me coming to terms with being a father, maybe it wouldn't have happened.'

She pulled back in his embrace to look up at him. 'You mustn't blame yourself. My father recently told me my mother had three miscarriages before she had me. I don't know if it's hereditary or not, but I'm sure we'll have a baby one day.'

'So you'll come back to me?' he asked.

She smiled as she linked her arms around his neck. 'I can't think of any place I would rather be than with you.'

His dark eyes melted as he looked down at her. 'I know someone who is going to be absolutely thrilled to hear you say that.'

She gave him a quizzical look. 'Who?'

'She's waiting in the car,' he said. 'She said something about BFF. What does that mean, by the way?'

Emelia's smile widened. 'It means best friends forever. She's really here? Izabella came all this way?'

His smile was self-deprecating. 'She didn't trust me to be able to convince you to come home. She said if I didn't succeed she would come in and do it for me. Do you want me to call her in?'

'Of course I do.' She ran to the window and, finding the hire car, waved madly to the young woman sitting inside chewing her nails.

Javier's gaze warmed as he came over and looped an arm around her waist. 'There's just one thing I need to do before she gets here,' he said, turning her around to face him.

'Oh,' Emelia said, smiling brightly. 'What's that?'

'I think you know,' he said and, before she could admit she did, he covered her mouth with a kiss that promised forever.

THE KONSTANTOS
MARRIAGE DEMAND

BY
KATE WALKER

Kate Walker was born in Nottinghamshire, but as she grew up in Yorkshire she has always felt that her roots are there. She met her husband at university, and originally worked as a children's librarian, but after the birth of her son she returned to her old childhood love of writing. When she's not working, she divides her time between her family, their three cats, and her interests of embroidery, antiques, film and theatre, and, of course, reading. You can visit Kate at www.kate-walker.com.

For Abby Green with thanks
for the inspiration over Kir Royales
in the Shelbourne and for sharing Delphi Lodge

CHAPTER ONE

IN SPITE OF the driving rain that lashed her face, stinging her eyes and almost blinding her, Sadie had no trouble finding her way to the offices where she had an appointment first thing that morning. From the moment that she left the tube station and turned right it was as if her feet were taking her automatically along the route she needed, with no need to look where she was going.

But then of course she had been this way so many times before. In other days, some time ago perhaps, but often enough to know her way without thinking. Of course then she had been heading in this direction in such very different circumstances. In those days she would have arrived in a taxi, or perhaps a chauffeur-driven car, with a uniformed driver sliding the limousine to the edge of the kerb and opening the door for her. Then, the offices towards which she was heading had belonged to her father as the head of Carteret Incorporated. Now they were the UK headquarters of the man who had set out to ruin her family in revenge for the way he had been treated.

And who had succeeded far more than he had ever dreamed.

Burning tears mingled with the sting of the rain as Sadie forced her feet towards the huge plate glass doors that marked the entrance to the elegant building, blinding her so that she almost stumbled across the threshold. Bitter acid swirled in her stomach as the doors slid open and she recognised the way that the words Konstantos Corporation were now etched in big gold letters on the glass where once she had been able to see her father's name—her family name—displayed so clearly.

Would she ever be able to come back here and not think of her father, dead and in his grave for over six months, while the man who had hated him enough to take everything he possessed from him now lorded it over the company that her great-grandfather had built up from nothing into the multi-million corporation it now was?

'No!' Drawing on all the determination she possessed, Sadie shook her head, sending her sleek dark hair flying, her green eyes dark with resolve, as she stepped into the wide, marble-floored foyer. Her black patent high-heeled shoes made a clipped, decisive sound as she made her way across to the pale wood reception desk.

'No!' she muttered under her breath again.

No way was she going to let cruel memories of the past destroy her now. She couldn't let them take away the hard-won strength she had drawn on to get herself here. The resolve that was holding her upright and, she prayed, stopping her legs from shaking, her knees from giving way beneath her. She had come here today because it was her last—her only chance. She had to brave the lion in his den and ask him—beg him—to give them this one small reprieve. Without it the thought of the consequences was impossible to bear. For herself, her mother and her small brother. She couldn't let anything get in the way of that.

'I have an appointment with Mr Konstantos,' she told the smartly dressed young woman behind the reception desk. 'With—Mr Nikos Konstantos.'

She prayed that no tremor in her voice gave away how difficult she had found it to say the name—his name. The name of the man she had once loved almost to the point of madness. The name she had once believed would be hers too for the rest of her life—until she had realised that she was just being used as a pawn in a very nasty power game. A cruel game of revenge and retribution. A settling of scores from wounds that had originally been inflicted long ago and had been many, bitter years festering viciously, until they had poisoned so many lives. Her own amongst them.

'And your name is?' the receptionist enquired.

'Carter,' Sadie supplied, hoping that the sudden dropping of her green eyes to examine some non-existent spot on one of her hands didn't betray how difficult she had found it to come out with the lie. 'S-Sandie Carter.'

She had had to resort to the subterfuge of a false name, she acknowledged inwardly, a nasty taste in her mouth at having been reduced to it. She knew only too well that if she had tried to gain an appointment with him under her real identity then Nikos Konstantos would never even have given her a moment's consideration. Her request to see him would have been refused with cold-blooded arrogance and unyielding rejection. Her attempt to contact him would have been squashed dead under his arrogant heel before it had even struggled into life and she would be back where she had been at the start of this week: lost, desperate, penniless, and without a hope in the world.

She didn't have much of a hope now, but at least the receptionist was checking through a list of names and times on her computer, smiling her satisfaction as she found the fictitious one that Sadie had given her, and making a swift click with her mouse as she checked it off.

'You're a little early…'

'Not to worry—I can wait…' Sadie put in hastily, knowing

only too well that 'a little early' was a major understatement. She was way too early—by more than half an hour. But nervousness and a real fear that she might have backed out of this if she hadn't left home just as soon as she was ready had pushed her out of the door well before the time needed for her journey.

'No need,' the other woman assured her. 'Mr Konstantos's first appointment cancelled, so he can see you straight away.'

'Thank you,' Sadie managed, because it was all she could say.

She'd committed herself to this interview and she had to go through with it. But now that the time had come she felt sick at just the thought of confronting Nikos here, in what had once been her family's offices. What had possessed her to do this? To think that she could cope with seeing Nikos for the first time in five years, and come back into the building that did so much to emphasise how far her family's fortunes had fallen—both at the same time.

'I think perhaps…' she began again, her already shaky courage deserting her, meaning to say that she'd changed her mind—she had another appointment, or her mother had just called…anything to give her an excuse to leave, get out of here now. To run and hide before she had to come face to face with…

'Mr Konstantos…'

The receptionist's tone, her sudden change of expression, would have alerted Sadie to just what was happening even without the use of that emotive name. The other woman's eyes had widened, her gaze going straight to a point over Sadie's shoulder, behind her back. And the expression in it, as in the way she had said the name—*that name*—told Sadie without another word needing to be spoken just who had come up behind her, silent as a hunting jungle cat, and possibly just as deadly.

'Has my ten-o'clock appointment arrived?'

'She's right here…'

The receptionist smiled as she indicated Sadie standing before her desk, and she clearly thought that Sadie would smile back. Smile and turn. Possibly say hello or some such.

But Sadie knew that she couldn't move. Her legs seemed to have frozen to the spot. Her mind too had iced up, leaving her incapable of registering a single thought other than the fact that he was behind her.

That *Nikos Konstantos* was right behind her. And that at any moment he would see her and realise who she was.

It was the voice that had done it. Just those few words in those deep, sensually husky tones had short-circuited her brain waves, making it impossible to think of anything but the shivering sensations that ran up and down her spine. Once she had heard that voice whisper to her in the darkness, murmuring sounds of delight and promising her the very best—the world—the future. And, entranced by that sexy accent, lost in the world of sensuality that just being with him had always created around her, she had foolishly, naively believed in every word.

Every lying word.

'Mrs Carter?'

Her silence had gone on too long. It had had the opposite effect to the one she had hoped for. What she had really wanted was to become invisible. Or for the beautiful marble floor to open up so that she could fall right through, out of sight. But instead, by standing still and silent, she had puzzled and confused the other woman so that she frowned in faint enquiry, making a slight nod of her head to draw Sadie's attention to the man behind her.

A man who couldn't possibly be unaware of the way she was standing there, stiff and awkward and with blatant disregard for normal polite behaviour.

'This is Mrs Carter…' The receptionist tried again. 'Your ten o'clock…'

She had to move; she had no choice. Any more delay and she would raise all his suspicions, put him on edge. Drawing on all her strength and squaring her shoulders, Sadie snatched in a deep, sharp breath and turned on her heel. The effort she put into the movement made it far too strong, too wild, so that she whirled round, almost spinning out of control as she came suddenly face to face with the man she had once believed she was destined to marry.

He recognised her instantly, of course. No matter how much she might have changed over the past five years—and she had changed—she knew that. She had to have changed. There was no way she could still be the younger, more relaxed, far happier Sadie who had first met Nikos. But there was no doubt, no hesitation in his recognition of her. She saw the way that his face changed, the sudden tightening of his mouth, the flare of something wild and dangerous in his eyes, and her blood ran cold inside her veins at the sight.

'You!' he said, and that was all. The one word was riddled with all the disgust, contempt and obvious hatred that he felt for her, making her shiver inwardly in fearful response.

'Me,' she managed, sheer nerves making her tone inappropriately flippant, so that she saw the way that anger snapped his dark straight brows together in an ominous glare. 'Hello, Nikos.'

'My office—*now*,' he said, and spun on his heel, striding away across the foyer, never once looking back, and obviously believing that she would follow. That she would have no option but to obey the harshly muttered command he had flung at her.

And really, she did have no option. It was either that or leave, with her mission unaccomplished. And now that she had braved the lion in his den, surely she had the worst over with?

Or did she? It was true that she'd been pushed into this meeting she'd been dreading, but she had had no time to prepare, or even to think about what she was going to say. And she had hoped to approach Nikos as calmly and quietly as possible. Instead she had done just the opposite.

She'd knocked him off balance too, and he was angry as a result. Coldly furious.

It was there in every inch of his long, powerful body as he strode across the foyer towards the lifts. It stiffened the straight spine, tightened the powerful shoulders and held his dark head so arrogantly high that she felt it gave him an even more impressive height than usual.

It was impossible not to reflect on the sheer impact of that stunning frame, the width of chest, narrow sexy hips and long, long legs. She had rarely seen him quite so formally dressed when she had known him before, and the effect of the severely tailored outfit was to turn him into a distant, unapproachable figure. Deep inside there was an ache in her heart at the memory of the younger, warmer, kinder Nikos.

At least he had seemed warmer and kinder then. It was only later that she had discovered the truth about how he really was.

'Are you coming?'

The sharp question dragged her back to the present with a jolt. *Warm* and *kind* were not the words to use about Nikos now. In fact, in everything about him he was the exact opposite. As he stood just inside the lift, one long finger jammed hard on the button that held the door open, he directed a cold, icy glare at her face that had her jumping into action fast, almost scurrying the last few steps into the compartment and huddling back against the wall.

Nikos's only response was a sharp movement that released the button, letting the door slide to, shutting them in.

'I…' Sadie tried, but another of those arctic glares froze the words on her tongue.

She had forgotten how deep a bronze his eyes could be in

certain lights. In others they could be almost molten gold, the colour of the purest honey and just as sweet—or they had been once upon a time. There was nothing sweet in the look he turned on her now, nothing to melt the knot of ice that seemed to have clenched around her stomach, twisting it brutally until she felt raw and nauseous deep inside.

And Nikos clearly had no intention of even attempting to lighten the atmosphere or to make her feel any better. Instead he simply leaned back against the wall of the compartment, folding his strong arms across the width of his chest as he subjected her to the sort of savage scrutiny that made her feel as if the burn of his gaze might actually shrivel her where she stood. Why she didn't just collapse into a pile of ashes under it she didn't know. Instead, she shifted awkwardly from one foot to another then, unable to bear the terrible silence any longer, forced herself to try again.

'I—I can explain…' was all she managed, before he made a slicing, brutal gesture with his hand that cut off all attempt at speech.

'In my office.'

It was tossed at her, almost flung into her face, no hint of expression or trace of warmth on his features. His expression was a stone wall, no light in his eyes, his jaw set and hard.

'But I…' she tried again.

'In my office,' he repeated, and his tone left her in no doubt that he would brook no argument so there was no use in even trying.

Besides, the confined space of the lift was too small, too claustrophobic for her to want to risk confronting him while she was trapped there. She might have been prepared to face him in his office—in more civilised surroundings—but not here, not now. Not like this.

And, seeing the burn of icy anger in those golden eyes, she

felt a shiver creep across her skin at the thought that *civilised* no longer seemed an appropriate word to describe Nikos Konstantos, either.

'In your office, then,' she muttered, determined not to let him have the last word, and the glance she turned in his direction had the flash of defiance in its green depths.

That glance challenged him to take things further, Nikos acknowledged grimly as he adjusted his broad shoulders against the mirrored wall of the lift. But if she knew just what sort of taking it further was actually in his thoughts then he suspected that she would back down pretty hastily. Back down and back away.

It was what he should do too. The back away part at least. He should back away, back off, get his thoughts under control. He had been rocked, knocked mentally off balance by the speed and intensity of his response to discovering that she was in the building. That his ten-o'clock appointment was actually with none other than Sadie Carteret.

With the woman who had once taken him for a fool, used him, fleeced him, damn nearly been the death of his father, and then walked out on him on what had been supposed to be their wedding day. Bile rose in his throat at just the thought. The memory should have been enough to blast his mind with black hatred, drive any more basic, more masculine response right out of it.

But instead it was desire that had hit. No—give it its proper name—it had been lust. Pure, driven, primitive male lust. Though of course there had been nothing at all pure about the thoughts that had sizzled through his mind. And that had been from only seeing her from the back.

He had taken one look at the tall, slender frame of the woman in front of him, gaze lingering on the swell of her hips, the pert bottom under the clinging navy blue skirt. The contrast between the very feminine curves and the surprisingly matronly clothing, the soft flesh pushing against the restricting material, had had a sensual kick that had made his head spin and he had known that he was resolved to get to know this Sandie Carter well—very well—as swiftly as possible.

But then she had turned and he had seen that she was not Sandie Carter at all but Sadie Carteret, the woman who had torn his world apart five years before and was now, it seemed, back in his life.

For what?

'I suppose things will be more private there,' she added now, smoothing a hand over her hair and then, more revealingly, down the sides of her hips, as if wiping away some nervous perspiration from her palms and fingers.

She was not as much in control as she wanted to appear and that suited him fine. He wanted her off balance, on edge with her guard down. That way she might let slip the truth about what she was after. Because she was after something—she had to be.

'And you'd prefer to continue this interview in private?'

'Wouldn't you?'

It was another challenge, one that brought her head up, green eyes flashing, her neat chin lifting high.

'That is why you want to continue things in your office, isn't it?'

'I prefer not to have the whole world knowing my business.'

He'd had enough of that when she'd swept into his life like a whirlwind and stormed out again, leaving everything turned upside down and inside out. It had been bad enough that the financial newspapers had delighted in reporting the downfall of the Konstantos business empire with barely disguised glee, but the memory of his personal humiliation at the hands of the gossip columns and the paparazzi made acid burn in his stomach as the bitter taste of hatred filled his mouth.

'Me too.'

Something in his words or his tone had hit home, making her change her stance and drop her eyes suddenly, looking down at the floor.

So did she have something to hide? Something she would prefer the papers never got their hands on? Something he could use to bring her down as low as she had brought him? A rich sense of satisfaction ran darkly through his blood at the thought.

'Then in this at least we are in agreement.'

And he would have to control his need to know more, to understand just why she was here. To stamp down on the sudden rush of anticipation that was almost like an electrical charge along his senses. A call to battle and a challenge to be met. Once they were inside his office things would be different. Then he would get the truth from her.

Although the fact was that he already largely suspected he knew what that truth would be. Deep down he knew just why she was here because there really could only be one answer to that question.

She had to be here for money.

What else would bring her here, knocking at his door? That was what she would have most need of after all. When he'd brought her father down, he'd destroyed her luxurious way of life too. And now that Edwin Carteret was dead, there was no one else she could turn to.

But she must be desperate to think of asking him for help. Just how desperate she'd shown by lying about her name. She'd known that there was no way that Sadie Carteret would ever have been allowed to set foot over the threshold.

So why was he taking her up to his office instead of having Security eject her—forcibly, if needed—from the building?

He wasn't prepared to admit even to himself that the decision had anything to do with the instant physical response he'd felt in the first moments when he'd seen her. And now, in this small compartment, with the tall, slender lines of her body, the sleek, shining mane of dark hair and the porcelain smooth pallor of her skin repeated over and over in the multitude of reflections in the walled mirrors, it was so much worse to handle. The scent of her skin came to him on a waft of air with each movement she made, and when she shook back that smooth bell of hair it was mixed with a soft, herbal essence that made his head and his thoughts spin. Primitive hunger clawed at him deep inside, and the clutch of desire that twisted low down made him shift uncomfortably, needing to ease the discomfort.

Thankfully at that moment the lift came to a halt and the heavy metal doors slid open on to the grey carpeted corridor that led to his office. Deliberately Nikos stood back and gestured to indicate that Sadie should precede him, refusing to allow himself to look anywhere but at the top of her shining dark-haired head as she moved past.

'Left,' he said sharply, then swallowed down the rest of the directions as to how to reach his office. Because of course she didn't need them. She knew the way to what had once been her father's office probably better than he did, and she was already heading in that direction without any help from him.

She'd made a *faux pas* there, Sadie admitted to herself. She'd probably infuriated him by not standing back and waiting for directions but setting out at once in the right direction. But she'd just turned to the left automatically, following her path from so many other times in the past. She could only be grateful for the fact that walking ahead of Nikos gave her a moment or two to adjust her expression unseen, to control the sudden waver in her composure, the instinctive tightening of her mouth at the faint shiver that ran down her spine.

She had to remember that she no longer belonged here. That she wasn't on her home territory but in Nikos's domain. This was where he belonged now, where he ruled like some king of ancient Greece, absolute monarch of all he surveyed.

Absolute monarch—and possibly a tyrant too? She didn't know what Nikos was like as a boss, but he had to be a ruthless and highly efficient one. It had only taken him five short years to turn round the fortunes of the Konstantos Corporation from the weakened position in which his father's wild gambling on the stock exchange had left it. He'd turned the tables on *her* father, exacting a brutal revenge for the way Edwin had treated him in the past.

'I'm sorry…'

Carefully she adjusted her pace so that she was no longer leading but had made space for Nikos to walk alongside her, take the lead if he preferred. But he didn't take advantage of the change. Instead he stayed just behind her, a dark, looming shape at her right shoulder. Impossible to see. Impossible to judge his mood.

He was so close that she could almost feel the heat of his body reaching out to her. The scent of some cool, crisp after-shave tantalised her nostrils with thoughts of the ozone tang of the clear blue sea off the shores of the private island that the Konstantos family had once owned. That island had been part of the property empire Edwin had taken from them, so she supposed that it must now be once more back in Nikos's hands—unless her father had sold it on to someone else.

Her conscience gave an uncomfortable little twist at the thought, knowing how much Nikos had loved that island. It had meant as much to him as Thorn Trees, the old house that had been part of her family for so long, meant to her mother. So surely he would understand why she had come here today.

'Here…'

The touch of Nikos's hand on her arm to bring her to a halt outside a door was soft and swift, barely there and then gone again, but all the same the faint brush of his fingers against her elbow sizzled right the way through to her skin underneath the fine navy wool, making her almost stumble in reaction. She had known that touch in the past, had felt it so intimately on her body, on her hungry flesh without any barrier of clothes. She'd felt his touch, his caress, his kiss along every yearning inch of her, and now, like a violin fine-tuned to a maestro's hand, she felt herself quiver deep inside in shivering response as much to her memories as to the heat of his hand that barely reached her in reality.

'I know!'

Unease pushed the words from her, as she faked impatience and irritation as an excuse to snatch her arm away from his hand as she twisted the door handle with unnecessary force and wrenched it open.

'Of course you do.' Nikos's response was darkly cynical, the rough edge to his voice a warning that she had over-stepped the mark as he reached a long arm across her shoulder and pushed at the door. 'But allow me…'

Could the words be any more pointed? Could he make it any plainer that he was emphasising the fact that *he* owned this place now? That he, and not she, was in the position of power. Very definitely in charge.

And she would do well to remember that, Sadie told herself, pulling her scurrying thoughts back under control, forcing herself to take a couple of deep, calming breaths and remind herself just why she was here. She needed Nikos on her side and she would be foolish to anger and alienate him before she had even had a chance to put her case.

'Thank you.'

Somehow she managed to make it polite, careful. Not quite

the polite, submissive murmur she suspected would be more politic, but politic was beyond her. Her heart was pounding, ragged and uneven, so that her breath was jerky and raw. Tension, she told herself. Pure, unadulterated tension. She was nervous about what was coming, fearful about what she had to say and the way he might receive it.

It couldn't be anything else, she told herself. It had to be that, could only be that. She wasn't going to let it be anything else that was affecting her in this way. But with the heady scent of clean male skin in her nostrils, the brush of his hand along her neck as he reached for the door, the memory of those long ago sensual touches and caresses coming so very close to the surface of her mind, she knew that something else was knocking her dangerously off balance. Something she didn't want to look at too closely for fear of what she might find.

'Come in.'

Nikos was still keeping to that excessively polite tone, the one that warned her that she was in the presence of real danger. That she was trapped with a dark and menacing predator, one that had simply been biding its time before it decided to turn and pounce. And once inside this office, in the privacy that he had declared he was determined on, with no one close at hand to hear or to intervene should she need them, that surely would be the moment that he finally resolved to attack.

That thought made her legs suddenly weak as cotton wool beneath her as she stumbled into the room, coming halfway across the office before they gave up completely and brought her to nervous halt, not knowing what to do next. And as she stood there, her thoughts whirling, trying to find some way of beginning, an opening that would start her off on the path to saying what she had come to say, the words to ask for what she needed so badly, she felt Nikos brush past her. He strode towards the big desk that dominated the room, his movements brusque and controlled, his long body held taut with some ruthlessly restrained emotion. And it was as he swung round to face her that she saw the dark expression etched onto his stunning features and felt her heart lurch painfully just once, before it plummeted downwards to somewhere beneath the soles of her neat patent court shoes.

Anger. The whole set of his face was tight with icy fury, his golden eyes blazing with it. Away from public scrutiny, from everyone else who might see them together, hear what he had to say, he had thrown off the careful veneer of civilised, cultured politeness. The real Nikos—dark, primitive and very, very angry—was exposed in total clarity, without any pretence to mute the shocking impact of the rage that gripped him. A rage that was directed straight at her.

The predator had decided to pounce—and this time he was very definitely going in for the kill.

CHAPTER TWO

'YOU LIED!' NIKOS said, flinging the accusation at her almost as soon as the door had swung closed behind her, shutting them in together. 'You lied about who you were—gave a false name.'

'Of course I did!'

Sadie prayed that the control she was forcing into her voice kept it steady. She hoped that she had at least held it down so that it didn't go soaring up too high under the influence of the panic that was tying her insides into tight, painful knots.

'I had to. What else could I do? If I'd given my real name then there's no way you would have ever agreed to see me, would you?'

'You're damn right I wouldn't. You wouldn't have got across the threshold. But the fact remains that you are here—and that you lied in order to get here. Which means that you have something you want to say. Something that is important enough for you to use that lie in order to get to say it. So what is that, I wonder?'

The look he turned on her seemed to sear right through her, the blaze of his eyes so intense that Sadie almost expected to see her clothes scorch and burn along the path that it traced over her body.

Nikos was behind his desk, and he leaned forward to stab

one long finger down on a button by his phone. Sadie heard a woman's voice, faintly blurred by the nervous buzzing in her head, respond almost immediately.

'No calls.' It was a command, and clearly one he meant to have obeyed. 'And no interruptions. I am not to be disturbed until I say.'

And if the secretary or PA goes against those instruction, then she's a braver woman than I am, Sadie told herself. But the next moment any other thoughts fled from her mind as Nikos nodded his satisfaction and turned his attention back to her.

'So why are you here?'

'I...'

Faced with that arctic glare, the ferocious bite of his demand, Sadie found that in that moment she couldn't actually recall precisely why she *was* there, let alone form her response into any sort of coherent argument. One that might actually impress him, persuade him on to her side when she knew that he was guaranteed to take the opposite stance, simply because he was who he was and she was the one doing the asking.

She was suddenly very glad of the expanse of polished wood of his desk that came between them, acting as a barrier between the powerful dynamic force that was Nikos Konstantos.

It was totally irrational, but when he glowered at her like that she suddenly felt as if the room had shrunk, as if the walls had moved inwards, the ceiling coming down, contracting the space around her until she felt it hard to breathe. She felt trapped, confined in a room that had suddenly become too small to hold them both.

She had been shut in with him in the lift, in a far smaller space, but somehow, contradictorily, this seemed so much worse. Now Nikos seemed so much bigger, so much more powerful, dominating the space in which he stood and hold-ing her captive simply by the pure force of his presence.

Or was it about the room? Because it was the office that had once been her father's? But there was no sign at all of the previous occupant. Every last trace of anything that was per-sonal to Edwin had been removed and replaced with some-thing much more modern, more stylish—and much more expensive. Even in the good days of Carteret Incorporated the office had never looked like this.

The heavy, dark desk and chairs had all been removed and replaced by modern furniture in a pale wood. Thick golden rugs covered the floor, and in the window area there was a comfortable-looking settee and armchairs for relaxing.

It spoke of Nikos Konstantos of Konstantos Corporation. The man who had taken everything her father had thrown at him and refused to go down under it. He had seen everything his own father had worked for snatched away, had stared bankruptcy and total ruin in the face and still come out fight-ing. And in five short years he had built up his business empire to what it had once been—and then outstripped that. The Konstantos Corporation was bigger, stronger, richer than it had ever been. And it had swallowed up Carteret Incorporated and absorbed it whole on its way to the top.

And Nikos *was* the Konstantos Corporation.

As she hesitated, Nikos shot back the cuff on his immacu-late white shirt and glanced swiftly and pointedly at his watch.

'You have five minutes to explain yourself—and that is more than you would have had if I'd known it was you,' he stated curtly. 'Five minutes. No more.'

Which was guaranteed to dry Sadie's tongue, make it feel as if it was sticking to the roof of her mouth, and no matter how hard she swallowed, she couldn't quite force herself to speak.

'Could—could we sit down?' she tried, looking longingly

at the cream cushions on the padded chairs. Perhaps with her attention taken off the need to concentrate on keeping her legs from shaking so that she could stay upright she might manage to put her thoughts—and the necessary arguments to convince him—into some sort of coherent order.

Sitting down was the last thing Nikos had in mind. He had no intention of letting her get settled, allowing her to stay a moment longer than he had to. Just seeing her here like this was making him feel as if the room was suddenly at the centre of a wild and dangerous hurricane, with the day he had been living being picked up and whirled around, turned inside out.

And the sound of her voice was raking up memories he had pushed to the back of his mind for so long. He wanted them to stay there. He had never wanted to speak to Sadie Carteret ever again.

'Tell him to go away, Daddy.'

The words she had tossed down the staircase at him, the last words he had ever heard her speak on the day that had been the worst day of his life, came back to haunt him, making savage anger flare like rocket fire inside his head.

'Tell him the only interest he had for me was his money, and now that he has none I never want to see him again.'

And he had never wanted to see her, Nikos acknowledged, his whole body taut with rejection of her presence in his life once more. The disturbing tug of sensuality he had felt in the lift had evaporated, he was thankful to find. The memory of her callous rejection, the cold tight voice in which she'd flung it at him, not even bothering to come downstairs and tell him face to face, had driven that away, leaving behind just a cold savagery of hatred.

The sooner she said what she had to say and got out of here, the better.

'Five minutes,' he repeated with deadly emphasis. 'And

then I get Security to escort you out. You've wasted one of them already.'

'I wanted to talk to you about buying Thorn Trees!'

That got his attention. His dark head went back, eyes narrowing sharply.

'Buying? What is this? Have you suddenly come into a fortune?'

Belatedly Sadie realised her mistake. Nerves had got the better of her and she'd blurted out the first thing that came into her mind.

'No—of course not.'

'I didn't mean buy—I could never afford that. I just…'

The sudden drop of those bronze eyes down to the gold watch on his wrist, watching the second hand tick by, incensed her, pushing her into rash, unguarded speech.

'Damn you, you took everything we had. Every last thing my father had owned—except for this. I just hoped that I might be able to rent it from you.'

'Rent?'

Her antagonism had been a mistake, sparking off an answering anger in Nikos, one that tightened every muscle in his face, thinning his lips to a hard, tight line.

'That house is a handsome property in a prime position in London. With some restoration—a lot of restoration, admittedly—it would sell for a couple of million—maybe more. Why should I want to rent it out to you?'

'Because I need it.'

Because my mother's happiness—possibly even her sanity—her life—might depend on it. But Sadie wasn't quite ready to expose every last detail of the worries that had driven her to come here today to plead with him. Not with Nikos standing there, dark and imposing, arms now folded across the width of his chest, jaw clamped tight, eyes as cold as golden ice, looking for all the world like the judge in some criminal court. And one who was just about to put the black cap on his head, ready to pronounce the sentence of execution.

Besides, her mother had already lost so very much. She wouldn't deprive her of the last shreds of her dignity, her privacy, unless she really had no choice.

'As you've admitted, it needs a great deal of restoration. There's no way you would be able to get the market value for it right now.'

'And no way I can get the necessary renovations done with you and your mother there. I thought I'd given instructions to my solicitor…'

'You did.'

Oh, he had. She knew that only too well. The letter advising her family that Nikos Konstantos now owned Thorn Trees and that they should vacate the house by the end of the month had arrived a few days before. It had only been by a stroke of luck that Sadie had managed to intercept the envelope before her mother had shown any interest in the post. That way she had succeeded in keeping the bad news from Sarah for a while at least.

But not for good. Within twenty-four hours, her mother had somehow found the envelope and read its contents. Her panicked reaction had been everything Sadie had anticipated— and most dreaded. It was the final straw that had pushed her into action, bringing her to the realisation that there was only one way she could hope to handle this and that that was by going to see Nikos himself, appealing directly to his better nature in the hope that he would help them, let them stay at least until things improved just a little.

Not that Nikos, as he was now, looked as if he had a better nature at all. His face was set and stony, his eyes like glowing flints.

'Your solicitor did exactly as you told him—don't worry about that.'

'Then you know what I have planned for the house. And it does not include a couple of sitting tenants.'

'But we don't have anywhere to go.'

'Find somewhere.'

Could his voice get any more brutal, any more unyielding? There wasn't even a flicker of emotion in it, nothing she could hope to appeal to. And what made it so much worse was the way a memory danced in front of her eyes. An image of the same man but five years younger. And so unlike the cold-faced monster who seemed intent on glaring her into submission that he looked like someone else entirely.

She'd loved that other man. Loved him so much she'd broken her own heart rather than break his. Only to find that in the end he hadn't had a heart to break.

A terrible sense of loss stabbed at her and she felt bitter tears burn at the back of her eyes. She only managed to hold them back by sheer force of will.

'It isn't as easy as that,' she managed, her voice rough and uneven. 'In case you hadn't noticed, the economy…'

She swallowed down the last of the sentence, knowing that finishing it would only give him more ammunition to use against her. Of course he knew all about the economy, and the way things had changed so dramatically in a couple of years or so. It was what he had used against Edwin, manipulating the wild fluctuations in the stock market to his personal advantage and against the man he had hated so bitterly.

'I thought that you had a business of your own,' Nikos said now.

'A small one.'

And one that wasn't doing very well at all, Sadie acknowledged privately. With things as tight as they were for most people, no one was indulging in the luxury of having a wedding planner organise their 'big day'. She hadn't had an enquiry in weeks—and as for bookings, well, the last she'd had had cancelled the next month.

'Then get yourself another house. There are plenty on the market.'

'I can't afford—'

'Can't afford a smaller house but yet you want me to rent you Thorn Trees? Have you thought about this? About the sort of rent that can be asked for a place like that?'

'Yes, I've thought about it.'

And had quailed inside at the realisation of the fact that just the rent on her family home would probably be far more than she could possibly manage to rake together every month.

'Or did you perhaps think that I might be a soft touch and give it to you for—what is that you say—mate's rates?'

The slang term sounded weird on his tongue, his accent suddenly seeming so much thicker than before, mangling the words until they were almost incomprehensible. But even more disturbing was the knowledge that there was no way at all that they applied to the relationship between herself and Nikos. Whatever else they had been, they had never been 'mates'. Never truly friends or anything like it. Hot, passionate lovers, fiancés, prospective bride and groom—or at least that was what had been intended.

Or had it? She had been overjoyed to accept Nikos's proposal. Had looked forward to her wedding day with joyful anticipation and had wept out her devastated heart when she had been forced to cancel it. But what she had thought had been a broken heart had been as nothing when compared to the misery she had endured later, when she had learned the truth about what Nikos had really been planning.

The shattering of her dreams had coincided with such a

major crisis in her family life that she had barely known what
she was doing from day to day. In the end she had resorted to
the policy of least resistance, letting her father dictate everything she did, the way she behaved. He had written the script
for those appalling days and she had followed it exactly. At
least that way her mother had been safe, and Edwin Carteret
had made sure that Nikos had failed in his attempts to get back
into her life, to try and see Sadie—and no doubt hurt her even
more.

'I…'

'Get yourself another house, Sadie,' Nikos commanded.
'Nothing else is on offer.'

'I don't want another house—I want…'

I want Thorn Trees was all she had to say. And then he
would ask her *why*.

And if she answered with the truth, how would he react?
Would he sympathise, as the Nikos she'd thought she had
known all those years ago would have sympathised? Or would
the Nikos he was now see yet another opportunity to further
deepen his revenge against the family who had ruined his
father and taken almost everything from him?

Not knowing whether telling him the truth would help or
simply put another weapon into his hands, she swallowed
hard against the uncomfortable dryness of her throat.

'Look…'

Her voice croaked embarrassingly.

'Do you think I could have a coffee or something? Even
some water?'

Seeing the look he gave her, she felt her heart clench at the
savage contempt that burned in his eyes.

'Of course not,' she commented bitterly. 'That would eat
into the paltry five minutes you've allotted me. It's all right.'

Despair blurred her eyes, tiredness making the room seem

to swing round her. Why didn't she just admit defeat, give up and go home? But the memory of her mother's face as she'd left the house was there, urging her to try again. Sarah needed a home and so did little George. And right now Sadie was their only chance of keeping the house.

'Here…'

The abrupt word made her start, jump back slightly. Nikos sounded suddenly so very close. Disturbingly so. She blinked hard to clear her vision and found herself staring at a glass filled with water, bubbles rising inside, beads of moisture sliding down the sides. Feeling as she did, it had the effect of discovering a cool oasis in the centre of a blazing desert.

'Thank you.' It was genuinely grateful.

Reaching out a hand to take the glass from him, she misjudged the distance, the right approach, and found that although she aimed to grasp it at the base, well below his hand, in fact she closed her fingers over his, feeling their strong warmth in contrast to the cold hardness of the glass.

'I'm sorry!'

A sensation like the shock from a bolt of lightning shot up all the nerves in her arm, so that she wanted to snatch her hand away, and yet at the same time it seemed that the sudden heat had welded their fingers together, so she couldn't peel hers away without a terrible effort.

Nikos seemed to have no such problem, though his eyes held hers, darkly mesmeric, as he adjusted his hold on the glass, eased his hand away, waiting just a moment to make sure that she had a good grip before he finally let his arm drop to his side.

Still with their eyes locked together, Sadie lifted the glass of water to her parched lips, swallowed a mouthful, finding it suddenly intensely difficult to force the cool liquid past the disturbing knot that seemed to have closed off her throat.

She wished he would look away, and yet at the same time she knew that she would feel lost and strangely bereft if he did.

'Thank...'

Her voice failed her, seeming to shrivel in the heat of that intent gaze. Something had happened to his eyes, so that the colour of the iris seemed to have disappeared and there were just the deep dark pools of his widened pupils, edged only at the rim with burning molten bronze.

Almost snatching at the glass, she drank again, gulping down water that did nothing to cool the sudden heat that had flooded her body or ease the sudden heavy pounding of her heart.

'Thank you.'

At least her voice sounded stronger now, without that appalling crack in the middle that gave away far too much of what she was feeling.

She held out the glass to him, expecting him to take it back, check his watch again to see just how long of her allotted time she had left. But instead, to her total shock, he ignored the gesture and, extending one long, tanned finger, reached out to touch it to her cheek just below the corner of her right eye. Instinctively Sadie flinched and would have backed away, but once more something in that intent expression caught and held her frozen where she was.

'Tears?' he said on a softly spoken note of blank disbelief. 'Tears—for a *house!*'

Tears?

Sadie's hand flew up to her face, the backs of her fingers brushing her cheek to discover the shocking truth of his words. Tears that she had been totally unaware of having shed had slipped onto her skin, moistening her eyelashes. But even as she recognised that they were there, she looked deep into Nikos's darkly assessing gaze and knew a terrible sense of despair as she acknowledged that he couldn't be more wrong about the reason why they were there.

'Not just a house.'

Had she said the words aloud or just heard them inside her head? She couldn't tell, only knew that they blazed so hard they seemed to be etched into her thoughts in letters of fire.

Not just the house—not even though it was the home that she loved, that her mother needed. It wasn't anything to do with Thorn Trees or even her angry frustration at not being able to persuade Nikos round to her way of thinking that was twisting a brutal knife in her devastated heart. Instead it was the sudden terrible sense of loss that she'd known in the moment she'd looked into Nikos's eyes as he came close to her.

She'd armoured herself against this meeting. Told herself that what she had once felt for him was all over, that time had healed the scars and put a distance between her and the love she had once felt for this man. That his final betrayal and the way he had behaved since, the terrible revenge he had exacted so cold-bloodedly, had left her immune to him, not even hatred surviving of the onslaught of feelings she had been through.

But if this was immunity, then she would hate to have to try and face a fully developed fever! Her whole body was fizzing with awareness, coming to burning life in response to just that one, tiny touch.

No—not just the touch. She was responding to the look in his darkened eyes, the scent of his skin, the sound of his voice, even of his soft breathing, his very presence. Everything about him made her burn as if she stood in the direct line of the sun. And yet, contradictorily, it held her frozen to the spot, unable to move or look away. And hunger, dark and disturbing physical craving, throbbed like a heavy pulse in her blood.

'It's not just a house,' she tried again, hoping to stir him into movement, away from her.

But it seemed that Nikos too had fallen under something of the same spell. After that one harsh question he stood as transfixed as her. His eyes locked with hers, his burning gaze so fixed, so unwavering that it seemed he barely even blinked. And Sadie sensed rather than actually saw the way his long tanned throat moved as he swallowed deeply.

'Sadie…' he said at last, his voice seeming to be becoming unravelled at the edges.

And the sound of her name on his lips had the effect of stabbing a stiletto dagger right into the centre of her heart, so that it jolted once, violently, then started pattering rapidly, high up in her throat, making it so very difficult to breathe naturally. His accent had deepened shockingly on the sound, making it raw and rough, disturbingly like the times that she heard him speak her name in the burn of passion, deep in the darkness of the night.

Memory dried her mouth again and nervously she licked her lips to ease the sensation. The water seemed to have done nothing at all to ease her thirst, or if it had then the moisture had evaporated in the heat that his touch had sent rushing through her.

'Sadie…' Nikos said again, and at long last the finger that rested so lightly on her cheek moved softly.

But not to move away from her, not to break the contact with her skin. Instead, his touch simply shifted, adjusted slightly, smoothing down one side of her cheek to curl under the fine line of her jaw, lifting her chin. She heard his harshly indrawn breath, watched those heavy black eyelashes close slowly, then open again as the burning bronze of his gaze blazed into her.

And he bent his head to kiss her.

It felt as if she had been waiting for it for so long. As if it was the kiss she had been waiting for all her life. It was shocking, heart-stopping in its gentleness. In anyone else she might even have called it hesitancy, but there was nothing hesitant about Nikos's taking of her mouth. It was slow, it was sensual, it was totally sure of what he was doing—the effect it was aiming for. It was pure seduction, aimed right at her libido and having exactly the effect that he wanted.

Sadie's fingers softened, her grip on the water glass loosening so that it fell to the floor. She vaguely heard the splash of water, the thud of the tumbler bouncing on the thick wool of the rug.

But after that she knew nothing else. Nothing but Nikos and the warmth of his body all around her. The strength of his arms as they gathered her close. The pressure of his mouth on hers and the magic it was working as he eased her lips open, slid his tongue along the edge and into the warm softness of her mouth.

His hands slid up her back, into her hair, tangling in the dark silky strands. He twisted his fingers around them, using them to hold her head just where he wanted as he increased the pressure, forcing her to open to him even more.

She was drowning in a dark, heady world of sensuality. Lost to reality and aware only of the responses of her body, following blindly where Nikos led. She was soft and malleable in his hands, unable to think for herself or find any trace of will to call her own. Her own hands lifted, arms winding themselves around his neck, drawing his proud head down even closer, taking the kiss into another dimension, another stage of hungry sensuality.

'Nikos…' she murmured against his cheek as he turned his head, his wicked, beguiling mouth finding the fine, taut line of her throat and kissing his way down it to the spot where her pulse throbbed frantically at the base of her neck.

When his warm lips pressed against the tiny point, she felt

her breath catch in her throat, the electric shocks of response sparking its way along every nerve, flashing down to pool in liquid heat in the most intimate spot low in her body, between her legs. Restlessly, she moved against him, pressing her body close to the hardness of his and feeling the heated swelling of the erection that marked his undisguised response to her. That pressure was what she wanted. That and more—so much more—and it was obvious that Nikos felt the same as one large hard hand came down to curve over her buttocks, bringing her into even more intimate contact and holding her there.

'Nikos…' Once more she choked out his name, restless fingers clutching in his hair, pressing against his scalp, holding him against her.

It seemed that the heat of their bodies had melted her bones, so that she swayed against him on unsteady legs. She heard his breath hiss in sharply between his teeth, and the hand that had been in her hair released her to slide, hot and sensuous, down to her ribcage to cup the side of her breast, his thumb stroking tormentingly over her nipple, bringing it to springing, tightened life underneath the cotton of her blouse. Sadie's own breath caught in her throat, making her gasp in shocked delight and wriggle even closer, pressing her sensitised flesh against the heat of his palm.

'Yes, Nikos, yes. This—'

But the words died on her tongue, crushed back down her throat by the way that he suddenly stopped, his whole mood changing.

'No!'

His body stiffened, the dark head going back violently to look down at her with a new and devastating hostility, brutal rejection blazing in his eyes.

'No!' he said again, more forcefully this time.

The hands that had held her close were now moving her

away from him, setting her aside with cold precision. The fingers that had tangled in her hair were tugged free with a speed and roughness that brought pinpricks of tears to her eyes, though she was too stunned, too bewildered by the sudden change in mood to have even the energy needed to let them fall.

She couldn't find the strength to speak, either. Shock deprived her of her voice, so that even though she opened her mouth twice to try to protest she had to close it again when all she managed was an embarrassing croak. Stunned, she could only stand and watch in blank bewilderment as Nikos adjusted the fit of his jacket that her clutching fingers had knocked askew, smoothed his hands over his hair to bring it back into sleek order rather than the wayward tangle she had made of it.

And then, to her total consternation and horror, he actually checked his watch once again.

'Your time is almost up. You have just fifty seconds left,' he declared with flat detachment, completely devoid of emotion. 'Was there anything else that you wanted to say before you leave?'

CHAPTER THREE

HE SHOULD NEVER have touched her, Nikos told himself. Never been such a damn fool as to bridge the gap between them, do something as crazy as to put his finger on her face, feel the softness of her skin underneath his.

He should never have let himself get close enough to her to catch the scent of her skin, the clean softness of her hair.

Just a couple of steps forward was all it had taken. And, with the electrical sting of response to the moment their hands had touched around the glass still sizzling up his arm, he had already been halfway towards the madness of arousal that she had always been able to spark in him so instantly in the past.

And still could, damn it, it seemed.

He had spent the last five years trying to put her part in his life behind him, out of his mind. He had managed to get the taste of her out of his mouth and now it was right back there, sensual, intoxicating, driving him insane.

He had to be insane. How the hell else could he have let her get to him so far, so fast?

One touch and he had been right there, back in the maelstrom of searing hunger that tightened his throat, made his heart pound in his chest, made him hot and hard and hungry in the space of a single devastating heartbeat.

Just the feel of the soft flesh of her cheek under his finger-tip had brought a memory, fast and dangerous as a bolt of lightning, of the way it had felt to have her naked, all that softness underneath him, warm and willing, yearning for his touch, his caress…opening to him…

Thee mou, no! He was not going down that dangerous path again, sensually enticing though it was.

'I repeat,' he said, injecting every ounce of control he possessed into the ruthless command of his voice, 'is there anything else that you want to say before you leave?'

Was there anything?

Sadie felt as if her head was spinning, reeling as if from the force of a sudden fierce blow.

Her shocked, numbed brain wouldn't focus, and all she could think of was the feeling of Nikos's arms around her, the pressure of his body against hers. Her heart was still thudding ferociously and the taste of him was still on her lips. And deep in her body the yearning hunger that had uncoiled in those few fraught, dangerous moments was still burning, still stinging at her senses and making her feel miserably restless with unfulfilled need.

The clamour of every aroused cell made her feel as if she was being assailed by some appalling fever. One that had her burning up in one moment and then shivering in wretched cold the next.

'Well?'

Nikos's tone was harshly impatient, and damn him if he didn't flick another glance at that hateful watch, driving home his message without needing to say another word.

'I…'

Still unable to collect her thoughts, Sadie resorted to desperate measures, giving her head a rough little shake in an attempt to clear it. The movement caught Nikos's attention, making him frown ominously.

'And what does that mean?' he questioned sharply. 'Is it supposed to be no, you have nothing more to say? Or no, you have no plans to leave? Because I can tell you that you may not have plans—but I certainly do. I have another appointment in fifteen minutes, and a business lunch and an afternoon conference call after that. I don't have time to waste standing here, waiting for you to make up your mind and realise that you've had your chance—you made your plea and you lost.'

'Lost?' Sadie echoed dejectedly, recollection of why she was here coming back to her in full—and leaving her feeling worse than ever at the realisation that Nikos was dismissing her for good, with no chance at all of saving their home for her family.

'There is no way that I am going to sell you Thorn Trees,' she heard him say now, confirming her worst suspicions. 'Or rent it to you. My plans for the house remain just as they were when you—'

'Oh, please!' Sadie broke in on him, the thought of going home and telling her mother that she had failed driving her to one last desperate attempt to get him to show some compassion. 'Please don't say that! You have to understand—there has to be something I can do for you.'

'And what makes you think that? What the devil could I want from you? Believe me, there is nothing—'

'But there must be!'

'Nothing.'

His tone warned her not to argue further. And the way he raked both hands through his hair, pushing it back into its sleek control, spoke of a ruthless determination to be back on track, ready for the next move, that next appointment. This one was over and he was done with her.

'But that—what happened just now—surely...?'

Her words died as she looked into his face and his expression told her the terrible truth.

'What happened just now?' Nikos echoed cynically, his burning gaze searing over her from the top of her ruffled dark head to the toes of her black patent shoes.

The look of dark contempt that filled it made her shiver, feeling as if a much needed protective layer of skin had been stripped from her body, leaving her raw and exposed, frighteningly vulnerable.

'And what makes you think that what just happened had anything to do with anything?'

'But—you… I thought…'

Her tongue seemed to tangle up on itself, tying itself in knots so that she couldn't get the words out.

'You thought…?' Nikos prompted harshly when she fought with herself, trying to speak.

'I thought that that—that when you…'

When you kissed me. She just couldn't make herself say it. She knew that she would give herself away if she did. She had thought—had *hoped*—that the way he had kissed her so passionately meant that he still felt some trace of something for her. That, if nothing else, at least he was still attracted to her. And she had little doubt that that hope, that illusion—because his face made it plain it *was* an illusion—would show in her voice if she said anything more.

'When I kissed you?' Nikos drawled mockingly. 'Is that what you mean? So tell me, my sweet Sadie, just what did you think was happening? What do you think that was?'

'I—' Sadie tried to begin, but he ignored her stuttering attempt at speech and talked across her quite deliberately.

'Did you think it was warmth? Was that it? Or perhaps affection? Or perhaps…'

He actually had the nerve to stop, appear to consider, even

look suitably surprised, when deep down inside she knew damn well that the brute wasn't surprised at all but had been aiming for this right from the start.

'*Thee mou*, you didn't think it was *love*, did you?'

If she'd found it hard to speak before, then now Sadie found it absolutely impossible. She could feel the hot colour flaring in her cheeks and knew that her furiously embarrassed reaction had given her away completely.

'Then I'm sorry—'

'No, you're not!' Sadie broke in, finding her voice at last in the strength of the wave of anger that swept over her. 'You're not sorry at all. And I know it wasn't—wasn't anything like love.'

It couldn't have been. There was no way anyone could switch on love like that and then immediately turn it off right away.

'It certainly wasn't,' Nikos confirmed coldly.

'So what was it?'

Cruelty? Deliberate manipulation? Some sort of hateful test?

'Isn't it obvious?' Nikos questioned softly. 'I couldn't help myself.'

He'd shocked her there. It wasn't at all the answer she'd expected. But he'd anticipated her response and knew that he had her when her head went back in amazement, green eyes opening wide. A smile that did nothing to light up his face and had no effect at all on the coldness of his eyes flickered across his beautiful mouth as he noted her response.

He paused just long enough for his words to sink in and hit home before moving in for the kill.

'Lust will do that,' he declared, making sure that his words were totally clear. 'You always spoke to my most basic masculine nature—my libido—you still do. I find it hard to keep my hands off you.'

'Is that supposed to be a compliment? Because if it is you need to work on your technique.'

But Sadie's sarcasm, her attempt to hit back, simply bounced off Nikos's impenetrable hide without, apparently, even leaving a mark.

'Lust I can handle,' he went on, as if she had never spoken. 'It's something I can decide to indulge or not as I choose.'

'And you—decided to indulge it just now when you *pawed* me—'

'Not pawed, Sadie,' Nikos corrected, shaking his head almost as if in sorrow at her interpretation of his actions. 'I do not paw women. And if I had then you would not have responded as you did.'

'I—' Sadie tried to protest, but the sudden rush of confidence to speak seemed to have deserted her.

'If you want the truth,' Nikos continued, 'I wanted to know if you tasted the same. And you do.'

'Taste?'

It was the last thing she had expected.

'You still taste *exactly* the same.'

Nikos's mouth twisted on the words.

'I may not have recognised it before, but I see what it is now—the taste of lies and deceit—the taste of betrayal.'

Sadie flinched inwardly as he flung the words in her face. She wished she could deny them, throw her refutation right back into his dark, contemptuous face. But how could she when deep down she knew that they were nothing but the truth? She'd been forced to betray him, but he had planned his own betrayal with cold-blooded cruelty and with no one twisting his arm up behind his back—emotionally, at least. It had all been precisely what he had wanted all along.

'It wasn't exactly as you think. But I don't suppose you want to hear about that, do you?'

'You're damn right I don't. In fact, I do not want to hear another single word from you.'

'But the house…' Despair forced her to say it, pushing the words from her mouth when she just wanted to keep quiet and get out of there with some shreds of dignity intact. But she had her mother and her little brother to think of, and she couldn't let them down.

'*Gamoto!*' Nikos flung up his hands in a gesture of total exasperation. 'How many times do I have to tell you that I will not sell you Thorn Trees? Nor will I rent it to you—not at any price. Not if you were the last person on earth.'

'But there must be some arrangement we can come to! Surely there's something I can do—anything…'

The words shrivelled and died when she saw the fiendish light in his eyes and knew that she had made a terrible mistake.

'And exactly what sort of services did you have in mind? What exactly are you offering…?'

'Not that! Never!' Sadie flung at him, seeing the way his dark and cruel mind was going. 'If you really think that I'd sell myself…I'd rather die!'

'That was not the impression you were giving a few minutes ago,' Nikos returned, his voice sounding soft and silky but with an effect as brutal as a sharp stiletto sliding in between her ribs to stab at her heart. 'Then it was *Oh, Nikos—yes, Nikos…*'

'And you fell for it, didn't you?'

The words had flashed from her mouth before she had time to consider if they were wise or even safe. She only knew that she couldn't take any more of this black mockery. Of the appalling insults he was tossing in her direction with almost every word that came out of his mouth.

'You really thought that all you had to do was to touch me—kiss me—and I would be putty in your hands.'

'You were. That is exactly how you behaved.'

'I made it *seem* as if I was but you're pretty easy to fool. All I had to do was to let you cop a feel…'

The way that his black brows snapped together in a furious frown made her heart lurch in panic, cutting her words off short. Deciding hastily that it was probably safer not to think about the real reason why he looked so furious, instead she opted for a less contentious option and flashed him a mocking smile.

'Ask someone to translate,' she suggested wickedly.

'No translation necessary, believe me,' Nikos flung back, cold as ice. 'None at all. But if you think that that was what was happening then you are the one in need of an interpretation. And a reality check.'

'Oh, yes?'

'Oh, yes. If you think that all it takes is a flash of those stunning green eyes or a wiggle of your sexy little behind, then you really don't know me at all.'

'It felt—' Sadie began, but Nikos cut in on her, bringing one long-fingered hand down in a slashing gesture to emphasise his interruption.

'I was fool enough to go that way once before and I have no intention of ever putting my head into the noose all over again.'

'And you've made us pay for it ever since!'

Sadie was beginning to feel as if she was on some dangerous emotional rollercoaster. And it was all her own fault. After all she'd started this, with the pretence that she'd only been playing him along.

Playing him along—hah! That would be the day. She hated to admit it, even to herself, but the truth was that she *had* been putty in his hands. One kiss, one caress, and she had lost all grip on her sanity and been spun into a world of hot sensation and even hotter need. At least she had had the sense to realise that those casually tossed compliments—stunning green eyes and sexy little behind, indeed!—were not meant at all. They were just the practised flattery of a consummate womaniser. He probably rolled them out to whichever woman he happened to be with, changing the colour of their eyes where appropriate of course.

'You've had five years of taking your revenge. Haven't you done enough, had enough?'

'If you want the truth, then the answer is no,'

It was a flat, hard statement, his tone as harshly unyielding as his face, and when she looked into the deep pools of his eyes she saw no spark of warmth, no hint of humanity. Instead they were as cold and unresponsive as ice, his opaque, blanked-off stare shocking and frightening.

'What more can you have? There's nothing left. My father's dead—his fortune, his company are yours. Isn't that enough for you?'

'No, it is not.'

Nikos's golden eyes flicked over her face, catching and locking with her furious gaze just for one moment. Then he looked away again, heavy lids coming down to cut him off from her.

'I thought it was, but now I find it just won't do. It isn't enough. It doesn't give me the satisfaction that I wanted. I need to find some other way of making sure of that.'

And then she knew. With a terrible, sinking sense of despair she realised just what was going on here. Nikos Konstantos had always been determined to have his revenge for the way that Edwin had ruined his family. He had worked for that and for nothing else all the five years since she had last seen him. He'd taken the Carteret name, the Carteret business and stamped them into the mud, drained them of every last penny they possessed. He was even prepared to take the family home from them and throw her and her mother and little George out into the street.

And she had done the worst thing possible, made the most terrible mistake imaginable, by coming here to plead with him for a chance.

Because that had given Nikos one more chance to exact revenge on the member of the family he had the most personal reasons to hate. The one that he hadn't yet crushed beneath his heel and laughed in triumph as he did so.

He hadn't truly had his revenge on Sadie herself. Until now. And now it was strictly personal and totally ruthless. This wasn't about the house or the past except as it pitted the two of them against each other. This was the last part that would make his campaign of revenge complete.

He had her in his sights and he wasn't letting go.

'And the way you've found is by making sure that my family don't have a home to live in. How can you live with that on your conscience?'

'No problem.'

Nikos's shrug dismissed the question as being of no importance to him whatsoever. He didn't care and he had no intention of caring.

'I live with it as easily as you and your father could walk away from the devastation you made of my life—and my family's.'

'And you think that gives you the moral high ground? You were pretty damn good at playing games at that time, if I remember rightly.'

'Not games, Sadie.'

Nikos shook his head, his expression almost sorrowful, but Sadie knew that sorrow was the furthest thing from what he was feeling. He might hide it well but she knew that deep inside he was probably taking a cruel delight in tormenting her like this, having her with her back to the wall, nowhere to run.

'Believe me, I was serious. Deadly serious.'

'Oh, yeah, deadly serious about perpetuating that damn family feud. And look what that did to you. It almost ruined your family.'

'Almost,' Nikos echoed with deadly emphasis. 'Almost—

but it did not actually ruin us, did it? Not totally. And now the shoe is very definitely on the other foot.'

'As I'm only too well aware,' Sadie muttered belligerently.

She wondered what would happen if she told Nikos that the only reason that *'almost'* was even there was because of her. Because of the choice she'd made.

He'd probably never believe her. The mood he was in, he wasn't going to listen to anything she said.

'So this is checkmate, is it?' she went on. 'You must know that I can't leave it like this—without persuading you to let us stay in Thorn Trees….'

'That isn't going to happen,' Nikos stated with cold obduracy.

'So what do I do?'

Once more those powerful shoulders under the superbly tailored jacket lifted in an unfeeling and dismissive shrug.

'You said you were prepared to do anything to get what you wanted,' he drawled heartlessly. 'Turn those wiles that you were using earlier on someone else and you might have more success with someone who doesn't know you as well as I do.'

'Wiles…' Sadie spluttered in furious indignation. He really thought that she had set out to seduce him as a way to manipulate him into giving her what she wanted. 'How dare you…?'

But Nikos ignored her angry interjection.

'Find yourself another rich man and beg him to give you a chance to earn the price of the house. He might not find the offer so distasteful—his standards may not be as high as mine.'

Sadie gritted her teeth against the need to refute the implications of that cynical *'earn,'* though her fingers twitched sharply at her side with the urge to lash out and swipe that cold sneer from his arrogant face. Whatever momentary satisfaction it would bring—and it would be very satisfying—it would also make things so much worse and only succeed in angering Nikos even further.

'And if I did then you would only put the price up higher and higher each time.'

Nikos's smile was pure cold evil. The smile of the devil.

'How well you understand me, *glikia mou*. And, knowing me as you do, I am sure that you will recall that once I have made up my mind on a matter then I never change it. No matter what the temptation.'

And he had made up his mind on this, so it would be like battering her head against a brick wall if she continued to try to persuade him.

'And now, as you have had more than twice the amount of time allotted to you, I really would prefer it if you left immediately.'

Striding across to the door, Nikos pulled it open and stood pointedly, waiting for her to leave.

'I am sure that both of us would prefer to avoid the publicity that my calling Security might create.'

Knowing Nikos, Sadie recognised when she had come to the end of the road and there was nowhere else she could go. Defeat was staring her in the face and the only thing left to her was to accept it with as much dignity as she possibly could. Though the thought of going home and telling her mother…

Putting her head up high, stiffening her back and straightening her shoulders, she forced her feet to take her towards the door he had indicated. She had fully determined that she wouldn't say another word. That she wouldn't show him any weakness. She wouldn't even look at him. But somehow as she had to pass him her footsteps faltered, and in spite of her determination her reluctant gaze was drawn to his dark, stunning face, meeting the icy glare of those golden eyes.

'Is there nothing I can do…?' she began and knew her mistake as she saw his face harden even more, hooded eyes closing off from her.

'Yes,' he said coldly, unbelievably. 'The one thing you can do is go home and start packing—I want you out by the end of the week.'

It was the final blow, but at least his vicious tone was enough to stiffen her resolve.

'I'll do that,' she flung at him, refusing to let him see the terrible sense of defeat that was tearing at her soul.

'I'd appreciate it.'

Another couple of strides and she was beyond him, out of the room at last and marching straight down the long, soulless corridor, staring straight ahead.

She'd taken it better than he'd thought, Nikos admitted as he watched her go. Just for a moment there he had suspected that she was going to show him that she meant her declaration that she would do *anything* and turn back to him, coming close with smiles and deliberate kisses in an attempt to seduce him into giving her what she wanted.

And if she had done just that? The way his heart kicked and his body tightened gave him his answer.

Gamoto! Was he really going to let her walk out of his life once again, just as she had done five years before? With the taste of her still on his lips, with his body still in the grip of the burning arousal that just that one kiss had sent flaring through him, he knew that the answer was no. For almost five years he had tried to put this woman out of his mind and now, after less than an hour in her company, he knew why he had never fully managed to do it.

He still wanted her.

He wanted her like hell, in the way that he had never wanted any other woman in his life. And even the knowledge of the vile way she had behaved, the way she'd used an e-mail message to tell him she was backing out of their marriage—less than twenty-four hours before the ceremony—the cold-voiced rejection that she'd tossed down the stairs, couldn't erase the yearning hunger that plagued his senses. Watching the sway of her hips, the swing of the glossy dark hair as she walked away from him, he found he was actually considering calling her back, offering to renegotiate.

'You've had five years of taking your revenge. Haven't you done enough, had enough?'

The echo of her angry voice, just moments before, sounded inside his head. And his own answer came back at him fast, forcing him to face the truth.

'I thought it was, but now I find it just won't do. It isn't enough. It doesn't give me the satisfaction that I wanted. I need to find some other way of making sure of that.'

When Edwin Carteret had died, he'd thought he was done with the whole, hateful family. He'd clawed back every last penny of the fortune that had been taken from them and doubled it. He'd taken every asset the Carterets had owned— Thorn Trees being the last on the list—and seen his hated enemy reduced to total bankruptcy and ruin. To the black despair that his father had known and had barely even recovered from now. And he had thought that it was enough.

But one meeting with his nemesis in the seductive form of Sadie Carteret had brought that belief crashing down around him. Now at last he could put his finger on the feeling of restlessness and dissatisfaction that had plagued him in recent months. Before then he had been working too hard, barely even raising his eyes from his desk, from the files of stock market dealings, the takeover details and investments that had brought him to where he was now. It could never be enough because he hadn't dealt with the one remaining insult the Carterets had dealt him. Only this time it wasn't 'the Carterets' he had in his sights, but one member of that family in particular.

This time it was personal. Personal between him and seductive, manipulating Sadie Carteret.

And by coming here today Sadie had handed him just the weapon he needed. She was desperate to get her hands on her ancestral family home. Almost as desperate as he was to get his hands on her silken skin, her feminine curves. To have her under him in his bed once more. And the way she'd responded to his kiss had left him in no doubt that she still felt the passion that had brought them together in that one explosive weekend that had just been enough to awaken his appetite, never enough to sate it.

She would do anything she could to get Thorn Trees, she had said. Well, now he'd see how far she was prepared to go to do just that. If things went the way he planned, then she would get the damn house, and he could find the satisfaction he needed and get Sadie Carteret out of his system once and for all. In the most enjoyable way.

For a moment he thought about calling her back, and then paused, shaking his head as he rethought. If he sent a message down in the executive lift then she would get it before she left the building.

Kicking the door shut, he went back to his desk and reached for pen and paper.

The long, long corridor ahead of her blurred and danced as Sadie fought with the tears that burned at her eyes, but this time she was not looking back, she told herself. Not a single glance. Even when it seemed to be an extraordinarily long time before she finally heard the door to Nikos's office bang shut behind her.

Somehow she made it to the lift, and only once inside did she let herself collapse back against the wall, her whole body sagging limply and her head dropping forward as her eyes closed. It was some moments before she could even think of pressing the button for the ground floor.

She'd tried her best, given it her best shot. And she'd failed. Nothing, it seemed, could prevail against the black, brutal hatred that Nikos had let fester for all these years. Nothing could change him, restore him to the man he had once been. The man who had stolen her heart. The man she had been going to marry.

No.

Shaking herself roughly, she snapped her head up sharply, forcing herself to face facts once and for all.

She had to stop deceiving herself. That Nikos was a fantasy, a deception—a lie. The Nikos she had loved had never truly existed; he had simply been playing with her, manipulating her until he got exactly what he wanted. If her father hadn't moved in to protect her then the end result could have been far worse than it had. And it had been terrible enough.

The lift came to a halt, the doors sliding open, and Sadie pushed herself into motion, now desperate to get away, to be free of the tainted atmosphere of hatred.

It was as she crossed the wide, marble-floored foyer that she heard the beeping sound from her mobile phone. A text message. She knew who it would be from even before she had taken it from her bag, though the sight of 'New message from Mum' on the screen almost made her switch it off and not look.

But that would be the coward's way out. She had to face her family and let them know that she had failed some time. Taking a deep breath, she pressed the 'view' key.

How did you get on? her mother asked, as Sadie had known she would. *Have you got good news? Can we stay?*

Standing in the middle of the foyer, Sadie could only stare at the tiny screen until the backlighting blinked off and the whole thing went black. How was she going to do this? What could she say to soften the blow?

'Miss Carteret?'

It took a moment or two to register that the voice was speaking to her. That the receptionist she had talked to earlier had come up behind her and was now trying to get her attention.

'Excuse me, Miss Carteret, I have a message.'

'A message?'

Sadie stared blankly at the folded sheet of paper the other woman held out to her.

'From who?'

But even as she asked the question she knew there could only be one person who could have sent it. Only one man who could have dashed off the note and had it brought down to her in the executive lift, so it had caught up with her before she left the building.

Nikos. Just the thought of his name made her hand shake as she reached for the note.

'Thank you.'

She barely noticed the receptionist move away, her attention closely focussed on the piece of paper she held. After the way she had left Nikos upstairs, the brutal harshness of that final 'nothing', this was the last thing she had expected. He had been adamant that he was not going to help her, so why…?

Her fingers fumbled with the note as she unfolded it, tension blurring her vision as she tried to focus.

The note had neither greeting nor signature, but it didn't need one. There was no mistaking Nikos's dark, slashing scrawl. Just four brief words, dashed off in haste, and the sight of them made Sadie blink hard in bewilderment and confusion.

Cambrelli's 8:00 p.m. Be there.

Be there.

It was a blunt decree, a command that she would be wise to obey—or risk the consequences.

Be there.

And Cambrelli's. Dear heaven, but the man knew how to stick the knife in. Cambrelli's was the small Italian restaurant he had taken her to on their very first date.

Rebellion rose hotly in Sadie's heart. Who the hell was this man that he could issue such an order and expect to have it obeyed? Her fingers tightened on the paper, the impulse to crumple it into a ball and toss it away from her almost overwhelming. She was damned if she…

But even as she lifted her hand to do so, common sense reasserted itself and froze the defiant gesture. What was she thinking of? She knew exactly who this man was.

He was Nikos Konstantos, and he was in the position of having every command he issued obeyed at once, without any hint of a question. He also held all the cards very tightly in his hands.

'And, knowing me as you do, I am sure that you will recall that once I have made up my mind on a matter then I never change it.'

The words that Nikos had flung at her sounded so clearly inside her head that she almost believed that the man himself had come up behind her and spoken them out loud.

He had sworn that he would not help her and made it plain that every one of her entreaties had fallen on totally stony ground.

And yet…

Her gaze went back to the note in her hand as she smoothed it out and read over once again.

Cambrelli's 8:00 p.m. Be there.

She didn't know what it meant, but it seemed that Nikos had tossed her some kind of lifeline. It wasn't much but it was all she had, and she would be a fool not to grab at it while she could.

The receptionist was still hovering close at hand, obviously waiting for an answer. Glancing down at her phone, reading the message from her mother again, Sadie drew in a deep breath and came to a decision.

'Tell Mr Konstantos that I will meet him as arranged.'

CHAPTER FOUR

CAMBRELLI'S RESTAURANT HAD changed very little in the past five years. It was perhaps a little cleaner and brighter—they had obviously put a fresh coat of paint on the walls—but not much else had altered.

There were the same dark wood tables and chairs, some in small booths with red fake leather banquettes on either side, the same red-and-white checked tablecloths, the same candles stuck into empty wine bottles on each table, with wax dripping down the neck and over the label. She was sure that there were even the same rather worn and faded posters on the walls. One of the Colosseum in Rome and one of St Mark's Square in Venice. It was like stepping back in time and reliving a small part of her life.

If only she really could do that, Sadie thought as she followed the waiter to one of the booths near the back of the room, well away from the window, she noted. If only she could be arriving here as a rather naive twenty year old, still at university, her head in a whirl of excitement and her feet barely seeming to touch the ground as she headed for a date with the most exciting man she had ever met. Anticipating the most wonderful night she had ever known.

And it had been just that. That night and the days, the

months that had followed had been the happiest, the most glorious times Sadie had ever known. But if it was at all possible, if she really could go back in time, then she would grab hold of her younger self, try to shake some sense into her.

'Poor stupid little fool,' she muttered to herself, the bitterness of memory pushing the words from her mouth in spite of the fact that she wasn't really speaking to anyone.

'I beg your pardon, *signorina?*'

The waiter had heard her, and paused in his progress across the room to glance at her questioningly.

'Oh—sorry—nothing…'

She had to get a grip on herself, Sadie thought, managing an embarrassed half-smile. The stress of the day and anxiety about the evening ahead was getting to her and making her control of her tongue slip slightly. She needed to have her thoughts and her feelings totally under control.

But oh, how she wished that someone had taken charge of her younger self. That they had warned her not to trust Nikos, not to believe a word he said. Better that she should have faced the inevitable disillusionment then, before their affair had truly begun, rather than go through the whole terrible process of falling hopelessly and mindlessly in love and then being bitterly disappointed. The appalling sense of loss and betrayal had been all the worse because of the wonder and joy that had gone before.

But of course then she wouldn't have believed anyone who had tried to convince her that Nikos was not what he seemed. She wouldn't have listened to a single person—probably not even herself if she had managed to appear to give a warning message. At twenty years old she had been naive, gullible, and totally starry-eyed, and she would have thought that it would be well worth a broken heart at the end if she could only have that night.

She had never expected it to last anyway. She had only ever

thought that she would have that one night, one date. At the end of the evening she had fully expected that Nikos would take her home, say goodnight, and that would be that. She had been overjoyed, and unable to quite believe it, when he had asked to see her again—and again.

'Good evening, Sadie.'

Sadie had been so lost in her thoughts that she hadn't noticed they had reached the booth. It was already occupied, she realised, as in the shadowy darkness Nikos rose to his full height and faced her across the table.

This was not the man she had confronted in his office earlier that day. This Nikos was not the sleek suited businessman who headed the Konstantos Corporation. Instead he was darkly devastating in a soft black shirt, open at the neck with no tie, and worn black denim jeans that hugged the lean hips, the narrow waist that was emphasised by a heavy leather belt.

And just what was the message he intended her to read into that? Or was she reading too much into it because she had spent so long worrying about what she should wear herself— opting for a pair of smart black trousers with a deep red shirt and loose jacket so that she neither looked as if she had dressed up or down for this meeting? She was too acutely sensitive to the hidden clues in what Nikos had chosen to wear.

'Won't you sit down?'

The pointed question brought home to her the fact that she had been standing, still and silent, staring at him as if she had never seen him before in her life while he waited with carefully controlled patience for her response.

'Thank you.'

It was as she sank into the seat directly opposite him that she recalled how she had once been told that when eating out in a restaurant Greek men usually seated themselves with their backs to the wall, their guest facing them. That way the host could see everything that was going on, the coming and going in the main body of the restaurant, but their companion's attention was forced to be concentrated solely on them.

Not that Nikos's attention seemed to be anywhere else other than on her. Those bronze eyes were fixed on her face in a way that made the tiny hairs at the back of her neck lift in the uncomfortable reaction of a wary cat, faced with a threatening intruder into its space.

'So you came,' Nikos commented when the waiter had handed them menus and left them to decide on their meals.

'Of course I came. As you knew I would have to. I had no other choice. Not unless I wanted to stay at home and pack, as you'd already ordered me to do.'

'Not ordered. It was the logical next step if things stayed as they were,' Nikos corrected softly, earning himself a sideways glare that Sadie hoped made it clear that she was not in the least convinced by the apparent conciliatory tone in his voice.

There was no way that he was here to do any peace-making. Why should he when he held all the cards in his hands—and most of them were aces?

'And I suppose you are going to claim that you didn't order me to meet you here?'

'I merely invited you. So, what would you like to eat?'

Nothing. Sadie felt that she would be unable to swallow a single mouthful. Besides…

'Did you really invite me out for a meal?'

Nikos glanced up from his study of the menu, one black brow slightly lifted in mocking enquiry.

'Why else would we be in a restaurant, with menus to choose from?'

Because he wanted to prove that he had so much power over her that he could say jump and she would ask how high. Because he wanted to emphasise, by choosing this particular restaurant, just how very different things were now from the way they had been in the past, when they had been here together before.

'And why are we in this particular restaurant? Why here and nowhere else?'

'Because I know you like it here.'

If she didn't know better, she might almost believe in the innocence in his eyes, his voice. But she had no doubt that it was more than that. Nikos Konstantos never did anything without considering all possible outcomes and planning for the one that was exactly what he wanted.

'I liked it once,' she said coldly, pointedly. 'My tastes have changed since then.'

'Mine too,' Nikos drawled cynically.

So how was she supposed to take that? Was he, like her, thinking of the first meal they had eaten here? She hadn't known who he was then. Only that she had fallen for the most devastatingly handsome and attractive man she had ever met. If she had known would she have been more careful, more on her guard? Maybe even held back and never agreed to go out with him?

If she had then things would have been so much easier. She would never have become tangled up in Nikos's schemes—and those of her father. She would never have become a pawn in their hateful feud, never been used by each of them against the other. Because that had been all she was to them. A weapon which they could use to inflict as much damage on the other as possible.

'I understand that the calamari here is very good—unless you prefer—'

'What I'd prefer…' Sadie put in sharply, having foolishly let her eyes wander over the menu so that she spotted the delicious shrimp dish she had eaten that first time she had been here. She could almost taste it in her mouth, the memory was so clear and devastating. 'What I'd *prefer* is that you tell me exactly why I'm here and what you want from me.'

'Some wine first?' Nikos returned imperturbably, lifting one hand to summon the waiter.

The response was immediate, as of course it always was with Nikos. He only had to make the slightest gesture, look as if he might need something, and there was always someone there, right at hand, ready to provide whatever he needed.

But the presence of the waiter and his enquiring glance in her direction, the way he brandished his notepad and pen, meant that she couldn't pursue the topic she wanted with him standing there listening. Feeling cornered, with her back against the wall, she snatched up the menu again and chose a pasta dish completely at random, only wanting the man to be gone so that she could confront Nikos and find out just what was going on.

'I don't for one moment believe,' she began as soon as they were alone again, 'that you have invited me here simply to spend an evening together and eat pasta—however good it might be.'

'You're right...'

Nikos set his own menu aside and folded his hands together on the tabletop. The movement made a sudden flash of gold catch the light from the candle flame, and Sadie felt her heart thud just once, hard and sharp against her ribs, as she realised that she had no idea whether Nikos was married or if there was a woman in his life.

Someone to replace her.

Outside a heavy rumble of thunder announced the fact that a storm was approaching. Sadie noted it with only half her mind, the rest of her attention focussed on those long, strong, tanned fingers resting on the red and white checked cloth. Fingers where she now saw the gold was just a signet ring, worn on Nikos's right hand. At the realisation her breath escaped her in a rush. Breath that she hadn't even been aware of holding in.

'I haven't just invited you here to spend the evening with me. I asked you to meet me because I wanted to offer you a job.'

'A job?'

And now the waiter was back with the wine, interrupting them again. Was Nikos really making a particular thing about checking the label, having the bottle opened, tasting the small amount the waiter poured into his glass? Or was it just that it seemed that way to her, with every long drawn out second seeming to grate more on her already overstretched nerves, making her want to scream or make some protest. Instead she had to settle for waiting, her back tense, teeth digging into the softness of her bottom lip, until he had nodded his satisfaction and indicated that the waiter should pour her a drink.

'No, thanks,' Sadie put in hastily, pressing her hand over the top of her glass. She needed to keep a clear head until she found out just what Nikos was up to. If he pressed her...

Nikos took her decision with surprising equanimity, sipping appreciatively at the rich red liquid in his own glass, once again taking his time before he moved the conversation on at all. Sadie couldn't stand the waiting any longer.

'What sort of a job?' she demanded when the silence had stretched out just too long to bear. 'Why would you want to employ me? And what makes you think that I would ever want to work for you?'

'You did,' Nikos told her coolly, taking another swallow of his wine.

'I never!'

'Oh, yes, you did.'

And when she frowned in blank incomprehension, he shook his head slightly, as if in disbelief.

'What a very short memory you have, Miss Carteret. What-ever happened to "There must be some arrangement we can come to! Surely there's something I can do—anything"? *Any-thing,*' he added, with soft menace and deadly emphasis.

Recalling the interpretation he had put on that *'anything'* earlier that day, Sadie suddenly wished she had accepted some of the wine. Right now it might ease the painful knot of tension tight in her chest, ease the uncomfortably jerky pound-ing of her heart. She knew she would do anything in her power to gain some extra time that her mother and George could spend in the home that meant so much to them. But did Nikos really mean…?

'What exactly did you have in mind?' she managed to croak, another rumble of distant thunder seeming to under-line the apprehension in her tone.

Once more Nikos took his time in replying, stony, hard eyes never leaving her face as he leaned back in his chair and seemed to consider his response. Not that he had any need to, Sadie re-flected. She had little doubt that he knew exactly what he was going to say and how it would affect her. She had the most un-comfortable feeling that she was as powerless as a puppet, with its strings dangling from the hands of a ruthless and cruel master.

'We'll come to that in a moment,' he said evenly. 'But first I want you to tell me exactly why you want the house so much.'

'Isn't it obvious?' Sadie hedged, unwilling to expose her mother's story to his pitiless gaze.

'Oh, yes, totally obvious.'

Could his tone get any more cynical?

'Young woman with no money, a not very successful busi-ness as a wedding planner…'

Seeing her start of surprise, he gave a tight smile.

'I make sure I keep up to date with what is happening to anyone I have had dealings with in the past.'

So how much did he know? The idea of being kept under surveillance like that when she hadn't known he was watching made her skin crawl.

That smile grew darker, more dangerous, the blaze of the candles reflected in the depths of his penetrating gaze.

'I always thought that it was something of a very black irony that someone who walked out on her own wedding just the day before it was due to take place should now make her living organising other women's "big days."'

Nikos's sensual mouth twisted on the words.

'But then the one thing I could never deny is that you always had that very special sense of style. When other people were paying, of course.'

'I had to do something to earn a living,' Sadie managed from between tight lips. 'And that at least was a way of using my design course.'

The one her father had paid for as a reward for doing as he asked of her. She wouldn't need it, Edwin had told her. After all, she was going to be a great catch—a very wealthy young woman now that he had seen off the opposition, which was the way he had described his takeover of almost everything the Konstantos family had owned.

But Sadie had known that she couldn't just sit around at home. For one thing, the atmosphere there between her parents had been so poisonous that it had been an endurance test simply to breathe the same air. And, for another, the last thing she had wanted to do was to consider the prospect of another suitor who would only want to marry her because of the huge inheritance that was going to come to her when her father died.

She'd been through that once. And once was more than enough.

'And it was something I could do from home.'

Nikos nodded slowly, turning the stem of his glass round and round in his tanned fingers.

'And of course Thorn Trees is a prestigious address from which to run a business that would attract society brides and their wealthy families.'

'But that isn't why I want to keep the house!'

A deliberately lifted eyebrow questioned her over-emphatic outburst.

'Then why would you want to live in a huge London mansion with—what?—seven bedrooms and an indoor pool? Preferably for free, or at the most for a tiny rent. So, tell me exactly why you need a house like Thorn Trees? Do you plan to sleep in each of the bedrooms on a different day of the week?'

'Oh, now you're just being ridiculous! Of course not! And I wouldn't be living there on my own.'

That had his attention. She could tell by the way his back stiffened, cold eyes burning into her as the swept over her face. Sadie felt she could also tell just what was going through his mind—clearly his 'keeping up to date' hadn't resulted in him finding out the story about her mother. At least that was one thing her father had done properly before he died.

But the waiter was back again, this time bringing their meals, and Nikos was forced to sit and wait—obviously burning up with impatience—to be served before he could find out more. The man barely had time to put the plates on the table before Nikos was waving him away, ignoring his questions as to whether there was anything else they wanted.

'Who?' he demanded, and Sadie allowed herself a moment or two to prolong the tension, knowing it would provoke him even more.

'Did you have to send him away like that?' she complained. 'I might have wanted some parmesan…'

A flick of Nikos's hand dismissed her protest as irrelevant and unimportant.

'*Who?*' he repeated.

'Well, not what you're thinking—so you can get your mind out of the gutter. Do you really think that I would ask you to finance my love life by providing a home for me and my lover?'

He wouldn't put it past her, Nikos acknowledged to himself. Sadie Carteret had had a liking for the good things of life, always provided someone else was paying. The way she had discarded him so quickly when his family had been ruined and he had lost his personal fortune had been proof of that. And of course she had deliberately distracted him so that her father could work behind the scenes, planning hostile takeovers, finding ways to bring the Konstantos empire down. She had even been prepared to sacrifice her own virginity to ensure that the destructive plan succeeded.

Beyond the windows, yet another distant rumble of thunder after what he assumed was the flash of lightning just seemed to underline the point of her corruption.

'Nothing would surprise me.'

'Well, for your information, I share the house with my mother and little brother.'

That was so unexpected that it seemed to hit like a blow between his eyes, making his head go back in shock, eyes narrowing assessingly. This was information he had not been given.

'You don't have a brother.'

The look Sadie turned on his was wide-eyed, innocent, sharply contrasting with the way that her chin came up and she faced him defiantly over the table.

'Well, that just goes to show that your amazing spy network isn't as good as you thought. For your information, I *do* have a brother—a little brother called George. He was born— He's not quite five.'

Five. Why did it seem that everything that had turned his life upside down had happened at the point not quite five years before? So her mother had been pregnant around the time when they had been together and planning to get married, or just after. And little George had been born into the maelstrom of action and reaction once her father's plan to bring down the house of Konstantos had been put into motion.

And of course in those months he had been focusing only on holding things together. On keeping the corporation from going under and taking his beleaguered father with it. At the time he had felt that if he thought about anything else, focussed on anything else, then the dark waves of total disaster would break over his head and he would definitely go down for the third time—and never come up again.

But the fact that she had a brother put a different complexion on the fact that Sadie wanted to keep the house. This George was so young that there was no way he could have ever been involved in anything the adult Carterets had planned and implemented against his family.

'I see,' he said, the words loaded with dark meaning. 'That explains why I never got to hear of it. So tell me…'

'No.'

Ridiculously buoyed up by the small triumph she'd had in putting him mentally onto the wrong foot for once, Sadie waved the hand that had picked up her fork to dig into her pasta to silence him.

'My turn.'

He might hold all the aces, but that didn't mean that she was going to let him get away with monopolising the conversation and treating the meal as if it was a trial for fraud with him as the counsel for the prosecution.

'I get to ask some questions too.'

Was that a grudging respect in his eyes, the inclination of

his head? Just the possibility gave her a little surge of confidence as she forked up a mouthful of her pasta.

'What questions?'

'Well, the obvious, for a starter. Like—you said you wanted to talk to me about a job. What sort of a job could I do for you? I mean—what need would you have of a wedding planner?'

'That really is asking the obvious,' Nikos commented. 'To plan a wedding, of course.'

The impact of his response hit home just in the moment that Sadie popped the forkful of pasta into her mouth and chewed. Too late she realised that she'd been in such a state of apprehension when she'd arrived at the restaurant that she'd blindly ordered her meal with an *arrabiata* sauce, instead of the one next to it on the menu. She loathed chillies, and this was heavily laced with them.

'A wedding?' she croaked through the burn in her mouth, tears of reaction stinging her eyes.

'Here…'

Leaning forward, Nikos poured a glass of water, held it out to her, watching as she gulped it down gratefully.

'You hate spicy food,' he said, when she finally started to breathe more easily. 'Particularly chillies.'

Did he remember everything about her? It was a scary thought.

'So why order something that you were going to hate?'

'It's almost five years. I might have changed—people do.'

'Obviously not that much,' Nikos drawled, his dry tone making her wonder if there was so much more than her reaction to the chilli sauce behind his comment. 'Would you like something else?'

'No—thank you.'

Any appetite she had had fled in the moment he had made that stunning announcement. But at least the impact of the chillies had disguised the fact that a lot—oh, be honest!—most of her reaction had been in response to his declaration. Her heart was still thudding from the shock of it, her thoughts spinning, whirling from one emotion to another and back again.

And none of the reactions was one that she really wanted to take out and examine in detail. Not here, not now. Not with Nikos lounging back in his chair, watching every move she made.

'Whose wedding?' she managed to croak. 'Are you telling me that you are getting married?'

Once more Nikos inclined his dark head in agreement.

'Who to?'

'I prefer not to say. One never knows when the paparazzi might be hanging around, looking for a story. I prefer that they do not find out about this just yet. I want to protect my fiancée.'

A protection he hadn't offered her, Sadie recalled with a stab of bitterness. Then he had been happy that the world should know about their engagement, their upcoming wedding. With the result that she had begun to feel she was living her life in a goldfish bowl, with a huge, powerful spotlight directed right at it all the time.

Which had made their final break-up into a media circus that had left her shattered and devastated.

'And you don't trust me?' she asked, as much to distract herself from the particularly vivid, particularly painful memories that had risen to the surface of her mind, no matter how much she tried to push them down.

'You will find out soon enough—when the time is right for you to know.'

It seemed that Nikos too had abandoned all pretence at having an appetite for his meal. His ignored sea bass was rapidly cooling on his plate as he focussed only on her.

'And of course when you are in Greece…'

'What?'

She couldn't have heard that right.

'No—wait a minute—back up a bit here. What was that? I thought you said… I'm not going to Greece!'

'Of course you are.'

Nikos's half smile was perfectly composed, totally in control.

'How else will you organise the wedding?'

'Your wedding?'

The croak in her voice was worse than the one inflicted by the bite of the chillies. She could hardly believe that she had heard anything right. Had he really said?

She couldn't… She *wouldn't!* How could he expect her to organise and arrange a wedding at which he—the man she had once been going to marry herself—would become someone else's husband? He couldn't ask it of her! It was too cruel. Too monstrous.

But the reality was that Nikos wasn't *asking*. He was simply stating a fact. As far as he was concerned this was what was going to happen. She was going to take on the arranging of his wedding—to his fiancée. Because he said so.

'No…'

It was all she could manage. Even after a long, shaken gulp of cooling water, her throat refused to allow her to say any more.

'I said that I had a job for you.'

'*This* is the job? This is what you brought me here to talk about?'

And what sort of twisted vindictiveness had driven him to bring her here, to the restaurant where they had shared their first meal together, and where, barely two months later, he had proposed to her in one of the other candlelit booths?

'Well, thank you for the offer, but I'm afraid I'm going to have to decline the commission. I can't go to Greece.'

And she couldn't possibly work with him on his plans to marry someone else.

'I'm afraid that you do not have that option.' Nikos's tone took his response to a place light years away from any real regret. In fact, it made it only too plain that the very last thing he was was sorry. 'This is not a job that you can turn down—or even stop to think about. Not if you really meant what you said when you told me you would do anything if I would just let you live in Thorn Trees.'

'So…' Sadie drew in a slow, deep breath and let it out again on a thoughtful sigh. 'This is your price for what I asked? I work for you—plan your wedding—and you'll allow me to stay in…'

'I'll allow your mother and brother to stay in the family home. For now,' Nikos put in, making it plain that his concern was only for them.

'What made you change your mind? Only this morning you were saying that you wouldn't even consider it.'

'Your mother played no part in what happened in the past. Neither did your brother. Because of that I am prepared to make some concessions for them.'

Which once again put the emphasis of what he was doing firmly on the personal, between Nikos and herself. And what he wanted from her was for her to organise this wedding for him and so rub her nose in the fact that he had not only moved on but totally replaced her in his life. The cruel sting of that thought made her wish again that she had let him pour her some wine. At least then she could have lifted her glass, sipped from it—even if she was only pretending to drink. She could have fiddled with the glass, hidden her face behind it, anything that would distract him from the hurt, the feeling of being at a loss, she knew must show in her face.

'But I don't know anything about Greek weddings—

you would do better with someone else, someone who knows all about—'

'I don't want anyone else. I want you.'

'Surely your bride-to-be will have some say in the matter?'

'My bride-to-be will leave things entirely in my hands.'

'Oh, she will, will she? What's this—you're reverting to type and determined to get yourself a sweet little innocent wife who daren't say a word against you.'

'Unlike the wife I would have had if I'd married you?' Nikos drawled cynically, swilling the rich red wine around in his glass before taking a long drink from it. 'No one could ever have described you as "sweet"—or "innocent."'

'But then you never really wanted to marry me in the first place,' Sadie flashed back, still fighting with the pain of her memories.

She'd been an innocent when he'd met her—still a virgin at twenty. But naively, crazily, head over heels in love, and thinking she was going to be married to the love of her life, she had thrown that special gift away, giving it to the man who she believed loved her but who had in fact just been using her cynically and cruelly as a way to get at her father.

'On the contrary…' Nikos countered. 'I wanted you very much indeed. So much so that I was out of my head with it.'

'So that's all I was to you—a mental aberration?'

She had needed the reminder of how ruthlessly he had behaved. He might have wanted her, all right, but only physically. And she had offered herself to him on a plate, pushing to anticipate their wedding vows.

It was that same night when she had discovered just what Nikos had really been up to when he had claimed he wanted to marry her.

'You certainly drove me crazy. Are you going to eat that?'

He nodded his dark head towards the plate of rapidly

cooling pasta that now was beginning to look nastily congealed and even more unappealing.

'No chance.'

Sadie gave an exaggerated shudder, and to her astonishment a smile flickered on Nikos's lips. Brief, barely there, but it did at least have a trace of real warmth, real amusement.

'I knew that would happen when you ordered it. Remembering how much you hate chillies...'

'Then why didn't you say something?' she demanded, causing Nikos to hold up his hands in front of himself in a gesture of appeasement.

'I also remember what you were like when anyone tried to tell you what to do,' he said dryly.

And for a moment, as their eyes met across the table, it was as if the years had fallen away and they were back on that very first date, with every part of their relationship brand-new and fresh. When they had both been just learning about each other and everything had seemed bright and clear, with so much potential lying ahead.

As the flickering candle-light played over Nikos's stunning face it emphasised shadows, showed up lines that she hadn't seen before. Lines that five years of experience had put on his face, under his eyes, around his mouth. But somehow the marks of time seemed only to enhance rather than reduce the powerful masculine appeal of his hard features. At this time of day his strong jaw was already shaded with the darkness of a day's growth of beard and, seeing it, Sadie suddenly had a rush of vivid, painful memory of just how she had loved the feel of that faint roughness against her skin when he kissed her, the lightly stinging response it had always left behind.

Nikos's eyes were dark, deep pools above the broad slash of his cheekbones, and his sensual mouth was stained faintly by the rich red wine he had just drunk, his lips still moist from it.

As their gazes clashed, froze, locked together with an intensity that made it seem as if the whole of the restaurant and everyone in it had faded into a hazy blur, the murmur of conversation blended together until it made a sound like the distant buzzing of a thousand bees—there, but making no real sense at all.

All the breath seemed to stop in her throat, making her lips part in an attempt to snatch in air that she had almost forgotten how to breathe. She felt as if she was drowning in those eyes, losing herself and going down for the third time as hot waters of sensuality swirled around her head, making her senses swim dangerously. Outside, in the darkened rainswept street, the lightning flashed again, but Sadie barely saw it. It was only when a growl of thunder made her jump that she came back to herself in a rush.

'Nikos…'

She barely knew she had spoken, only that the sound of his name had escaped on a breath that had somehow formed into the word. And when she looked around, with things coming back into focus again, she saw how she had actually put her hand out to him, trying to make contact. Her arm lay across the gingham tablecloth, her fingers stretched towards his, almost making contact.

In the space of a jolting heartbeat she knew what a mistake she had made. She saw the way the man before her blinked hard, just once, and when he opened his eyes again it was as if all trace of any emotion, any warmth, had been washed from them leaving them, opaque and cold as a pebble at the bottom of a mountain stream. With that blink the silent connection that seemed to have formed between was broken, shattered, and Nikos suddenly straightened up, reaching for his napkin and dabbing it to his mouth.

'Then we'll go. I've said what I wanted to say and you will need to get home and pack. We leave for Athens in the morning.'

'Leave…'

Indignation and exasperation burned away any last remaining shreds of the disturbing sensual response she had just felt, leaving her feeling uncomfortable and totally on edge.

'But I haven't said I'll come yet. You can't just—'

'There's nothing for you to say,' Nikos cut across her attempt to protest, pushing back his chair and standing up as he did so. 'It's make your mind up time, Sadie. You either pack to come with me to Greece in the morning—or you pack up everything for yourself, your mother and brother and leave Thorn Trees. So which is it to be?'

It was the reminder of her mother and George that decided the question, as Nikos had obviously intended it should. He had held out the offer to let them stay, but only on his terms. And those terms involved her going with him to Greece and working to arrange Nikos's wedding to his new bride.

'Your choice, Sadie,' Nikos prompted harshly when she still hesitated.

Which, of course, was no choice at all. There was only one thing she could say. Only one way she could keep her mother and George safe and happy. No matter what the personal cost to her.

'I'll come,' she said. 'It seems I have no choice.'

'None at all,' Nikos assured her. And the really disturbing thing was the total lack of any sort of triumph or satisfaction in his tone.

He had planned for just this result and things had worked out exactly as he intended. He had expected nothing else. Because he knew exactly where he had her—dancing on the end of the strings that he was holding, in total control of her life. And there was nothing she could do about it.

CHAPTER FIVE

'WE WILL BE preparing to land soon.'

Nikos's accented voice broke into Sadie's concentration, making her jump.

'You'll need to put that away.'

His gesture indicated the laptop on which she had been working ever since the private jet had levelled out on their flight to Athens, her attention totally focussed on the screen.

'What are you working on anyway?'

'Greek wedding customs—what else?' Sadie swivelled the machine round so that he could see the site she had been studying.

She had been glad to disappear into her need to concentrate on the reason she was on the plane in the first place. It had meant that she could try at least to ignore Nikos's long, lean form sprawled in one of the soft leather seats on the opposite side of the cabin.

But the truth was that her mind hadn't really been on her research. Instead, it had insisted on taking her back into the past, replaying scenes of the times she had spent with Nikos when the only wedding she had been planning had been her own. She had desperately needed a real distraction from that.

'I take it that you are planning a traditional wedding,

seeing as you have insisted on dragging me out to Greece with you?'

Nikos shrugged off the question with an indifferent lift of one shoulder.

'Have you even given your bride a choice? Or will you just dictate how things are to be?'

That brought his eyes to her face, coldly probing, as if he was trying to read what went on behind her eyes. And she could see the flash of something fierce and dark in their golden depths.

'Are you saying that this is how it was with you? That I dictated everything?'

'No.'

How could she claim that? He had insisted she should have everything exactly the way she wanted. It was her choice, he had told her, her wedding. She should choose everything. And as a result it had really been the way her father had wanted things, not her choice at all.

But then, of course, that had been because he had never truly meant to marry her. All the time Nikos had been planning on using her to distract her father while he and his family worked to ensure his downfall, the ruin of his company. It was only when she found out the truth that she had realised why he had been so unexpectedly easygoing, so unconcerned about having an Orthodox wedding.

'Of course you didn't dictate anything. Because nothing mattered enough to you to bother with that.'

'You couldn't be more wrong.'

Nikos's smile sent a shiver down her spine.

'Oh, of course, there was one thing.' She flung the response at him. 'I know only too well just what mattered to you. You wanted me in your bed and that was all.'

'And I had you there without too much trouble, as I recall. You practically threw yourself at me.'

She had played right into his hands there, Sadie admitted. At first determined that she would wait until her wedding night to give her virginity to the man she adored, she had completely lost her head just a short time before the big day. So she had hired a cottage, enticed Nikos away with her for a long weekend of blazing passion.

Instead it had turned into a dreadful time when her dreams had started to unravel and she had finally begun to learn the truth.

These were the memories that had plagued her as the plane sped towards Greece. Echoes of the time when Nikos, thinking she was asleep, had gone downstairs to answer a call on his mobile phone. But Sadie had only been dozing and, missing him, had crept down after him. Before she'd opened the door she'd caught a drift of his conversation and had stopped to listen. And what she'd heard had shattered her illusions and fantasies, making them tumble in pieces all around her.

'Don't worry,' she'd heard Nikos say, a thread of dark, cruel laughter in his voice. 'There is more than one way to skin this particular cat. When my ring is on his precious daughter's finger and she's part of the Konstantos family too, then Carteret will soon come to heel. We'll have him exactly where we want him.'

'It was what I wanted at the time,' she said now, matching Nikos with an equally dismissive shrug.

Somehow she managed to make her voice hard enough to conceal the way that her memories tore at her heart. She even added a curl of her lips, as if in contempt at her younger self.

'Don't forget I was naive and innocent then. I had nothing to compare you to.'

'Inexperienced, maybe—innocent, never,' Nikos scorned. 'You knew exactly what you were doing and you played your virginity as your trump card.'

'It wasn't like that!'

'No? So are you going to tell me what it *was* like? Are you going to claim that you were truly as crazily in love with me as you pretended to be?'

She was heading into dangerous waters here, Sadie told herself. If she admitted the truth, that she had adored him, that he had been her life, then he would want to know why she had turned on him as she had done. And she still had enough pride to want to hide from him just how much she knew of the way he had used her callously in his determination to bring down her family.

And she needed to tread carefully while Nikos was in total charge of the situation. For his own private reasons he was prepared to be unexpectedly generous. He was letting her mother and George stay in the house for now. But she was terrified that if she rocked the boat in any way he might change his mind. Just the memory of the way her mother's face had lit up when she had been able to give her good news last night was enough to keep a careful check on her tongue.

'*Crazy* would be a good way to describe it,' she hedged carefully. 'You were pretty hot back then, Nikos, and I was tired of being a virgin. But don't kid yourself that you were anything special.'

'Oh, I won't.' Nikos's response was darkly dangerous, the savage edge to it slashing like a cruel knife. 'Believe me, I never did. Now, are you going to switch that thing off or not?'

'Oh—sorry…'

Hastily, she closed down the site she had been studying, saving her notes before switching off the whole computer. Her movements clumsy, partly from haste and partly because of the burning intensity of his scrutiny, she shut it up and bundled it into the case on the floor beside her seat.

'I'll take that.'

Nikos leaned over to pick up the case.

'Oh, but…' Sadie tried to protest but he dismissed it with a gesture.

'The staff will see to our luggage and this will go with it. You will get it back when it's necessary. And what about your phone? Your mobile will need to be switched off.'

'Of course.'

The phone was in her bag, and as she pulled it out she saw that the words telling her she had a newly arrived text message were on the screen.

'It's from my mother. Can I just see this…?'

Another flick of his hand urged her to do just that and be quick about it, his impatience making her all fingers and thumbs as she checked her message.

It was a long one, and she had to scroll down to read it all. Then scroll back again to reread, not quite believing what she had seen.

'Sadie…'

Nikos's hand was held out towards the phone. He didn't quite click his fingers in impatience, but that mood was very much in the air as he waited for her to respond.

'But…'

Sadie's eyes were still on the text message.

'Mum says that she's had a letter from you—a courier delivery. And you…'

She had to spin round, had to look straight into Nikos's face to try to read his expression.

'Is this true? Have you really sent my mother written notification that she can stay in Thorn Trees for now?'

The answer was there in his face, in the swift, darkened glance that he directed briefly at the phone and then at Sadie once again.

'I instructed my solicitor to send a letter this morning.'

'But why?'

'I told you. Your mother and brother played no part in what happened in the past. It would be inhuman to take revenge on a child.'

Which once again brought a shiver of apprehension at the thought that revenge was in his mind at all.

She was here to organise his wedding, wasn't she?

'And this is in return for my helping to plan and arrange your wedding?'

The bronze eyes that met her questioning glance were cool and opaque, all emotion blanked out so that there was nothing to read, nothing to give her any help.

Nothing to ease that cold edge of uncertainty that had shivered down her spine.

'Our arrangement is that you will do a job for me. As long as you carry out that job to my satisfaction then your mother and brother will be able to stay in the house without harassment or upset. I have sent them a letter informing them of that.'

'Thank you!'

After the fear and uncertainty of the moment she had left his office only the day before the rush of relief was so great that it pushed aside all sense of restraint, driving her into instinctive action without a thought of the consequences. With her phone still in her hand, she bent forward, lifting her face to press a swift, light-hearted kiss on Nikos's lean cheek.

'Thank you!' she said again. Then froze as reaction hit home.

It had been meant to be light-hearted. Rationally, that was what she had told herself. But what thumped straight into her heart was a response that was very far from rational.

Just the scent of his body in her nostrils, the taste of his skin on her lips, the faint rasp of stubble breaking through the olive-toned flesh, went straight to her head like the most potent alcohol. Her mind swam, her vision blurring so that every other sense came into sharper focus. She couldn't stop herself from letting her tongue slip out to experience, very softly, the faintly salt taste of his skin, knowing in that moment such a sudden rush of memories and sensations that she felt as if the plane they were in had hit sudden violent turbulence that swung them up and down and from side to side until she was dizzy with shock and sensation.

She wanted to press herself up against the hard strength of his body, wind her arms up and around his neck, fingers tangling in the jet silk of his hair. She wanted to turn her head just an inch or more, so that it met with the warm temptation of his lips. She longed to deepen the taste of him as their mouths joined, opened…

She knew her mistake even before the thoughts had fully formed in her mind. She felt his sudden tension, the stiffening of that long body, the way his jaw tightened until his whole face was just one rigid mask of rejection, so cold and unyielding that it was almost like kissing the carved, immobile face of some marble statue. She felt as if her mouth must be bruised by slamming up against it.

'No!'

Nikos's response was sharp and violent. The swift jerk of his head repulsed her foolish gesture, and he wrenched himself away from her with a force that had her almost losing her balance. Instinctively, her hand went out to grasp at Nikos's arm for support, then immediately released it again as she felt the even more powerful rejection that stiffened it against her.

'I'm sorry!'

Somehow she managed to stay upright. But the fight for equilibrium in her mind was harder won as she struggled with the terrible sense of loss that seared through her with the force of a lightning strike. She had forgotten that Nikos had told her he was marrying someone else, that he was committed to another woman. It was no wonder he had reacted so forcefully to her impulsive response.

'That wasn't any sort of come-on—truly it wasn't. It was only a thank-you!'

Could the look he turned on her be any colder, any more distant? Was it possible that she could endure the icy contempt that seemed to strike with the force of an arctic blast and not shrivel under the force of it, crumpling where she sat?

'It won't happen again.'

'You're damned right it won't happen again.' Nikos turned on her in dark fury. 'If you thought that you could win me round to giving you whatever you want by seducing me then you couldn't be more wrong. I may have been caught that way before, but never again.'

'You were caught?' Sadie scorned. 'In my opinion it was exactly the opposite way round! I was the one caught in your trap. The one you hunted down. You could never have been caught because I'm not sure you ever intended to marry me. You simply wanted to use me in your damned family feud with my father.'

'Oh, I would have married you, all right,' Nikos tossed back, the words hitting her like a slap in the face. 'By then I was so completely obsessed with you that I would have done anything—however stupid—to have you in my bed. One night with you was not enough. Could never be enough. I would have put my head right back in the noose if only to have another one.'

What else had she expected? Sadie asked herself, struggling with the bitter pain that had put a taste like acid in her mouth. Had she really believed that Nikos would deny the accusation she had thrown at him? That he would claim— pretend—he had actually felt something for her? That he would even declare that he had loved her?

She'd known the real truth all along. Ever since her father

had enlightened her. And yet it still hurt so terribly, ripping great raw and bleeding holes in her heart.

'But not now,' she managed.

'Not now,' Nikos confirmed darkly.

'Of course you have a new fiancée now. A new lo…'

But her voice failed her then. There was no way she could form the word *love*. It didn't belong on her tongue and it seemed to have formed a cruel knot in her throat, so that she could barely manage to breathe.

'I will do my very best to create a wonderful wedding for you both.'

It was the only way she could thank him for the reprieve he had offered her and her family. The chance to try and make sure that her mother survived the upheavals in their life and maybe found a future to look forward to. The thought of her mother twisted on nerves deep inside her. She had made the best provision she could for Sarah, and that text at least made it seem that she was coping for now. But Sadie had never been away from home for more than a day since the truth about George had burst on the family. She could only pray that her mother would cope.

'When will I meet your fiancée?'

Or even get to know her name? It was the first time she'd ever taken on a commission with so little information and no chance to meet the bride-to-be. She had never encountered a set-up like this.

'You'll have all the information you need when the time is right.'

At that moment a bell sounded and a light came on over the seats, an indication that they should fasten their seatbelts. Immediately Nikos held out his hand, palm upwards.

'Phone…' he snapped, with an impatient beckoning gesture of the hand that was between them.

Her mind still half on her mother and George, Sadie blindly

followed the command that was in his rough, irritated voice. She had dropped her mobile phone into his upturned palm before it occurred to her to question what he wanted with it.

'Hey—hang on…!'

But she had spoken too late. Even as she opened her mouth Nikos's long fingers had snapped shut over her phone, and without another word he dropped it swiftly into the pocket of his jacket, out of sight and out of reach.

'You can't do that!' she protested. 'That's my property!'

The look he turned on her said that he could do whatever he wanted and she couldn't stop him.

'I prefer to have your communication with the outside world under my control.'

'But how can I keep in touch with my mother—with home?'

A touch of panic made her voice raw. How would her mother cope if she wasn't at the end of a line to offer help if she was needed? The rough and ready support system she had been able to set in place might be enough, but only if Sarah could contact her daughter at any moment she felt she needed to.

'You will be able to phone Thorn Trees once a day to see how things are. But other than that—'

'It isn't enough!'

'It will have to be enough. Because that is how it is going to be.'

'But my mother—is unwell.'

She was severely tempted to move forward, try to snatch the phone from the pocket of his immaculately tailored jacket, but the urgent sense of need warred uncomfortably with a strong sense of self preservation. She was here, on her own, in his plane, thousands of feet up in the air. If she caused a scene, started a struggle, then she was at a disadvantage from the off. Nikos would only have to raise his voice and call his staff…

No, don't be ridiculous. He wouldn't even need to call

anyone, she acknowledged to herself. Nikos could see off her feeble attempt at resistance so easily that she would be a fool even to try it. But even so she still couldn't give in to such domineering behaviour.

'You have no right—!'

'I have every right. I am the one who makes the rules, not you. You are here because I allow you to be here—no other reason. And you are here to do a job.'

'A job I can't do without a phone…'

Her eyes went to the laptop case still in his possession, carefully tucked under his arm, and a shiver of cold panic ran along every nerve. Did he really mean to isolate her totally, have her under his complete control?

'Or my computer.'

'Any information or help you need will be provided once we are in my villa. All you have to do is ask.'

'I can't work that way.'

'You work any way that I ask of you.'

It was a deliberate verbal slap down, reminding her harshly just who was in charge here. And she would be every sort of a fool to forget that, Sadie reminded herself miserably. She had been in grave danger of forgetting just how important this job was to her.

She was grateful for the lifeline he had tossed her, the chance to let her mother stay in the only place where she felt safe. And now here she was, risking everything by setting herself against the only man who could ensure that would still happen. She should be thanking him, agreeing to go along with anything he suggested. But still—stealing her phone…!

'I do not want the paparazzi finding out anything about this,' Nikos went on, snatching the conversational rug from under her feet and stunning her into silence in the space of a single heartbeat.

That she understood. She had no argument against it, and she couldn't even try to find one. The paparazzi and the popular press had been the bane of their lives when she and Nikos had been together. They had plagued them incessantly, day in and day out. They had never had a moment's peace or time to themselves. She had hated it, been made miserable by the constant hounding, the pushing and shoving, the shouted demands and the incessant flashing of a hundred or more cameras.

And at the end… Sadie shivered at just the memory. At the end the relentless attentions of those snoopers had made everything a thousand times worse.

She understood why Nikos couldn't let his new fiancée go through that. But she wouldn't be human if she didn't feel a pang of jealousy at the protective way he was determined to shield her.

'You can trust me!'

The look he turned on her told her that he felt the opposite was true.

'Trust…' he said, drawing out the word until it was a sound of pure doubt, cynical and rough. 'Ah, yes, we had such a trusting relationship, didn't we?'

Sadie winced away from the contemptuous mockery of his tone. She had trusted him with her heart, her future, her life. And he had torn it all to pieces and tossed it back in her face.

'This isn't about you and me. And I wouldn't—'

'I trust no one.' It was a flat, cold statement. No room for negotiation. 'I find it's better that way. Now, if you will fasten your safety belt…'

'What a terribly sad way to live your life,' Sadie flung at him, but she knew that she had no option but to do as he said. The seat belt light was still flashing and the jet was already beginning to alter its path to turn in the circle needed for descent. Personal safety, if nothing else, demanded that she acted sensibly.

'That is my phone,' she managed, determined to keep the defiance up as she sank back into the soft leather of her seat and reached for the belt. 'And, paparazzi or not, you have no right…'

Except the right of possession, she acknowledged to herself as Nikos blatantly ignored her, strapping himself in. And in this case possession was all, because she had no hope that he would return the phone to her, no matter how she pleaded.

Miserably she yanked the seatbelt tight, tighter than it needed to be. And she forced herself to stare out of the window, blinking fiercely until the tears that burned at the back of her eyes ebbed away, leaving them dry and unfocussed. She wished she could do the same with her thoughts, driving away the bitter sting of the slap of reality right in her face.

Because nothing could bring home to her more definitely or more cruelly the way that, in Nikos's mind, she was now no longer part of his life than the nasty little exchange she had just endured. Nothing could make it plainer that she was firmly on the outside, kept from the centre of his world by high, strong fences, the 'Keep Out' signs clearly and forcefully displayed. He didn't even trust her, putting her so far outside any circle that could be termed his friends that she could only assume her place was amongst those he considered his enemies. And the thought of being considered an enemy by him made a sensation like the crawl of something cold and slimy slither down her spine.

Out beyond the window she could see the land below becoming clearer and clearer as the plane continued its descent. Down there was Greece, Venizelos Airport and the city of Athens itself. The last time she had been here it had been as the newly engaged fiancée of Nikos Konstantos. She had stared out of the window with keen interest, bubbling with excitement at the thought that she was going to set foot in the homeland of the man she loved for the very first time. How different was this arrival, with no sense of excitement or joy, only a terrible feeling of oppression and apprehension, uncertainty about what was to come.

Then she had felt as if she was coming home. As if she was launching a new beginning, one that would put the tensions and stresses that had ruined her family life behind her and put her on the path to a much happier future.

This time she had no idea what to expect. The prospect of what was ahead of her made her insides twist into tight knots of panic at the realisation that this time she was truly alone, without a single ally on her side. No one she could turn to for help or support.

She might understand, rationally at least, just why Nikos had felt that he needed to take her phone and her laptop. But that didn't stop the nasty, creeping sense of fear that there might be more to it than he was letting on.

Just what did he have planned for her? And why did she have the terrible feeling that in coming to Greece like this she had made the terrible mistake of jumping right out of the frying pan and into the fiercely blazing heart of a savagely burning fire?

CHAPTER SIX

MAY WAS SUPPOSED to be the best possible time to visit Greece. A time when the sun shone but the weather had yet to heat up to the baking temperatures of summer. Sadie had experienced some of that heat when she had visited Greece before and she had found it hard to cope. But then they had only stayed a couple of nights in the capital before flying to the tiny island of Icaros that had been owned by Nikos's family for generations going way, way back. Once there, she'd found the breezes from the sea had helped to ease the scorching temperatures and made life more enjoyable.

But Icaros was no longer owned by the Konstantos family. Sadie's father had seen to that. And the memory of just what Edwin had done was a troublesome worry, like the ache of a sore tooth, nagging at her mind all the time.

'How are you this morning?'

Nikos's voice startled her from her thoughts, making her jump nervously as he strolled out of the living room on to the wide main balcony where she had been trying to at least make a pretence of eating some of the breakfast that had been laid out on a table in the sunshine.

'I trust you spent a comfortable night?'

'That depends on what you mean by comfortable.'

Dressed more casually in the warmth of his native country, he was devastatingly dark and stunning in a soft white shirt and loose beige trousers. His feet were bare, lean and bronzed on the white stone of the balcony, so that he moved as silently and easily as some loose-limbed cat, every bit as lethally elegant and striking.

'The room was not to your satisfaction?'

Nikos strolled over to the table and picked up a bunch of grapes, plucking one from the stalk and tossing it into his mouth.

'My room was fine. As you know it had to be. This is a beautiful house.'

And if she needed anything to bring home to her just how far the Konstantos family had come since their lowest point five years before then this was it.

The villa had been a real surprise. The first of many. The first time Nikos had brought her to Athens they had stayed in his large apartment in the Kolonaki district, overlooking the Parthenon. That apartment had been impressive enough, but it was nothing when compared to the Villa Agnanti, where they had arrived late yesterday afternoon. Built into the side of a hill, the huge white house was on several levels, each one going lower down the cliff from the main road. From the lowest level you could walk out through the back gate, step out on to Schinias beach, where the crystal clear Aegean Sea lapped against the shore just metres away. Every single one of the bedrooms had a balcony that overlooked the ocean, but even the gentle sigh of the waves against the sand had not been soothing enough to ease Sadie into sleep last night. Instead she had lain awake and restless, wondering just what she had got herself into and how she was going to manage to handle things here.

'It has everything I need,' Nikos responded, but the flat, un-emotional level of his voice somehow communicated far more than what he actually said. It was what he had not said that seemed to reverberate underneath the words and gave them a very different emphasis from the one he had used.

'But you must know that I wouldn't be able to rest properly without knowing what was going on at home.'

Sadie adjusted her position against the balustrade, turning so that she was resting her back against the white stonework and looking straight into Nikos's dark, sculpted face, feeling the warmth of the morning sun beat down on the back of her head.

'You phoned Thorn Trees just before dinner. All was well then.'

'But I only had five minutes.'

Five minutes during which the door to the room she had been in was left open and she had been painfully aware of the way that Nikos was waiting for her beyond that door, no doubt listening to every word she said. She had felt like a prisoner under careful observation, unable to manage more than a few stilted sentences in response to her mother's unrestrained delight at knowing that she was safe in Thorn Trees for the time being at least.

Not that Sarah fully understood that their reprieve was only temporary. The joy that had rung in her mother's voice had been another twist of the knife in Sadie's already worried and aching heart. Her mother might think that Nikos had been wildly generous and unbelievably forgiving, she might believe that the stay of execution was permanent and for all time, but Sadie knew it was just that—a stay. And the way Nikos had behaved on the flight here, the fact that her phone and her laptop, her only means of communication with the outside world, were still firmly in his possession left her in no doubt that he wasn't planning on being forgiving or even kind, but on holding her ruthlessly to their bargain for as long as it took. And then…

And then?

The truth was that she had no idea at all what would happen next. When her time in Greece was up, when she had fulfilled her contract and Nikos and his fiancée were married, then what would happen?

Was the reprieve that he had granted them only for the length of time that she was working for him? And when that was done would he let them stay in Thorn Trees? She couldn't see it happening.

'Long enough to assure yourself that your mother is well. You are here to work.'

'Then let me get some work done! There's no way I can do anything without my laptop. And without meeting your bride.'

That came out more pointedly than she had planned. The truth was that just the thought of him marrying someone else twisted up her feelings so badly that she didn't know what to think or how to feel.

'My bride will not be here for some time. You will not be able to talk to her.'

'But that's ridiculous! How can I work on your—? We—'

To Sadie's horror her mixed up feelings seemed to have tangled on her tongue, making her stumble over the word.

'Your wedding—when I don't know who she is or what she likes? I need to talk to her.'

'You will talk to me.'

Nikos tossed another grape into his mouth and chewed on it before swallowing it down. Sadie found that the simple movement held her gaze transfixed on the lean line of his throat, the muscles moving under the smooth olive skin. She felt her own mouth dry in response, her own throat move as she swallowed too.

'I will tell you everything you need to know.'

'You will?'

Was that embarrassing croak really her voice? Sadie moved to the table set out on the balcony and reached for a glass of orange juice, gulping it down to ease the tight constriction of her throat.

'A wedding is a woman's most special day. She would want it to be absolutely perfect.'

'And it will be,' Nikos returned with smooth arrogance, clamping sharp white teeth down on another beautifully fresh grape. A tiny trickle of juice slid out on to his lips and he swept it away with a slick of his tongue.

Sadie forced her eyes down to study the surface of her drink as if it held the answer to some vitally important question. Anything to distract herself from the way that her thoughts were heading. Deep inside she was having to struggle with the wild, crazy impulse to move forward, press her mouth to that one small spot on his lips, to savour the sweetness of the grape combined with the intensely personal taste of Nikos's lips.

She was still fighting the sensual need, her fingers gripping her glass tightly, when Nikos spoke again.

'I will see to that.'

In the face of his cold confidence the rush of physical response faded as rapidly as it had come, leaving her feeling shivery and unsure, as if in the grip of a sudden fever. For a moment she had let herself forget how icily controlling and ruthless Nikos could be. And forgetting that was not a good idea.

'And you think that everything you do is so perfect? That you can never make a mistake?'

'Not perfect, no.'

Nikos pulled out one of the chairs and lowered himself into it, stretching out long legs in front of him, crossing them at the ankle. The change of position should have made him look more relaxed, at ease, but strangely it had exactly the opposite effect. He looked like nothing so much as a hunting tiger, lazily settling down to keep a watch on its prey before it decided whether it was worth the effort to pounce or not. The glass in her hand shook with the tremor of her grip and she hastily banged it down on the table, so as to avoid spilling some of the juice on to the stones of the balcony.

'And as to making mistakes, well, if I was immune to them then I would never have had anything to do with you.'

'But you can't take control of someone else's life like this. I would never let you get away with it… What?' she questioned in surprise as Nikos's low laughter broke into her outburst.

'I am only too well aware of that, *agapiti mou.*' The cynical emphasis on that *my dear* turned it into the exact opposite of any term of affection and the gleam in the golden eyes as he laughed up at her was totally lacking in any sort of warmth. 'Why do you think that I would prefer I kept you to myself while we work on plans for the wedding?'

'If you intend to go ahead and marry this girl this time.'

No sooner had the words escaped her than she wished them back. Too sharp, too bitter, they revealed far more of her personal thoughts than she had ever wanted. The last thing she wanted was for Nikos to feel there was any lingering bitterness about the fact that their marriage had never taken place. She was free of that—wasn't she?

'Do you doubt it?'

'What do you think? I have personal experience of just how much you mean your marriage proposals, remember?'

Nikos's mouth twisted slightly, his penetrating stare seeming to burn right into her soul.

'But I always intended to go ahead and marry you.'

'You did?'

Nikos swallowed some of his coffee, then grimaced in distaste.

'This stuff is cold. But no matter.' Pushing back his chair, he got to his feet again. 'We should be heading out anyway.'

'Heading out? Why? Where are we going?'

'You said that you wanted to know more about the wedding. What better way to start than with the place I have in mind for the ceremony? Go and collect whatever you will need. We leave in ten minutes.'

It was going to be a long day, Nikos reflected as he watched Sadie's retreating back, the sensual sway of her hips, as she made her way into the house. The morning sun beat down on his head and down below, at the bottom of the cliffs, the roar of the surf pounding against the shore was a constant background sound to everything.

A sound that fitted the restless hammering of his thoughts as he fought a constant battle to keep his more primitive male impulses under control. He was beginning to wonder just how long he could keep up this pretence of wanting to work with her on the wedding. The truth was that work had nothing at all to do with what he wanted to do with Sadie Carteret.

When he had walked out on to the balcony and seen her standing there, it had been all that he could do not to march across and grab her, pulling her hard against him and bringing his mouth down roughly on top of hers, kissing her until they were both reeling with hunger, their thoughts obliterated in the need that he knew would flare between them.

The sun had gleamed on the dark gloss of her hair, gilding the pale shoulders in the sleeveless red sundress. A red sundress that had big black buttons all the way from the dipping neckline right to where the hem swirled around her slender shapely calves. Those buttons had put the devil's torment into his mind, tempting him almost beyond endurance with images of closing his fingers over each one, sliding it carefully, slowly from its fastening, and then moving down. Exposing first the soft creamy curves of her breasts, the shadowed valley between them. A valley that he knew from experience—all too short an experience—would be warm and slightly moist, the intimate scent of her skin heightened by the heat of her body, reaching out to him and then falling away with each hasty, unevenly snatched breath she took.

And then moving lower, down to her waist, letting the folds of the soft material part over her hips, where the shadow of her sex showed beneath the delicate covering of her underwear. Lower still, until it fell away from her body, leaving her exposed and revealed to the hunger of his eyes, the touch of his hands.

No! With a rough jerk of his head, he pulled his mind away from the sensual thoughts that plagued him and forced them back on to the here and now.

Because here and now he had to concentrate on other things. But it was damn near impossible to concentrate on anything when all he wanted to do was to take Sadie to bed and spend the rest of the day sating himself in the soft warmth of her body.

She would let him too. Or at least she wouldn't put up much of a fight. He had seen it in her eyes when they had been on the balcony. The sensual awareness that she hadn't been able to hide. The way her head had gone back, her lips parting slightly, softly. The way that the dark pupils of her eyes had enlarged until her eyes were almost all black, only the faintest trace of mossy green at their edges.

If he had walked across to her then, taken the glass from her hand and replaced it against her lips with his own mouth, then she would not have protested. Or not much.

It would be that moment in his office all over again. The response that neither of them could hide. That he was damn sure he didn't want to hide. And that he knew Sadie was fighting to conceal from him now because she believed he was going to marry someone else.

A faint smile crossed his mouth as he followed Sadie inside. He was enjoying watching her struggle with the flames that flared between them and the feeling that she could not, must not act on them. He would keep her on that particular rack for a while longer. The end result, when he finally let her off, would be well worth waiting for.

'We're here.'

Sadie had to struggle to bite back the exclamation of relief when Nikos made his announcement perhaps fifty minutes later. Helicopter flights were not her favourite form of travel, and from the moment Nikos had led her from the house to his private helipad, where a gleaming machine that looked like nothing so much as a giant black dragonfly had waited for them, her stomach had been twisting tight with tension. And that sensation had been made all the worse by the way the limited space inside had forced her into close confinement with Nikos for the length of the flight.

He'd piloted the helicopter himself, and every movement of his tanned, muscular arms, the strength of his long fingers on the controls, had her mouth drying in sensual response, her own hands tightening on each other where they lay in her lap. So it was with a sense of escape that she watched the land, the first they had seen for the last twenty minutes of a journey which had been mostly over sparkling blue sea, come closer and closer as the helicopter descended.

'Where are we?' she asked when at last they were on the ground, with the engine turned off, and she was able to look around.

But Nikos was already out of the craft and, ducking to avoid the slowing blades, coming round to open the door on her side. It was as she set foot on the ground, the blast of heat hitting her after the controlled temperature inside the plane, that recognition hit, and with it a cruel wave of desperate memory. She knew this rugged shoreline, the steep cliffs that rose above the sea. And there in the distance was the low, white-painted, unexpectedly simple house where she had once spent a magical couple of days when Nikos had first brought her to Greece and to his family home.

'This is Icaros!'

She knew she looked as startled as she sounded, her head coming up sharply in surprise, green eyes locking with cool gold. And it was then that she realised he had been aiming for just this response.

'You got the island back?'

Nikos's response was a curt nod.

'I got the island back,' he confirmed.

'Oh, I'm so glad about that.'

That made his eyes narrow in frank disbelief.

'You are?'

'Of course! I know how much this island means to your family.'

It was in the tiny chapel here that his father and mother, his grandparents and every great-grandparent they could remember had been married. A tradition that was vital to the man Nikos was. And his sister, who had died as a baby, was buried in the chapel grounds.

'So did your father.'

Nikos's tone was so savage that Sadie actually flinched away from it, recoiling in her chair as if from a blow to her face.

'That was why he sold it to someone else instead of keeping it for himself. An extra fortune for him, and more of a problem for me to get it back if I ever tried it. I would have to negotiate with someone else and he thought he would be able to watch.'

Sadie shivered both at that icy tone and at the thought of

how her father had behaved. The island had been one of the weapons Edwin had used against her when she had refused to believe that Nikos didn't really love her. If it was a love-match, her father had said, wouldn't she be marrying in the little island chapel, like every other Konstantos bride before her? And faced with that and so much other evidence, she had had no choice but to believe him.

She hadn't wanted to think that her father was right. Hadn't wanted to accept his bitter, cynical way of thinking about everything. He had been so totally obsessed with getting revenge on the Konstantos family that it had taken over his life. But she had no idea why.

'Do you know what started this crazy feud in the first place?' she asked impulsively, not caring if the question was wise or if it would push her even further into trouble with Nikos, raking up old bitter memories that were far better left buried.

'There was always rivalry between the families—in business dealings. But then it became personal, when the woman my grandfather was supposed to marry ran off with your grandfather instead. *Pappous* never forgot—or forgave. And he made sure that the Carterets paid for it financially. After that, if one family could attack the other in any way, they did.'

Nikos moved away from the helicopter and paced over to the edge of the cliff to stand staring out at the sea. His long body was silhouetted dark against the sunlight, the width of his shoulders seeming even more impressive than ever.

Suddenly, painfully, Sadie was reminded of the days when they had been together. When, if she had seen him like this, she would have been able to go up to him, slide her arms around that narrow waist until they met over the flat stomach. She could have rested her head against the powerful back, felt the heat of his skin through his shirt and inhaled the rich, intimate scent of his body.

That was how she had always dealt with difficult times in the past. Whatever mood he had been in, she had always been able to bring him round that way, to make him relax and smile again. More often than not he would turn in her arms, gathering her close to kiss her fiercely, until her head was spinning with happiness and desire.

That was how they had ended up in bed together the first time on that weekend before her wedding…

No, no, no!

Desperately she dragged her thoughts back from the painful path they were following. She must not let herself remember how it had once been. It was too cruel, too distressing. And all those 'once had beens' had never really existed. She had been living in a dream world, swallowing every deliberate lie that Nikos tossed her way and believing she had found the love of her life. The risks of even allowing such memories back into her life was too great to contemplate with any degree of safety. If she let them back into her mind, into her heart, then she would never be able to cope.

'There was more to it than that.' She tried to continue the conversation in order to distract herself from the torment of her memories. 'Something more recent that had made things even worse. My father was…*obsessed* is the only word. He'd always perpetuated the feud in a business sense, but something new happened to drive him even further into the depths of hatred for the Konstantos family. Into a determination to ruin them once and for all.'

'And you didn't know what that was?'

'No,' Sadie managed, her eyes now fixed on the horizon. Her heart was thudding erratically, making it difficult to breathe. She was too much on edge, too aware of the difference between being here now like this and the way things had been that first time to manage to control her voice.

'But I do know, in the end, it never truly brought him any real satisfaction. He drove his family and friends away because nothing else mattered to him. And he broke my mother's heart. I found out later that my mother had had an affair. It destroyed their marriage, but I'm sure it was because she felt neglected, abandoned because he was so obsessed.'

It was so much easier to talk like this when Nikos had his back to her. When she couldn't see his dark, stunning face and the cold contempt that burned in his eyes, thinned his beautiful, sensual mouth. Like this she could still pretend that they had some sort of a civilised relationship.

'We could—we could end it,' she suggested, buoyed up on a sudden rush of hope. 'We could say it stops right here and now and—'

'And what?' Nikos enquired, turning suddenly to face her again. 'And what, Sadie, *agapiti mou?* Hmm? We end it now and—what? Become close friends?'

He didn't have to explain how he felt about that. It was there in the disgust stamped clearly onto the beautifully carved features, in the twist to his lips, the bite of the words he flung into her face.

'No—not friends. We could never be that…'

'Not friends,' Nikos repeated with a brutal emphasis, his tongue curling in distaste on the word. 'Because friends would never turn friends out of their home. Because friends would waive the cost of the rent—or even the purchase price of a very expensive house.'

'No!' Sadie shook her head violently so that her dark hair spun out wildly in the sunshine. 'No—nothing like that!'

Did he really think that that was why she had proposed ending the feud? So that as her 'friend' he would feel obliged to let her off her debts and hand Thorn Trees over to her at a peppercorn rent? In the back of her mind she could hear once more that mocking 'mate's rates' that he had tossed at her in his office a couple of days before.

'You're right! We could never be friends. And I wouldn't want to be. All I meant was that we could call a halt to these stupid hostilities and—and live totally separate lives. There's no way we ever have to even see each other again.'

The thought seemed to stop her breath in her throat. She'd managed to get on with her life these past years by refusing to let herself even think about Nikos and pushing away every memory when it tried to surface. It had nearly broken her but she had managed it. Now it would all be to do again. And, knowing how hard it had been the first time, she flinched away from the prospect of going through it once more.

'And the sooner that happens, the better as far as I'm concerned.'

He was supposed to respond to that. She even paused, waiting for him to say something but Nikos remained strangely silent. Silent and still. Only the burn of his eyes, fixed on her, unblinking, seemed alive in his set and rigid face.

She should take that as a yes, Sadie decided. It certainly wasn't any sort of a no. Nothing like a rush to say that, no, they must not separate, must not be apart again. Of course not. But she wished he would say something. Anything.

And suddenly she had to speak again, if only to break the disturbing, nerve-stretching silence that had been going on for far too long.

'We'd better get this job done so that I can get out of here and be on my way.'

She would be professional if it killed her, she told herself. It was the only way she was going to get through this. She would do the best damn job she could, never put a foot wrong, and then Nikos would have no reason at all to find fault. No reason to go back on his word to let her mother stay in Thorn Trees.

But it was one thing to make that sort of a resolve, quite another to stick to it when every place they walked held a memory of the time when they had been together. Every path, every cove, even every rock, spoke of a happier time, a time when she had known the joy of love, even though it had all been a bitter deception and not the delight she had thought it to be.

It was almost as if Nikos knew what was in her thoughts, what had been in her heart when she had visited Icaros with him all those years before, and was now using it to torment her with the fact that this was where he would be marrying his new fiancée, the woman he loved. And it was when they crossed the little wooden bridge that led from the main island to the high headland, where the tiny chapel stood, that she knew she couldn't hold back any more. Coming to an abrupt halt, she turned to Nikos, brushing back the dark silk of the her hair that the winds had whipped into wild disorder around her face.

'Just why am I here?' she demanded, not caring if the words were wise.

Had she gone completely mad? the look he turned on her said. Did he have to explain everything to her? In words of one syllable?

'You are a wedding planner. I need to plan a wedding.'

The exaggerated clarity with which he spoke, a deliberate slowing down of his words, grated on her already over-wrought nerves. He sounded as if he was having to explain to someone simple. Someone who would have difficulty in understanding what he said.

'But you could have anyone you wanted. There must be much more established—more successful—fashionable—wedding planners you could hire.'

'But I want you.'

What was it in his voice that made a shiver run over her skin, lifting the tiny hairs in a rush of apprehension? Sadie

couldn't define it, and she wasn't sure that she really wanted
to dig too deep and find out more than she wanted to know.

'Why me? Why none of the others?'

Nikos pushed open the door of the little chapel, the wood
making a harsh scraping sound over the stone-flagged floor.

'You owe me,' he declared harshly. 'They don't.' And then,
with an abrupt turn onto another conversational path that
threw her completely off balance, he continued, 'Now, come
inside and see the chapel.'

She didn't want to see the chapel, felt that it would destroy
her totally to do so. It would take what was left of her shattered heart and grind it in the dust beneath Nikos's soft
handmade boots. If the rest of the island had bitter memories
for her, then the inside of the chapel belonged purely to Nikos
and the woman he now planned to marry. He had never
brought her in here when they had visited Icaros in the past.
In fact, the tiny building had stayed securely locked and shuttered, and she had never even set foot on the worn wooden
bridge that led to it. Further evidence, her father had said, of
the way Nikos had never planned to make her his wife.

But when it came down to it, what choice did she have?
She was here to do a job, as Nikos had just reminded her so
brutally. And on that job depended her mother's peace of
mind—possibly even her sanity, with the resulting repercussions for her small brother's happiness. She couldn't let them
down. And so she drew in a deep, hopefully strengthening
breath, squared her shoulders and made herself step over the
threshold into the cool, shadowed interior of the little church.

After the brightness of the sunlight outside, it was all so
dark and dim that she was almost blinded, barely able to see
a metre or two ahead of her down the single narrow aisle
between the rows of rough wooden pews. Nikos himself,
standing before the simple altar, was once more just a sil-

houette, a solid more substantial shape in the hazy light that came through the narrow windows.

Perhaps it was because of the blackness, because she couldn't see his face or read his expression clearly. Perhaps it was that she had no choice but to accept that in planning to marry someone else Nikos had demonstrated so clearly that he had moved on from the bitter past they had once shared. But suddenly Sadie was hearing again her own voice inside her head.

We could end it, she had said, referring to the terrible feud between their families. The feud that had taken away too much and given nothing. *We could say it stops right here and now…*

If only they could. If only she and Nikos could find a way to start again, so that each of them could go on and live their lives without the terrible black shadow hanging over them. But how could she begin? If she could just get Nikos to trust her, even in the tiniest degree, then that would be a start.

A sudden rush of new-found determination pushed her up the aisle towards the still, silent figure standing by the altar steps. Face unreadable, arms folded across the width of his chest, Nikos watched her come.

'If you really want to employ me as your wedding planner then you have to let me do my job properly,' Sadie managed once she had drawn level with him, the words spluttering from her in a rush to get them out. 'You really don't need to keep my phone and my laptop under lock and key—I'm not going to sell your story.'

The cold-eyed look he turned on her told her that there was no way he believed her declaration.

'You did damn nearly everything else in the past,' Nikos flung at her. 'So you'll have to forgive me if I'm in no rush to believe you can be trusted now. We do this my way or not at all. And if you can't agree then you'll be on the first plane out of here….'

And if she was on the first plane out of Athens, then what would happen to her mother and George? Nikos had said that he would not take revenge on a child, but if she did not fulfil her part of the contract then what was to stop him going back on the deal and throwing her mother and brother out of the only home where they felt safe? Her insides knotted in raw panic at the thought.

She had promised her mother that she would keep her safe in her home for as long as she possibly could, and she would keep that promise if it killed her, she told herself. The one thing she had going for her in this situation was the fact that Nikos was getting married and, for reasons known best to himself, he wanted her to plan the event for him.

She was just going to have to ignore the fact that even thinking about it brought with it a sensation like a cruel knife being scraped over raw, sensitive skin. That the concern that Nikos showed for preserving his fiancée's anonymity, his involvement in this early stage of things, rubbed her face right in the difference between this wedding and the one he had been planning with her.

Had *appeared* to be planning with her, she corrected painfully.

She needed to put all those difficult feelings out of her mind. She had to refuse to let herself remember that she was trapped here, isolated with the man who had ruined her life and her family's. A man who now seemed hell-bent on using the hold he had over her to his own advantage, and taking a cruel and sadistic pleasure in doing just that.

Somehow she was going to have to pretend to herself that Nikos was just a client. Sighing inwardly, Sadie faced the impossibility of that task. Nikos could never be 'just' anything. But that was her only way through this situation. The only way she could handle this. Because she did have to handle this.

The truth was that Nikos held all the cards and he could

play them as he chose. The only single option left to her was to do the best job she could—and hope that Nikos had some sort of kind cell in his body that would push him to help her when she was done.

Otherwise she would be right back where she had started—or worse. And all of this would have been for nothing.

CHAPTER SEVEN

'YOU WILL WANT to phone your mother.'

After a journey back to the villa that had been completed in almost total silence, Nikos's first words on their arrival caught Sadie distinctly off balance, so that for a moment or two she could only stare at him in confusion, not quite sure she had heard him right.

'Did you not tell me that you needed to check on your mother and brother?'

'Oh, yes—but…' But she hadn't expected him to remember or, if he did, that he would be the one to prompt her into action rather than the other way about. After everything he'd said, she had never thought that he would be so generous— or so trusting.

'You can use the phone in my office—it's just through here.'

He led the way into a room at the back of the villa. One that had disturbing echoes of the office at the Konstantos building in which she had faced him—was it really only a couple of days before? Memories of that encounter threatened to drain the strength from her legs as she followed him, putting a fine tremor into the hand she held out for the phone he snatched up and passed to her.

'If you need the code for England then this is it…'

Nikos scrawled a number on a piece of paper and pushed it towards her. Then he pulled out a chair at the head of the desk and dropped down into it, switching on the computer before him as he did so.

Not quite so generous or so trusting after all, Sadie acknowledged privately to herself. He might have handed her the phone, but he was still staying around in the office to make sure that she didn't say anything he objected to. She was not to have any privacy with her phone call.

But she wasn't going to look any gift horses in the mouth. Her mother's mental balance and her own peace of mind were too important for that. So she pulled the sheet of paper towards her, punched in the numbers and pressed 'Dial'. Perching on the edge of the desk, with her back to Nikos, she waited anxiously for her mother to answer. She would know how things were from the moment that happened.

'H-Hello?'

Oh, no! Sadie closed her eyes briefly in distress, her shoulders tightening as tension held them taut. She knew that tone of voice and it meant there was a problem. Her mother was clearly in a very different frame of mind from the previous night.

'Mum, it's me—Sadie. How's things?'

'Sadie—where have you been all day. I've been expecting you to call…'

'I had things I had to do, Mum.'

Sadie kept her voice low, hunched herself over the phone, as if by doing so she could cut herself off from the man at the other side of the desk, where she hoped that the click of keyboard keys meant Nikos was concentrating on what he was doing and so wouldn't catch anything of her mother's words.

'I'm here to do a job, remember?'

'I know you said that—but do you have to be away so long?'

Sadie's heart sank at the querulous note in her mother's

voice, the way it rose so sharply on the final words. She was very much afraid that, without her there to supervise, Sarah hadn't taken her medication and so was worryingly off balance.

'It's only a couple of days.'

But that was longer than her mother had been left alone at any time since George's birth, she acknowledged. And clearly the older woman was finding it hard to cope.

'What is it, Mum? What's wrong?'

And suddenly it was as if her question had pressed a switch, making the words flow. Sadie could almost see her mother perched on the edge of her chair, her fine-boned face drawn taut with nervous tension as she gave voice to her fears. She couldn't believe that the letter Nikos had sent yesterday was real. It seemed impossible that it was true. Impossible that they wouldn't be forced out of their home after all.

'It will be fine, Mum.' She could only pray that she sounded convincing. That there was enough conviction in her words to get through the panicked haze inside her mother's head and reassure her. 'I promise you that everything's going to be fine.'

If she could believe that herself then everything would be so much easier.

'But how do you know that, Sadie? How can you be sure? How do you know that Nikos Konstantos will keep his word? What if he changes his mind?'

'That isn't going to happen. I won't let it happen, Mum. I've made sure of that.'

What else could she say? she asked herself. When she was so far away from home, how else could she persuade Sarah to calm down? And it seemed to have worked. The nervous questions eased, and she could hear her mother's breathing settle from the frantic, uneven gasps that had so worried her.

'I've got everything in hand,' she said again. 'You know you can rely on me.'

'You're sure? We can stay?'

'Mmm…'

The non-committal sound was all Sadie could manage. Painfully aware of Nikos's dark, silent presence behind her, she didn't dare to try for more. And even more than before she prayed that nothing her mother had said could reach him.

When she had explained the situation to Sarah on that first evening after her meeting with Nikos at Cambrelli's, she had deliberately aimed to emphasise the positive. Nikos was letting them stay in the house for now. And at least as long as Sadie was working for him they were safe. That was what she had to hold on to until she had any sort of a chance to think of any other way out of their situation. But she knew that by highlighting the good things she was risking letting her mother think that all was completely well and their future in Thorn Trees was assured.

But she hadn't dared risk anything else.

If Nikos had caught her mother's words then what was he going to think? Would he believe that she had taken too much for granted? That she had assumed he would hand over a house worth millions simply because she was doing a job for him, planning his wedding? A sneaking cold shiver ran down her spine at the thought of his possible reaction.

'Promise me.'

'I promise, Mum.'

And now at last it seemed that Sarah was convinced enough to let her go. Reluctantly, Sadie managed to say goodbye, switching off the phone as she fought to get her own disturbed and shaken mood back under control.

'Is something wrong?'

Nikos had caught her sigh, and it made her stomach lurch in apprehension at the thought that he might also have heard her mother's unwary comments after all.

'No—nothing. Everything's—fine.'

Her voice caught on that word, but she pulled herself together and returned the phone to its stand on the desk. The movement brought her close to an array of family photographs nearby. Some of them looked familiar, but she couldn't quite place why.

'Who's that?' She waved her hand in the direction of one particular frame.

It was a question she was obviously not supposed to ask, judging by the dark frown that Nikos turned in her direction.

'My father.'

'Really?'

Sadie's eyes went back to the man in the picture. A man who looked so very different from the one time she had met Nikos's father—thinner and older, and with his black hair almost totally grey—that she shook her head in confusion.

'He's changed a lot.'

'He's been ill.'

Nikos clearly had no intention of explaining further, and Sadie was about to give up on the photos when something about another picture tugged on her attention again.

'And the one behind it…?'

'My uncle Georgiou. He died five years ago.'

And that was all he was going to tell her.

'So—do you have any questions about the wedding—other than who exactly the members of my family are?' he prompted harshly, cutting across her hasty, uncomfortable apology in a way that made it plain that she had been slapped down, verbally at least.

She was to keep her mind on her job and nothing else. Besides, if Nikos's uncle had died so long ago then she had obviously never met him.

'Well, yes, lots—starting with the obvious. You know it's

ridiculous to expect me to work on this without any idea about your—your bride. I understand your need for privacy—but surely just a few basic facts…?'

She pulled a notepad towards her, picked up a pen.

'Like her age, colouring, name.'

'Why the hell do you do this?' Nikos said, so suddenly and unexpectedly that the pen that was resting on the notepad jerked sharply in her hand, shooting up across the page and etching a wild straight line into the paper.

Hastily she recovered herself.

'What?'

Did she know what it did to him, Nikos wondered, when she looked at him like that, with her eyes wide and shocked, blinking in confusion? Very possibly she did, and that was exactly why she reacted in that way—wide-eyed and inno-cent, like a startled deer.

'Why do I do what?'

'Why does a woman who walked out on her own wedding spend her time planning other people's big days?'

'Because I believe in marriage.'

She was definitely on edge as a result of his question, ten-sion showing in her shoulders and the elegant line of her beautiful neck. It was just a damn torment that the way she held her head, the rapid rise and fall of her breathing, brought those creamy breasts into his line of vision, creating a devas-tating temptation with every breath she took.

'Marriage?' he scorned. 'Do you really? Why would you of all people think that marriage is important? Ah—but of course…'

He snapped his fingers, as if he had really just come to the realisation but the way that Sadie's eyes flared in response made it clear that she knew only too well the way his thoughts were heading.

'Marriage as a dynastic arrangement. Preferably with plenty of money as a sweetener and perhaps a lot of hot sex in order to avoid any boredom.'

'It's nothing of the sort!'

She was getting to her feet again, her eyes flashing fury, cheeks pink with indignation. The way her breathing had accelerated meant that her chest rose and fell rapidly and unevenly, pushing her breasts against the v-neck of her red dress with every movement. The heated clutch of lust low down in his body in response was hard and immediate, making him draw in his breath in a sharp, uncontrollable response.

'I also happen to believe in love—I do!' Sadie flung at him, when the effort to drag his gaze away from the creamy swell that rose and fell so distractingly made him glance at her with what she obviously saw as disbelief in his eyes.

And he didn't believe her. Why should he believe her? How could he believe someone who had manipulated and schemed so that her own wedding was just a distraction of his own attention that her father needed to complete his plan for the destruction of the Konstantos family? A plan that had very nearly achieved more destruction than it had ever aimed for when his father had tried to take his own life.

And Sadie had played her part in that too.

'Love!' Nikos scorned. 'What do you know about love? Have you ever felt real love for anyone—anyone but yourself?'

'Of course I have! You know I have! I—'

'Oh, don't try to tell me that I know you've loved because of the way you were with me!'

Unable to believe how outrageously she was still prepared to lie, Nikos flung the words at her in a black fury.

'*Thee mou,* don't you dare claim that you loved—even still love—me!'

Sadie's head snapped back, eyes closing briefly as if he had actually slapped her in the face. But she recovered quickly enough and turned on him instead.

'No, I'm not claiming that! I don't love you. If you want the truth…'

'Oh, by all means, let us have the truth,' Nikos drawled, when an unexpected catch in her breath had her stumbling over her next words. 'It is time there was a little honesty in this relationship.'

'Honesty?' Sadie echoed, injecting the word with so much cynicism that she almost felt it sharp as a razor on her tongue, ready to cut her to ribbons. 'If you want honesty, then I'll give you *honesty*.'

Once more she had to pause, to draw in a needed calming breath, and Nikos watched her with burning eyes, no trace of emotion on the stone wall of his face. And the need to drive something past that armoured wall drove her to lose control completely.

'The honest truth is that I don't love you. Of course I don't. The only feeling I have for you is loathing. I *hate* you. I would never have come to you, never have sought you out unless you were my very last chance. The only hope I had.'

The way his eyes narrowed, black brows snapping together in a dark frown made Sadie's stomach clench in sharp unease. Had she taken several steps too far, saying that? Given him too much ammunition to use against her if he wanted to? But then there was no way he couldn't know that she'd had to be desperate, on her very last chance, to be prepared to come to him, practically begging for a way to stay in Thorn Trees. He could never have doubted how worried she had to have been to turn to him. Nikos, of all people, would know that if she had had any other possible alternative then she would have used it if she could.

And it had felt so good to actually spit the words out and toss them in his face. To say the things that she had wanted to say five years before and never had the chance. When Nikos had come to the house that one last time, and her father had opened the door to him, she had been upstairs with her mother. Sarah had been pregnant with George and had been in such a state that there'd been no way Sadie could have left her, not even to face the man who had broken her heart and destroyed her life. So she had tossed down the stairs the lines that her father had given her to use and at the time had been thankful that that was all she'd had to do. That she hadn't had to actually confront Nikos about the things he had done. Because that would have been more than she could bear.

But this time it felt good to actually have the words on her tongue and to give them free range. So good that for a crazy, wild moment she didn't stop to think of what she was doing or of how dangerous it might be to let rip.

'And the only reason I'm here is because you asked me to do a job—to plan and organise your damn wedding! We had an agreement on that.'

'We did.'

Nikos's tone was surprisingly mild, but the burn of his eyes seemed to flay away a couple of precious layers of her skin, leaving her raw and hurting without even trying.

'And I will stick to that agreement, no matter how I feel about you personally. I'll give you every last bit of my expertise. I'll do the best job I can. Because that's what I promised.'

She had no other choice. If she didn't fulfil her side of the bargain, then what was to stop Nikos from reverting to the 'no way, no chance…go home and pack' stance that he had taken with her at first. Before his unexpected and almost unbelievable change of heart.

'But I'll not do it for you. I'm doing it for your bride, so that she can have a wonderful day even if—even if she is marrying you. And in order to do that…'

What had changed in his face, altered his expression? Some shift in his muscles or a different light in those searing eyes. Something very subtle but definitely there. And it changed everything in the space of a single heartbeat, disturbing the atmosphere so that she felt herself floundering, suddenly gasping for air as if she had gone down under water and her lungs were filling up with liquid.

'In order to do that?' he prompted smoothly as she fought to find her voice again.

'In order to do that I will need to meet her—talk with her.'

'No way.'

Leaning back in his chair, Nikos laced his hands behind his head, lifting his legs so that they rested on the polished wood surface, feet crossed at the ankles.

'But that's ridiculous. Impossible!'

His one-sided shrug dismissed her protest as totally irrelevant.

'That's how it's going to be.'

'But there's no way I can do my job if you won't tell me anything, not even her name.'

But once again they had reached a sticking point. She could see it in his eyes, in the set of his stubborn jaw. She had had all the factual information he was going to allow her.

But there was one more thing he wanted to tell her.

'All you need to know is that she is the only woman I have ever wanted to marry.'

Nikos was still lounging back in his chair, feet still on the desk. He looked supremely at ease, totally relaxed. But there was nothing comfortable or casual about the way that he added that final comment. Instead, he slipped it into her hard-won composure like the sharpest stiletto blade, sliding in between two of her ribs, aiming straight for her heart.

And it hurt so much that it destroyed every last trace of the already precarious self-control that she had been fighting to maintain ever since this conversation had started.

'I can't do this!' she declared, shaking her head in despair at the situation in which she found herself. 'I really can't! You have to see that. Here I am, trying to arrange a wedding for a bride who to all intents and purposes doesn't seem to exist.'

A stunning thought hit her, and she turned to glare into Nikos's watchful face, green eyes clashing with gold in deliberate challenge.

'She does exist, doesn't she?' He couldn't have brought her here on some sort of wild goose chase, could he? And if he had, then why?

Nikos adjusted his position, taking his hands from behind his head and raking both of them through his hair, ruffling its sleek darkness in a way that was dangerously appealing. Sadie's hands itched with the recollection of how it had felt to have the freedom to smooth through the black silky strands, curling them round her fingers.

'Oh, she exists,' he assured her. 'She's very definitely real.'

'Then I want you to get in touch with her.'

Reaching for the phone, she snatched it up and held it out to him.

'Get her on the phone—talk to her. You don't even have to let me speak to her. I'll just ask you the questions I need and you can get me her answers. At least that way I'll know she's been consulted—go on!' she insisted, when Nikos simply stayed where he was, watching her without moving.

But now the relaxed sprawl of his long body had changed, much as his expression had changed only moments before. There was a new tension in the muscular limbs, a tautness like that of a wary hunting animal, waiting and watching before it pounced upon its prey.

Furiously, she waved the telephone receiver in his face, not caring that the wildness of the gesture gave away far too much of the turmoil raging inside her.

'Talk to her!'

Another of those long silences, then at last Nikos shook his head, slowly and adamantly.

'No,' was all he said, making her stare at him in stupefied bewilderment.

'What do you mean, no?'

'I mean, I cannot call my prospective bride on the phone.'

'Why not? Where is she?'

'Right here.'

'What?'

The answer was so totally unexpected that Sadie actually jumped, looking round in shock. She almost expected to see Nikos's fiancée standing right behind her.

'There's no one—just me.'

A terrible, unbelievable thought dawned on her as she spoke, and slowly she turned back to face Nikos again.

'There's no one else here,' she said again, but this time it was a challenge.

'Exactly.'

Nikos removed his feet from the desk, stretched lazily and stood up, every moment slow and leisurely.

'The woman I want is right here.'

'But your fiancée…'

'There is no fiancée.'

He couldn't have said… Sadie found it impossible to believe that she had heard right. Desperately she shook her head, trying to clear her muddled thoughts.

'You brought me here to plan your wedding,' she protested,

knowing she was grasping at straws. Nikos's blank, emotionless face told her that he was not going to help her out in any way. 'You told me you had a fiancée…'

'If you remember rightly, I never said anything of the sort,' Nikos put in, with the sort of cold reasonableness that made her head spin in disbelief. 'I said that I wanted you to come here to arrange a wedding. But I never said who I planned to marry. And I never said that there was any other woman involved.'

The room seemed to be swirling round Sadie, blurring dangerously, setting off a terrible nausea in her stomach that she could barely control. Fearfully, she pressed her hands to her head, fingers tight against her temples, feeling worryingly as if her head might actually explode.

'You can't mean— You don't…'

'I can and I do.'

Nikos prowled closer, silent, deadly… And Sadie could only watch transfixed as his hand came out and touched her cheek, cupping her jaw softly as he lifted her face so that their gazes locked and held.

'What you are saying,' he said quietly, even gently, 'or trying to say, is that you are here because the one woman I have ever planned on marrying is you.'

CHAPTER EIGHT

THE ONE WOMAN I have ever planned on marrying is you.

The words pounded against Sadie's skull, making sense in a literal way, and yet stopping short of any possible sort of reality.

The one woman I have ever planned on marrying is you.

How could Nikos say that when it was so blatantly obviously not true? He had never really meant to marry her in the past, so why should anything be different now?

'No.'

She shook her head violently, but that only seemed to make the spinning sensation so much worse. It didn't even free her head from Nikos's grasp. Instead it seemed to bring her into closer contact with the warmth and strength of that hand, those long, powerful fingers closing over her jaw, firmer but not harder, warm and strong and shocking sensual. Shockingly welcome.

In the middle of all the chaos of her thoughts, the only thing that she could grab hold of was the way she wanted that hand to be there. She wanted to turn her head, her cheek, into the warmth of his palm, and feel the heat of his skin, taste it against her mouth.

And that was the exact opposite of how she thought she should be feeling. The way that she wanted to be feeling. The way that, rationally, she felt it was safe to be feeling.

It wasn't safe, it wasn't wise, it wasn't even damn well rational. But rational was so far from the way she was feeling that she frankly didn't care.

She only knew that all the time they had been in this room, when he had been standing or sitting so far way from her, she had wanted, needed to bridge the gap between them. Had longed to come close and feel the heat of skin against skin, the pressure of hard bone under cushioning flesh. But it was only now, when he had made the move, that she actually realised that was what she had been feeling.

'No…' she tried again, but her voice had no more strength than the first time she had tried the word, less if anything, so that it croaked and broke in the middle as she spoke. 'You can't mean that.'

'Can't mean what, *glikia mou?*' Nikos questioned softly, the words seeming to shiver over her skin.

You can't have brought me here to—to…'

That word wouldn't form, and she didn't know whether it was because she didn't dare to face it or because of the way his thumb began to move, stroking slowly, delicately, over the angled line of her cheekbone and down the line of her jaw. Her legs were trembling, turning to cotton wool beneath her, and she felt as if the heat from that one small touch was radiating through her body, firing her blood, melting her bones. With a raw, jolting effort, she wrenched her head up and away from it, green eyes blazing into cloudy gold.

'You brought me here under false pretences!' she accused him furiously. 'You conned me—you've *kidnapped* me!'

'Kidnapped?'

Those beautiful eyes were deliberately wide and deceptively clear, with the look of the devil's innocence.

'Kidnapped you, *agapiti mou?* So tell me—when did I

force you, drag you on to my plane? When did I hold you hostage—lock you in your room, imprison you in the house?'

Strolling across the room to the door, he flung it open, gestured to indicate that she should walk past him if she wanted, out of the room, out of the villa…

And she very nearly took the option he offered. It was only as she made a single step forward that the rush of realisation came. He hadn't forced her in any way except mentally. He had told her that if she came with him to Greece he would let her mother and little George stay in the house that meant so much to them.

'You may leave any time you want.'

'No, I can't—and you know it! You made sure of that from the start. But I also know that I can't go through with what you have planned. And I really don't think that you can, either.'

'Why not?'

His question was so impossibly pleasant-toned that it was obvious the smoothness of his voice was hiding the dark, dangerous bite of something else. Something that Sadie shrank away from and yet was irresistibly drawn towards like a needle drawn to the most powerful magnet. She couldn't take her eyes from the sexy mouth that spoke those words, couldn't pull away from the sensual aura of his long, lean body that seemed to reach out to enclose her, holding her fixed as if her feet were nailed to the floor.

'Because what you said just does not make sense. You can't possibly want to marry me.'

'I can if that's what it takes.'

That had her frowning her total lack of understanding.

'Takes to do what?'

'To deal with what is between us.'

'There's nothing between us! Nothing at all.'

'Oh, but there is.'

When had he moved again, coming even closer, those soft boots making no sound on the polished floor?

'No!'

Sadie's hands came up between them, trying to push him away. But Nikos simply smiled and curled his fingers around hers, twining them together, soft and warm.

'There's this…'

Sadie's breath hitched in her throat as he lifted her hands to his mouth and pressed kisses on to each finger in turn. Her heart thudded hard in response to each warm, soft pressure of his mouth and she slicked a soft tongue over her own lips, easing the sudden disturbing dryness there.

'And there's this…'

Still holding both of her hands enclosed in one of his, he lifted the other to her head, stroking it down softly over her hair until she arched her neck to press herself against the caress, practically purring like a contented cat.

'And this…'

With a gentle but powerful tug, he jerked her close, so that the softness of her breasts was crushed against the hard wall of his chest, her hips cradled against his pelvis. The heat of his body flooded hers, making every nerve tingle into life, the pressure and the closeness making it impossible to be unaware of the swollen evidence of his arousal so close to where an answering need was already beginning to uncoil low in her body.

'Nikos…' she murmured, and her voice had changed, softened, the dryness of her throat making it husky and raw.

'Yes, *glikia mou?*'

Nikos sounded much the same, his words almost seeming to fray at the edges in the soft roughness of his tone. And, hearing it, Sadie knew that she had used up her ability to speak, her voice totally deserting her as she shook her head slowly, uncertainly. Unable to meet the fierce burn of that golden gaze, she lowered her eyes to look away. But that only meant that she was now staring straight at where their hands were still linked between them, his strong and dark against the paler slenderness of her own.

For a moment she froze, aware of the man who held her with every cell of her body, of the heat and hardness of him that seemed to surround her totally. If she breathed she inhaled the warm musky scent of him. She could see nothing but him. The bulk of his body enclosed hers so that she couldn't look past him to any other part of the room. And even though he hadn't kissed her she almost felt that if she ran her tongue over her lips once more she would taste the essential flavour of him.

'Sadie?'

Nikos's voice was a warning and an invitation all rolled into one. The same warning, the same invitation that his body held for her. The warning said that if she backed away now then this chance would never come again. The invitation was to all she wanted and more.

Deep in a corner of her mind some tiny shred of common sense cried a warning. But Sadie crushed it down until it was buried completely. She had no intention of heeding it or going along with common sense. This was what she had wanted from that moment in Nikos's office, and again in the plane on the way to Athens.

Then, the kiss, the caresses had been forbidden to her, because she had believed that he had a fiancée. Now there was no one to come between them, nothing to stop her. And she didn't want to stop.

The invitation was what she wanted. And the invitation was what she was going to accept.

Slowly, she lifted her head. This time her eyes met his full on and she didn't blink or look away.

'All right,' she said softly, but clearly, angling her head even more so that her mouth was his for the taking. 'Let's deal with what there is between us.'

The words were barely out of her mouth before they were crushed back under the pressure of his lips. But where she was expecting hard force, powerful passion, what she actually felt was slow, sensual enticement. The taking of her mouth with knowing skill. The wicked exploration of every inch. The slide of his hot tongue along the division between top and bottom lip, into the crevice at the corner and then back again, probing softly but insistently until she had no option but to let her head fall back and open to him completely.

And as she did so everything took fire. The slow, seductive moments were gone and all was heat and hunger and blazing, stinging passion that had her whimpering underneath his kiss, writhing up against him. Her breasts were crushed against his chest, her hips against the heat of him, and she flung her arms up and around his neck, holding his proud head down and close to her to prolong the kiss.

A kiss that now was no longer slow and seductive but hot and hard and demanding. A demand that she met willingly, gave back willingly. She felt Nikos's heart kick against his ribcage, lurching into a heavy pounding that she heard echoed in her own bloodstream as the heat of hunger flooded through her. Her hands clutched in his hair, her body writing against his as she felt the burn of his fingers trailing over her naked shoulders, down the length of her spine. His palms clamped over the swell of her buttocks, drawing her closer than ever before.

'Nikos…'

This time his name was a whimper of need against his mouth. A sound of encouragement driving him on. And she heard him mutter something in raw thick Greek as he adjusted his position, made it possible for him to obey her needy urgings.

She was spun round, lifted from her feet. The next moment she found that she had been deposited on the polished surface of the desk, the skirts of her red dress pushed up around her waist, the smooth wood cool against her legs. Nikos took advantage of her change in position as, one hand supporting her back, the other worked fast and urgently to unfasten the black buttons that held the sides of the dress together. And all the time his mouth followed the path of his hand, imprinting burning kisses over her skin.

The red linen fell away, exposing the creamy slopes of her breasts in the soft blue bra. Nikos's breath hissed in sharply between his teeth and he lifted his head slightly, one long finger reaching out to trace the outline of the scalloped edge, making her shudder in agonised response.

'Nikos…' she said again on a sound of protest, of need, and the shivers came again, harder, fiercer, as he cupped one aching breast, slipping his thumb inside the lacy material, stroking over her breast, circling a tightening nipple until she cried out in shocked response.

That cry was captured in his mouth again, swallowed down as he pulled her closer once more, angling her halfway down to the desk, supported only by the strength of his arm at her back. The heat of the other hard palm burned against her sensitive flesh as he pushed the pale blue cup aside, wrenching the straps of the bra over her shoulder and partway down one arm, imprisoning it against her side.

But her other hand was free and could reach out to the buttons on his shirt, wrenching them open with rather less finesse than the way he had dealt with unfastening her dress. She heard the material of his shirt rip slightly, the clatter of a button landing on the table, but couldn't find it in herself to care.

All she wanted was the feel of his skin, hot and silky, hazed with body hair, underneath her questing fingertips. A gasping sigh escaped her as she clawed at his chest, fingernails scraping lightly over the tight buds of his male nipples. Her mouth curled into a knowing smile as she heard a muttered imprecation in his native language, felt his strong body jerk in uncontrolled response.

'Yes, *gineka mou*,' he told her roughly, the movement of his mouth tormenting that achingly aroused tip of the breast beneath his lips, the heat of his breath feathering delight over the sensitised bud, making her writhe in delicious torment on the desk.

She heard the clatter of something—perhaps the pencil pot—being knocked aside, the thud of something landing on the floor, and Nikos's dark laughter against her skin was just an intensification of all the sensations that assailed her already.

'You are my woman,' he repeated. 'Mine.'

'Yours.'

It was a whispered echo, one that was choked off on a note of abandoned ecstasy as that hot and hungry mouth found her pouting nipple, sucking it deep into its moist heat and swirling a tormenting tongue around its yearning peak.'

'Yours!'

She arched up towards him, needing to intensify the sensations, the pressure, and felt his teeth gently scrape the distended tip. For a moment she completely lost herself, almost swooning away in pleasure and only coming back to herself when another new and stunning sensation hit.

Those knowing fingers had reached the heart of her, stroking tormentingly along the fine stretch of fabric between her legs, making her gasp aloud, her one free hand clutching at the fine cotton of his shirt, holding him when she feared he might move away. But all he planned to do was hook his fingers in the sides of her knickers, tugging them down along her thighs to expose her to him more openly. At first it was easy, but when they caught and tangled just below her knees he swore roughly and gave up trying for any sort of finesse. A couple of hard tugs and they had ripped apart at the seams, tossed away in an impatient, careless movement.

His mouth was where his fingers had been, kissing a burning path through the dark curls clustered between her legs, the wicked torment of his tongue swirling over delicate, receptive tissue, making it unfurl and respond like a rosebud opening towards the sunlight.

But she had had enough of waiting, had enough of the sensual agony of anticipation, delicious though it was. Her hands were shaking as she fumbled with his belt, clumsy with need and a desperate urgency. She was making a total hash of things when he laid a restraining hand over hers, and his hot mouth kissed the moans from her lips.

She heard the rasp of a zip and knew a moment of agonising tension, her breath held in her lungs, before he came back to her again. Lifting her so that she was half on, half off the edge of the desk, he opened her legs wide, knees bent, feet braced against the polished wood and moved between them. His mouth took hers again, his tongue probing deep, in the same moment that he used his hands on her hips to lift her, move her, then draw her down on to his hard, heated length.

'Nikos!'

His name was a long drawn out sigh of pure satisfaction and delight, and for a moment she would have been content to stay like that, close to him, filled with him, abandoned to him. But Nikos was not prepared to stay or wait. Already he was moving, stroking deep inside her, in and then withdrawing almost to the end, before plunging in deeply over and over again. Her hands were around his neck, fingers digging into his shoulders, her mouth moving against his jaw, kissing, licking, nipping at the stubble-roughened skin, tasting the salt of his sweat against her tongue. After only a very few seconds she had lost herself, unable to do anything other than absorb herself into the moment, giving herself up purely to sensation. Mindlessly, blindly, she was moving with him, on him, feeling him inside her, taking her higher, higher, until he finally pushed her over the edge into the blazing, whirling oblivion of total ecstasy.

She heard a voice cry out aloud, and from a distance vaguely realised that it was her own, but she was too far gone to care if anyone had heard. A few seconds later she heard Nikos too give a raw, exultant sound as he followed her, and for a long time after that she knew nothing at all. Only the slow, slow drift back to a form of reality, a sort of return to consciousness, but one that kept floating to and fro, coming back to her and then swirling away again. Taking her into the glowing darkness where all she was aware of was the strength of Nikos's arms around her, the heave of his chest as he fought for control of his breathing, the thud of his heart underneath the powerful ribcage, the scent of his skin where her head rested, totally limp and spent against his shoulder.

It was a good thing there was the desk here to support them both, Nikos reflected, when some of the thundering haze had left his head and he could finally begin to think again. At least it was there to take some of Sadie's weight and allow him to prop himself up on it until he recovered. After the onslaught of wild and uncontrolled passion that had taken him—taken them both—by storm, he seemed to have lost the ability to focus, to recognise reality when it came back to him. He felt as if he had been at the centre of some furious whirlwind, snatched out of reality and spun around in a spiralling, blazing typhoon of feeling, then dumped back down on still not quite steady ground again, not knowing which was up and which was down. His arms were shaking, his legs unsteady beneath him, and he still couldn't manage to get enough air into his raw and aching lungs. He was quite sure that the racing of his heart would never ease so that his pulse rate could return to anything approaching normal.

And Sadie was in no better state than he was. In fact, she seemed barely conscious, her head dropped on to his shoulder, her breath scorching his skin as she too struggled to breathe normally. Her whole body sagged against him, limp as a marionette with its strings completely snapped in two, nothing to hold her upright. And the only noise in the room was the raw, unsteady sound of their breathing, that and the faint splash of the waves coming in to shore out beyond the open window, where ordinary everyday life was going on as normal, oblivious to the wild and sensual storm that had raged inside the villa.

But they could not stay shielded from reality for ever. Sooner or later life must start again. Someone might come in. They had to collect their thoughts and return to normality, for the time being at least.

And then they would have to face the repercussions of what had just happened here.

He for one would have to face the fact that he had stupidly, blindly, rashly rushed into this without a thought, without a moment's consideration for common sense or practicality. Or even, *Thee mou,* even safety.

He had just had sex with the woman he had hated for the past five years, a woman he had learned the hard way not to trust. And he had done it without even the use of a condom to protect him now and against the future. He hadn't paused to think about such things but had been totally at the mercy of his body, his libido, as lust-crazed as a newly horny teenager—and every bit as mindless. Both of them had been wildly out of control, responding in such a white hot fury of desire that any weak attempt at a rational thought had been burned away, reduced to ashes in the blazing conflagration they had lit between them.

And the worst, the most stupid thing of all was that he would do it again at the drop of a hat. Even now, with his breathing barely back under control, his pulse-rate still far from normal, she only had to move and he could inhale the clean, fresh scent of her skin, overlaid with some delicate flowery perfume, or feel the brush of her soft hair against his cheek and the heavy throb of blood would start to rise within his body. If she sighed, exhaling warm breath against his shoulder, so that it slid in to caress the skin at the open neck of his shirt, then he was still tempted to turn and take her in his arms once more, to kiss her hard and strong. Kiss her until their senses woke again, fought off the lassitude of satiation, destroyed all rational thought, and the heated hunger and yearning took possession of them once more.

She would go with him too. He knew that without thinking. Knew that he had only to touch her and both of them would go up in flames, the most basic, most primitive parts of their natures responding to the instinctive demands of their bodies.

And that would be the most damnably stupid way to behave imaginable.

He had to get a grip and fast, before things got completely out of control.

'Sadie…'

At first he found that his voice wouldn't work and he had to clear his throat and try again.

'Sadie.'

This time she heard and lifted her head, slowly and with difficulty. Her eyes, still hazed by the storm that had assailed her, the explosive climax that had erupted like a volcano in her slender form, blinked and tried to focus, almost but not quite succeeding.

'We need to talk—' Nikos began, then broke off as the sound of the phone ringing broke through the silence, tearing apart the atmosphere that was rich with the heavy clouds of sensuality and jolting them back to the real world in a second.

Automatically Nikos reached for it, lifted the receiver.

'Yes?'

Hearing his father's voice, he knew that he had no alternative but to deal with whatever Petros had on his mind.

'I have to take this,' he said to Sadie. 'And I may be some time.'

She looked as if she needed the time anyway. How could they talk when she was so clearly not yet capable of doing so? Besides, he would prefer to have some time to collect his thoughts himself. Decide just where he was going to go from here.

But first he had to deal with his father. And if Petros discovered who was with him—if Sadie spoke or gave herself away—then they would be back on the terrible old treadmill of the family feud before he could stop it. That had complicated his relationship with Sadie once before. He was not about to let it happen again.

'Go and clean yourself up…'

His eyes swept over her dishevelled state, the red linen dress hanging open heavily crumpled and creased, her bra half on and half off, and her knickers discarded in two separate tiny pieces on the office floor. Stooping, he picked them up and dropped them into her hand while she was still clearly gathering her thoughts.

'But…' she began, but Nikos shook his head, hunching one shoulder to hold the phone between it and his ear as he turned her and propelled her firmly towards the door.

'Take a shower—or maybe swim in the pool. I'll come and find you when I'm ready. What?'

The sound of his father's voice drew his attention back to the phone conversation.

'No,' he said, in response to the older man's enquiry as to whether the person he was with should take priority over him. 'No one important. Nothing that can't wait.'

It was only when the door slammed closed behind Sadie that he realised that he had spoken in English. Even when talking to his father.

CHAPTER NINE

Well, that was her well and truly dismissed.

Finding herself in the corridor outside the study door without quite realising how she had got there, Sadie did not quite know whether to explode in fury or to burst into shocked, bewildered tears. She was quite capable of both, and the resulting combination was so volatile that any one tiny incident would be enough to spark it off.

For a moment she actually considered spinning round, marching back into the room and confronting Nikos over what he had said. Snatching the phone receiver from his hand and tossing it well out of reach if she had to. She even half turned, ready to do just that. But the thought of the danger she might put herself in—and her mother and George—as a result stayed her movement and kept her feet moving right in the direction that was safest: away from the office and back up to the safety of her bedroom, moving as quickly as she could for fear that she might meet some member of staff which, in her present dishevelled and disreputable state, would be just the worst thing possible.

It couldn't be more obvious just what she had been up to. Her crumpled dress was still gaping over her exposed breasts and her underwear barely existed. Looking down at the totally destroyed knickers she held in her hand, she couldn't suppress a shudder of revulsion at the sight of them and the thought of just how they had got into that appalling mess.

And she had only herself to blame.

'All right.' She could hear her own voice in her thoughts, husky and inviting—seductively so. 'Let's deal with what there is between us.'

And of course Nikos had taken her at her word. Who could blame him? She'd handed herself to him on a plate, without a care or thought for the consequences.

Reaching her bedroom, she hurried inside and slammed the door shut, leaning back against it as the last of her mental strength deserted her, leaving her shaking and distraught.

She hadn't even had the sense to insist that he use a condom! She had made every possible mistake in the book. The sort of thing that even her twenty-year-old self had managed to handle so much better in the past. So she had no right to complain if Nikos had treated her like the easy conquest he obviously believed her to be.

The easy conquest she had let herself be.

With a cry of disgust and horror, Sadie flung the ruined knickers into the wastepaper bin, not caring that one part of them fell far short, fluttering down on to the deep gold carpet like a wounded and dying bird. A moment later the dress and bra followed them, tossed aside in total revulsion. She couldn't wait to get out of them as soon as possible. Just the thought of ever wearing them again made her stomach heave.

Take a shower, Nikos had said. He was damn right. She would take a shower. She needed to wash the scent of him from her body, the taste of him from her mouth. If only she could erase her memories as easily, she told herself as she stood under a hot shower, letting the water pound down on her head, sluice over her skin. She scrubbed every inch of her body, shampooed her hair twice, but she still couldn't get rid of the feeling of having been used and then discarded without a second thought.

'Damn him!'

Finally having to get out of the shower, before she reduced her skin to the state of a prune, Sadie rubbed at her hair with a towel, ruffling it impossibly.

'Damn, damn, damn him!'

She was strongly tempted to put on fresh clothes, stamp back down to the study—but to do so would reveal to Nikos just how much his behaviour had upset her. That and the fact that as long as she didn't push things to the ultimate extreme then her mother and George were still safe in Thorn Trees. If she made one mistake, took a wrong step, then she had little doubt that Nikos would carry out his threat to have them thrown out of their home and on to the streets.

Or would he do that anyway? The frantic movements of Sadie's hands stopped and she stared at herself in the mirror, looking anxiously at her face where the flush of colour from the heat of the shower was now fading rapidly from her cheeks. Just what did Nikos plan to do next?

He had got her here under false pretences, claiming that he needed her to plan and organise his wedding. But there had been no wedding to organise at all. It had been nothing but a deceit from start to finish. So had this really been his plan? To get her back into his bed—not that she had actually been in his *bed*, she acknowledged grimly. She had fallen right into his hands like a ripe plum the first time he had kissed her in his London office and that must have given him the cue he had needed—if in fact he'd needed any such thing—to go ahead with the scheme that she now saw was his ultimate attack on her family and his personal revenge on her.

'But there must be some arrangement we can come to!

Surely there's something I can do—anything…' Her own words came back to haunt her, making hot colour flood every inch of her body. She could see just how that had sounded—and how Nikos would naturally have interpreted it.

'And exactly what sort of services did you have in mind?' he had come back at her. 'What exactly are you offering…?'

She'd denied it furiously at the time, but obviously she had put a seed in his mind and he had determined that the real price of letting her stay in Thorn Trees was to be paid in kind.

If she had any sense, she'd be out of here—fast. She had her passport. She might just be able to afford a plane ticket home on the little that was left on her credit card—she hoped.

If she had any sense, or any choice. Because she could be in no doubt as to what would happen if she did run out on Nikos now. Just the thought of her mother being thrown out of her home after the delight of thinking that she had been given a reprieve made the tears burn at the back of Sadie's eyes. She couldn't even call the police and tell them how Nikos had kidnapped her. As he had pointed out, he had used no sort of force, and she had come with him only too willingly.

And if they heard about what had just happened in Nikos's office…

She was trapped, but that didn't mean she had to sit back and take whatever Nikos tossed her way. A quick glance at the clock revealed how much time had gone by since he had bundled her—as 'no one important'—so unceremoniously out of his office. Any minute now, she was sure that he would be coming looking for her.

She didn't want him to come here and think that she had been sitting waiting for him. Sitting on the bed waiting for him. What she wanted him to think was that she didn't care. That the words he'd said had had no effect on her.

Take a shower he'd said—or have a swim.

She'd do that. Moving hastily to one of the drawers in the wardrobe, she pulled out the swimming costume she had tossed into her case at the very last minute, never really expecting that she would ever have a chance to wear it, and hurried herself into it. When Nikos came to find her, she wouldn't be here. She would be in the pool—swimming and relaxing in the sun, without a care in the world. And not sparing a single thought for the heated scene in the office.

It almost worked. The warmth of the sun beating down on her head, the cool clarity of the water, the regular physical activity of the strokes up and down the pool soothed her jangled nerves. She actually managed to empty her head of the anxious thoughts that preyed on her mind and focus only on what she was doing. Until the moment that a dark shape blotted out the sun and there was a splash, a brief glimpse of a powerful form slicing into the pool in a perfect dive. A few seconds later, Nikos surfaced, dashing water from his face, tossing back his wet hair as he trod water beside her.

'So this is where you've been hiding yourself.'

'Hardly hiding,' Sadie managed with careful insouciance. 'It's a hot day and I didn't want to waste the luxury of having a pool at my disposal.'

She prayed that he would take the ragged edge to her voice as being the result of the exertion of her swimming and not what it truly was—an uncontrollable response to his closeness. To the sight of the powerful chest and shoulders that showed above the surface of the water, black body hair slicked against the tanned skin under which the strong muscles flexed and bunched as he balanced carefully, keeping himself from going under.

'After all, it's not every day I see a pool like this. And I do love swimming.'

In spite of her effort to control it, a note of longing slid into her voice. For years now there had been no time for this sort of relaxation, not even in the local public pool. Her mother's illness and the need to look after George had taken up any free time she had from running the business.

'You should have stayed with me.'

Nikos pushed both hands through the darkness of his hair that lay sleek and black, plastered to the strong shape of his skull by the weight of the water. Drops of moisture still lay along the broad slash of his cheekbones, sparkling in the sunlight as he turned towards her.

'You should have stayed with me, *glikia mou,*' he returned sardonically. 'Then you could have swum in a pool like this every single day.'

'Not if I'd married you when it was originally planned— five years ago.'

The memory of the way that Nikos had trapped her, making her believe that he was going to marry someone else, made her voice sharp. No matter how much she tried to push it out of her mind that telling phrase, *'The one woman I have ever planned on marrying is you'* just would not be pushed away. She knew he didn't mean it—how could he mean it?—but still her brain just wouldn't let it go. And she was forced to face up to the appalling possibility that in a moment of weakness, of longing for it to be so, she had let that lying declaration influence her earlier, when he had kissed her.

Was it possible that she had actually let herself believe that he meant it? And that that was the reason—part of the reason—why she had given in so easily—too easily—to his passionate seduction?

'You weren't in such good financial shape then, were you? Or why else would you have come after me in the first place?'

One corner of Nikos's sensual mouth quirked up into a half

smile. Seeing it, Sadie couldn't help but remember the sexual devastation that mouth had worked on her hungry body when he had kissed every inch of her while she had lain, aroused and yearning, on the polished surface of his office desk. The heat that raced through her veins at the memory had no chance at all of being cooled by the lapping water of the pool.

'Didn't what happened earlier give you the answer to that?' he drawled softly, the wicked gleam in his eyes heightened by the glare of the sun. 'Surely that would have shown you that you have no need at all of false modesty?'

'There's nothing false about it,' Sadie flashed back. 'Or modest. I'm simply being realistic and honest—and I wish that you would do me the courtesy of being the same. The fact is that if I had not been Edwin Carteret's daughter and the heiress to his fortune then there is no way you would ever have sought me out at the start.'

'I—' Nikos began, but she had seen the look in his eyes, the subtle change in his expression, and knew that, in spite of the way that he tried to hide it, he was thinking through his response very carefully, planning exactly what to say.

'Honesty, Nikos. You owe me at least that.'

For a long moment his golden eyes locked with hers and she could almost hear his clever, ruthless brain working through the possibilities and coming to a decision.

'Honestly, then…' he said at last. 'The answer is no. If you had not been your father's daughter, then I would never have sought you out in the first place.'

If he had reached out and grabbed her hard by the shoulders, wrenching her towards him and pushing her down hard underneath the cool water, then he couldn't have caused more of a shock to her heart. *But, be honest with yourself too*, Sadie reproached her foolish mind. *Did you really think there would be any other answer*? Hoping for a different response was such a foolish weakness. A wishful fantasy that could never be achieved.

'And, yes, I lied to you—or at least kept from you the fact that the Konstantos finances were not in the best possible shape. But who can blame me when I already had overwhelming evidence of the way your father was working to bring the corporation down?'

'You could have confided in me. Trusted me.'

'Trust!' Nikos scorned, throwing back his dark head in a laugh that seemed to turn the air around them into ice and then splinter it into a million tiny pieces. 'You dare talk to me about trust when all the time you were part of the whole conspiracy your father had set up. When I was fighting for my life—for my family's life—you were there, just waiting to stab me in the back.'

That was more than Sadie could take. In the past she had been forced to play along with her father's wicked plans, forced to keep silent about everything that was going on in order to keep her mother and her as yet unborn baby brother safe. Now that part of the problem, at least, was all over. Her father was dead; he couldn't hurt anyone any more.

'If I hadn't done what I did, then you would have lost your fight.'

'What?'

Nikos's intent stare from swiftly narrowed eyes made her wish that she could duck down into the water to escape it. But she'd embarked on telling at least this part of the truth. She couldn't back down now. She doubted that Nikos would let her do it even if she tried.

'And just what is that supposed to mean?'

Dredging up her courage, Sadie faced him across the clear sparkling surface of the water. Pride stiffened her spine and brought her chin up defiantly.

'You talk about fighting for your family's life, but it was really just to preserve some part of the family fortune.'

She'd missed something there. The sudden hard blink of those amazing eyes told her that she wasn't actually in possession of all the facts. Once again Nikos had adjusted his expression, so that the one he showed to her was a carefully assumed mask, a polished veneer that hid reality behind it. But she couldn't stop to think about what it might mean. So far Nikos had seemed to hold the upper hand, but in this at least there was something he didn't know and she was determined to make sure he knew it.

'And if I hadn't done what I did then you would have lost everything. As it was, you were at least left with the Atlantis.'

As she named the one rather run-down hotel that was all her father had let Nikos and his family keep from their ruined estates, she knew that she had hit home. If her words had been a slap in his face, then he couldn't have reacted more strongly. His whole body stilled in the water, his face freezing into a hard, set façade that gave away nothing of what he was thinking.

'And what do you know about the Atlantis?'

But the sense of injustice that had buoyed her up until now had abruptly deserted Sadie, taking all her courage with it. She couldn't take any more, couldn't face that ruthlessly probing look, the way that his amazing eyes seemed to burn right into her.

'Enough,' was all she could manage, and at the sight of his frown, the way that his mouth opened to demand more of an answer, her nerve broke completely and she made a swift dive into the water, kicking out her legs and turning to swim away, heading for the far side of the pool as fast as she could.

But of course Nikos came after her, his stronger stroke and more powerful muscles driving him through the water so that he came up behind her fast, long arms reaching out to grab at her. He caught her just as she was about to scramble up the ladder on to the side, hauling her back against him and twisting her round in his arms so that she was forced to face him.

'Explain,' he snarled, issuing an order with no doubt at all that it would be obeyed.

But Sadie's throat seemed to have closed up over the words she needed and she couldn't get them out. She could only shake her head in despair, sending her soaking wet hair flying so that drops of water spun off and landed on Nikos's face, close to his eyes. He dashed them away with a brusque movement of his head, refusing to let go of her arms in order to brush them aside. Instead his grip around her arms tightened and he gave her a rough little shake, pushing her to give him the answer he wanted.

'Explain,' he said again, and to her astonishment just a little of the attacking quality had gone out of his voice. 'What you are saying doesn't make sense. When your father set out to bring down the Konstantos Corporation, he damn nearly succeeded. In fact, we thought that he had done just that—taken everything. It was only later—after…'

Again he made a slight adjustment, as if there was something he was covering up, hiding from her.

'Afterwards that I discovered Carteret had not quite managed to take everything. There was one little piece of the company left—something that had either been too small or, in his mind, not important enough to bother with…'

As he paused to stare into her eyes, Sadie found the strength to fill in the gap.

'The Atlantis.'

Nikos nodded sombrely, his eyes never leaving her face. But she felt the way his hard grip on her arms had eased and knew it meant his mood had changed.

'And you can only know about this because you were

somehow involved in making sure that it was still ours. That it was the one thing your father didn't get his hands on.'

It was a statement not a question. His tone of voice and the dark-eyed look was levelled on her face told her that he already knew the answer but he wanted her to confirm it.

'Yes.'

As she nodded her head in response, she suddenly felt a rush of pride and determination come back to bring new strength to her mind and body.

'Yes, I was involved. I could have saved the island for you—my father actually gave me the choice, and I considered it at first—but at the time I felt choosing the one small hotel that was the other thing he had been prepared to concede might actually be more practical help than the sentimental attachment you had to Icaros. And I was right, wasn't I?'

Nikos nodded slowly, his expression unreadable, bronze eyes clouded and hooded, hiding his real feelings from her.

'You were right.'

'Of course I was right—and bloody stupid at the same time. I knew you and so I chose the Atlantis, giving you at least a small business—something to keep you and the Konstantos Corporation one step away from complete bankruptcy. I chose that and I gave you a small start on the path to building your fortune back up again. Of course I didn't know how quickly and easily you would do it. Or how you would then use all that you'd gained—all the money, all the power—to turn the tables on me and my family. To have your revenge—'

'My revenge on your father,' Nikos put in, but she was too caught up in what she was saying, fighting too hard against the tide of pain and bitter memories that threatened to swamp her, to hear what he was saying or to understand the tone in which he'd said it.

'And then when you'd succeeded in getting back everything

you'd ever lost—and more—when you'd finished taking your revenge on my father—when he was dead and free from your cruel quest for vengeance—that was when Fate really dealt you an ace card. Because when you moved to take possession of Thorn Trees you just thought that you were going to throw us out. That you would kick us out of the family home and never see any of the damn Carterets any more. But of course I had to go and turn up in your office, begging for a chance to stay in the house—offering to do anything. And that...'

Her voice cracked on the words so that she had to struggle to go on.

'And that was when you decided you could have it all. The money, the businesses, the house—and the ultimate satisfaction: your final, personal revenge on me.'

Nikos's hands had fallen from her arms, setting her free, and so now, unable to bear the closeness to him any longer, she pulled away, swallowing hard to fight against the tears clogging her throat.

'Well, you got what you wanted, Nikos—every last little bit of it. Two days ago you said that you weren't satisfied—that the revenge you'd taken hadn't been enough. Well, I hope to hell you're satisfied now—you damn well ought to be, because to be honest there's nothing left for you to take!'

She had to get away. Had to. If she stayed any longer then she was going to give herself away completely. Eyes stinging, vision blurred, she somehow managed to find the ladder out of the pool and scrambled up it.

'No!'

But Nikos was only seconds behind her, vaulting out of the water and coming after her. He quickly caught up with her, grabbing her arm again to whirl her round to face him.

'No, you're wrong. Revenge doesn't come into it any more.'

'It doesn't?'

'No. It may have started that way but along the way things changed.'

'Changed how?'

Nikos's mouth twisted slightly, and just for a moment that clear golden gaze didn't quite meet hers.

'Along the way I abandoned revenge for something far more basic.'

Sadie frowned her confusion.

'Basic? So tell me what is more "basic" than revenge?'

Nikos didn't answer. But then he didn't have to. Looking into his eyes, Sadie saw just what he meant. It was written there, clear and plain to see.

What was a more basic drive than revenge? There was just one answer. Lust. Physical desire. Sexual passion. That was what had driven him from the start and what was still behind everything he did. An intense, searing physical need that obliterated everything else, burning it up in its heat. She recognised that, and understood it. Because didn't she feel the same whenever he touched her? Hadn't she just been so driven out of her mind with the same overwhelming hunger that she had let him take her on the desk in his office without a hint of a thought?

'So…' Her throat was painfully dry, cracking on the single word. 'So the whole story of a fiancée?'

'I told you. It was a pretence from start to finish. It had to be.'

Nikos dropped his head, resting his forehead on Sadie's so that his eyes burned into her from mere inches away.

'How could there be someone else when I never got you out of my head? You ruined me for any other woman. You got under my skin and I never got rid of you.'

'No—no one else?'

That was so much more than she had ever anticipated that her head swam under the impact of it.

'How could I kiss you like this…?'

His mouth took hers, slow and sensual, heating her blood in an instant and making her sway unsteadily on her feet.

'…if there was anyone else? How could I touch you…?'

If his kiss had been a sensual assault then his caress, the way his hands swept over her body, was like throwing a lighted match on to bone-dry tinder, making her skin flame in a second, setting her pulse racing between one uneven breath and another.

'And how could I ever think of taking another woman to my bed when the only one I ever wanted is right here…?'

The one woman I have ever planned on marrying is you.

The words that Nikos had spoken in his office came back to tempt and torment her. Tempting because she so wanted them to be true. Tormenting because she could scarcely begin to imagine that he could actually mean them.

And yet when she had insisted that he tell her about his imaginary fiancée—oh, dear heaven—he had also said: *She is the only woman I have ever wanted to marry.*

Was the world really spinning round her as she felt it was? Had she been out in the sun too long? Or was it really possible…? Could she believe a word he was saying?

But then Nikos took her lips again and she suddenly knew with a sense of total conviction that deep down she really didn't care. All she needed, all she ever wanted most in the world, was right here before her in the shape of this man. The man she had fallen for five years before. And she had never managed to recover from that infatuation ever since.

She was sinking deep into the spell of sensuality he was weaving, definitely going down for the third time. But at the same time a tiny, barely audible voice of instinct was whispering inside her head that there was something wrong, something missing, but she couldn't begin to think what. And quite frankly she didn't even want to try.

His hands were hot on her body, smoothing over the tingling flesh exposed by her plain black swimming costume. The stretchy material had almost totally dried in the sun, but the heat of the day was as nothing when compared with the flames that were flaring inside, burning her up with the yearning need that he could create so easily. One broad palm cupped her breast, the thumb stroking wickedly erotic circles over her nipple so that she shuddered in uncontrolled response, feeling that she might actually collapse into a molten pool right at his feet. Against her stomach she could feel the hard ridge of his erection, and moist heat flooded between her legs in response.

'So…'

Nervously, she slicked her tongue over her lips to moisten them enough to get the words she needed out of her mouth.

'So—when we first met—would you have married me?'

'Hell, yes. I'd have done anything to get you into my bed.'

That scorching, exciting mouth was doing amazing things to her. Tracing a burning path down her throat, over the exposed slope of her breast. When it caught one pouting nipple into its moist heat, suckling it through the black material of her costume, she cried aloud in response to the stinging pleasure-pain that sizzled through every nerve, destroying thought, leaving only space in her mind for the throbbing need she couldn't deny.

'Do you doubt it?' Nikos questioned against her skin, his breath on the question feathering over the moistened nipple, making it burn with even greater need.

'No…'

It was a moan of response and she shook her head vigorously, well past the point of being able to think about doubting anything. Her world was made up of just three things—herself, this man, and the wild sexual hunger that was blazing between them.

'Then come with me now—come back to my bed, *glikia mou,* and let me show you exactly what I mean.'

She meant to answer, Sadie told herself. She had to answer—because there was only one possible response she could give him. But she wasn't completely sure whether the wild, fervent *yes* that was burning in her thoughts had actually translated itself into sound or not.

But obviously it had—or it just didn't matter and the way that she returned his kiss gave Nikos the answer he'd been waiting for. Because he didn't ask any more questions or hesitate for a second. Instead he swung her up off her feet and into his arms and carried her out of the blazing sun into the coolness of the house and up the stairs, heading for his bedroom.

CHAPTER TEN

THE LATE MORNING sun coming through the window and onto her face finally dragged Sadie from the deep, exhausted sleep into which she had fallen well after midnight. Yawning and stretching, she felt the faint aches in her body after the night of passion she had shared with Nikos.

A long, long night of passion that had followed on from the equally ardent afternoon they had spent in bed too. At some point they had emerged to eat a meal, drink some wine, but the food had barely been touched before Nikos had leaned across the table, catching her chin in his hand and drawing her face towards him to plant another long, lingering kiss on her partly open mouth. Sadie had responded with equal enthusiasm, and soon they had abandoned all pretence of wanting to eat and headed back to the bedroom.

She could still feel the places where Nikos had kissed her, caressed her, finding pleasure spots she hadn't known existed, opening a world of sensual delights to her with every second that had passed. The scent of his body still permeated the sheets, and if she rolled over she could see the indentation on the pillows where his head had rested when they had finally succumbed to sleep.

And she could even still taste him on her mouth. If she

licked her lips then her tongue caught the faint flavour of Nikos's skin, the salty tang of his sweat, the deeply personal memory of his tongue tangling intimately with hers.

Sighing contentedly, she stretched again, savouring the memory that the taste brought back to her.

The taste of her first, her one and only lover.

The taste of the one man she had ever loved.

Her heart kicked hard and sharp at the thought, pushing her upright in the bed, staring sightlessly out of the window to where the clear blue Aegean Sea lapped lazily against the shoreline below.

The one man she had ever loved and the one man she still loved with all her heart.

She drew in a sharp, raw-edged breath at the realisation that this was how it was, and nothing she could do would ever change it. She had fallen head over heels in love with Nikos in the first moment she had met him and nothing had changed since. All that had happened, all that had come between them, had never managed to destroy the way she felt, even when she'd believed it had. Deep in her heart, the feelings had remained just the same. She still loved him; she would always love him.

And Nikos?

Now she realised just what she had been trying to grasp hold of in her mind yesterday by the pool, when Nikos's kisses and caresses had driven her so distracted with need that she hadn't been able to think of her own name, let alone grasp the elusive, whispering little voice that had tried to warn her that not all was well. That there was something she really should be thinking of before she jumped in too deep and let the dark waters of sexuality close right over her head.

Now, too late, she knew what it was—and she also knew that it meant that her life would never be the same. She also knew that it had been too late yesterday, too late from the moment she had confronted Nikos in his London office, seeing him again for the first time. Too late to go back to her old way of life, to managing to live without Nikos in it, without knowing that she still loved him. From the moment she had set eyes on him again she had fallen right back in love with him—though in those first days she had never realised the truth.

If, in fact, she had ever really fallen out of love with him. She had been terrified of being in love with a man who didn't love her at all. And so she had forced herself to believe that she hated him because it was safer for her, easier that way.

'Safer!'

Sadie actually spoken the word aloud, the way she was feeling turning it into a sound of shaken laughter. *Safer* just didn't come into it. *Safer* wasn't possible. Because the truth was that she had done exactly that, no matter how careful her personal safeguards had been.

She was in love with Nikos Konstantos and Nikos... Well, Nikos *wanted* her. He desired her intensely sexually; she could be in no doubt about that. He had spent last night and half of yesterday proving just that to her. He might even want to marry her. But only to get her into his bed and keep her there. He'd said as much yesterday.

'Hell, yes. I'd have done anything to get you into my bed.'

But he had spoken no word of love. Had never shown any sign of even considering that such an emotion existed. And probably, for Nikos, it never had. He had never loved her in the past, didn't love her now. And there was no hope that he would ever come to love her at any time in the future—if they had one together.

'Oh, Nikos!'

Sighing, Sadie forced herself to throw back the covers and get out of bed. What was it they said about the cold light of dawn? Yesterday had been wonderful, the night a sensual fantasy come true. But now, with the morning light shining bright on the new day, and with Nikos no longer in her bed to kiss her distracted, keep her thoughts from the 'what nexts' and 'if onlys' that plagued her, she was forced to face the probability that last night had not been a beginning, a start to a future, but instead a one-off final fling.

Wasn't it far more likely that Nikos had seen last night as a way, as he had said, 'to deal with what is between us'? To get her out of his system once and for all. He had made no promise, offered her nothing else. And she would be all kinds of a fool if she looked for anything.

But for now she'd take what was on offer, she resolved as she headed for the bathroom and the shower. The truth was that she was weak enough to admit to settling for anything. Just one more day…just one more time…

That phrase was still repeating inside her head when, fresh from her shower, naked and with dripping hair, she wandered back into the bedroom. Only to stop dead at the sight of the dark figure standing by the window.

'Nikos!'

With the sun blazing behind him, his imposing frame was just a black silhouette, his face a shadowed blank. But there was something about the way he stood, a tension in the broad shoulders under the soft blue linen shirt, in the way his hands were pushed deep into the pockets of his pale trousers, that warned her about his mood. He was not here for light conversation, and if she was any judge he was definitely not here to resume the lovemaking that had occupied so much of the night.

'What is it?' she asked sharply in the same moment that he spoke too.

'We need to talk.'

It clashed with her own words, but she caught it and it sent her spirits, already only precariously balanced between good and low, plummeting right down on to the floor beneath her bare feet. How many ominous, difficult conversations had begun with just those words? *We need to talk* implied that something had gone wrong—or was about to go wrong.

But what?

'OK.'

It was all she could manage, and in a way that was totally ridiculous after the night they had just spent together she found herself wishing that she had wrapped a towel around her before she had left the bathroom. Standing here like this, totally naked, she felt so vulnerable and exposed, needing to hide. She certainly didn't feel up to any 'we need to talk' type of discussion anyway.

'Not like this. Get some clothes on first.'

Obviously Nikos felt the same about her appearance. Which should have been a relief but, in fact, only added to her tension. Last night, nothing would have distracted him from the fact that she was naked—or from taking full advantage of it. Now it was an awkward obstacle in the way of what he wanted to get done.

Which didn't promise well for this talk.

'Of course.'

But her clothes were in her room, not here in Nikos's bedroom where they had spent the night.

'I'll…'

But Nikos was already moving, heading for the door as if he couldn't get out of there quickly enough.

'I'll be in my office,' he tossed over his shoulder at her.

'I'll be there.'

Somehow Sadie managed to keep her tone buoyant, when in fact, it should have been sinking with her spirits. She had admitted to herself that she expected her dismissal from his life to come sooner rather than later, but not this soon. She doubted if Nikos even heard her anyway, as the door swung to behind his hasty exit.

He was a fool, Nikos told himself as he headed for the stairs, the pace of his steps matching the state of his thoughts. A stupid, total fool and he had just proved it to himself.

He should have known. He did know, damn it! He'd left Sadie sleeping in his bed this morning and she had been totally naked then. And then, when he had gone into the room and heard the shower running in the bathroom, any idiot would have assumed that when she emerged she was not likely to be wearing any clothes.

But he had not been thinking straight. With his mind so full of the news he had been given this morning, he hadn't been thinking about anything else at all. And so when Sadie had finally emerged, beautifully naked, with her soft skin still pink and glowing from the shower, the sight had hit him like a blow to his already unfocussed head. And that was something he didn't need. In two ways.

He already had the image of Sadie's naked body in his mind. *Gamato*, after last night he knew that it was etched there permanently, never to be erased. If he had hoped that the sensory indulgence of the past eighteen hours or so would sate him on her charms and leave him free to live his life again, then he had been very badly mistaken. There was no way he was sated at all. The truth was that he doubted if he ever would be. There was no way he could have enough of Sadie Carteret, and one passionate night of total abandon had done nothing to appease the appetite he had for her.

If anything, it had only whetted it so that he was far hungrier now than he had ever been in the years they had been apart.

And that was why the article he had read in the English gossip columns had sent his mental temperature soaring, making any sort of rational thought impossible.

'*Gamoto!*'

It was also impossible to sit down and wait for Sadie to appear. The thought that he might have actually started to trust her when the truth was that he was being led around by his nose—or another part of his anatomy—twisted cruelly in his guts.

She was down quicker than he had anticipated. And where he had been sure that, realising something was up, she would dress carefully for maximum impact—something like the fantasy come true of that red dress came to mind—he found he couldn't have been more wrong.

Sadie had clearly rushed into her clothes, grabbing at the first thing that came to hand. And the first thing was a pair of worn denim jeans and a plain white v-necked tee shirt, her face clear of any make-up, pale against the still-damp darkness of her hair. Not that it helped any. The truth was that she was hellishly sexy in anything. And with the memory of her gloriously naked body in his arms, in his bed—underneath him, warm and willing all through the night and again in the bedroom just now—he had to make a fearsome effort to keep his eyes on her face. Because it was her face that he needed to see. He needed to look into her eyes, read her expression. That way he might have some chance of finding out what was going on in her conniving little mind.

'What is it?'

So she was going for wide-eyed innocence. With just a touch of defiance. It was the look she'd had on her face the last time he'd seen her five years before. He didn't want to look too closely at the memories that dredged up.

The newspaper was still lying on the desk, exactly as he had left it to go upstairs. He picked it up and tossed it towards her.

'Read that.'

He knew exactly the moment she registered what the photograph showed by the way that the colour shifted in her face and she bit down hard on her lower lip, white teeth digging into the soft pink. With an effort Nikos suppressed an urge to go to her and tell her to stop, to run his thumb over the damage she was inflicting on herself.

'Well?' he barked, when she had obviously taken in all she needed to, had dropped the paper back on to the desk and was preparing her answer.

'Well, what?'

What did he expect her to say? Sadie asked herself. And, perhaps more to the point, was there really any point in saying anything? From the thunderous dark frown on his face, he had clearly already tried her, acting as judge and jury, found her guilty and was now prepared to pronounce sentence.

'I don't know anything about this.'

A wave of her hand indicated the incriminating photograph. And she had to admit that she understood only too well just why he was so angry.

She had come downstairs, feeling shaken and on edge, apprehensive as to what was ahead of her. From the mood Nikos was in it was obvious that something had gone terribly wrong, though she had no idea what. The only thing that she could think of was that Nikos had had second thoughts about the passion they had shared in the night and was going to tell her it was all over. That had been bad enough. But this she was totally unprepared for.

'I *don't!*' she repeated when he turned a frankly sceptical look on her, making it plain that he had no intention of believing a word she said.

The picture was of the two of them in Cambrelli's just a few nights before. And it had been taken in the moment that she had leaned forward, stretched out a hand to touch him.

She hadn't actually made contact at the time, but from the angle the photograph had been taken it looked as if she had. And in the way their heads were inclined towards each other, eyes locked, seeing nothing else, no one else, the picture seemed to tell a story. A totally inaccurate story, but one that was encapsulated in the headline that ran along the top of the page.

'Together again!' it read, and the rest of the short article interpreted the scene in the way that she supposed it must have looked to an outsider. The sexy Greek billionaire and his marriage-shy ex-fiancée seemed to be back together, it claimed. They had met for a secret tryst in a down-market restaurant where they'd appeared to be getting closer by the second.

'Well, I don't see why you're so angry that we were seen together. I mean…'

Desperate to lighten the atmosphere, she tried a flippant shrug and knew immediately that she'd hit the wrong note.

'Look, it's not as if you really have a fiancée who would be worried or hurt by it.'

'Do you think that I give a damn about that?'

Sadie had no answer for him. Instead, she was busy trying to work out just what had happened.

'The storm…' she said slowly as realisation dawned. 'There was a storm that night, and what I thought was lightning…'

'Was in fact the paparazzo you had tipped off that we would be there.'

'What? No—of course not! How could you think that I would do that? Why would I do that?'

'Two words,' Nikos stated with deadly venom. 'Thorn Trees.'

'Th-Thorn Trees?'

Sadie frowned disbelievingly, rubbed hard at her temples where a headache was beginning to form. The abrupt transition from waking up happy and sensually contented to this fraught and tension-filled atmosphere was a terrible shock to her system. And now that Nikos seemed even more aggressive and antagonistic she was finding it even harder to think straight.

'I don't understand—why would this have anything to do with Thorn Trees?'

'Don't play games, *agapiti mou,*' Nikos scorned savagely. 'Do you think that I cannot add two and two together?'

'And come up with five, obviously!' Sadie flung back. 'Or more like five hundred. I don't see how you can make the connection, but I'm sure you're going to tell me.'

'Isn't it obvious?'

'Not to me. You're going to have to explain yourself.'

Nikos flung up his hands in an exaggerated expression of exasperation and his breath hissed in through his teeth in a sigh of dark irritation

'"I won't let it happen, Mum,"' he said suddenly. '"I've made sure of that. I've got everything in hand."'

For a second Sadie didn't realise what was happening, couldn't understand where the words had come from. But then she realised that he was quoting her own conversation with her mother on the phone the day before.

'I was talking about the wedding planning job I was doing—I thought I was doing—for you.'

Her legs felt distinctly unsteady beneath her so she pulled out the chair from the desk and rested her hands on the back of it, letting it support her as she faced him.

'I don't know what else you think I had planned.'

The furious glare Nikos shot her told her that he still believed she knew exactly what he was saying, but she refused to be intimidated by it, staring him out though it took all her courage to do so. Eventually he raked both hands through his hair again and muttered something dark and hostile in thickly accented Greek.

'The dinner at Cambrelli's was after you came to my office to ask—to beg—for a way of staying in Thorn Trees.'

'I know. And after you refused to help at all.'

'Exactly. In response to which you said that you would do anything—anything at all—if it meant you could stay in the house.'

The realisation of the truth hit her in the face like a slap, and she was so very grateful for the fact that she was supporting herself on the back of the chair as the shock of it made her head spin nauseously.

'You really believe that in order to get what I want I alerted the press to the fact that we were meeting—gave them a photo opportunity?'

The swift, sharp inclination of his dark head to one side was Nikos's silent acknowledgement that she was on the right track. But it still didn't make any sense that she could see.

'But I don't understand—why would that help me twist your arm over Thorn Trees?'

'Because we had been seen together. Because it was assumed—implied—that our relationship was back on.'

'But it isn't—wasn't…'

Which did she mean? Which was right? She really didn't know.

'We knew that. No one else. And not knowing that, how would it have looked if it became known that I had taken possession of Thorn Trees after all. That I had thrown my fiancée's mother and little brother out of their home? Perhaps out of spite for the fact that you had refused to get back with me again…'

'You think that I would have used this picture as some sort of moral blackmail—a bargaining tool to get what I wanted?'

'Why not? It is a technique worthy of your father at his best—or do I mean his worst? He would be proud of you, Sadie *mou*. You have clearly learned a great deal from him.'

'I've learned nothing!'

Raising her voice like this was probably a big mistake, but to be honest she didn't really care. She wanted to make her point as emphatically as she could.

'I've learned nothing from my father—and I wouldn't want to! The cold-blooded way he went about everything appalled me. I hated it. My father thought he could run people's lives—rather like you, in fact. It made my life a misery—my mother's too—and everyone else's around us!'

'And you expect me to believe that?'

'Do you know what?'

Sadie flung up her arms now, in a gesture that was very similar to the one that Nikos had used a few moments earlier—and expressing the same sort of exasperation.

'I don't really care! You're so obviously dead set against me—and so convinced that you're damn well right—it seems to me there's very little point in even trying to explain. I'm never going to persuade you of anything else. So I might as well just stop trying.'

And she'd have to admit that she lost Thorn Trees too, she acknowledged privately to herself. There was no way Nikos was going to let her stay in the house now, under any circumstances. She didn't dare to let herself consider that thought any further for fear that it would take all the strength from her. And she already felt as if she was fighting for her life.

'You're right,' Nikos conceded unexpectedly, shrugging his broad shoulders in a way that made her mouth drop open slightly in astonishment and disbelief. 'It really doesn't matter any more now. If anything, it makes things easier.'

And that was the last thing she had expected. So much so that she took a step back in shock, eyeing him warily, as if she believed that he might have changed shape and persona right in front of her, turning into some totally different, totally alien being right before her eyes.

'Easier in what way?'

He looked straight at her, those gleaming golden eyes locking with her confused green ones. And he actually smiled. But it wasn't a smile that warmed her in any way, or even lifted the atmosphere in the room. Instead it sent a cold, creeping sensation sliding down her spine in dread of what was coming next.

'When we marry, it won't be such a shock to the world—the gossip columns will already have had a field-day.'

Sadie shook her head in confusion. She couldn't have heard right.

'We aren't getting married.'

'Oh, but we are.'

Nikos put one hand down on the top of the desk, pressing hard on it as he leaned towards her.

'It's the obvious solution, isn't it?'

'Not to me. You haven't even asked me!'

'Do I need to ask?' he stunned her by saying. 'I told you—you are the only woman I've ever wanted to marry.'

And he truly thought that that made it all fine. The belief was stamped onto his dark features, drawing the muscles tight around his mouth.

'Yes, in order to have me in your bed!'

If she'd expected him to look mortified, even disconcerted, then she was very badly mistaken.

'And what better reason is there for being together?' he countered dismissively.

There's love, and caring for each other... But she didn't dare say it, couldn't even find the strength to open her mouth to speak the words. Obviously they had never crossed Nikos's mind, and were never likely to do so at any point in the future.

'We're great together sexually,' Nikos went on, confirming her fears. 'The best. You have to agree there. Last night proved that. I want more of that.'

'And me?' Sadie had to force the words from her tight and painful throat so they sounded raw and rusty, breaking apart at the edges. 'What do I get out of this?'

Again he looked stunned that she had to ask.

'Do I really have to tell you? You get to be my wife—to have all the wealth and luxury you could ever want. Everything you've ever dreamed of. I'll never look at another woman as long as we are together. And I'll give you Thorn Trees too—as a wedding gift. I'll sign it over to you on our wedding day.'

It was the fact that he thought it was enough that finished her. Nikos obviously felt he was offering her everything she wanted, so why was she even hesitating?

Because what he was offering was everything he thought she had ever dreamed of but nothing that she truly wanted.

She couldn't do it. It was her worst nightmare come true, possibly even worse than the last time he had wanted to marry her. Because at least then she had believed—had deceived herself—that he loved her. Now she no longer had even that comforting delusion.

'No.'

The stark rejection was all that she could manage. Besides, what else was there to say? There was no point in even trying to explain. The two of them were on opposite sides of a huge, gaping cavern, and there was no way at all of bridging the gap that yawned between them.

'Why not? After all, you were prepared to marry me for money once before. What's different now?'

If he had tossed a bucket of icy water right in her face then he couldn't have brought her to her senses any quicker. What was she doing even standing here like this, listening to him?

She had lost. That was the plain and simple fact. And the only thing she could hope for now was to get out of here with a shred of her dignity intact.

'What's different? Everything. Every damn thing. But I couldn't expect you to understand that.'

'Try me.'

Sadie had turned on her way towards the door, but those two words had her swinging back, looking him straight in the eye. If she had seen any sign there then, damn it, she might actually have tried. But Nikos's gaze was pure golden ice, no trace of emotion, no flicker of doubt to give her hope that they were even speaking the same language.

'You can't even see that it's the fact you have to ask that is the problem. If you think any woman would accept a proposal like that then you have to be out of your mind.'

Then, knowing that she had well and truly burned her boats, that she had to get out of here before she collapsed completely, she forced herself to continue her walk to the door, not daring to spare him even the briefest of glances.

'I'm going to my room to pack—and then I'm leaving—getting out of here. But don't worry. I don't expect you to get out the executive jet just for me. If you can order me a taxi to the airport, then I'll take it from there.'

CHAPTER ELEVEN

HE LET HER go.

Nikos made no response to her outburst, and he didn't even attempt to come after her, to try to stop her. He just stayed exactly where he was and watched in total silence as she walked away from him, down the corridor and up the stairs. And for that Sadie could only be intensely grateful.

If he had made one move to stop her or even said a single thing then she knew that she would have fallen apart, gone to pieces in the space between one heartbeat and another. But when he said nothing and simply let her go she managed to get to the top of the stairs before the tears that had been pushing at the back of her eyes spilled out on to her cheeks, and she had to pause for a moment to draw in a shaky breath, fight with herself for control.

He hadn't even thought her worth fighting for. She had turned down his proposal of marriage—such as it was—and that was that. There was nothing more to do or say. She had said that she was leaving and that was the only alternative left open to her. She didn't dare to think of what would happen when she got home and told her mother that they had to move out. But she would face that when the time came. For now, she had to pack.

It didn't take long. She hadn't brought very much with her, and she certainly wasn't going to stay around to make sure everything was put neatly in the case. As long as she emptied the room and got out of here, that was all that mattered. She didn't even expect to see Nikos again.

So it was a shock to her when, after a brief knock, the door swung open and Nikos came into the room. Sadie's heart jolted against her ribs at the sight of him. Just for a moment she couldn't stop herself from wondering…

But, no, of course he hadn't come upstairs to try and persuade her not to leave, or even to talk to her. Instead, his face more shuttered and closed off than ever before, his eyes hooded, he waved a hand towards the case that she had just fastened where it lay on the bed.

'This ready?'

'Yes.'

'Then I'll take it down for you.'

So he had come to help her on her way. To make sure that she left the villa as speedily as possible. At least she didn't feel she had to thank him for his consideration.

Instead she grabbed her handbag and jacket and followed Nikos down the stairs to the hall. No taxi, Sadie noted. Obviously it hadn't yet arrived. She just wished it would hurry up and get here. Every moment that she had to stay seemed to be dragged out beyond endurance, stretching her strength to its limits.

'You'll need these.'

Nikos was holding something out to her. Her laptop and her mobile phone. It was as she took the latter, preparing to drop it into her bag, that realisation dawned with a kick of shock.

'My mother!'

In the heady intoxication of the previous afternoon and night, the shock to the system that this morning had become, she had forgotten to phone and check how her mother was.

And now, checking her phone, she saw that she had forgotten to charge it up too. The battery was completely dead.

'Use the phone in the office.'

Nikos's voice make her start, glancing up at him with wide startled eyes.

'Are you sure?'

'Of course I'm sure. Do you think that the price of a phone call bothers me?'

The office was just as they had left it, the newspaper still lying opened on the surface of the desk. But somehow it was the other, earlier time they had been in there that now burned in Sadie's mind. She couldn't push from her thoughts the memory of how she had been half on and half off that polished surface, her clothes wildly disordered and her senses spinning off into ecstasies as she clung to Nikos's powerful form, her mouth melded to his.

Feeling the fiery colour rush up into her cheeks at just the thought, she grabbed at the phone in a fury of embarrassment. But just as she did so Nikos's hand came down on top of hers, making her start as the heat of his skin burned into hers.

'One thing,' he said abruptly, his voice harsh. 'This feud stops now. Here. It's over.'

'Do you think that I would say something to my mother that would incite that appalling hatred all over again? I just want to put it all behind me.'

She knew that the way she snatched her hand out from under his looked antagonistic, even hostile, but she felt as if her fingers might actually be scorched by the touch of his, so that she would branded for life if she didn't pull away.

Luckily Sarah was back on good form again, so the phone call to her mother took only minutes. Feeling both relieved and ill at ease, Sadie carefully replaced the receiver, glancing at the clock as she did so.

'What time is the taxi coming?'

'It isn't,' Nikos stunned her by saying. 'At least not yet. We still need to talk.'

'Didn't you say everything? No?'

She was stunned to see him shake his dark head. But then she thought she saw where he was going with this. The conversation she had just had with her mother.

'I know I didn't tell her—and I'm sorry. I couldn't do it like that, over the phone. But I promise you'll get the house back. We'll be out of there before you blink. We'll…'

The words faded into oblivion as some subtle change in his expression told her that that was not what this was about. He wasn't angry that she hadn't told Sarah they had to leave Thorn Trees. There was something else.

'Nikos…'

'Tell me about your mother.'

It was the last thing she had expected, and she knew that her consternation must show on her face as she stared at him.

'Tell me about your mother,' Nikos repeated. 'It seems to me that your problems with her are at the bottom of this situation. I know the signs.'

'What signs?'

'Tell me about your mother.'

He was clearly not going to concede an inch on this. And what could it hurt to tell him now? He had said the feud was over. She prayed that, for her mother's sake, he had meant it.

'She's ill,' Nikos said now.

'How did you…? Well, yes. She's—emotionally fragile. If you must know, she's agoraphobic—desperately so. She hasn't been out of the house in years. Not since George was born.'

She glanced nervously at Nikos, watching for his reaction. If he so much as looked shocked…

But Nikos simply nodded, his face calm, his expression attentive. With an elegant economy of movement he perched on the edge of the desk, one leg still resting on the floor, and waited.

'She—she had a breakdown after George was born—terrible postnatal depression combined with…with…'

'With the fact that her baby was not your father's,' Nikos put in, making Sadie blink in astonishment.

'How did you know?'

'It's the only thing that makes sense—all the secrecy about the child, the way your father behaved. Like a man betrayed. A man out to make the world pay for what had happened to him.'

'That was just how it was.' Sadie nodded sadly, remembering the dreadful fights, the constant yelling and screaming.

'Why didn't your mother leave him? Had her lover abandoned her?'

'He was dead. He died in an accident just before Mum found that she was pregnant. That was when my father found out too—and, well, everything together was just too much.'

'Did you ever find out who she had been seeing?'

'No. She would never say. And my father had made her promise that she never would. That was his condition for letting her stay. For not divorcing her. The only thing she ever told me was that he—her lover—drowned in a boating accident.'

'Over five years ago?'

What had she said to sharpen his tone, narrow his eyes like that?

'Is that important?'

But Nikos didn't answer her. Instead he was on his feet, pulling open a drawer in the desk.

'Do you have a photo of your brother?'

'Of George? Of course…' Rooting in her bag, she pulled out her wallet, opened it to where the passport-size picture was kept. 'But why?'

She took out the picture in the same moment that Nikos placed a large album on the desk, flicking through it until he found the photograph he wanted, one long bronzed finger pointing it out to her.

'Oh, my…'

Sadie let the picture she was holding drop down beside the one Nikos was indicating.

'It's George.'

'It's my Uncle Georgiou,' Nikos said flatly. 'When you were in here yesterday you commented on it specially, and since then it has been nagging at me. It was just before Georgiou died that your father really started to stick the knife into my father's company—it was one of the reasons why he was able to succeed so well so fast. Because when Dad was in mourning he was badly off balance—not focussing on business.'

'And my dad was hell-bent on revenge for Georgiou's affair with his wife!'

So much made sense now, in a way that it never had before.

'It wasn't just the feud—or rather it was that plus this new reason for anger, for revenge.'

And they had got caught up in it.

'That damn feud tainted every person it touched.'

Nikos's voice was filled with black anger and a touch of something else—something that Sadie would almost have labelled despair as he shook his dark head in disbelief over what had happened.

'But it really does end here.'

Suddenly he looked up, amber gaze burning straight into hers.

'It stops,' he said fiercely. 'And from now on things will be different. For a start, you will have no need to worry about Thorn Trees. The house will be my gift to your mother—and my cousin. And there will be more. Little George should have inherited all that his father had, and if he really is my uncle's son—and looking at this photo, I am sure that he is—then I will make sure he has what is his by right.'

'Thank you.'

Sadie made herself say it, though her tongue tripped up over the words. She found that her mind was seesawing from one emotion to another. She was full of relief for her mother, delight for George—but there was a terrible sense of uncertainty about what this would mean for herself. She had had to acknowledge that she had lost her chance of ever having Nikos love her. She had faced up to the prospect of a future without him and she had been prepared to leave. To head out into that future and try to cope with it as best she could. Now she saw that everything was going to be so much different. That with Nikos being George's cousin—George's family— inevitably he would want to be in the little boy's life. It was only right, only fair.

But it meant that she would frequently be forced to see this man she loved and who had never loved her. And she didn't know how she could handle that.

'It—it will mean a lot to my mother. She admitted to me recently that she adored George's father. That he was the love of her life. She was devastated when she learned he'd died.'

Suddenly something Nikos had said to start off this line of conversation came back to her, making her frown in confusion.

'When you asked about my mother—you said you knew the signs.'

The question she needed wouldn't form properly, but the urgency in her voice obviously hit home to Nikos and he nodded his understanding without her having to say any more.

'My father. I know what it's like to have to watch someone break down—to always feel that you need to check if they are all right. To worry that perhaps the depression will come back.'

'And this all stems from the same vile mess.'

She didn't have to ask, just as Nikos hadn't needed to ask her. His clouded eyes gave her the answer without words.

'When he lost everything—when your father took over everything and bankrupted him—it was soon after he'd lost his brother. Like your mother, he broke down. I came home one evening and found him…'

The way his face had lost colour warned that there had been something very wrong. Suddenly Nikos pushed himself from his seat on the desk and paced restively about the room, his actions like those of a wild hunting cat, caged up for far too long.

'I was early. I wasn't supposed to be there. He thought he had time.'

Suddenly Sadie thought she knew exactly what day Nikos had been talking about, and all the tiny hairs on the back of her neck lifted in fearful apprehension as Nikos paused in his restless pacing, standing by the window and staring out at the sea. But she was sure that those beautiful golden eyes saw nothing of the clear blue waves with their foamy white tops, the golden sands of the beach.

Nikos pressed his forehead against the window glass, closing his eyes in despair at his memories, and, seeing that, Sadie could not stay still at the other side of the room. In a rush she crossed to his side, reached out a hand and touched his arm, just above the elbow. It was all she dared do, even though her heart ached with misery at the way things had turned out.

Like their parents, both of them had been wounded, scarred by the dreadful feud between their families. But as a result of the fallout of that feud, a fallout that had tangled up their own lives, creating the mess they now lived with, neither of them could comfort the other properly.

'That was the day I rang you…'

The day when she had had second thoughts about her

father's warnings that Nikos was simply out to use her, to make her part of his revenge on the Carteret family because of the feud. She hadn't known then of his personal motives for making everything worse. She had broken off her engagement, cancelled her wedding at a day's notice, but she had wanted to at least try to talk to Nikos himself....

'You told me to go to hell.'

'I know.'

Nikos's sigh was weary, dragged up from somewhere deep inside him, and as he turned to her, his movements were slow and heavy, like those of a much older man.

'But what the hell else could I have done? I was there in a room with my father who thought he had lost everything. He'd got a gun from somewhere and he meant to use it on himself.'

'Oh, Nikos, no!'

It was worse than she had thought. Worse for Nikos and worse for herself.

Because of that phone call, and the way he had turned on her, she had moved herself firmly onto her father's side.

'I didn't know—and I believed that my dad was right. I begged him to help me, asked him to tell me how to handle things. He said that if I did as he told me, said exactly what he wanted me to say, then all would be well. He would even look after my mother, let her stay in the house. He would raise her baby as his own.'

And her father had given her the final, cruel words that she had tossed down the stairs to where Nikos was standing in the hall on that final day.

'I'm so sorry—I don't know how I could have said those dreadful things.'

'I do,' Nikos astounded her by replying. 'I know because I ended up getting caught in the same terrible mess. I was supposed to be helping my father, but I ended up getting so

obsessed with you that I couldn't think straight. I took my
eye off the ball—focussed on you, not the business. And then
when I found that while you and I were in that cottage, away
for the weekend…'

The look in his eyes told her without doubt exactly which
weekend. The one she had arranged. The one where, half
crazy with her physical hunger for this man, she had pushed
him into anticipating his marriage vows. The resulting explosion of passion had kept them both locked in sensual obses-
sion, barely even surfacing for food for the three days they
were there.

For the space of the three days in which her father had
finally made his move.

'I should have been there, checking on things, making sure
he made no mistakes. Instead, I was the one who made the
worst mistake.'

The 'worst mistake' being spending time with her. Sadie
flinched inside at the pain of his words.

'I felt so terribly guilty as a result. I *was* guilty, and that
guilt twisted me up inside. I blamed your family for everything that had happened—I blamed you.'

Pushing his fingers through his hair, Nikos pressed the
heels of his hands against his temples, as if to ease some in-
tolerable ache.

'So when you came to me for help—because your mother
needed a home where she could be safe—I just saw the opportunity to take my revenge. *Thee mou*, my darling, I thought
that I was immune to this damn feud and I was so proud of
being so. Now I see that I was eaten up with it all the time. I
thought the worst of you because that was what I expected
from a member of the Carteret family. But I wasn't dealing
with just one of the Carterets—I was dealing with you.'

Did he know what he had said? Sadie wondered, not daring

to ask the question for fear that, with the raw pain thickening Nikos's accent, she had misheard him and that 'my darling' had been something else entirely.

'You—you weren't completely to blame,' she stammered, feeling as if she was treading over delicate eggshells with infinite care. 'I had said some terrible things—done some…'

But Nikos was shaking his head again, his eyes dark and shadowed in a way that made her heart twist in pain.

'And even then I was deceiving myself. Even then I wasn't admitting to my real motives. I wasn't even acknowledging that revenge had nothing to do with it, not deep down. Deep down, from the moment I saw you again, I knew that I couldn't live without you in my life. That once I had you again I could never let you go. So I resorted to stupid subterfuge to get you here and keep you. I was sure that if we could just spend time together then it would be as it had always been.'

'It could—it was!' Sadie couldn't bear to let him go on berating himself any more. 'Didn't yesterday—last night— tell you something? That I wanted to be with you.'

'In my bed, perhaps,' Nikos responded heavily. 'But I wanted more than that. I wanted you in my life for good. And I was so desperate to do that that—to keep you with me—that I offered you anything—everything that I thought might keep you there. But I offered all the wrong things. You didn't want the house—or money…'

'No,' Sadie put in softly, her voice breaking suddenly as he reached out and took each of her hands in his, pulling her gently towards him. Her heart was racing so hard that it set her blood pounding in her ears, the sound like thunder inside her head. 'No, I don't want those.'

The hands that held hers tightened, drawing her even closer, so that they were almost touching, only their clasped hands coming between them, holding them just a breath apart.

The eyes that looked down into hers were blazingly intent, blindingly so. But now they were wide and clear, the clouds and the darkness burned away by the open sincerity that told her everything she needed to know.

'So now I'm going to offer you the only thing that really matters,' Nikos told her, his voice so deep, so serious, that it took her breath away, made her freeze into immobility, unable to blink or look away. 'Though the truth is that the only thing I have to give you, you already have. I gave it to you in the moment we met, but I never really knew it until now. As a result I've been lost and wandering—not knowing who to be or how to live.'

Suddenly, unexpectedly, he lowered himself slowly to the floor until he was on one knee at her feet, looking up into her face with his feelings clear and open for her to read.

'You have my heart, Sadie,' Nikos told her. 'You have my heart and my love—they are yours for ever, no matter what answer you give. I am yours. There is no other woman in the world for me. What I'm asking is will you be mine? Will you be my wife and help me to put this dreadful feud far behind us, to heal the hurts that it brought and create a future that is so different, so loving, that there will be nothing but bright days ahead of us?'

'Oh, Nikos…'

Sadie turned her hands in his so that she could hold him, draw him up again to face her, until she could look deep into his eyes and see the way they changed as she gave him her answer.

'You have my heart too, and I never, ever want it back. All I want is a chance to go into that future with you, to create those bright days and to love you as I have always wanted to do. And so of course my answer is yes. It never could be anything else. It's—'

But she never managed to get any more words out. Whatever she had been about to say was crushed into silence by the force and passion of the kiss that Nikos pressed against her lips. And as he swept her up into his arms, crushed her against him, she knew that no words were needed anyway.

Words were totally redundant when there were much better ways to express the way they were feeling.

'Can we go yet? Can we go?'

Little George was almost dancing on the spot in impatience, tapping his smart patent shoes on the floor and risking crumpling his crisp white shirt and pressed black trousers as he chanted his request over and over again.

'Can we go, pleeeease? I want to see Niko.'

'So do I,' Sadie told him, her smile mirroring that on her brother's face at the thought of the way that Nikos would be waiting for them, just a very short distance away on this special morning. 'And we'll be leaving very soon.'

George had adored his big cousin on sight, and in the time since they had first met that love had grown into a sort of idolatry as Nikos filled the role of the father the little boy had never had.

'But we just have to wait for—'

She broke off as the door opened and her mother, elegant in peach and cream, stepped into the room. Her eyes went straight to her daughter, taking in the full effect of the simple white sheath dress with its overskirt of lace, the simple wreath of flowers on Sadie's shining dark hair.

'You look gorgeous, my darling—every inch the beautiful bride. Nikos is going to be knocked for six when he sees you.'

'I hope so…' Sadie smoothed a hand down her dress as she drew in a deep calming breath. 'And what about you— are you OK, Mum?'

It was impossible to iron out the edge of concern in her voice as she studied her mother's face. Sarah looked calm and in control, but underneath her carefully applied make-up she was still slightly pale and drawn, revealing the effort she had made to be here. The therapist Nikos had found for her had worked wonders, and that, together with the new-found happiness that came from knowing all their worries about Thorn Trees and everything else were far behind them, had created an incredible transformation in her mother's life. But all the same the journey to Greece, to Icaros, was more than she had ever been able to imagine her mother could manage.

'I'm fine,' Sarah assured her now. 'I'm exactly where I want to be—by my daughter's side on her wedding day.'

'And I'm so happy that you're here with me.'

Happier than she could possibly put into words, Sadie told herself as she collected her bouquet of creamy roses. Today was literally the happiest day of her life. The day on which she was marrying the man she adored, and the day that marked once and for all the final ending of any last trace of the feud that had threatened to tear her and Nikos and their families apart.

Not only had she been welcomed into the Konstantos family, but George too had brought a new happiness to Nikos's father, the little boy's uncle. Petros had been overjoyed to find such a special link to his beloved dead brother in the little boy, and Sarah, as George's mother and the woman Georgiou had loved, had been gathered into the warmth and welcomed too.

'Can we go now?' George was chanting again. 'Is it time? I don't want to wait another minute.'

'It's time,' Sadie told him, keeping her bouquet in one hand as she held the other out to her mother. 'And I don't want to wait another minute, either.'

Arm in arm, with the little boy dancing around them, she and Sarah made their way out into the sunshine, taking the short walk towards the ancient wooden bridge, now beautifully decorated with flowers and ribbons that fluttered in the gentle breeze, leading to the open door of the tiny private chapel where Nikos waited for her.

Just for a moment, as she paused on the worn stone steps that led into the church, Sadie had a momentary flashback to the first time she had set foot inside the chapel. But that only lingered long enough for her to be able to drive it right out of her mind, knowing that such moments of doubt and insecurity were so far behind her now it was almost as if they had never happened. The promise of the happiness of her new life was now stretching out in front of her.

It took a moment for her eyes to adjust to the darkness inside the old building, but as soon as they did her gaze went straight to the tall, dark and powerful figure of the man standing at the altar.

Standing at the altar, waiting to make her his wife.

Immediately it was as if there was no one else in the place. As if the world and everyone in it had faded away and there was only this one man. The man to whom she had given her heart so completely that it was no longer a part of her but his to keep, to hold with him for ever.

'Nikos,' she breathed, tears of pure joy blurring his beloved image just for a moment.

It was impossible for him to have heard the sound of his name on her lips, but all the same in that instant something made Nikos turn and glance towards the back of the chapel. And the transformation that came over his face when he saw her standing there made her heart soar, her feet feel as if they were not touching the floor but floating inches above the worn stone flags.

'Sadie…'

She saw his lips move on her name, saw the smile that made his stunning eyes burn like bronze fire.

'Sadie—*kardia mou*—my love, my heart…'

When he held out both his hands to her, opening his arms wide to welcome her home, she didn't hesitate but practically flew the short distance down the aisle towards her future with the man she loved.

FOR REVENGE OR
REDEMPTION?

BY
ELIZABETH POWER

Elizabeth Power wanted to be a writer from a very early age, but it wasn't until she was nearly thirty that she took to writing seriously. Writing is now her life. Travelling ranks very highly among her pleasures, and so many places she has visited have been recreated in her books. Living in England's West Country, Elizabeth likes nothing better than taking walks with her husband along the coast or in the adjoining woods, and enjoying all the wonders that nature has to offer.

For Carol, Sheila and Roy

CHAPTER ONE

'OPENING nights are always nerve-racking, Ms Tyler,' the red-haired young woman with the clipboard told Grace reassuringly, pinning a microphone to the pearl-grey lapel of her designer jacket. 'But this gallery's going to do well. I just know it is!' Her raised eyes skimmed a wall of contemporary paintings, signed prints and ceramics in the tall, glass case immediately behind Grace. 'We're doing the exterior shots first, so you won't be on for a while yet.' She tugged gently at the lapel, running deft fingers over the smooth sheen of the expensive fabric, brushing off a pale strand from Grace's softly swept-up hair. 'There! The camera's going to love you!' the woman enthused.

Which was more than the press did! Grace thought, remembering the hard time they had given her after her split with her fiancé, wealthy banker's son Paul Harringdale, four months ago. Then the tabloid's comments about her had ranged from "butterfly-minded" and "fickle" to "the tall, slinky blonde who wasn't capable of making the right decision if her life depended upon it". It had all been cheap reporting—and the fact that that last remark had come from a journalist who had pursued her romantically without success wasn't worth losing sleep over—but it had hurt nevertheless.

'Good luck,' someone said in passing as the doors opened

and invited guests, critics and members of the art world started pouring in.

'Thanks. I'll need it,' Grace laughed over her shoulder, realising it was her friend, Beth Wilson, a curvaceous and vertically challenged brunette, as she liked to call herself; at four-feet-eleven, she assured everyone that life for her was always looking up. Also loyal and efficient, she was the woman Grace had appointed to run her small London gallery while she carried on with her main objective in life, which was to try to keep afloat the nationally renowned textile company that her grandfather had founded and which had run into serious problems since his death just over a year ago. And with no moral support from Corinne.

Since inheriting her husband's share of the company, Corinne Culverwell had made it clear that she wasn't interested in being actively involved in the business. Now, with showers of congratulations and good wishes seeming to come at her from every angle, Grace darted a glance around her as the launch party got under way, wondering why her step-grandmother—a name that always seemed inappropriate for a woman who was barely three years older than herself—had claimed that a prior engagement at the last minute prevented her from coming tonight.

Directing two well-wishers to the table where the champagne was being served, Grace noticed the camera crew packing up outside. She had to stay focused, she told herself firmly, steeling herself for the interview that was now imminent. *Stay calm. Relaxed.*

'Hello, Grace.'

A prickling tension stiffened her spine as those two softly spoken words dragged her round to face the man who had uttered them.

Seth Mason! She couldn't speak—couldn't even breathe for a moment.

She would have recognised him from his voice alone, a

deep, rich baritone voice with no trace of any accent. Yet those masculine features—strongly etched and yet tougher-edged in their maturity—were unforgettable too. How often had her dreams been plagued by the stirring images of that hard-boned face, those steel-grey eyes above that rather proud nose? The slightly wavy, thick black hair still curling well over his collar, with those few stray strands that still fell idly across his forehead.

'Seth…' Her voice tailed away in shock. Over the years she had both longed and dreaded to see him again, yet she had never expected that she would. Especially not here. Tonight. When she needed everything to go right for her!

From his superior height, his penetrating gaze locked onto hers and his firm, well-defined mouth—the mouth that had driven her mindless for him as it had covered hers—twisted almost mockingly at her discomfiture.

'How long has it been, Grace? Eight…nine years?'

'I—I don't remember,' she faltered, but she did. Those few fateful meetings with him were engraved on her memory like her five-times table. It had been eight years ago, just after her nineteenth birthday, when she had thought that everything in life was either black or white. That life was mapped out for her in just the way she wanted it to go and that anything she wanted was hers for the taking. But she had learned some hard lessons since then and none more painful than the ones she had suffered from her brief liaison with this man—when she had discovered that nothing could be taken without there being a price, and a very high price, to pay.

'*Don't* remember, or don't want to?' he challenged softly.

Flinching from the reminder of things she didn't want to think about, she took some consolation from realising that they were concealed from most of the party by the tall case of ceramics. She ignored his velvet-sheathed barb and said with a nervous little laugh, 'Well…fancy seeing you here.'

'Fancy.'

'Quite a surprise.'

'I'll bet.'

He was smiling down at her but there was no warmth in those slate-grey eyes. Eyes that were keener, more discerning, if that were possible, than when he'd been...what?... twenty-three? Twenty-four? A quick calculation told her that he would be in his early thirties now.

The tension between them stretched as tight as gut, and in an effort to try and slacken it she tilted her small pointed chin towards a display of watercolours by an up and coming artist and asked, 'Are you interested in modern art?'

'Among other things.'

She didn't rise to his bait. He had an agenda, she was sure, and she wasn't even going to question what it might be.

'Did you just walk in off the street?' His name certainly hadn't been on the guest list. It would have leaped out at her instantly if it had been. Nor was he dressed to kill like a lot of the other guests. He was wearing an open-necked white shirt beneath a leather jacket that did nothing to conceal the breadth of his powerful shoulders, and his long legs were encased in black jeans that showed off a lean waist and narrow hips, a testament to the fact that he exercised regularly and hard.

'Now, that would be rather too much of a coincidence, don't you think?' he supplied silkily, although he didn't enlarge upon how he had managed to cross the threshold of her little gallery, and right at that moment Grace was far too strung up to care.

Making a more obvious point of looking around her this time, she asked, 'Is there anything you fancy?' And could have kicked herself for not choosing her words more carefully when she saw a rather feral smile touch his lips.

'That's a rather leading question, isn't it?' Rose colour deepened along her cheekbones as images, scents and sensations invaded every screaming corner of her mind. 'But I think the answer to that has to be along the lines of once-bitten, twice shy.'

So he was still bearing a grudge for the way she had treated him! It didn't help, telling herself that she probably would be too, had she been in his shoes.

'Have you come here to look around?' Angry sparks deepened her cornflower-blue eyes. 'Or did you come here tonight simply to take pot shots at me?'

He laughed, an action that for a moment, as he lifted his head, showed off the corded strength of his tanned throat and made his features look altogether younger, less harshly etched. 'You make me sound like a sniper.'

'Do I?' *I wonder why?* Grace thought ironically, sensing a lethal energy of purpose behind his composed façade, yet unable to determine exactly what that purpose was.

The dark strands of hair moved against his forehead as he viewed her obliquely. In spite of everything, Grace's fingers burned with an absurd desire to brush them back. 'Still answering every question with a question?'

'It would seem so.' She was amazed that he remembered saying that, even though she hadn't forgotten one moment of those torrid hours she had spent with him. She met his gaze directly now. 'And you?' He'd been a boatyard hand from a poor background, manually skilled, hardworking—and far, far more exciting than any of the young men she'd known in her own social sphere. 'Are you still living in the West Country?' His nod was so slight as to be indiscernible. 'Still messing about with boats?' It was only her nervousness that made it sound so detrimental, but by the way those steely eyes narrowed he'd obviously taken it exactly the wrong way.

'It would seem so,' he drawled, lobbing her words back at her. 'But then, what did you expect from a young man with too many ideas above his station? Wasn't that what you as good as said before you went on to make me look an utter fool?'

She flinched from the reminder of things she had done when she had been too young and wrapped up in herself to know any better.

Defensively she said, 'That was a long time ago.'

'And that excuses your behaviour?'

No, because nothing could, she thought, ashamed, and it was that that made her snap back, 'I wasn't offering excuses.'

'So what are you offering, Grace?'

'You think I owe you something?'

'Don't you?'

'It was eight years ago, for heaven's sake!'

'And you're still the same person. Rich. Spoilt. And totally self-indulgent.' This last remark accompanied a swift, assessing glance around the newly refurbished gallery with its pricey artwork, fine porcelain and tasteful furnishings—which owed more to her own flair for design than to cost. 'And I'm still the poor boy from the wrong side of town.'

'And whose fault's that?' His whole hostile attitude was causing little coils of fear to spiral through her. 'It's hardly mine! And if you persist in this—this—'

'Dissecting of your character?' He smiled, clearly savouring her lack of composure.

'I'll have you thrown off the premises,' she ground out in a low voice, hoping that no one else could hear.

The lifting of a thick eyebrow reminded her of how ridiculous her threat was. His commanding height and solid frame gave him strength and fitness that put him light years ahead of anyone else milling around her little gallery. That oddly feral smile pulled at the corners of his devastating mouth again. 'Going to do it yourself?'

Unwelcome sensations ripped through her as she thought about physically handling him, about the way his hard, warm body had felt beneath her hands: the strength of contoured muscle, the sinewy velvet of his wet skin.

'I didn't think so,' he breathed.

He seemed so confident, so sure of himself, Grace marvelled, wondering what made him think he could just march in here and start flinging insults at her; wondering in turn why he hadn't moved on. He had seemed so ambitious—full of high expectations, determined. And it was that determination to have what he wanted that had made him so exciting to her...

'Why the Mona Lisa smile?' he asked. 'Does it give you some sort of warped satisfaction to know that life didn't turn out the way we thought it would—for either of us?'

Grace lowered her gaze so as not to see the smugness in his eyes. If he thought—quite wrongly—that she'd been mocking him for not amounting to much then he was clearly enjoying reminding her of a future she had taken so much for granted when she had been young and so stupidly naïve.

Trying not to let him get to her, and still wearing a wistful little smile, she uttered, 'Not as much satisfaction as it's clearly given you.'

He dipped his head in an almost gallant gesture. 'Then that makes us even.'

'Really?' She grasped a flute of champagne from the tray of drinks being offered to them, even though she had decided earlier to keep a clear head tonight. She noticed Seth shake his head quickly in silent refusal. 'I hadn't realised we were clocking up a score.'

'Neither did I.' His sensuous mouth curved from some inward amusement. 'Are we?'

The pointed question caught her off-guard and before she could think of a suitable response to fling back he went on. 'I stopped envying you, Grace. And people like you. I never did manage to master the art of using others in my bid to get the things I wanted, but I'm learning,' he told her with scathing assurance. 'Nor did I ever find it necessary to do what was expected of me just to impress my own elite little circle of friends.'

Her interviewer had finished his piece outside with the film crew and was talking to the producer on the pavement. Any minute now he would be in to talk to her.

How must she look? she thought, panicking, feeling totally harrowed after coming face to face with Seth Mason.

'If all you want to do is take out your frustrations and your disappointments on me just because things didn't turn out for you the way you thought they would…' Flushed, uncomfortably sticky, she inhaled deeply, trying to stay calm, stay in control. 'Then you could have chosen a more convenient time to do it! Or was your intention behind coming here tonight simply to unsettle me?'

He smiled, and his face was suddenly a picture of mock innocence. 'Now, why would I want to do that?'

He knew why; they both knew why. She wanted to forget it, but it was obvious that he never had. Nor was he going to, she realised despairingly.

'I was merely interested to see the newsworthy Grace Tyler's new venture for myself, although I understand that it isn't entirely new. I know that you inherited this shop some years ago and only recently had it transformed from a run-down, barely viable concern to this temple of fine art I see before me today.'

It was information he could have got from any sensation-seeking tabloid, Grace realised, but still she didn't enjoy the feeling that he, or anyone, for that matter, knew so much about her.

'Quite a diversion for you from the world of textiles,' he commented. 'But then you showed promise…in an artistic sense…' His marked hesitation told her exactly what he thought about the other traits of her character. 'Eight years ago. Let's hope you have more success with this—' his chin jerked upwards '—than you've had managing Culverwells—or any of your relationships, for that matter.'

Stung by his obvious reference to her recent broken engagement as well as the company's problems, Grace looked up into that hard, cold but oh, so indecently handsome face with her mouth tightening.

Had he come to gloat?

'My relationships don't concern you.' The only way to deal with this man, she decided, was to give back as much as he was giving her. Because it was obvious that a man with such a chip on his shoulder would never forgive her for the way she had treated him, even if she got down on her knees and begged him to, which she had no intention of doing! 'As for my corporate interests, I don't think that's any of your business, either.'

A broad shoulder lifted in a careless shrug. 'It's everyone's business,' he stated, unconcerned by her outburst. 'Your life, both personal and commercial, is public knowledge. And one only has to pick up a newspaper to know that your company's in trouble.'

The media had made a meal of the fact, accusing her and the management team at Culverwells of bringing the problems about, when everyone who wasn't so jaundiced towards her knew that the company was only another unfortunate victim of the economic downturn.

'I hardly think a boat hand from…from the sticks is in a position to advise me on how I should be running my affairs!' She didn't want to say these things to him, to sound so scathing about how he earned his living, but she couldn't help herself; she was goaded into it by his smug and overbearing attitude.

'You're right. It is none of my business.' His smile was one of captivating charm for the redhead with the clipboard who was standing with the gallery manager a few feet away, gingerly indicating to Grace that they were ready to interview her. 'Well, as I said, I wish you success.'

'Thanks,' Grace responded waspishly, aware of that undertone of something in his voice that assured her his wishes were hardly sincere. Even so, she plastered on a smile and crossed over to join her interviewer, wishing she was doing anything but having to face the camera after the unexpectedly tough ordeal of meeting Seth Mason again.

Outside in the cold November air, Seth stopped and watched with narrowed eyes over the display of paintings in the window as Grace faced a journalist who was renowned for making his interviewees sweat.

Smiling that soft, deceptive smile, she appeared cool, controlled and relaxed, answering some question the man asked her, those baby-blue eyes seeming to flummox her interviewer rather than the other way around.

She was as sylph-like as ever, and as beautiful, Seth appreciated, finding it all too easy to allow his gaze to slide over her lovely face, emphasised by her pale, loosely twisted hair, and her gentle curves beneath that flatteringly tailored suit. But she hadn't changed, he thought, as he felt the inevitable hardening of his body, and he warned himself to remember exactly what type of woman she was. She would play with a man's feelings until she was tired of her little game. The way she had dumped him and the last poor fool, her fiancé, was evidence of that. She was also still an unbelievable snob.

What she needed was someone to let her know that she couldn't always have her own way; someone who would demand respect from her, and get it. In short, what she needed was someone who would bring her down a peg or two—and he was going to take immense satisfaction in being the one to do it.

CHAPTER TWO

THE interview was over, and so was the party.

Grace breathed a sigh of relief.

The evening had gone well. In fact, Beth had taken several orders for quite a few of the paintings and sold one or two of the ceramics. The interview, too, had turned out satisfactorily, without her having to face any of the awkward questions she had been dreading. She should have been happy—and she was, she assured herself staunchly, except for that meeting earlier with Seth Mason.

She didn't want to think about it. But as she went upstairs to the flat above the gallery, having locked up for the night, long-buried memories started crowding in around her and she couldn't stop them coming no matter how hard she tried.

It had been shortly after her nineteenth birthday, during the last few weeks of her gap year between leaving college and starting university, when she had first met Seth in that small West Country coastal town.

She'd gone down from London to stay with her grandparents who had brought her up and who had had a summer home there, a modern mansion high in the wooded hills above the little resort.

On that fateful day that would stay for ever in her memory, she'd been out with her grandfather when he had decided to call into the little boatyard on the far side of town. She couldn't even remember why, now. But, while Lance Culverwell had been in the scruffy little office, she had noticed Seth working on the hull of an old boat. She'd noted the way his broad back moved beneath his coarse denim shirt, the sleeves of which had been rolled up, exposing tanned, powerful arms as he'd driven rivets hard into the yielding metal, unconsciously raking back his untameably black hair, strands of which had fallen forward tantalisingly as he worked.

When he turned around, she looked quickly away, though not in time for him to fail to register where her gaze was resting on the hard, lean angles of his denim-clad hips.

He didn't say anything. He didn't even acknowledge her presence with a smile. But there was something so brooding in those steely-grey eyes as she chanced another glance in his direction that she felt herself grow hot with sensations she'd never experienced before just from a man looking at her. It was as though he could see through her red crop-top and virginal-white trousers to the wisp of fine lace that pushed up her suddenly sensitised breasts, and to her skimpy string, the satin triangle of which began to feel damp from more than just the heat of the day.

The faintest smile tugged at one corner of his mouth— a sexy mouth, she instantly decided, like his eyes, and the prominent jut of his rather arrogant-looking jaw. She didn't acknowledge him, though, and wondered whether to or not. But then Lance Culverwell came out of the office with the owner of the boatyard, and she gave her smile to the two older men instead.

She didn't look back as she walked over to the long, convertible Mercedes that was parked, top down, the gleaming silver on the gravel like a statement of her family's position in life beside the older, far more modest vehicles that were parked there. Instinctively, though, she knew that his eyes were following her retreating figure, the way her hair cascaded down her back like a golden waterfall, and the not entirely involuntary sway of her hips as she prayed she wouldn't miss her footing in her high-heeled sandals all the way back to the car. She even begged Lance Culverwell to let her drive, and she pulled out of that tired-looking little boatyard with her head high and her hair blowing in the breeze, laughing a little too brightly at some remark her grandfather made, wanting to get herself noticed—wanted—and by *him*.

He wasn't right for her, of course. He was a mere boat hand, after all, and far removed from the professional type of young men she usually dated. But something had happened between her and that gorgeous hunk she'd exchanged glances with that day, something that defied cultural and financial differences, and the boundaries of class and status. It was something primeval and wholly animal that made her drive back from town in a fever of excitement, guessing that Lance Culverwell would be appalled if he knew what she was thinking, feeling—which was an overwhelming desire to see that paragon of masculinity who had made her so aware of herself as a woman again, and soon.

She didn't have long to wait. It was the following week, after she had been shopping in town.

Laden with purchases for a party her grandparents were giving, she was just starting up the hill, wishing she hadn't decided to walk down that morning but had brought her car instead, when one of her carrier bags suddenly slipped out of her hand just as she was crossing the road.

Making a lunge for it, and dropping another bag in the process, she sucked in a breath as a motorbike suddenly cruised to a halt in front of her and a black-booted foot nudged the first errant carrier to the side of the carriageway.

'Hello again.' The sexily curving mouth of the leather-clad figure on the bike was unmistakable: Seth Mason. She remembered her grandfather casually referring to him on the way home the previous week, and had hugged the name to her like a guilty secret. Her heart seemed to go into free fall as he spoke to her, then felt like it was beating out of control.

'You've bitten off more than you can chew.' He looked amused at her plight. His voice, though, was deep and so warm that she fell in love with it just standing there on that rural road as he bent to pick up the one bag she still hadn't retrieved and restored it to her flustered arms. 'You look as though you could do with a lift.'

Every instinct of survival screamed at Grace to refuse, to listen to the nagging little voice of wisdom that warned her that involving herself with this man would definitely be biting off more than she could chew! But everything about him was exciting, from his dark, enigmatic features to his hard, lean body and the heavy pulsing of the motorbike's engine between those powerful, leather-clad thighs.

'I'm Seth Mason…if you're wondering,' he stated dryly, after she deposited her bags in the pannier and sat astride the bike.

'I know,' she said, easing down her mini-skirt that had ridden up to reveal more golden thigh than she wanted him to see.

'Aren't you going to tell me your name?' A distinct edge crept into his voice as he added, 'Or do you think I should know it?'

Grace had laughed at that. 'Don't you?' she asked cheekily.

From the look he sent over his shoulder, he wasn't particularly impressed.

'I'm Grace,' she told him quickly in the light of his challenging, brooding gaze.

'Here.' He thrust a crash helmet into her hand. 'Put this on.'

'Do I have to?'

'If you want to ride with me, you do.'

He was responsible for her safety, that was what he was

saying. The thought of having his protection sent a little frisson through Grace.

Somewhat nervously she said, 'I've never been on a motorbike before.'

'Then hold on to me,' was his firm command.

Even now, letting herself into the flat, Grace could still remember the thrill of putting her arms around his hard, masculine body. Of laying her cheek against the warm leather that spanned his back while the bike had throbbed and vibrated like a live thing beneath them.

'Lean when I do!' he shouted back above the engine's sudden roar. 'Don't pull against me.'

Never in a million years! the young Grace sighed inwardly, utterly enthralled, though she kept her feelings to herself for the unusually lengthy journey home.

'You took the long way round.' She pretended to chastise him, stepping off the bike. Her legs felt like jelly and for more reasons than just the vibration, or the speed with which he had driven the powerful machine along a particularly fast stretch of road.

Something tugged at the corners of his mouth. 'Well, they do say a girl always remembers her first time.'

Her cheeks felt as though they were on fire as she took off her helmet and handed it back to him. 'I will. It was truly unforgettable. Thanks.' But her voice shook at the images his comment about a girl's first time gave rise to. What would he say, she wondered, if he knew that there never *had* been a first time in that most basic of respects? That she was still a virgin? Would he lose interest in her? Because she was sure there was interest there. Or would he regard her as a challenge, like a lot of the men she'd dated had, backing off when they'd realised she wasn't an easy lay?

He was looking at the impressive security gates, and the big house with its curving drive visible behind them, but as she moved to retrieve her purchases from the pannier he said, 'Would you like a hand carrying those in?'

Setting the electric gates in motion, she laughed, saying, 'I don't think that's really necessary, do you?' But then, impelled by something outside her usually reserved nature, she was shocked to hear herself adding provocatively, 'Or do you?'

It was a game she had been playing with him; she knew that now—in hindsight. Now that she had the benefit of maturity on her side. But she had wanted him, so badly, even while she'd known that a relationship with a man like Seth Mason was strictly taboo.

She cringed now as she thought about her behaviour at that time. Even so, she couldn't stop the memories from spilling over into every nook and cranny of her consciousness, no matter how much she wanted to hold them at bay.

'Exactly what do you want from me, Grace?'

She remembered those words like they'd been spoken yesterday as, helmet removed, he'd come round to the rear of the bike and helped recover the last of her bags.

She took it from him with a hooked finger, laughing, but nervously this time. 'Who says I want anything from you?'

He studied her long and hard, those penetrating grey eyes so disquieting that she was the first one to break eye-contact. Distinctly she remembered now how vividly blue the sky had been behind his gleaming ebony head, and how the colours of the busy Lizzies in the borders along her grandparents' drive had dazzled her eyes almost painfully with their brilliance as she averted her gaze from his unsettling regard.

'You know where to find me,' he drawled, turning away from her with almost marked indifference, so that she felt deflated as she moved along the drive.

The starting up of his bike was an explosion of sound that ripped through the air and which brought her round to see only the back of his arrogant figure as he shot off like an avenging angel down the long, steep hill. The roar of his engine seemed to stamp his personality on every brick and balcony of the quiet, prestigious neighbourhood, and seemed to linger long after he had gone.

She didn't go down to the boatyard again. She couldn't bring herself to be so totally brazen as to let him think she was actually chasing him, even though it was torture for her not to make some feeble excuse to her grandparents and sneak down into town to see him.

In fact it was completely by accident when she met him again. With her grandparents visiting friends farther afield for a couple of days, she was out walking alone, exploring the more secluded coves along the coast.

Climbing over a jutting promontory of rocks, she clambered down onto the shingle of a small deserted beach some way from the town. Deserted, except for Seth Mason.

On the opposite side of the beach, wearing a white T-shirt and cut-off jeans, he was crouching down, his back turned to her, doing something to the lowered sail of a small wooden dinghy.

Grace's first instinct was to turn and head quickly and quietly back in the direction she had come from, but in her haste she slipped, and it was the crunch of her sandals on the shingle as she fought for her balance that succeeded in giving her away.

He looked round, getting to his feet, while she could only stand there taking in his muscular torso beneath the straining fabric of his T-shirt and the latent strength of his powerful, hair-covered limbs.

'Are you going to join me?' he called across to her, sounding unsurprised to see her there, as if he had been expecting her. 'Or are you just a vision designed to lure unsuspecting sailors into the sea?'

She laughed then, moving towards him, her awkwardness easing. 'Like Lorelei?'

'Yes. Like Lorelei.' He was watching her approach with studied appreciation. 'Have you been sent here simply to bring about my destruction?'

She laughed again, but more self-consciously this time, because his masculine gaze was moving disconcertingly over the soft gold of her shoulders above her strapless red top, travelling all the way down to her long golden legs exposed by what she suddenly considered were far-too-short white shorts. 'Why do you say that?'

'Didn't she have a song so sweet it could make any man lose his course?'

She wondered if he was applying that analogy to her, and knew a small thrill in guessing that he probably was.

'And do you have one, Seth Mason?'

He turned back to the dinghy perched on its trailer, and started to hoist the sail, checking something in the rigging. With a hand shielding her eyes from the sun, Grace watched the breeze tugging at the small orange triangle.

'Do I have a what?'

Turning her attention to the bunching muscles in those powerful arms, she said, 'A course.'

Solid and purposeful, his work taking all of his attention, he didn't say anything until he'd drawn the small sail down again.

'Why,' he enquired suddenly, turning back to her, 'does everything you say sound like a challenge?'

She remembered being puzzled by his remark. 'Does it?'

'And why do you answer every question with a question?'

'Do I?' she'd exclaimed, and then realised what she'd said and burst out laughing.

As he laughed with her it seemed to change his whole personality from one of dark, brooding excitement to one of devastating charm.

Caught in the snare of his masculinity, she could only gaze

up at his tanned and rugged features; at the amusement in those sharp, discerning eyes; at those strong, white teeth and that wide, oh, so sexy mouth. Madly she wondered how that mouth would feel covering, pressing down on, plundering hers.

'Do you do anything else but mess about with boats?' Her voice cracked as she asked it. In her heady state she wondered if he might have guessed at the way she was feeling and wondered, mortified, if he might take her question as another kind of come-on, because where he was concerned she couldn't seem to help herself.

'That's about the size of it.' His tone reverted to that familiarly curt and non-communicative way he had of answering her, like he was challenging her to criticise all he did—the person he was.

She walked round to the other side of the dinghy. 'Is this one yours?'

A hard satisfaction lit his face at that. 'She's not worth much.' Lovingly he ran a hand over the boat's smooth contours, a long, tanned hand that had Grace speculating at how it might caress a woman's body. 'But she delivers what she promises.'

She sent him an oblique glance. 'And what's that?' she quizzed, wondering instantly why she had asked it.

Heavy-lidded eyes fringed by thick, black eyelashes swept over her scantily clad body, and there was a sensual curve to the hard, masculine mouth as he uttered in a deeply caressing tone, 'Just pure pleasure.'

And he wasn't just talking about sailing his boat! There was a sexual tension between them that screamed for release, unacknowledged but as tangible as the hard shingle beneath her feet and the sun that played across her face and bare shoulders.

To break the dangerous spell that threatened to lead her into a situation she didn't know how to handle, she searched desperately for something to say. Remembering his reference to the sea-nymph, earlier and deciding that there was much more to him than she could possibly guess at, without thinking she found herself suddenly babbling, 'Where did you study the romantic writers?'

'I didn't.' He started pushing the boat towards the water's edge. 'Not everyone's lucky enough to go to university.' She wondered if that remark was a dig at her, and her family's wealth and position, but she let it go. 'I have a widowed mother.' Foster mother, as it had turned out. 'And foster siblings to support.' The boat was down in the water then, released from its support, bobbing on the gentle waves. 'I pick things up.'

Nothing would escape him, Grace decided, before he said, dismissing the subject, 'Right. She's ready.' He was holding the rope that was still attached to the trailer. 'Do you like the water?' he threw back over his shoulder. 'Or would it be another first for you if I took you out for a spin around the bay?'

'Are you asking me?' Her heart had started to beat like crazy.

'Is that a yes?'

She nodded, too excited because he'd asked her to say anything else. But quickly, as he leaped into the boat, she slipped off her sandals and started wading in.

'You're right, this is a first. I've never been in a dinghy before,' she gabbled, too conscious of the callused warmth of the hand he extended to help her, although she couldn't avoid adding with a provocative little smile as she was climbing in, 'My grandparents have a yacht.'

Suddenly she was being yanked down so forcefully beside him that she gave a little scream as the boat rocked precariously, and she had to make a grab for the soft fabric of his T-shirt to steady herself.

'Now why doesn't that surprise me?' he drawled.

Caught for a moment in the circle of his arms, aware of the deep contours of his chest and the heavy thunder of his heart beneath, she thought that he was going to kiss her as he dipped his head.

Instead, with his lashes coming down to hide any emotion in those steel-grey eyes, he said, 'Take the rudder while I get the sail up,' before moving away from her, leaving her fiercely and inexplicably disappointed.

It was an unforgettable afternoon. They sailed until the sun began to dip towards the sea while they seemed to talk about nothing and everything. She learned about his background—how he had never known his father and how he had been given up by his mother when he was three years old; about the orphanages he'd lived in and the foster homes. He had been with the family he was living with now, he told her, since he was fifteen. Now they were *his* responsibility, he stated with a surprising degree of pride. Just as they had made him theirs in the beginning.

He reminded her of how she had asked him earlier if he had a course, and he told her of his interest in architecture and his intention one day to build a new house for his foster mother. Marina-side, he said. With a view of boats from every balcony.

She laughed at that and said, 'All yours, of course!'

He didn't share her laughter, lost as he was in his personal fantasy. 'I think I'll put it there,' he speculated, pointing to the piece of derelict industrial wasteland where the tall chimneys of a disused power-station created a blot on the landscape.

'There?' She frowned, wrinkling her nose in distaste. 'I don't think she'd thank you for that!' She laughed again.

'And what about you? Do you have a dream, Grace?' His tone was slightly off-hand as though he didn't think too much of her making fun of his dreams. 'Or do you have so much that there's nothing left worth striving for?'

'No. Of course not!' she stated indignantly. 'I intend to settle down. Marry.'

'What—some ex-public-school type that Daddy's vetted who'll give you two-point-five children and a houseful of business associates to entertain?'

She didn't tell him that her father didn't figure in her life, that he'd given up his paternal duties after she'd caused her mother's death simply by being born. Those things were too private—too personal—to share with a total stranger, however handsome or amazingly sexy he might be.

Instead, guessing that it was mere envy that made him speak so derisively of her future, she asked, 'And what's wrong with that?'

'And that's all you intend to do?'

'No,' she argued, wondering why he made it sound so mundane, unromantic, as she watched him lowering the sail. 'There's the company. I'm earmarked to follow in my grandfather's footsteps one day.'

'Ah, yes, the company. And that's it—cut and dried? With no deviating from the pre-arranged course, no surprises, no dreams of your own?'

'Dreams are for people who crave things they haven't a hope of ever attaining,' she stated, feeling a little piqued. 'We inhabit different worlds. In mine the future's carved out for us, and that's the way I like it.'

'Suit yourself,' he said dismissively, giving all his attention then to securing a rope around a mooring buoy, while Grace had been glad to let the subject drop.

A little later, when he was leaning back relaxing for a few minutes with his face to the sun, she took a small sketch-pad from the big silver beach-bag she'd brought out with her that morning and drew a cormorant sitting on a rock drying its outstretched wings in the early-evening sun.

'You're good. You're very good,' Seth praised over her shoulder, making her clasp the drawing to her, warmed by his compliment, but suddenly terribly self-conscious at her efforts.

'You're too talented to be embarrassed about it. Let me see,' he insisted, but in reaching for her pad his fingers accidentally brushed the soft outer swell of her breast beneath her top, and it was that which had put the spark to the powder keg waiting to blow.

'Would you care for a swim?' His voice was suddenly thickened by desire, the grey eyes holding hers communicating a message that was as sensual as the feelings that were raging through her.

'I—I don't have any swimwear,' she responded, excitement coiling in her stomach.

His mouth compressed wryly. 'Neither do I.'

She looked away from him, suddenly nervous as she'd laid down her sketch pad. 'OK. But turn around.'

He laughed, but did as she requested, while she made short work of stepping out of her shorts and pulling her red bandeau-top over her head.

Without looking at him, she stepped nimbly out of the boat and plunged into the sea, gasping from the unexpected coldness of the water.

Coming up for air some way from the dinghy, she heard the deep plunge of Seth's body breaking the surface of the water just behind her.

They were moored near a small cove with a beckoning crescent of soft golden sand. Above and around it rose the sheer rugged face of the cliffs, making the small beach inaccessible to anyone without a boat.

Scrambling ashore first, Grace stood there on the wet sand in nothing but her flesh-coloured string, wondering how she could feel so free, so uninhibited. What she hadn't reckoned on was the impact of Seth's masculinity as he emerged from the water, hair plastered to his head, rivulets cascading over his hair-coarsened chest and powerful limbs; he was like some marauding sea-god, bronze from head to toe and unashamedly potent in his glorious nakedness.

None of the men Grace knew would have dared to walk naked like this, and she could only stand there and let her eyes feast on the sheer perfection of his body.

She should have crossed her arms over her own nakedness, turned away, but it didn't even occur to her—and anyway, she couldn't have torn her eyes away from him even if she'd wanted to.

Instead, raising her arms, she slipped her hands under the wet sheet of her hair, lifted it up and let her head tip back, revelling in the proud glory of her femininity.

She knew how she would look to him with her body at full stretch, the opposite to everything he was. Her long legs were silky and golden, her flat stomach smooth between the gently curving bowl of her hips and her breasts high and full, their sensitive tips hardening into tight buds from the excitement of all that she was inviting.

He came up to her and she lifted her head, her blue eyes beneath her long, wet lashes slumberous with desire, a desire such as she had never known before.

He didn't say a word and Grace gasped from the wet warmth of the arm that was suddenly circling her midriff, pulling her against him. The damp matt of his chest hair was a delight against her swollen nipples; he was already erect, and she'd felt the thrusting strength of his manhood against her abdomen.

His breath was warm against her face as his other hand shaped its oval structure; his fingers, first tender, then turning into a hard demand as they capped the back of her head, tilting her mouth upward to accept the burning invasion of his.

His hands moved over her with such possessive mastery that she became like a wild thing in his arms, her pleasure heightening out of control, as he slid down her body to take first one and then the other of her heavy, throbbing breasts into his mouth.

There was no need for words. She scarcely knew him, but she didn't need to know any more. From that first instant when their eyes had met in that boatyard, she had known instinctively that he was destined to be the master of her body. And when he peeled off her wet string and laid her down on the sand, positioning himself above her, she knew that every glance, every word and every measured sentence that had passed between them since they met had all been a prelude to this moment—the moment when he pushed through the last boundary and the taboo that separated them to claim the surprisingly painless gift of her virginity.

It had all been her own fault, Grace thought now as she went through into her rather bijou kitchen to fix herself some supper, berating herself, as she had done so many times over the years, for the way she had encouraged him. But as she filled her kettle, reached into the fridge and took out a carton of milk, some cheese and margarine, then hunted around for her tin of crackers, she knew that she hadn't had it in her power to stop it happening.

Her lower abdomen tightened almost painfully as she recalled how tender a lover Seth Mason had been even then, as a very young man—which led her to the reluctant speculation of just how experienced he would be now, until she realised what she was doing.

Did she care? He might be married, for all she knew. And, even if he were, what was it to her? Now? After all these years?

Finding the crackers, she started to spread margarine over one of the small discs with such vehemence that it split in several places, sending a shower of brittle crumbs across the worktop.

A mild little curse escaped her as she went to grab a piece of kitchen roll and dampen it under the tap.

What she had felt for Seth Mason had been crazy and totally irrational, a teenager's crush on someone who merely excited her because she knew her family wouldn't approve. Forbidden fruit—wasn't that what they called it? Her brows knitted in painful reverie as she began mopping up crumbs from the work top.

In spite of that, though, she had made a date with him for the following evening, arranging to meet on the beach where his boat was kept, because her grandparents were back by then and she had strictly forbidden him to pick her up from the house.

But she had forgotten the dinner party that she had been expected to attend with her grandparents that evening, which she hadn't been able to get out of, and she'd had no way of contacting Seth without anyone finding out. She'd forgotten to get his mobile-phone number, and she hadn't been able to ring him at the boatyard as she'd learned that the owner— his boss—and her grandfather were old friends. So she had broken their date without a word—no message of regret, no apology. Which would have been rude enough, she thought, straightening up and dropping the soiled kitchen-paper into the bin, without that final blow to his ego.

The following day she had seen him again when she'd gone down to town with her grandfather and Fiona, the daughter of a neighbour just a couple of years older than Grace who had elected to come with them.

Having left her grandfather at the newsagent's, Grace was walking along the high Street with Fiona when she suddenly looked up and saw Seth coming out of a shop.

Seth saw her too, and started to close the few yards between them, but then he held back, waiting for her to make the first move. She noticed the burning question in his eyes: *where were you last night?* No one with half an eye could have mistaken his smouldering desire for her that he made no attempt to hide.

A flame leaped in her from the memory of their mutual passion, of his hard hands on her body and the thrusting power of his maleness as he had driven her to a mind-blowing orgasm. But panic leaped with it, along with shame and fear of anyone finding out that she'd been associating with him and telling her grandfather. Fiona Petherington was a terrible gossip, as well as the biggest of snobs. 'Look at the way that boy's looking at you!' she'd remarked witheringly. 'Who is he? Do you know him?'

'Oh, *him*,' Grace remembered answering, as coolly as she was able to. 'Just some boat boy who's been sniffing round me. Quite sexy, if you don't mind slumming it.' Then she'd cut him dead and walked straight past him—and as she passed she realised from the look on his face that he'd overheard.

The memory of her behaviour that day still made her cringe. But she had paid for it less than ten minutes later. Having left her snobbish companion talking to two other neighbours that they had bumped into outside the chemist's, she popped across the road to the bank. She didn't know whether Seth had followed her or not but as she came out of the building he was striding up the steps outside.

She could still feel the angry bite of his fingers around her wrist as he drew level with her, could still see the condemnation in those angry eyes.

'Slumming it, were you? Is that what you thought you were doing with me down there in the sand?' It was a harsh demand, but low enough so that anyone passing couldn't hear. 'You think you're so high and mighty, don't you?' he breathed when she struggled free without answering, shockingly aware of Lance Culverwell coming up the steps to meet her. 'Well, go ahead, have your five minutes of amusement. But don't think that anything we did on that beach was for any other reason than because I knew I could!'

Those words still lacerated her as much as they had then, even though at the time she had known she deserved them.

Making love with him had been so incredible for her that, crazily, even after her shameful treatment of him, she'd wanted to believe that they had been incredible for him, too.

But Lance Culverwell had had his suspicions about what had gone on. His interrogation had been relentless, and there had been rows back at the house. The following morning she had been packed off to London with her grandmother and she had never seen Seth again. Until today.

Pushing back the plate of crackers and cheese that she suddenly had no appetite for, she tried telling herself not to think about Seth Mason, to forget about him altogether. She hadn't seen him in eight years before he had turned up at the gallery this evening, so there was no reason why she was ever likely to see him again.

Yes, she'd acted abominably, Grace admitted, but that was before she'd learned that pleasure, however fleeting, had to be paid for. Because six weeks after their uninhibited passion on that beach she had discovered that she was pregnant. That she was having Seth's baby. Seth Mason, who wasn't good enough even to be seen out with in her and her family's opinion, was going to be the father of her child!

CHAPTER THREE

'WHAT do you have to say about the dawn raid on Culverwells, Ms Tyler?' A microphone was thrust in her face and cameras flashed in a bid to capture the slim young blonde in the scooped-necked black t-shirt, combat trousers and trainers whose arm, draped with a casual jacket, was already reaching out to the revolving door.

'No comment.' She'd come straight in from New York and she couldn't deal with the press now, not while she was tired, jet-lagged and wondering what the hell had been going on while she had been away. She would deal with them later, she decided, when she had had a chance to speak to Corinne. But her grandfather's widow hadn't been answering her calls, either at home or on her mobile. Grace knew that the only way anything could have happened to Culverwells was if Corinne had been behind it.

'Surely you must have some statement to make? There will be changes in management—redundancies—surely?'

'I said, no comment.'

'But you can't really think…?'

Their persistent questions were mercifully cut off by the revolving door. She was inside the modern, air-conditioned building, the head office of the company that still bore her grandfather's name, even though it was in public ownership.

The silver-haired, moustached features of Lance Culverwell gazed down at her from the huge framed portrait in the plush reception area and, grabbing a moment to steady herself, Grace gazed back at it with tears of anger and frustration biting behind her eyes.

Oh, Granddad! What have you done?

It had been a shock to everyone when he had died last year and left everything he had, including his company shares, to his bride of two years. Not that Grace had begrudged Corinne anything; she'd been Lance Culverwell's wife, after all. But her grandfather had been so smitten by the ex-model that he couldn't have—or wouldn't have— even contemplated anything like this happening, Grace thought despairingly.

A *dawn raid*, that journalist outside had called the takeover, giving rise to a picture in Grace's mind of masked men on horseback brandishing rifles, intent on plundering the company's safe.

If only it were that simple! she thought giddily, clutching her bum bag—which was the only piece of luggage she hadn't instructed the taxi driver to drop off at her flat—as she took the executive lift to the top floor.

'Grace! I tried and tried to reach you...' The portly figure of Casey Strong, her marketing manager, rushed forward to meet Grace before she had barely stepped out of the lift. Grey-haired and due for retirement any day, he was flushed and out of breath. 'Your phone was off.'

'I've been in the air!' She had come straight from the airport, having spent most of her time in New York trying to persuade one of their best customers not to take their business away from Culverwells. It was a PR job that hadn't yet produced the result she wanted, as the company's governing body was taking time to consider what its future action would be.

'Grace! You're here at last!' It was Simone Phillips, her PA, who knew the problems that Culverwells was facing as well as anyone. It was the middle-aged, matronly Simone, who had finally managed to get hold of her with the shocking news of the takeover just as Grace had been coming through customs.

'It's Corinne. She's sold out!' the woman declared, confirming Grace's worst suspicions. 'And so has Paul Harringdale—your ex.' Paul had had a big enough stake in the company to give him and Grace an equal share with Corinne. Which was why Lance Culverwell had probably thought his company would be in safe hands and his granddaughter well provided-for, Grace realised bitterly; he would never have dreamed she would terminate her engagement as she had amidst a good deal of adverse publicity.

'We've got a new CEO, and there's already talk of a massive shake-up in upper management so he can get his own board up and running, like, *yesterday*!' she told Grace dramatically. 'The only up side is that he's gorgeous and single, which means he's probably as ruthless as hell and will probably be ousting us all at the first opportunity!'

'Over my dead body!' Grace resolved aloud, pushing wide the door to the board room which had been standing ajar. To meet a sea of new faces all swivelling in her direction as her fighting words intruded on something the new CEO had been saying.

'If that's the way you want it,' a deep voice, ominously familiar, told her from the far end of the table. 'But it's usually my method to do these things without anyone's actual blood on my hands.'

As the tall, impeccably dressed man in the dark suit and immaculate white shirt stood up, Grace's mouth dropped open.

Seth Mason!

'Hello again, Grace.' His deep, calm tones only emphasised the vortex of confusion that her mind had suddenly become.

It *was* Seth Mason. But how could it be? How could he have made the leap from a boat-fitter, or whatever he had been, to this international business-mogul? Because that was what Simone had called the man who had taken over when she had reached Grace so desperately on her mobile phone just after she'd stepped off that plane. And there was no doubt that Seth was the new CEO.

'Do you two know each other?' Grace wasn't sure where the question came from, only half aware that one or two of the older men had risen to their feet when they had realised who she was. She could feel everyone's eyes skimming over her crumpled and totally inappropriate clothes.

The dynamo at the opposite end of the table raised an eyebrow in mocking query. He was waiting for her response, which she was too dumbfounded to give.

'Oh, I think Ms Tyler will tell you—we go way back.'

She was still standing there near the door, unable to think properly, unable to speak; her only coherent thought was that Corinne obviously hadn't had the courage to speak to her until Grace had found out for herself what had happened.

'Can I have a word with you?' She couldn't believe how squeaky her voice sounded.

The subtle lift of a broad shoulder was the action of a man who couldn't be fazed. 'Fire away.'

In private, her eyes demanded.

The new man in charge glanced around at the others members of his team.

'Would you excuse us?' There was no disputing the depth of command in Seth Mason's voice.

Chair legs scraped over the polished floor as everyone complied. To Grace it seemed like for ever before they had all filed out.

'You had something you wanted to say?' he prompted when the door closed behind the last of them, leaving her alone with him in the room where all the major decisions were made.

Yes, she did, she had a lot to say to him! But his smouldering sexuality was something she hadn't reckoned on being so disturbed by, now that there was no one else around.

Images swam before her eyes of the way he had been eight years ago—of the feel of warm leather as he'd drawn her back against him where she'd sat astride that bike; of the warmth of his breath on her throat as one sure, strong hand had slid up to cup her breast, already too sensitive from his attentions...

'Why didn't you tell me?' she challenged angrily, dumping her jacket and bag down on the table and trying not to let his raw masculinity affect her. 'You must have known about this two weeks ago, that night you turned up at my gallery! Why didn't you say anything about this then?'

'And spoil the surprise?'

Of course. That was the whole point of takeovers like this—so the company being taken over wouldn't have time to organise any opposition to it. Grace gritted her teeth, her breathing shallow, breasts rising and falling sharply beneath her T-shirt.

'You led me to believe...' That he was still working in that boatyard. That he was...She couldn't think clearly enough to remember exactly what he had said. 'You let me think...'

'I did nothing of the sort,' he denied coldly. 'You jumped to your own conclusions with that discriminating little brain of yours.' A humourless smile curved his mouth as he came around the long table. 'What is it they say about giving someone enough rope?'

Grace raked her fingers agitatedly through her hair. It must look a mess—*she* looked a mess, she thought, standing there like a street urchin in her own boardroom. The hasty clean-up she had managed in the cramped washroom on the plane did nothing to make her feel adequately groomed beside his impeccable image.

'Well, you've come a long way, haven't you?'

'Not nearly far enough yet. Not by a long chalk.' Hostility seemed to emanate from every immaculately clothed pore.

'What do you mean?' Grace challenged, eyeing him warily.

He uttered a soft laugh. 'I mean I've waited a long time for this moment, and I intend savouring every satisfying minute.'

Unconsciously, she moistened her lips. 'Is that what this takeover's all about? Revenge?'

He laughed again, a harsh, curt sound this time. 'I prefer to call it making the most of one's opportunities.'

'What? Vindictively buying up enough shares so that you could steal my grandfather's company from under my nose?'

'Vindictive? Possibly. But not *stolen*, Grace, *acquired*— and quite legitimately. And hardly from under your nose. You've been enjoying yourself in New York for the past week or so, I understand, so you can hardly expect a man in my position not to salvage the spoils when you go off designer shopping—or whatever it is a woman like you does alone in the Big Apple—while your ship is sinking.'

'I didn't desert. And Culverwells isn't sinking.' *If only it wasn't!* she thought despairingly. *Nor was I 'designer shopping'!* she wanted to fling at him. But she decided that it wouldn't be worth the time or the effort, any more than it would be to tell him that she had sorely needed any free time she might have had in New York, as it was the first real break she had taken in the past eighteen months. 'OK. We'd hit a slump. But we would have pulled ourselves out of it eventually. We were surviving.'

'A pity your shareholders didn't share your confidence. It's clearly that bury-your-head-in-the-sand attitude that has put Culverwells into the state it's in today. Or have you been too busy with your rich boyfriends and your fancy little gallery that you didn't recognise disaster when you saw it?'

There was a glass of water on the table by the note pad in front of a vacated chair, the back of which she hadn't realised she was clutching. She had to restrain the strongest urge to pick the glass up and fling the contents right into his smug and incredibly handsome face.

'Don't even think about it,' he warned softly, disconcertingly aware.

'I've never buried my head in the sand. None of us has!' she retaliated fiercely, ignoring his pointed reference to the company she kept. 'It's been down to global forces and the dropping off of sales because the market's been depressed. It still grates, doesn't it? That I was born to all this when you— you were…'

'What? Not good enough to tread the same ground you walked on?'

'I didn't say that.'

'You didn't have to.'

No, she had made her opinion of him quite clear with those disparaging comments she hadn't meant him to hear before simply ignoring him in the street!

She couldn't deal with thinking about that right now. In fact, she could only deal with the shame of it by tossing back, 'So you think my team and I are just going to lie down while you sit at that table, lording it over us and throwing your weight around?'

'I don't actually care what you do, Grace,' he assured her, his body lean and hard as he moved purposefully towards her, as hard as those grey eyes that didn't leave hers for a second. 'And may I remind you that there was a time—however short—when my weight wasn't something you were totally averse to?'

A rush of heat coursed through Grace's veins, bringing hot colour up over her throat into her cheeks. Unbidden, those images surfaced again, and she saw him as he had been on that beach, those long fingers marked with grease as he'd worked on his dinghy. She smelled the salt of the sea air, felt the sun's warmth caress her skin, and then felt the thrill of that hard, masculine body pressing her down, down into the sand.

'That was a mistake,' she said shakily.

'You're darn right it was. On both our parts. But, as the saying goes, None of our mistakes need ever be permanent.'

'Meaning?' He was so close now that her breath seemed to lock in her lungs.

'Meaning you taught me a lot, Grace. I should be eternally grateful to you.'

'For what?'

'For showing me exactly how to handle women like you.'

A sharp emotion sliced through her, piercing and unexpected. Evenly, though, she said, 'You don't intimidate me, Seth, if that's what you're trying to do. And, as for salving that macho ego of yours, I think you managed that quite adequately eight years ago.'

Grace wasn't sure if he needed to be reminded, but those heavy eyelids drooped and a cleft deepened between those amazing eyes.

Seth felt momentarily uncomfortable at the reminder of having said something that, even then, was beneath his usual code of ethics. He couldn't even remember the exact words he had used, only that they had been a flaying retaliation for the way she had treated him.

'Yes, well…' He was regaining his cool, reclaiming the upper hand—which was what he needed to do, he reminded himself, with this calculating little madam. 'No man appreciates being snubbed by someone who only forty-eight hours before was sobbing with the pleasure of having him inside her.'

A deep throb made itself felt way down in her lower body. Surely she couldn't still be attracted to a man who with one swoop had just seized all that her grandfather had worked for—and whose only motive, where she was concerned, was to seek revenge?

'So this is how it's going to be.' His abrupt return to business put her off-balance to say the least, before he went on to give her a brief résumé of his plans for Culverwell's. 'I shan't make any unnecessary redundancies, unless I see areas of overstaffing or anything that will be detrimental long-term to the company and its other employees if I desist. I'll keep you on as my assistant—I can't deny that your expertise in the field of textiles will be invaluable. If you co-operate and accept my leadership, you won't have anything to worry about where your job is concerned. If you don't...'

'You'll have me fired, right?'

He didn't affirm or deny that statement. His narrowing eyes, though, resembled hard chips of steel, and harsh lines suddenly bracketed his mouth.

'Like your grandfather was instrumental in doing to me?'

Grace frowned. 'What are you talking about? You didn't work for my grandfather.'

'Directly, no, but he had interests in that boatyard, and enough clout with its owner to see that I was swiftly dispatched for even daring to breathe on his precious granddaughter, let alone lay my rough, rude hands on her supposedly chaste little body.'

His derision at the kind of girl he thought she was stung more than she wanted to admit. He didn't know she'd been a virgin. It had all been so easy; how could he have known?

'I—I didn't know.' She was shaking her head now in horrified rejection at Lance Culverwell ever stooping to do what Seth was accusing him of—and because of her. 'Really, I didn't.' But it would explain Seth's driving motive all these years, she realised—to get even with her family.

'Is that contrition I see in your eyes, Grace? Surely not! It really doesn't become you.'

'Why? Because you think I'm not capable of any feeling?' Surprisingly, the notion that he could even consider that cut deep—but it was just her pride that hurt, she convinced herself. Nothing else. 'Anyway…' Her reluctant gaze swept over the thick, black hair, which even an expensive cut hadn't altogether tamed, over the designer suit and exclusive black shoes. Ignoring the sudden quickening of her heart-rate that just looking at him produced, she said waspishly, 'It doesn't seem to have hurt you any.'

'Not so much as my mother who was already struggling to make ends meet. But, hey! What's a man's job when you live in a nice, comfortable mansion with more food than you could ever eat and servants to fetch and carry for you at the snap of your fingers?' His hostility and resentment burned in him like an eternal flame. 'And you complain that I think you aren't capable of any feelings? I'm quite sure that you and your kind don't have any regrets about trampling on others to get what you want, particularly those worse off than yourself.'

She flinched from his continual need to verbally flay her.

'You don't know *my kind*, Seth Mason. You haven't the first idea what sort of woman I am.'

'Haven't I?' he grated. 'Then all the more reason why I should keep you around to discover this new Grace Tyler for myself—and I think it's going to be a very enlightening journey.'

'Get lost!'

'As much as you'd like that, Grace, I'm afraid that this time that isn't going to happen. I'm calling the shots now. Take it or leave it, but I don't think you'll walk away with your tail between your legs like a disciplined little lap-dog because you're way too proud and you've got far too much to lose. No. You'll take it, and, before I've finished with you, lying down!'

His innuendo was obvious. But he had her just where he wanted her, she realised, because as he had already made clear he knew she'd stick it out. It was the only way she would have any say in, or be able to hang on to, even a part of all that her grandfather had spent his life working for, she thought. She despaired at how the woman he had been so besotted by could have thrown her on the mercy of a man like Seth Mason. Nevertheless, that pride that he had spoken off a moment ago had her flinging back recklessly, 'You reckon?'

'Don't present me with a challenge, Grace. I think it only fair to tell you that I thrive on them.' Which was obvious, she thought, shuddering from the determination in him, otherwise he wouldn't have got to where he was today.

'That's big of you,' she retorted, knowing she was playing with fire but unable to let him have the last word. 'Well, let me tell you, I haven't worked my butt off getting where I have in this firm to be walked over by an arrogant, overbearing, jumped-up boatyard worker from the back of beyond! I'll work alongside you for the sake of the company, but let's get one thing clear—you might have pulled yourself up out of the next best thing to the gutter…' Angrily, she snatched up her jacket and bag. 'But you'll never, *ever*, get me into bed with you again!'

The walls seemed to shake as she slammed the boardroom door behind her.

'Wow! What, already? He's a fast worker!' That dry comment from Simone, who was just coming along the corridor, fell onto the deafening silence that followed.

'That isn't funny, Simone.' Hot and shaking from her outburst, Grace felt uncomfortably sticky beneath her travel-creased clothes.

'No, I can't say amusement was the overriding emotion coming out of that boardroom. Care to tell me where you know him from?'

'No.'

Her PA pulled a knowing face. 'That memorable, was it?'

'I'm sorry, Simone,' Grace apologised, not meaning to have spoken so sharply to her assistant. 'I guess I'm suffering from a chronic case of jet lag.' She shook her head to try and clear it. 'Among other things,' she exhaled, her eyes swivelling towards the room she had just so dramatically vacated. She couldn't believe that this wasn't some farcical nightmare that she would wake up from any minute. An inner anguish pleated her forehead as she tagged on, 'It was a long time ago.'

'Not long enough for him to bring out a side of your nature I've never seen—or heard.' This with a roll of her eyes towards the ceiling. 'Are you all right? Can I get you something?'

'Yes. Enough Culverwell shares to give me a majority holding.' *So that I won't lose all that was precious to my grandfather—to me—to a man hell-bent on revenge!*

Simone grimaced sympathetically. 'No can do, girl. I think all we can do is co-operate with him and the new management and pray that we've still got jobs this time next week.'

'How can I co-operate—?' The boardroom door suddenly opening left Grace's words hanging in mid-sentence.

Seth Mason emerged, appearing more dynamic and commanding in the narrower confines of the corridor, if that were possible. He sent Grace a stripping glance. She had been way too rude in there, and something told her he wasn't going to let her get away with it.

'Simone, I'd like you to bring your note pad in here. But first will you have a word with whoever it is you need to see about having self-closing hinges fitted on all principal doors?'

'Certainly, Mr Mason,' Simone responded with what seemed to Grace like annoying deference to the new CEO, before she caught the covert glance her assistant sent her. It conveyed the message already obvious from Seth's instructions; *he isn't going to take anyone slamming doors in his face!*

'I see,' she said, rounding on him as the other woman tripped off towards the lift. 'So she's your PA now, is she?'

'No,' he surprised her by answering, 'But I thought you wouldn't mind my making use of her until my own arrives.'

'It so happens, I do mind. And no one *makes use* of anyone in this company,' she enlightened him, piqued by the dismissive manner in which he had just spoken about a member of her team. 'I just thought I ought to warn you, otherwise you might wonder why you've got a full-blown mutiny on your hands.'

'Thanks for the warning.' He smiled indolently, making her body react to him in a way that made her brain chastise her for her stupidity. 'It was just a figure of speech. Why don't you go home, Grace?' Strangely, his tone had softened, become dangerously caressing in its sensuality. She had a feeling that it was some sort of mind game he was playing with her. 'Grab a couple of hours' sleep? Freshen up a bit?' His gaze raked with disconcerting thoroughness over her dishevelled appearance. 'We've got a lot of work to do and I'm sure you'll agree that no one can give their best if they aren't functioning on all cylinders.'

Was that concern in his eyes? she wondered, then dismissed the notion, deciding that it was probably pity. The type one would have for an animal one has just snared as one mulled over the most humane way to make the kill.

'Perhaps you'd prefer it if I didn't come back at all!' Her fighting spirit rose to her defence, challenging him.

'On the contrary,' he said, and this time his mouth curved in a fragment of a smile that did nothing to warm his eyes, just merely showed her how calm he was in contrast. 'As I've already explained, I'm going to spend every satisfying minute working with you.'

Don't imagine it will be a bed of roses! It took every gram of will power Grace had to bite the words back. This was her family's business, in name if nothing else, and she'd be darned if she would let Seth Mason goad her into throwing in her share and just walking away, as Corinne had done, or give him any reason to get rid of her which—unbelievable and humiliating though it was—he now had the power to do.

'You're right,' she accepted, deciding to ignore his last remark that made her blood pump heavily through her with its scarcely concealed implication. Her head was pounding too and she was longing for a shower. 'I think I will freshen up.'

But she didn't summon a taxi to take her home.

No way, she decided, was she going to take the advice of this conceited, over-confident, muscle-bound boat builder—or whatever he had been—and abandon her staff just when they needed someone to reassure them that all their hard work and their loyalty wasn't just going to be written off.

Instead, swinging away from him, she took the lift down to her own office. This time when she rang the Culverwell home, Corinne answered.

'How could you?' Grace breathed as the much-too-affected voice of her grandfather's widow started trying to placate her with some hollow, meaningless explanation. 'How could you? And without breathing a word of it to me?'

'Because I knew you'd react like this.' Corinne sounded irritated. Grace could almost see her sitting at her marble-topped dressing table in her transparent negligee, her short red hair gelled to look as though she'd just tumbled out of bed, a cooling mask on her face as she applied precise sweeping strokes of lacquer to her perfect nails. 'Be sensible, Grace.

I wanted to sell my shares—so did Paul—and you couldn't afford to buy them.'

'Paul?' The fact that her ex could have been complicit in trying to oust her from the board of the family company made her wonder if there was something going on between him and Corinne. 'Did you cook this up between you?'

'No, we didn't. I haven't seen Paul Harringdale since you broke up with him. He's not my type.'

No. Your type is more besotted elderly men who'll give you anything just to hear you flatter their diminishing egos! Grace thought bitterly.

'When you've calmed down a bit, Grace, you'll realise that I've done Culverwells a favour. The company needs a man like Seth Mason. When he approached me to see if I'd sell, what could I do? He can be pretty persuasive. Wow! I don't know what you're complaining about. I can't imagine it being that much of a punishment, taking orders from a man like that.'

Grace bit back the desire to tell her grandfather's widow that she could go ahead and take orders from him if she wanted to, because *she* wasn't going to. But then she would have to hand in her resignation and she had already promised herself that she wouldn't do that.

'Goodbye, Corinne.'

Ringing off, she stepped through into the adjacent shower-room and, stripping off her clothes, stepped under the refreshing spray of the jets, wishing she could cut off her thoughts as easily as she had cut the line to her grandfather's widow.

But the memories wouldn't leave her alone, and unwillingly she found herself reflecting on the emotional chaos of eight years ago: the shock of her pregnancy. Her shame and regret over the way she had behaved. The unbelievable anguish following a miscarriage at four-and-a-half months.

It was then that she'd realised that life wasn't just one big party; that there were debts to be paid and rules to be respected, and that some things in life had a far, far greater value than status or money.

But she didn't want to think about any of that. It was all because of seeing Seth again that the past had opened its floodgates, making her dwell on things that she wanted, needed, to forget: regret. Loneliness. Self-blame. The pain of her loss.

She didn't have to think about it, and she wouldn't, she told herself fiercely. She had enough worries with the company right now and the shock of Seth Mason taking over.

Towelling herself off, she went through into the dressing-room adjacent to her office and, sliding back the doors on the mirror-fronted cupboards, she scanned the shelves for fresh underwear. She always kept a change of clothes in the office in case of an unexpected out-of-hours meeting or dinner when she couldn't get home to change.

Now she pulled a silver-grey silk blouse and dark business-suit down off their hangers, donned clean underwear and drew a short pencil-line skirt up over her hips.

She couldn't, wouldn't, let him get to her, she determined as she slipped on her blouse and came through into her office to jot down a reminder to herself of a dental appointment that had almost slipped her mind. She couldn't help wondering what he would say if he ever found out that there had been repercussions from their love-making all those years ago. What he would think—that it had been her comeuppance for the appalling way in which she had behaved?

Fumbling with the top fastening of her blouse, she shuddered from the thought of how he might gloat. She was glad that he didn't know and would never know all that she had been through. Then she looked up, startled, her eyes dark and enormous, to see him striding into her office.

'Don't you ever knock?' she challenged, flustered, still trying to fasten her blouse which was gaping open, revealing too much of her creamy breasts in their black lacy cups.

'The door was open.' He looked as shocked and surprised

as she was to see him, while his eyes skimmed with barely veiled masculine interest over her state of undress. 'Anyway, I thought you'd gone home.'

'Because you ordered me to?' She couldn't seem to give him any leeway, even if she wanted to.

'Advised,' he corrected. 'Not ordered.'

'And leave my customers and all the people who depended on my grandfather and now me in the hands of…of…'

'The enemy?' he supplied mockingly when she couldn't think of a word strong enough to describe him.

She chose to ignore his remark and his coldly sardonic smile, relieved that she had finally managed to slip the top button of her blouse securely into place.

'What did you want?' she demanded, more ungraciously than she had intended, because the way he was looking at her made every betraying little cell in her body react to him in a way she wasn't at all happy about.

'The last five years' trading figures. Perhaps you could look them out for me, since you're here.'

She swept over to the desk, jotting down the appointment in her diary with hands that shook. 'Perhaps you could look them out for yourself since you've obviously given yourself licence to everything else in this building.'

'Not quite everything, Grace.' The way his eyes swept over her body needed no interpretation. 'Not yet.'

She stood facing him, trembling with anger and frustration at his audacity. How could he even think he could say such things to her, let alone imagine that she would gladly leap into his bed? Though she was certain most women would. But, while she was battling to find a suitably cutting response, he said, clearly aware, 'Are you going to fight me every step of the way?'

It was suddenly painful to swallow. Pulling herself up to her full height, which in her stocking-clad feet still left her well short of his six-feet-plus inches, she replied, 'If I have to.'

'That isn't very sensible.'

'Well, no. We both know I'm rather lacking in that department, don't we? Or, rather, I used to be,' she tagged on pointedly. One thing she had learnt from that encounter with him was wisdom, if nothing else.

'Really?' A masculine eyebrow cocked in disdainful speculation. 'And I've always believed I was the one lacking judgement in that regard.'

His tone, with his opinion of the fickle creature she had been, still had the power to flay. But if he thought making love to her had been an error of judgement on his part, then it must have meant something more to him than just a feather in his cap, as he'd claimed that day outside the bank, mustn't it? Grace reasoned wildly. She did not want to dwell on the fact that it was only her actions, and subsequently her grandfather's in getting Seth dismissed from his job, that had fuelled his determination to make the Culverwells pay.

'I think it only fair to warn you, Grace,' he said, his next words emphasising that determination, 'That if you continue to fight me then it'll be a fight you're going to lose. I can turn this company's fortunes around or I can break up Culverwell's piece by piece and sell off the most profitable areas at considerable loss to yourself and all those people you claim so depend on you. It's your choice.'

There was no point arguing with him. He was clearly wealthy and powerful enough to do exactly as he said by stripping the company of its assets. And where would she— and a lot of people who would lose their jobs because of it—be then?

Walking purposefully over to the bank of cabinets on the far wall, she opened a drawer and pulled out the file he had requested before propelling the usually smooth-gliding drawer back hard on its runners.

'There.' Ignoring the masculine hand waiting to take it

from her, she tossed the heavy file down onto the desk in front of him. 'Is there anything else you'll be requiring...*sir*?'

Thick black lashes came down over steely eyes as he moved to pick up the file. 'Just for you to control your temper,' he said. 'Much as I'm not wholly averse to a fiery nature in a woman, I much prefer it if she keeps such loss of control confined to bed.'

'That's just the sort of sexist comment I'd expect from you,' she flung at his broad back, because he was already heading for the door.

He turned as he reached it, his immaculately clad free arm lifting to the doorjamb. He was the hard-hitting executive, all flippancy gone.

'I've called an emergency meeting of all the major shareholders at two o'clock this afternoon. If you care as much about this company as you say you do, you'll be there.'

Then he was gone, leaving her staring after him in angry frustration, a knot of tension tightening way down inside her from his remark about being in bed.

Seth leaned back against the mirrored wall and closed his eyes as the lift doors came together behind him.

She'd looked so bleak in there when he had surprised her walking into that office, almost hollow-eyed, he thought. He wondered if there was more behind that lovely face and body of hers than just a fear of losing the lifestyle she was clearly used to if he took it on himself to get rid of her. Perhaps she had changed from the spoilt little rich bitch it had been his misfortune to get involved with, the girl he'd often read about with interest in the tabloid press. She had seemed genuinely shocked when he had told her how Lance Culverwell had been responsible for him losing his job.

But don't be fooled, he warned himself, in danger of finding himself being charmed by her femininity. She would eat a man for breakfast and spit him out again without turning a hair.

He couldn't help wondering, if he was honest with himself, if he hadn't seduced her all those years ago just to prove something to himself, as he'd let her believe. But, no; she had been utterly desirable. Just thinking about her then, and being faced with the reality of just how beautiful and even more desirable she was now, made him realise that he had never wanted anyone so much as he'd wanted Grace Tyler—then or now!

Over the years he had managed to achieve everything he had set out to and that he had worked for. His architectural studies had made him a natural in a profession he had striven to reach, a lucky break had taken him into full-blown developments and now he had everything he wanted: Money. Cars. Women. Power. And Culverwells. There was only one thing left to make his achievements complete and that was Grace Tyler. She belonged in his bed, whether she liked it or not. And he meant to have her—with or without her liking him, if that was the way it had to be.

But she still wanted him. He'd have had to be blind not to notice that betraying little flutter in her throat whenever he came within touching distance of her, the flushed cheeks and dilated pupils in the centre of her huge, man-drowning blue eyes. She still wanted him, as much as he wanted her —if that were possible—and he wasn't going to rest until her lovely legs were wrapped around him again and she was lying there beneath him, sobbing out his name.

CHAPTER FOUR

THE little art gallery was peaceful and soothing on Grace's jangling nerves now that Beth had closed up for the day and gone home; Grace needed peace as much as she needed some sleep after a day doing battle with the likes of Seth Mason.

Left to her unexpectedly four years ago by the father she'd scarcely known, the gallery had been a run-down little shop selling artists' materials, and had come with a sitting tenant in the flat above and a whole load of debt.

Never a fan of Matthew Tylers' for abandoning his daughter as he had, Lance Culverwell had urged Grace to give it up.

'It will only bring you heartache, child,' she could still hear her grandfather saying. 'Which is all that man ever brought you while he was alive.'

But something deep down inside Grace hadn't been able to let the gallery go and, refusing any help from her grandfather, she had started to pay the outstanding mortgage herself. Which had seemed quite feasible until Culverwell's had started getting into difficulty. Then her grandfather had died, leaving everything to Corinne, and Grace had been forced to give up the bright, modern apartment she had been buying and move into the rather dowdy and suddenly vacant flat above the gallery in a much more modest part of town.

Struggling to meet the cost of her planned refurbishments

for the flat and gallery, she'd looked like losing both. But her father's paintings, virtually unnoticed while he had been alive, had already started to gain unexpected popularity, as had his sculptures, several of which Grace had seen change hands in various auction houses for surprisingly high prices over the past couple of years. But it had been that one special bronze of Matthew Tyler's that had brought all her fears for her gallery to an end, helping her to clear her debts and carry out her renovations after it had sold to a telephone bidder and fetched a mind-blowing sum.

So, even if Seth Mason had taken Culverwells from under her nose, at least this gallery was hers, she thought fiercely, looking around at the fine paintings and ceramics. Lock, stock and barrel!

The fact that she had had to part with what the art world claimed was her father's prize piece to achieve it brought on those familiar feelings of regret, as well as a whole heap of conflicting emotions whenever she thought about her father.

With tears threatening to sting her eyes, she tried to banish any sentimental feelings towards Matthew Tyler from her mind.

Just looking at that little figurine had always made her feel sad—and angry too—hadn't it? she assured herself. Anyway, she'd had to sell it to stay solvent, and that was that.

The phone was ringing in the flat as she started up the stairs.

Exhausted from the day, she considered leaving the answering machine to take the call, but as it hadn't cut in by the time she crossed the lounge she picked the phone up, then wished she hadn't when Seth's deep tones came disconcertingly down the line.

'Just checking that you're in and planning on an early night,' he remarked with that infuriating audacity that had Grace instantly snapping back.

'No, as a matter of fact I thought I'd pop up to the West End, take in a show and then do a bit of clubbing for a few hours. I'm tired, jet-lagged and, if you hadn't noticed, my grandfather's company was taken over today! A company that's been in my family for over fifty years!' The emotion she had managed to rein in downstairs now welled up in her again, clogging her throat, making her voice crack from the struggle she was having to keep it in check. 'Of course I'm getting an early night. I'm not quite as robotic as you obviously expect your workforce to be.'

'Or as well, by the sound of it. You sound distinctly nasal,' he commented, much to Grace's alarm. She couldn't—wouldn't—let him know that it was taking every resource she had not to break down after the day she had had. 'You aren't sickening for anything, are you? A cold, perhaps?'

'As if you'd care!' She had slammed the phone down before she even realised what she was doing, and stood there, staring at it, shaking with rage.

How dared he? How dared he try to control her private life as well as her business affairs? she fumed as she continued to stare at the phone, both apprehensive and fired up, waiting for it to start ringing again.

Relieved when it didn't, yet feeling strangely as though she'd been left hanging by ending their conversation in the way she had, she went back across the tastefully though minimally furnished living room, kicking off her high-heeled shoes as she did so. They weren't designed for a day in the office any more than her trainers would have gone with the executive image she had been particularly keen to cultivate today. But her pumps had been in the suitcase which she'd instructed the taxi driver to bring on to the flat this morning in her haste to get to the office.

Now, going into the bedroom, she slipped off her clothes, pulled her hair free of its pins and was just reaching for the champagne-tinted robe she'd tossed down onto the bed when the bleeper in the hall announced that there was someone at the front door.

'Who is it?' she asked into the loud speaker, shrugging into her robe. She didn't feel up to seeing anyone tonight.

'Seth. Seth Mason.'

Grace's heart instantly lurched into a thumping tattoo. Had he just been round the corner when he'd phoned? 'What do you want?'

'Can I come up?'

She wanted to say no, but her tongue seemed to cleave to the roof of her mouth, and before she was fully aware of what she was doing she was pressing the button that opened the door to the street.

Hearing his steady tread on the stairs, Grace couldn't get over how her hands were shaking as she fumbled with the belt of her robe, only just managing to secure it as those footsteps stopped outside the door to her flat.

'What do you want? she demanded, wondering how he could look as fresh and vital as he had that morning, while stepping backwards to admit him since his dominating figure promised to quash any refusal to do so.

Surprisingly, he was bringing her suitcase up from the passageway. She'd been too tired to bother carrying it up tonight.

'I thought you'd had a pretty tough day.' Pushing the door closed behind him, he stooped to put the suitcase down in the little hallway, his cologne drifting disturbingly towards her. 'I felt something of a peace offering might be in order.' It was only then, as he straightened up, that her brain registered the bouquet of predominantly white-and-yellow flowers he was holding.

'Where did you get these?' She wasn't ready to be placated as he handed them to her. 'Late-night shop at the supermarket?' And instantly she regretted her caustic and rather childish remark when he made no reply.

The bouquet was fragrant and beautifully arranged and the name of an exclusive florist on the wrapping caused her eyebrows to lift in surprise.

Had he been planning to come round with these much earlier? Was that why he had telephoned just now—to check that he wasn't going to have a wasted journey?

'You think that this makes everything all right?' she uttered waspishly. 'That I'll be bowled over by an apology and a few expensive flowers?'

'I'm not trying to bowl you over.' His tone was self-assured, his jaw cast in iron. 'And it certainly isn't intended as an apology.'

Of course not. She laughed. 'No. How stupid of me,' she bit out, swinging away from him into the lounge.

'Why is it,' he asked, following her, his voice suddenly dangerously seductive, 'that when I'm around you you're always in a state of undress?'

An insidious heat crept along her skin, making her heart beat faster, her nerve-endings tingle.

Why? Grace similarly wondered and, caught in the snare of his regard, felt that same throb of tension that she'd felt from the very first instant their eyes had clashed eight years ago.

'Perhaps because I didn't invite you up here in the first place,' she returned heatedly.

Seth's mouth curved in an indolent smile. His senses absorbed the translucent quality of her skin; those blue eyes that could make a man drown in his own longing for her; that rather proud nose that mirrored her attitude towards her subordinates and made him want to drag her to her knees; that full, slightly pouting mouth. He wanted to taste that mouth until he was drugged by the potency of all it promised him, devour it with his own until she was begging him to take her as she had all those years before.

He saw her as she had been then, naked except for that

web of lace across her pelvis, offering herself to him like a beautiful, abandoned spirit of the sea. He had never known a girl as passionate as she had been, although he'd known enough in his time. When he had dropped her off the bike outside her grandparents' house that night, she'd seemed to leap at his suggestion to meet him the following day. He'd felt sick to the stomach when she hadn't turned up, although he'd waited for hours on that beach. And the day after that, when he had bumped into her in town, she'd treated him like he hadn't existed. No, worse—like he was scum. He had been just someone with whom to amuse herself, he thought with his mouth hardening. Just a substitute until she could get back to her richer, stuck-up friends back home.

For a long time afterwards all he could think of was of getting his own back—having his revenge on the Culverwell family for the humiliation they had caused him, and for the hardship they had inflicted on his mother and his foster siblings as a result. Well, now he had, he thought grimly. And it wasn't over yet!

He noted the way she was clutching the flowers to her breast as though to conceal the fact that she wasn't wearing a bra. But he could see that all too clearly from the way her nipples protruded tantalisingly through the satin robe, and he had to clench his fingers to control the urge to rip it from her body and replace it with his aching hands instead.

'You had your hair cut,' he commented with an unaccustomed dryness in his throat, thinking, as he had done when he had seen her again in the flesh that morning, that the mid-length silky cloud that gently brushed her shoulders added a sophistication that hadn't been there eight years ago.

Poignantly she said, 'I grew up.'

And how, he thought. Feeling the uncomfortable constriction of his clothes below waist level, he was annoyed at how she could still affect him without even trying.

'Why have you come?' she demanded, but Seth noticed that

those eyes he had drowned in all too willingly eight years ago were wary, as though she were afraid of him—or, amazingly, herself.

'I was naturally concerned,' he said against his better judgement. She had sounded ghastly over the phone. Now he could see the dark circles under her eyes that no amount of make-up could conceal. She had to be tired, and she was most certainly jet-lagged. But there was something else. Something that caused that same bleak look about her that he had noticed when he had strode into her office that morning, which surprisingly had caused a slight pricking of his conscience, making him feel less a conquering hero and more like a heel for what he had done. 'I thought I'd come and see for myself that you were all right.'

Grace wanted to respond with some cutting jibe, but the events of the day had taken their toll. She had no more energy left to fight him tonight.

'Well, now you've seen me,' she murmured with her shoulders slumping, the bouquet hanging heavily at her side. She felt fit to drop, and as she made to move away from him she tripped over one of the shoes she had left lying on the carpet and would have stumbled if he hadn't been there, reaching for her.

'I don't need your help,' she said despite herself as his long, tanned hands pressed her down onto the sofa, disposing of the flowers on the table beside it.

'Well, that's just too bad, because you're getting it.'

His forcefulness, his proximity and his pine-scented cologne made her weak with a heady excitement that quickly turned to panic when he came down beside her on the settee.

'Who invited you to sit down?' she croaked, breathless from the force with which her heart was thumping.

'Your good manners,' he drawled, half-amused.

His droll remark would have drawn some retort from her if

she hadn't been so keyed up, debilitated by the hot sensations that were pulsing through her.

Desperate to distance herself from him, she was all for leaping up.

As if he could read her mind, though, his arm suddenly sliced across her middle, preventing her precipitous flight.

Grace's gasped breath seemed to lodge in her lungs, every part of her burning with the fire that strong arm was igniting in her as its warmth penetrated the fine material of her robe. His other arm was stretched across the back of the settee, setting her head spinning in a whirl of fear and wild anticipation.

If he kissed her…!

Surprisingly, though, he made no other move to touch her beyond keeping her there.

Rigid with tension, her breasts rising and falling sharply, she breathed, 'What do you want from me, Seth?'

She caught his sharp intake of breath and wondered if that arm lying across her could feel the hard pulse that was throbbing away inside her.

'I believe I once asked the same question of you.'

Yes, he had, she remembered, recoiling from the reminder, because they both knew what it was she had wanted—and, heaven help her, still wanted—from him. In spite of the ruthlessness in his desire for revenge, in spite of all he had taken from her, because she couldn't deny it now.

Sexually, she was as attracted to him as she had ever been. More so, if that was possible. But it was just her flesh that was weak. It meant nothing beyond that, and she had to keep reminding herself of that. Seth Mason was a dangerous man and she'd be a fool if she were to allow herself to fall into his honey-tongued trap. Because that was all it was, she decided—the flowers. The apparent concern. Just ways of wearing her resistance down until he could claim the ultimate prize for himself: her surrender to his powerful sexuality. And what then? she wondered, shuddering.

She longed to put a safe distance between them, and common sense alone prevented her from making any sudden moves. That would have had the same effect as a mouse trying to escape the clutches of a prowling jungle cat, she realised hopelessly, knowing by instinct alone that if she attempted it then that arm would tighten mercilessly around her—and where would she be then?

Instead, her fine features ravaged by her darkest emotions and the things that she must never, ever tell him, and with her eyes fixed on a pastoral watercolour on the far wall that she had bought for next to nothing at a car-boot sale, she asked, 'Just how much persuasion did it take on your part to get Corinne to hand over her share of the company?'

'What is it you want me to say, Grace?' He inhaled deeply, sitting back, mercifully withdrawing his arm as he did so. 'That I'm sleeping with her?'

Unable to help herself, she sent a swift glance towards his hard-hewn face, breathing normally again now that he had released her, or as normally as it was possible to breathe in his devastating sphere. 'Are you?'

His lashes came down, veiling the perfect clarity of his eyes. 'You think I'd kiss and tell on any woman I bed?'

She laughed, a humourless sound strung with tension, as images of him naked on that beach, and as he would be in bed now—his long limbs entwined with others that were paler, more submissive in their passion—rose to threaten her far-too-vulnerable defences. 'Are you trying to tell me you have scruples?'

Seth's mouth compressed. 'No more than you.'

She turned away from him, her chin lifting in spite of the reminder. A cold feeling seemed to settle right in the place where his arm had lain.

'Does it matter to you, Grace?'

'What?'

'Whether I'm sleeping with her or not?'

'Hardly,' she sneered.

He laughed softly, the warmth of his breath stirring the fine hairs at her temple, making her stiffen. 'Such protestation!' he mocked. 'I just wonder why the lady deems it necessary to deliver it with such force.'

'I would have thought that was obvious.' She leaped up now, dreading that she might have given him cause to suspect how her body reacted to him against her will, against her rational thinking. 'You're despicable!' she breathed.

His mouth moved carelessly. 'Shouldn't you be saying that to those closer to home?'

He meant Corinne—and Paul.

Turning wounded eyes in his direction, she noticed the grace with which he moved, brought his tall, lithe frame to his feet.

'She sold you down the river, Grace.' His words were hard, blunt, unsparing. 'So did your precious Harringdale.'

'He isn't *mine*,' she flared, hurting, wondering how he—how both of them—could have pulled the plug on her and left her and the company to the mercy of a man like Seth Mason. 'It's over between us—as you so subtly pointed out at that launch party. It was over months ago.'

'Ah, yes. What really happened there? Did you just get tired of him?' he asked, sounding bored suddenly, while ignoring her barbed accusation. 'Or were you as butterfly-minded and fickle as Harringdale said you were? What was it?' His thick brows pleated as he pretended to search for the words which were obviously at the forefront of that shrewd, keen mind. '"Grace Tyler's only interested in having fun and when that wears off, which is surprisingly quickly, so does her sense of loyalty".' His mouth compressed. After all, hadn't he been on the receiving end of what could only be described as her capricious behaviour? Perhaps he did have reason to think badly of her, she accepted painfully. But that was all in the past.

'I don't think my relationship with Paul is any of your business,' she murmured, catching her breath after the hurtful remarks her ex-fiancé had made to the press when she had broken off their engagement only a few weeks before their wedding. Wearily, she added, 'Perhaps you're just too influenced by what you read.'

'Perhaps,' he concurred, without sounding wholly convinced. 'Perhaps Harringdale was just being spiteful, in view of the way you jilted him. Or perhaps he was right. Perhaps loyalty and respect are two things you still need to learn.'

His words had an ominous ring to them. 'Believe that if you want to,' she objected, so tense that she flinched as the clock on the mantelpiece suddenly struck the half hour. 'Just like every sensation-seeking journalist I've come across, you've got your own prejudiced opinions and nothing I say will change them.'

'Try me.'

'Why?'

He didn't answer, but his eyes were so commanding in their intensity that she found the words slipping away from her before she could stop them.

'If you must know, it was something I drifted into with Paul as much as anything else. I thought we had a lot in common, so it seemed like a good idea for the two of us to get engaged and to merge our business interests. It was what both our families wanted, my grandfather in particular.' She couldn't forget the hints Lance Culverwell had dropped, the silent but eternal pressure he'd applied to see her settle down with the heir to the Harringdale fortune.

'And, with dear Granddad out of the way, you didn't have to.'

'No, strange though this may seem to you, I consider principles to be more important than doing something just because it's expected of me.'

'Really?' Dark, winged brows lifted mockingly. 'And when did you first cultivate that admirable virtue?'

'You can scoff all you like. It's true.'

'And your stepmother?'

'Step-*grand*mother,' she corrected with emphasis.

The look he sliced her left no doubt that he had picked up on that unintentional censure in her voice, and his mouth pulled at one corner, as though he were weighing up the age difference between the ex-model Corinne Phelps and Lance Culverwell, questioning the whole viability of the match.

'It's peculiar how sex drives a man—or a woman, for that matter—isn't it, Grace?'

She regarded him warily. 'Meaning?'

'Meaning he wasn't prepared for someone from my background to soil the pedigree of his precious family, but he had no such qualms when it came to himself and a woman who didn't mind being photographed in some of the more, shall we say, *graphic* newspapers.'

'What my grandfather found out *after* they were married had no bearing on his judgement. And we aren't all like you, Seth Mason. My grandfather didn't marry Corinne for…' She couldn't even bring herself to say it, hating having to listen to someone else voicing the doubts about Lance Culverwell's good judgement that she had harboured in silence, alone. 'He married her because he was lonely.'

Those steely eyes seemed to strip her to the soul. 'If you believe that, then you still haven't grown up, Grace, despite all your claims to the contrary. He might have advocated high standards and good breeding—which he obviously found in the woman he spent most of his life with—but at the end of his life he was no more immune than any other man to the wiles of a pretty gold-digger who has about as much refinement as a bag of raw cane-sugar.'

'Coming from someone as basic as you, that's rich!' she

shot back, hating him for saying these things to her. 'All I can say to that is that it takes one to know one.'

From the anger that flared in his eyes, she realised she had hit a raw nerve.

Scared by the fury she had provoked, she started to move away, but he was too quick for her, and she gave a helpless little cry as he caught her, dragging her into his arms.

Her robe had slipped off one shoulder and, tugging it off the other so that her arms were trapped inside it, he pulled her towards him before his mouth came down hard on hers.

She struggled in his grasp, protesting little sounds coming from her captured lips, but her wriggling only made him more determined, his mouth growing more insistent in its demands.

Her fruitless movements caused her robe to separate. She could feel the rasp of his suit against her stomach, her thighs, her naked breasts.

She groaned again, only this time it was the muted sound of desire. She hated him and yet she wanted him! How sick was that?

The revelation shocked her even as she realised that he had recognised it too.

In response his arms came around her, pulling her into the hard warmth of his body, his mouth leaving hers only to force her head back for his teeth to graze with humiliating purpose over the far too sensitive column of her throat.

Sensations ripped through her such as she had never known for eight long years. Why him? she asked herself savagely, clenching her teeth against all that he was doing to her. Was he destined to be the only man that she could ever respond to?

Hating herself for her weakness, fingers curling tensely against the shoulders of his jacket, she battled with the traitorous responses of her own body so that she was standing breathless and trembling with her eyes closed when he finally lifted his head.

His face was flushed, his mouth taut from the desire he was holding in check, but his eyes were unmistakably smug.

Even so, he seemed to have a struggle drawing breath before he said in a voice that was softly mocking, 'Where are those principles now, Grace?'

'You bastard.' Her lashes parted to reveal the self-loathing in her eyes. 'Was that why you came here tonight?' she demanded shakily, pulling out of his grasp. 'To try to humiliate me?' Her hands were trembling so much she could scarcely do up her robe.

'If it's of any consolation to you, Grace, humiliating you wasn't my intention.'

'No? Exactly what did you intend? To try and soft-soap me with your supposed concern for my welfare, and hope that that and a few well-chosen flowers would have me falling at your feet?'

'Just let me remind you, Grace, that there were two of us involved in that kiss—and *you* responded to *me*. As for my takeover of Culverwells, one day you might just thank me for stepping in when I did.'

'Never!'

'Never say never,' he ridiculed. 'So, we can do this the easy way by being civil and trying to get on…'

'Giving in to your assaults, you mean?'

'Or we can go on just the way we're going,' he said, ignoring her remark, 'And keep up this pointless war. It makes little difference to me.'

'You started it,' she said, and couldn't help cringing at how childish that sounded even to her own ears.

'Oh, no. You began it, my love.' The endearment made its mark, but only because he spoke with such lethal softness. 'Way, way before I'd done anything to earn your contempt.'

'But now you have earned it, so will you just please leave?'

Stooping to pick up his car keys, he didn't stay to argue, only turning as he reached her sitting-room door.

'Get an early night. We've got a lot of work ahead of us,' he informed her with all the blandness of an employer to a subordinate.

A couple of seconds later she heard him close the hall door after him. Biting back tears of frustration, Grace spotted the flowers still lying on the table and, picking them up, hurled them across the room in the direction that he had gone.

CHAPTER FIVE

SETH wasn't in when Grace arrived at the office the following morning and she couldn't have been more relieved.

After all her protestations yesterday about not winding up in bed with him, it had taken only one kiss from him to show her that, where he was concerned, she had no more control over her physical responses than she did over the weather.

As she slipped off her jacket, hung it over the coat stand and then tried to settle down to work she wondered—just as she had done until she'd fallen into a heavy slumber the previous night—she wondered why she had responded to him so disgracefully. Why, when his only interest in her was to seek revenge?

Was it because all her emotions had been so highly charged yesterday—because she had been shattered from a sleepless overnight flight, even before she had suffered the shock of Culverwells being taken over? Or was it simply because she had no resistance whatsoever where Seth Mason was concerned, and that nature—or whatever one could call it, she thought witheringly—would try its utmost to get them into bed whenever they were alone together?

She groaned to herself as she opened her post, staring down at a letter she had unfolded and reading it without digesting a word.

She was still the same woman who had got into that taxi

yesterday morning, determined to fight Culverwells' new CEO for all she was worth, wasn't she? So, she might have played right into his hands and made a total fool of herself, but she still had her fighting spirit and her determination to do what was right for the company.

When the internal phone on her desk buzzed, though, and Seth's deep voice came over the line insisting that she came up to his office, Grace's heart started to pound.

Was he going to fire her, now that she had been weak and stupid enough to show him that she was still as affected by him as she had been as a senseless teenager? she worried. Or was he determined to hold out for the ultimate prize that would make his vengeance complete—her total capitulation in his bed?

He was rifling through the filing cabinet when she walked into his office and she gritted her teeth, steeling herself for the worst.

'Good morning, Grace.' He pushed the drawer closed without even looking up. 'I trust you slept well?'

Following his impeccably clothed figure with mutinous eyes, she had the strongest desire to hit him as he moved back to his desk.

Restraining the urge, she dragged her wayward appreciation from the silver-grey jacket spanning his broad shoulders to answer bitingly, 'I'd had less than three hours' sleep the previous night. What did you expect?'

He sat down, picked up a gold pen and began writing with it. 'Does that mean you're in better shape to deal with more pressing matters today?'

'What's come up?' She swallowed, despairing at the way her voice faltered. Did this mean that he hadn't summoned her here to fire her?

'The Poulson account. I believe you were dealing with it.' He looked up at her now, and she could have kicked herself from the way the smouldering intensity of his eyes made her stomach flip. 'It seems they're quibbling over assignment dates. It appears from previous correspondence that they can be very difficult to deal with. It also appears that they will only listen to you.'

Grace tried to steady her voice, even though her whole body seemed to be trembling. 'I've built up a rapport with them.' It seemed wrong, talking to him like this, discussing business like formal colleagues, as though those impassioned moments in her flat a little over twelve hours ago had never happened. 'They can be rather awkward at first, but I've found that with a little bit of diplomacy and persuasion they come around.'

From his position of authority his eyes made a cursory survey of her dark-blue slimline skirt, the rather prim little green and navy blouse and her neatly swept-up hair. 'Most people do.'

He applied just the right amount of sexual undertone in the way he said that to bring the colour flooding into her cheeks. There had certainly been nothing diplomatic or persuasive about the way he had urged her into responding to him!

Trying not to look at him, she moved around the desk to pick up the letter he had laid aside for her to look at, at the same time as he reached for his memo pad. His sleeve brushed her bare forearm, a touch so light and yet so sensual that she recoiled from the contact, feeling as though an electrical current was suddenly zinging through her.

Breath held, she urged her feet to carry her over to the filing cabinet, her head swimming. She couldn't concentrate, or even think straight, when he was near her.

'What's wrong, Grace?' He was there, his tanned, very masculine hand rammed flat against the drawer, preventing her from opening it. 'Unwilling to acknowledge what I can still do to you? What we still do to each other?'

Every muscle locking rigid, Grace could scarcely breathe from the alluring, masculine scent of him, from that lethal sexual magnetism that seemed to be pulling her into its dangerous sphere.

'If you're referring to last night, I scarcely knew what I was doing.'

'No?' He looked sceptical.

As well he might! she thought despairingly.

'Why would I want that?' she croaked, clutching the letter she was holding to her breast like it was a lifeline. 'Why, when I despise you? When there aren't words strong enough to describe what you're doing?' A jerk of her head indicated what had been her grandfather's desk and the power it gave the man who sat behind it.

'Because you can't help yourself, Grace, any more than I can.' He was leaning on the cabinet now, his indolent manner unable to conceal that underlying restless vitality about him as he stood supported by his bent arm, one long finger resting against his tough, implacable jaw. 'Oh, don't get me wrong— you aren't my idea of the perfect partner, either. But we aren't talking about a loving, trusting relationship, are we?'

As that finger moved to touch her cheek, Grace twisted her head away in angry rejection.

'I wouldn't have a relationship with you, Seth Mason, if you were the last man left on earth!'

'Such a cliché!' He laughed, a flash of perfect white teeth. 'But I'm not the only man left on earth, am I?' he drawled, that steely gaze dropping to the soft pink bow of her trembling mouth. 'Just the only one you want. And, if that response last night was anything to go by, in as intimate a relationship as it's possible to get.'

As if she needed reminding!

Her throat tight with tension, she flung back at him, 'I had no resistance. I was exhausted—jet-lagged, for heaven's sake!' She brought her chin up to face him squarely, trying to convince him, if not herself, that that was all it had been.

'And have you recovered from your jet lag?'

'Just about. But I…' The pale curve of her forehead puckered, and a guarded look sprang into her cool, clear eyes as she realised where his question was leading. 'Don't you dare,' she warned, backing away from him.

'I told you not to present me with a challenge, Grace,' he reminded her, his arm shooting out as she almost tripped over the waste-paper basket. 'And you seem to make a habit of not looking where you're going.' He laughed softly as that arm snaked around her, but it was the laughter of a victor, of the conqueror claiming his prize.

'Let me go!'

As he swivelled her round, he was still laughing, ignoring the pummelling of her fists against his shoulders as he took her mouth with his in a brutal kiss.

'Why must you always put up a show of fighting me when you know you'll only respond to me eventually?' he mocked softly, lifting his head when her hands gave up trying to make an impression on his hard shoulders. They were now clenched against them in a vain effort not to show him how much they wanted to slide over the smooth cloth spanning his broad back. 'You couldn't help yourself then, last night, and you can't help yourself now, can you?' She couldn't answer. She couldn't say anything, because right at that moment she was too affected by him to speak. 'Perhaps you're one of these women who get their kicks out of being subdued by a man? Is that what it is? Because I'll play that game with you if you want me to—only we'll both know that that's all it is, won't we, Grace? A game.'

Despising herself, Grace wondered how her body could still continue to react to him in the way it did in the light of what was only his need to avenge himself for what she—her family—had done to him in the past. She dragged herself up out of a cauldron of traitorous sensations to toss up at him, 'Go to hell!'

'Oh, I've been there, my love. And I can promise you,

it isn't very pleasant.' His features were chiselled into un-compromising lines. 'But, if making love to me is hell to your pride, then you're going to have to get used to it being scorched raw. Because we're going to burn this thing out between us until there's nothing left but cinders. So don't worry—what we want from each other is so fierce it can't fail to consume itself in the end.'

'And then what?' she asked, shuddering from his determi-nation and the furore of sensations his words were producing in her. 'We both walk away?'

His heavy lids drooped so that she couldn't see the expres-sion in his eyes. 'Naturally.'

Only she wouldn't be able to do that; she was jolted into realizing it. But why? Why, when he meant nothing to her, nothing beyond someone she had had the briefest fling with once? Yet someone whose child she had carried and then lost, as though life had been ridiculing her, exacting payment from her for her naïve and unfeeling indifference.

She closed her eyes against the memories, against the an-guish that remembering caused—the longing, the loneliness, the confusion.

'I can't do that.' Involuntarily, the words spilled from her lips; to deflect the meaning he might put on them, she quickly tagged on, 'Contrary to what you might think, I don't go in for casual relationships.'

His lips were but a hair's breadth from hers, so close that even the denial of their consummate touch was a turn on. She brought her eyelids down so that he wouldn't recognise the hunger in her eyes.

'Oh, I think you can.'

Her lashes fluttered apart. His face appeared out of focus, a dark, inscrutable image, mouth hard yet oddly vulnerable, cheeks taut, black lashes drawn down against the wells of his eyes.

He was so incredible. So uncompromisingly handsome. And yet so vengeful.

'Seth, please…' It was uttered from the depths of her longing for the warm and tender lover he had been all those years ago. A tenderness that had been destroyed by the way both she and her family had treated him. 'Don't do this.'

He moved back a little so that he could see her more clearly. 'Begging, Grace?'

That cruel curve to his mouth showed her, with deepening despair, that there was going to be no reprieve for her.

'No, just trying to appeal to your better nature, but that's obviously a waste of time!'

'Obviously.' He smiled, an action still devoid of any warmth. 'How can you expect restraint from someone who's… what was it you called me?…basic? Now, let me see: what does that mean? Rough? Primitive? Lacking in social graces? Well, don't worry. I'm sure I can knock all your ex-public-school lovers into a cocked hat! When I make love to you there's going to be none of the haste or urgency that we were driven by the first time. You're going to have all the benefit of my cultivated experience in a long slow night of love play befitting a woman of your…sophistication. And you're not going to get out of that bed until you're so drunk on sex with me you'll be unable to stand. Is that clear?'

The hot retort that sprang to Grace's lips was stalled by a sudden knock on the door.

Pulling out of his orbit, she was still tugging her blouse straight when Simone came in carrying some files.

'You wanted these, Mr Mason.'

Distractedly, Grace noticed her PA's eyes dart from her to Seth and then back to her again; she noticed, too, the crisp white handkerchief stained with her lipstick that Seth was pocketing as he turned round, calmly, coolly, as though the air wasn't charged with a sexual tension so thick that it left

Grace trembling, and which she knew the other woman must surely be able to feel.

'Yes, thanks, Simone. Did you bring your note pad as well?'

He had known her PA was coming up here, Grace thought, aghast, as the other woman laughed a little nervously at something else he said before sitting down. Yet he had still tried to seduce her again in spite of that? What had been his intention? she wondered, fuming—to hope that Simone was the type of tactless employee who thrived on office scandal and would let everyone in the office know that they were having an affair?

His upward glance at Grace from where he was sitting now was almost one of surprise to still see her there.

'Thank you, Grace, he said, his tone crisp, cold, formal. 'That will be all.'

He had the audacity to dismiss her, like she was some temp he could call up or dismiss whenever the fancy took him! Or, worse, some fawning little sex-slave at his beck and call.

Well, if he wanted office gossip, she decided, grabbing the letter off the top of the cabinet she realised he'd taken from her, then she'd let him have it.

'Don't keep him too long,' she uttered, bending, piqued, towards Simone. 'He's got a heavy appointment coming up this afternoon. Nasty maintenance case.' Voice lowered, she wrinkled her nose in a knowing little gesture. 'Best keep it under your hat.'

From Simone's obvious discomfort, the woman was clearly unsure whether Grace was joking or not. Although Grace knew that her PA would keep any personal information about her employers to herself, Seth didn't know that.

She didn't even bother looking at him again before sweeping out of the office, a tight little set to her mouth, her head held high.

* * *

The next couple of weeks passed in a hectic blur of board meetings, legal work and negotiations, then Seth was away for a few days, engaged in aspects of his diverse business-interests elsewhere.

There had been too much to do in the office for other, more personal distractions, and when Seth was called away unexpectedly to sort out yet another problem in his business empire that couldn't be delegated, Grace couldn't have been more relieved.

Just like everyone else, she had worked hard over that initial period to get the transition of management running smoothly, staying late at the office, sometimes going without meals—something she had often done in the past, much to her grandfather's disapproval. But Seth was a phenomenon with reserves of energy that outstripped hers and even the most dynamic of the other executives and she was determined, if she could, to try to keep up with him. How he managed to control his business interests, keeping them all running efficiently even from a span of hundreds of miles, was beyond Grace—although it did give credit to his judgement in engaging only the best staff needed to run each and every enterprise he presided over.

Which made his decision to have her working closely with him something she might have taken a pride in, if it hadn't been for the knowledge that he harboured a bitter desire to make her pay for her actions in the past—and in the most basic way possible. So whenever he was around, his presence alone seemed to shatter her equilibrium, stretching her nerves as taut as guitar strings, so that she began losing sleep as well.

'You look ghastly,' he remarked when he returned briefly late one afternoon on a flying visit to the office. 'Simone tells me you've been working all hours and neglecting to look after yourself—like missing lunch on more occasions than is healthy—and we can't have that, can we? I don't want a weak, undernourished lover in my bed.'

'Then you'll just have to find yourself one with more generous proportions, won't you?' Grace threw back, refraining from telling him that she'd had a recent stomach upset, which was probably why she looked so pale. She was unwilling to acknowledge how fit, strong and how terrifyingly attractive he looked in comparison, with the brilliant white collar of his shirt emphasising his olive skin and his black, untameable hair and that fine-tailored dark suit he was wearing accentuating the lean, hard lines of his body. 'I'm sure you'll find plenty at Weight Watchers!'

He laughed, as he always did when she tried to fend off his determined remarks about making her his mistress.

'You'll eat,' he ordered, catching her hand. 'Starting now.' A glance at the clock on the wall showed that it was already four-thirty.

'Not with you.' She tried to pull away but his grip only tightened in response.

'With me. And on my expense account. This is a business dinner, and one I expect you to honour.'

He meant it; she could always tell when business came uppermost on his agenda. Which was how, twenty minutes later, she found herself being handed out of the chauffeur-driven Mercedes he often used around the city and guided into the tastefully furnished little restaurant which was glowing with seasonal warmth and which, Seth had told her on hte way there, served exquisitely cooked meals throughout the day.

'I hadn't realised how hungry I was,' she accepted reluctantly as she tucked into a home-made lasagne with salad and huge chunks of crusty bread, while Seth had a gammon steak with all the trimmings.

'I thought you might want to see this,' he said when they had finished.

It was an email addressed to Seth, from the customers that Grace had visited in New York, agreeing to continue to trade with Culverwells now that it was under Mason's corporate umbrella.

'That must make you feel quite smug,' she remarked, unable to keep the edge out of her voice.

'Not at all.' He wiped his mouth with his napkin, laid it down on the table. 'The PR job you did in New York obviously paid off.' So he was acknowledging now that she hadn't flown off to the Big Apple just to go designer shopping, as he'd originally accused her of doing. 'And *I'm* in this simply to restore Culverwells to a healthy balance sheet.'

'And to make yourself even more millions while doing so.'

'Well, naturally. I'm a businessman,' he stressed, pushing his empty plate forward before sitting back on his chair. 'That would obviously come into the equation. But one thing I'm not in this business for is to antagonise you.'

'Really?' She looked at him dubiously, picking up her glass of sparkling water, which reflected the festive, coloured lights adorning the bar. 'You could have fooled me.'

'That's a totally separate issue,' he stated, ignoring the jibe. 'One thing I learned on the road to where I am now is never to let personal and business dealings overlap. Did you know your grandfather took risks in other areas that weren't always to the good of the company?'

His question, coming out of the blue, threw her for a moment. She looked at him over her glass, a mixture of puzzlement and wounded accusation in her eyes.

'My grandfather would never have done anything underhanded.'

'I'm not saying he did.' He had ordered one small glass of wine for himself—rich and ruby red—which left tears around the bowl as he finished drinking, and put the glass back down on the oak-stained table. 'He invested unwisely—with the best intentions, I'm sure, but against the advice of more circumspect members of his board. By then his judgement was probably clouded by more…personal matters.' Which, as he had already pointed out, he himself would never allow to happen. 'Ones that, I believe he realised at the end, hadn't really been worth risking his company for.'

He meant Corinne, but Grace wasn't sure what else he was driving at.

'What do you mean?' she queried, her forehead pleating.

'Did you know that your grandfather had made an appointment with his solicitor for the day after he died with the intention of changing his will?' Grace felt the colour drain from her face. 'You didn't.' Amazingly, that strong-boned face was etched with something almost close to commiseration.

She shook her head several times as though to clear it. 'How did you find out?'

'I have my sources.'

Of course. He would have access to everything now—letters. Files. Company diaries. Even her, if she allowed herself to succumb to that lethal attraction.

'Perhaps he realised the mistake he was making and had decided to do something about it,' he said.

But instead he had had that heart attack, and his real wishes had never been known. She wondered if Seth was thinking what she was—that if Lance Culverwell hadn't died when he had things could have been so different. Grace would probably have control of the company, and Seth could never have taken it over as he had.

'I'm afraid all your admirable efforts to save Culverwells wouldn't have amounted to anything without the injection of cash it sorely needed for reinvestment,' she heard Seth telling her, as if he knew the path her thoughts had taken.

Which only a man with his obvious wealth and influence could provide, she acknowledged reluctantly.

'Be careful,' she murmured. She was choked by her feelings for the grandfather she'd been unable to help believing had let her down, on top of a barrage of conflicting emotions towards the man sitting opposite her—although for reasons she didn't dare to question. 'That sounded suspiciously like a compliment.'

'Your ability as a businesswoman, Grace, has never been in any doubt.'

She made a sceptical sound down her nostrils. 'But other aspects of my character have?' When an elevated eyebrow was his only response, she went on, 'Anyway, that isn't what you said the day you took over Culverwells.'

'I know what I said,' he rasped. 'That was before I'd had a chance to study just how hard you've worked and how much you've put into the firm, given of yourself, to get the best out of your fellow directors and your staff.' He lifted his glass again. 'I salute you, Grace. It isn't every day, in my experience, one comes across such single-minded ded- ication—particularly in a woman. And before you say I'm being sexist—' he put up his other hand, staving off the retort that was teetering on her lips '—I'm not. I merely stated in my *own* experience. Most of the women I've known in top management have had to split their time between their jobs and their families, particularly their children, which makes it very hard to remain ruthlessly single-minded indefinitely. You, fortunately, have had no such distractions.'

'No.' With a rueful curl to her mouth she looked down at her glass, wondering what he would have said had he known that if fate hadn't intervened she would have had a child now. And not just any child. *His* child.

'Come on,' he said, surprisingly gently, perhaps sensing her sudden change of mood, probably thinking it was because of losing her previous position in the company. 'I'll take you home.'

The gallery lights below her flat had only just gone out when the huge white car pulled up outside.

'Beth's been working late,' Grace commented, getting out

of the car just as the gallery door opened and the curvy little brunette came out.

Exchanging a few words with her friend, Grace couldn't help noticing the way Beth looked appreciatively at Seth who was moving around the bonnet of the gleaming white Mercedes.

'How do you do it?' she whispered to Grace, clearly awe-struck.

Reluctantly, because Seth had overheard, Grace introduced Beth to him. What woman was safe from him? she despaired as the two of them shook hands and the gallery manager seemed to visibly melt beneath Seth's devastating smile.

'So, you're the Seth Mason I've been hearing all about!' All smiles herself, Beth sounded slightly breathless as she let Seth know with that unusually tactless remark that Grace had been discussing him with her. 'Didn't I see you at the open-ing night?' She looked at Grace then back to the tall, rather untamed-looking man beside her for confirmation.

'It's…possible,' Seth answered rather evasively.

'It's all right, Beth, I'll lock up,' Grace offered, relieved when her friend took the hint and tripped lightly away without causing Grace any further embarrassment, after falling over herself to express her pleasure at having met Seth.

'Going to ask me in for coffee?'

He was standing there just behind her and, after he had just bought her the meal, Grace didn't feel she could refuse.

When she complied somewhat uneasily, she saw him nod briefly to his driver.

'You said coffee—not breakfast,' she reminded him with her heart racing as the large saloon pulled away.

'He was parked on double yellows. He'll amuse himself without breaking any traffic regulations until I give him a call.'

Which told *her*, she thought, feeling suitably chastened. She was relieved though that the gallery door was still unlocked,

which meant that she could take him through to the small
sitting room at the back of the shop rather than up to the
crowding intimacy of her flat.

Flicking on the lights and securing the doors behind him
so that no one would think the gallery was still open, she left
him browsing the display of paintings while she went through
to the tiny kitchen behind the stock room and made two mugs
of instant coffee, pouring milk into her own and remembering
that, in the office, Seth always drank his black.

He was studying a simply framed pen-and-ink seascape
which was concealed from public view in a small recess
behind the counter when she came back. He stooped closer,
reading the scrawled signature at the bottom.

'Matthew Tyler.'

'My father.'

He took the mug she handed to him. 'Of course. I understand his paintings sell for thousands—tens of thousands—
these days.'

Grace nodded.

'I believe his sculptures aren't doing so badly, either.'
When she didn't respond with so much as a gesture this time,
he tagged on, 'You must be very proud of him.'

Was she?

To avoid answering, she took a hasty sip of her coffee and
burnt her tongue in the process.

'I didn't really know him,' she said, trying to sound non-
committal when she had recovered enough to speak.

'And is this the only thing you have of his?' He glanced
at her briefly.

'Besides this shop?'

She was reminded from his lack of surprise that he knew
about that already. 'No loft full of unsold masterpieces?'

'I should be so lucky,' she said with a grimace. 'I don't
think he'd done anything for a long time before he died.
Anything that wasn't unfinished or crossed through had been

sold, or thrown away. I've been told he was an obsessive perfectionist.'

'So this was all he left you to remember him by?' He was still studying the sketch, his Adam's apple working as he took sips of his coffee.

'Well, no, to be fair, there was one other item.'

He sliced her a glance, obviously expecting her to enlarge, but she didn't.

With her head tilted to one side, she gave her attention to the drawing. 'It's good,' she appraised a little stiffly. 'But it isn't one of his best.'

His best, according to the experts, was the bronze figure she had sold, created from a sketch that Matthew Tyler had made of his daughter during one of his rare and fleeting appearances in her life. He had only come to see her then, during those agonising weeks after her miscarriage, because Lance Culverwell had sent for him, because she had been so unwell, so low...

'The sculptures were his forte,' she told him with her gaze still trained on the wall, wondering if those intelligent eyes she could feel suddenly resting on her profile could guess at the tension behind her tightly controlled features.

How could she talk about that bronze to anyone—least of all him? Explain the emotions that had driven her to selling it?

She didn't even chance looking at Seth, afraid that he would see those emotions now scoring her face.

'What is it?' he asked quietly, far, far too aware.

She gave a gasp as the lights in the gallery suddenly went out, leaving them in darkness.

'Oh, no, not a power cut,' Grace groaned, though she was grateful for the diversion from his probing question in spite of the inconvenience of having no electricity.

'I...don't think so.' Seth was looking at the festively lit shops on the other side of the road and the street lamp that was glowing brightly immediately outside the gallery. 'It might be that something's blown your fuses,' he stated.

She uttered a nervous little laugh. 'Just my luck!'

'Do you know where your trip switch is?'

When she told him he went through without any hesitation to fix the problem. A couple of seconds later, the lights came on, but then instantly went out again.

'Do you have any other appliances switched on?' he queried.

'Only the fridge.'

'Anything upstairs?'

'Again, the fridge…'

'What is it?' he asked, seeing her frown.

'I put the dishwasher on before I left this morning. But that would have finished hours ago.'

'I think you'd better let me check.'

As soon as she opened the door of the flat to let them in, she could feel the heat coming from the kitchen.

Seth shot her an urgent glance. 'What time did you say you put it on?'

Grace looked at him anxiously. 'Before I left for work…'

Three strides brought him across her tiny kitchen. He cancelled the switch on the wall above the worktop before opening the door of the overheated appliance, stepping quickly aside as a cloud of steam gushed out.

'I don't think there's any doubt that your dishes are clean,' he remarked dryly. He was down on his haunches now, pulling the lower basket towards him, and Grace felt her gaze drawn to the way the dark-grey fabric of his trousers strained across his thighs as he inspected the shiny interior of her dishwasher for any obvious damage.

'It's been going all this time?' It was an amazed little utterance, dragged from a throat suddenly dry from a riveting sexual awareness.

'Seems like the programmer's stuck,' he diagnosed authoritatively. He was pushing the basket back in, but stopped in mid-action. 'Hardly a load worth putting on, was it?' he commented, noting the sparsity of dishes in both baskets.

Grace made a small gesture with her shoulders. 'Believe it or not, I don't spend all my time in this flat cooking.'

'Obviously not.' His speculative smile left little doubt as to what he thought she spent most of her time doing. Probably entertaining a steady stream of boyfriends! she thought hopelessly. 'But that doesn't alter the fact that you're not eating enough.' His eyes, skimming over her willowy figure beneath her black executive suit, admonished as much as they admired. 'Worrying about something, Grace?' The sound of the dishwasher door clicking closed only added to an air of menace Grace could almost touch as he got to his feet, so that she was far too affected by him to answer. 'We're going to have to do something about that, aren't we?' he said.

Aware of the worktop against the small of her back, Grace swallowed, feeling absurdly trapped. The way he was looking at her with that smouldering regard—as though he knew that the reason she couldn't eat or sleep properly was because she was so wound up over him—left her in no doubt, after that last remark, as to what he was going to do about it.

One of the sleeves of his suit was pushed up, exposing a good deal of immaculate white cuff. Those loose strands of hair that fell tantalisingly over his forehead even though he'd raked them back were curling damply from the steam. He looked flushed, dishevelled and incredibly sexy.

'Come here, Grace,' he urged softly.

CHAPTER SIX

SHE didn't want to. She wanted to ask him to leave. But his eyes were as compelling as his voice had been and, while her lips wouldn't move, her feet had no such reservations.

Fuelled by an inner fire that his masculinity had stoked, as much a slave to her desire for him now as that teenager had been all those years ago, she moved towards him, drawn by an insistence stronger than her will, stronger even than all her instincts of self-survival.

When she was but half a pace away he reached out and let his fingers curl around the nape of her neck, closing those extra inches as he brought his head down to hers.

Surprisingly, his lips grazed one corner of her mouth, so gently that Grace sucked in her breath from the exquisite tenderness of his action.

His breath was warm and so feather-light against the curve of her cheek that the sensuality of it sent shivers along her spine. She turned her head, her mouth aching for contact with his. He laughed softly, denying it, drawing a small, plaintive sound from her lips.

'Why rush it?' he whispered against her ear, and even the deep timbre of his voice was arousing her—as he knew it would, she realised helplessly, lured deeper into the sensual heaven he was creating for her.

With one hand resting against his shirt beneath his open

jacket, Grace could feel the warmth of him and the steady rhythm of his heart. His biceps flexed under fingers that were locked tensely onto his immaculate sleeve just below his shoulder. Even the cut and elegance of his clothes couldn't disguise his latent strength, the whipcord power of his body.

'Seth…' she murmured as wanting became a need that spread like bushfire, radiating excitement, heat and tension along her veins.

'Pleading?' he mocked softly. But then he was covering her mouth with his own, his arms coming fully around her, pulling her into the hard angles of his taut, aroused body, his groan lost in the warm cavern that was yielding to his sensual plunder now.

No man had ever made her feel like this, Grace acknowledged, her arms sliding up around his neck. No one! *Only this man!* And now she knew why all her potential relationships with other men had failed. Because after Seth she had wanted to feel like this with someone else, just once, and it had never happened for her. Never in eight long years.

The scent of him was intoxicating as her eager fingers slid into the dark strength of his hair, locking him to her to prolong the kiss, wanting it never to stop.

When he did it was only to allow his lips to follow the scented column of her throat, forcing her head back as her body reacted with a will of its own, arching, yielding, guiding him along its secret paths to unleash the pleasure to which only he had ever possessed the key.

Somehow he had tugged open her blouse and pushed aside the scalloped lace of her white bra, and as his mouth closed over the erect, tingling peak of her breast the pleasure spilled out in a spiral of throbbing need.

'Seth…'

She shouldn't be doing this! There was a frantic little voice inside her head: *he despises you!* she tried telling herself. But her feeble attempts to remind herself were lost in the delirious heat of all that he was doing to her as she helped him remove her jacket and blouse, and felt him release the button on her skirt and draw down the zip like it was second nature to him to be undressing her.

He murmured some appreciative sound as the clinging little garment slid to the floor, followed by the bra he had unclasped, so that she was standing there in only her white satin string and sheer black hold-ups.

Later she would regret this, she knew, but for now what did it matter what he thought about her? All that mattered was that she was in his arms, this man who had been born to be her lover, because he was right, she accepted with a painful intensity. He was the only man she wanted. The only man she had ever wanted.

His hands caressed her breasts, his slightly callused palms an excruciating pleasure as they teased and tormented the pale, swollen aureoles.

Wild for him, drugged with desire, she tugged at the buttons of his shirt, allowing him to help her in removing his jacket, dragging his shirt out of his waistband.

The feel of his taut, warm skin as he pulled her back against his hair-roughened body sent pulsing sensations rocketing through her.

Her breathing laboured, Grace caught his groan of need, her excitement a stifling heat that held her rigid as he moved to allow his tongue to travel down and down along her eager body.

He was on his knees, his long fingers caressing the gentle curve of her buttocks, playing across the smooth, pale flesh above the black lacy tops of her stockings.

She moved convulsively and he caught her to him, his mouth hot against the core of her femininity beneath the damp scented satin of her string.

She was on that beach again, paralysed by the depth of her

wanting, her body moving of its own accord, for him to douse the fire he had aroused in the only way it could be doused.

'Oh, mercy…' He shuddered violently against her and the next instant he was lifting her up, finding his way instinctively to the room with the big double bed.

Somehow they were lying there naked together and those hands caressing her body were as familiar as a pathway home.

She jerked against him, eager for his possession, but he was determined to make her wait, treating her to a practised and abandoned eternity of consummate love-play, just as he had promised he would.

A long time later when she was damp and sobbing with desire, thinking she would die of wanting if he didn't take her soon, gently he parted her thighs and with one rapturous thrust slid into the slick, wet warmth of her body, blowing her mind with his slow, calculated control.

With a driving need, she curled her fingers along the velvet-sheathed strength of his back, her body closing around his, writhing beneath him like a mad thing until the swift, sharp crescendo of orgasm that made her cry out. It seemed to go on and on, until the thrusts that were driving her became harder and more urgent, and the fluid warmth of him erupted and flowed into her, finally dousing the mutual fire of their passion.

Some time afterwards he raised himself up and looked at her. Her hair lay like a silver cloud over the pillow. Her face was flushed and damp from the ecstasy they had shared. Her eyelashes, though, were drawn down, as though she didn't want to look at him—or couldn't.

Marvelling at how beautiful she was, a warm pleasure curved his mouth from the way she had made him feel, as though he were the only man on earth—or, amazingly, the only one that mattered—and on a breath that seemed to shudder through him, he murmured, 'Look at me, Grace.'

The eyes she raised reluctantly to his were dark and slumberous from the aftermath of their love-making, but as they tugged over his face something clouded their depths and in a barbed tone she said, 'Why? So you can claim yet another victory for yourself?'

Her unexpected response surprisingly cut him like a whiplash.

Of course. She hadn't been able to help herself, any more than he had. They were bound to wind up in bed together whether they liked each other or not. And it was clearly "or not" in her case, he realised, mocking that moment's conceit when he had imagined otherwise.

So what had he been expecting? he challenged himself roughly. Declarations of undying love from her? His inward laughter was mirthless and cold. Of course not. He wouldn't have welcomed that from her in any case. Or would he? The thought struck him suddenly. He had to admit that it would be a rather ironic turn up for the books.

'If that's the way you want to view it.' Self-ridicule put a chill in his voice now. 'Although for one supposedly beaten you sounded pretty triumphant at the end.'

Shame scorched Grace's cheeks. How could she have let it happen? she remonstrated with herself, mortified that he had seen her so helpless and begging. But that was exactly what this whole seduction thing had been about, she realised hopelessly, wanting to bury her head under the pillow and never come up for air.

'I take it there's no chance of your getting pregnant?' Seth's question was curt, matter-of-fact.

Coldly reminded of all she had been through after the way she had behaved with him the first time, Grace pressed her eyelids closed, immensely relieved that at least she was protected by the Pill she had started taking shortly before her cancelled wedding.

Nevertheless, she couldn't help biting out, 'Isn't it a bit late to ask me that now?'

It was, and he could have kicked himself for not giving it too much consideration beforehand, but then she had blown his mind with her abandoned response.

'Well?' It was a hard, emotionless demand.

'Don't worry.' Rolling away from him, Grace leapt to her feet and self-consciously scrambled around for the robe that she'd left draped across the bottom of her bed that morning. 'I won't be coming after you with a paternity suit,' she assured him caustically, finding the robe in a pool of pale satin on the carpet. 'If that's what you're worrying about.'

'Do I take it then that you're on the Pill?'

Propped up on an elbow, he reclined there, watching her, totally unfazed by the fact that he was naked while she was struggling to bring both ends of her robe together, ridiculously embarrassed after what they had just done.

'Take it any way you like!' Finding it almost impossible to keep her eyes from those heavily muscled limbs and hard, lean torso, when he had just used that devastating masculinity of his to subdue her, she swung away from him towards the bathroom, not anticipating the speed at which he could come after her until he was pulling her round to face him before she was even halfway towards the door.

'What are you trying to do?' His fingers bit into her arm. 'Deny that it happened?'

How could she? She still wanted to slide her hands over his magnificent body, surrender to its warm strength and thrusting power with a pleasure unequalled by anything else in the universe.

'No,' she uttered shakily, looking past him so she wouldn't have to focus on the harsh sweep of his jaw and that hard, incisive mouth that had made her cry out with the screaming intimacy of its kisses. The musky scent of him that was filling her nostrils was a taunting reminder of how uninhibitedly their juices had fused. 'Just trying to come to terms with being such a fool.'

'Don't let it get you down.' He released her with almost careless indifference. 'The feeling does wear off eventually.' And on that scathing note he turned away, leaving her fleeing to the bathroom with the stinging reminder of how she had once made an equal fool of him.

Fortunately, Seth flew off the following morning to pursue some new accounts in the States, which gave Grace time to recover her composure and a little bit of dignity. She didn't know how she would have faced him, particularly in front of the rest of the board, Simone and other members of staff, knowing that she had played right into his hands and handed him on a plate the conquest he had been planning.

As she took telephone calls, attended meetings and made appointments for the week ahead, she kept asking herself—as she had been doing constantly since before she had come out of her bathroom the previous night and found that Seth had already left—why she had let things get so out of hand between them.

He had shown her a soft side of himself yesterday that had lured her into a false sense of security, and like a prize idiot she had fallen for it when she knew how much he despised her and how little respect he had for her. Consequently, she only had herself to blame.

She groaned at her senseless behaviour, so unable to think of anything else that she cut off a caller who wanted to speak to the marketing manager and got through the rest of her work like an automaton. Her only consolation, she thought, racked by shame and self-reproach, was that she'd learned her lesson the first time and that at least this time there wouldn't be any repercussions from their love-making.

Seth didn't return at all that week. Having already put things in place to keep the company running smoothly while he was away, he telephoned some time during the following week to say that he expected to be out of the country for the rest of the month.

He didn't speak to Grace personally, however, leaving the message with Simone. Hurting and angry, Grace decided that, having achieved everything he had set out to do—taking control of Culverwells, then securing her ultimate humiliation by taking her to bed—he was obviously now treating her with the contempt he thought she deserved.

Christmas came and went with still no word from him, and her wretchedness was only compounded by a heavy cold.

Having spent the holiday alone, being forced to miss a party at Beth's, and with Corinne having flown off to Madeira on Christmas Eve, Grace returned to work on a wet January morning feeling as though she was the only person in London that Christmas had done a detour round, and with the knowledge that Seth wasn't due to return for another week.

And, if that wasn't enough to deal with, her period was overdue.

At first she put it down simply to stress. Stress could be responsible for a lot of things and over the past couple of months she had had a lot of things to be stressed about.

No way could she be pregnant, she assured herself resolutely. Fate couldn't do that to her twice.

But, beneath her over-confident attempts to dismiss any possibility that she might be, lay the nagging truth that she was worried sick. She'd been protected, when she and Seth had made love, it was true, but she was only on a low-dosage Pill, and she had had a stomach upset a couple of days before. She hadn't even thought of it at the time, but of course something like that could render the Pill ineffective. It didn't help reminding herself that her periods were as regular as clockwork. That there was only one other time in her life that her period had ever been late...

Around mid-week, feeling queasy and off-colour, she

decided to buy a pregnancy test. And it was then, in the lonely privacy of her flat, where she had behaved so foolishly with the man whose only plan was to make her pay, that her worst fears were realised.

She was having Seth Mason's child—again!

'You OK?' Simone glanced up at her young boss with matronly concern as Grace emerged from the 'ladies' just outside her PA's office. She had darted in there a few minutes before, overcome by a bout of sickness.

'I'm fine, Simone.' Grace wanted to dismiss any suggestion that she wasn't, unwilling to draw attention to herself or her pregnancy. But she had just seen herself in the ladies' room mirror and had been shocked by how washed out she looked, with her black pin-striped suit emphasising the sickly pallor of her skin.

'Yeah?' Simone sounded as sceptical as she looked. 'And my name's Errrol Flynn and I swing from chandeliers for a living.'

Grace couldn't help but smile wanly at the images that conjured up. 'I'd like to see that,' she murmured, too under par even to want to talk right then. 'Honestly, Simone, I'm fine.' She managed to inject just the right degree of authority in her voice to silence her concerned PA; she was glad of her standing in the company which gave her the right to pull rank, that she seldom exercised, so that she could escape to the privacy of her own office.

The phone was ringing on her desk before she even had chance to sit down.

'How are you getting on with that hunk you're answerable to now?' Corinne enquired from her yacht somewhere in the tepid waters of Madeira, sounding far too breezy. 'And don't tell me you're not enjoying it, because he's the type of man that could satisfy even someone with as many sexual hang-ups as you.'

Sighing, Grace rued the day that she had confided in her grandfather's young wife about her lack of desire for the men she dated; she'd been especially worried when her real lack of enthusiasm had extended even to Paul.

'Did you know my grandfather knew of Seth Mason from years ago?' she asked the model, not feeling up to having this conversation with her. 'And that he would have done anything to keep him from pushing his way into his company's boardroom?'

'Not pushing, Grace, dear—storming it. And with all that lovely drive and crackling authority!' That the woman was smitten by Seth's looks and dangerous charm was obvious to Grace. 'Anyway, what do you mean?' She could almost see the redhead's green eyes narrowing in anticipation of some juicy snippet of information about him, and realised too late that she had said too much when Corinne, her voice dropping confidentially, enquired, 'What did he do? Try to have his wicked way with you?'

She laughed, supposedly at the improbability of it. But it was so on the mark that Grace couldn't contain the sharp little breath that escaped her. 'Good heavens! Is that it?' Corinne was far too shrewd not to have noticed. 'My word! Have I hit the nail on the head? Is that why you're so opposed to working for him? What did he do, Grace, spoil you for every other man?' Corinne's amused tones were just a little too loud, far too triumphant. 'You aren't frigid, love. You were just weaned on the wrong type of man far too soon.'

The wrong type of man full-stop! Grace thought, hating him, angry with him and with herself—for wanting him, for missing him like crazy, and for allowing herself to get pregnant—twice!—by the man she had once snubbed. Only now he was snubbing her, and it wasn't very nice. No, worse than that—it hurt like hell!

But why? she asked herself, agonised. She wasn't in love with him, was she? Or had she just been kidding herself all

along? Was that why she had never been able to indulge in
casual sexual relationships with men as some of her contemporaries did? Or even find the degree of pleasure she should
have found with the man she had been planning to marry?
Was it because she had found her soulmate in a man her
upbringing had forced her to reject? The man with whom
she had compared all other men she met, only to find them
lacking in every way?

'Stop dreaming up romantic dramas, Corinne,' she parried,
shaken by the possibility, and desperate to keep the ex-model
from realising that she had guessed the truth—or at least part
of it, at any rate. No way was she ready to accept that all her
problems with men stemmed from a void in her life that only
Seth Mason could fill.

'Granddad would have been appalled by what you did.
Culverwells is going to wind up being sold off. Seth says he
won't do that, but I don't believe it.' And in a sudden rush of
anger, because she hadn't seen him, because she didn't know
where he was and because she had been unfortunate enough
to conceive his child when he didn't even like her, she blurted
out, 'He's a money-making, social-climbing, mercenary opportunist! And if you ever see him again, you can tell him I
said so!'

'Why don't you tell him yourself?' Corinne's voice suddenly sounded sultry, oddly provocative. 'He's sitting right
here on deck beside me. It's Grace. I think she's missing
you.' There was no attempt on Corinne's part to cover the
mouthpiece.

In a mortified daze, Grace grabbed the edge of her desk
for support. Seth was on her grandfather's yacht? Seth was
in Madeira with Corinne?

'Hello, Grace.' As it started to sink in that he must have
heard everything that her grandfather's widow had been
saying about her, that deep voice coming down the line was
agonising torment. 'Is everything all right?'

No, it blasted well isn't!

Then, as it dawned that Corinne must know everything that had been going on between Seth and herself, in a voice raw with accusation she exhaled, 'Did you tell her?'

'Tell her?' He sounded puzzled. 'Tell her what?'

'About us?' She imagined them together, discussing her, laughing about it.

'What is there to tell?'

'For goodness' sake! Do I have to spell it out?' He was stalling for time, making her sweat—and enjoying every minute of it. 'You know exactly what I'm talking about.'

'Now, come on, Grace. You know what I said about kissing and telling.'

'Oh, thanks a bundle!' Now Corinne wouldn't be in any doubt about what had gone on between them. 'So now you've made sure she knows, if she didn't before!' The pain she felt inside was excruciating, but she forced herself to continue even as she collapsed, sick with herself, onto her chair. 'I suppose you're getting immense satisfaction out of this?'

'No more than you were when you tried to convince Simone—and probably the whole office—that I was involved in a paternity suit.'

His words made her flinch. Well the joke had backfired on her. And how!

'So that's what this is—tit for tat? Let the spoilt, stuck-up little brat stew while you're sunning yourself with Corinne and having a good laugh over it at expense? Why not just shout it to the crew? Why not tell everybody what we did? You're worse than unscrupulous, you're…!'

'Hold your horses, Grace. Corinne's gone below.'

'What for?' she enquired pointedly. 'Her bikini top?'

'You think I'm bedding your grandfather's widow?'

'Is that what they call it, lying bare-breasted on the open deck of a yacht? Or has she gone down to warm up that nice, big double bed for you?'

'What's really eating you, Grace?' He was beginning to sound annoyed. 'Are you jealous?'

'Hah! Don't be ridiculous!' she retorted, feeling a wave of nausea wash over her. She took a deep breath to try and stave off the feeling before she went on. 'It may surprise you to know that I don't care what you do. Just don't do it in my company's time!'

'It isn't your company—it's mine.' All levity had gone from his voice. 'And so help me, Grace, if I was in the building right now I'd come straight down to your office and take you over my knee.'

The anger trickling down the line from goodness knew how many miles away was a tangible thing in the silence that followed.

Through an imprisoning sexual tension, Grace could hear the water lapping against the side of the boat, hear the wind tugging at the rigging, a mixture of sounds confused and distorted by the ringing of a phone somewhere in another office and the deep, rhythmic sound of the photocopier on Simone's desk.

'I'm here to finalise a deal,' he stressed before she could recover her vexed and wounded pride enough to deal with that last sexist remark. 'But I'll be back in the office next week, and then I'll give both you and the company all the attention you need. Now, what was it you wanted?'

'Wanted?'

'Why did you ring me? Is there some problem?'

Trying to clear her head, Grace only then remembered that Corinne had telephoned *her*, whether to make her jealous, or in some weird, sadistic way to see how she would cope having her private emotions discussed in front of Seth, she wasn't sure.

'Yes,' she breathed, so humiliated now that she didn't care if she did ruin his week, wanting to make things as difficult and as painful for him as he was making them for

her in being with Corinne. That was impossible, though, she
thought, because nothing could hurt him as much as she was
hurting as she spat out bitterly, 'I'm pregnant!'

CHAPTER SEVEN

THE phone she slammed down started ringing almost immediately, and even without checking the number on the display Grace knew it would be Seth.

When she didn't pick it up, it continued to ring, a shrill insistence that cut through her tension, causing the embryo of a pain to start throbbing on either side of her temples. At last the ringing stopped.

Good; let him stew! she thought, gritting her teeth against her headache and her suffocating misery. But instantly the phone started ringing again.

When she didn't respond this time, the merciful seconds' silence that followed was immediately broken by her mobile phone ringing in her bag on the shelf behind her desk.

Grabbing the bag, she found the phone with fingers that shook, and with more than a degree of unusual force switched it off.

She couldn't—wouldn't—give him the satisfaction of venting his frustrations on her now. If she was going to have to suffer all over again for her stupidity in going to bed with him, then he was going to as well, she agonised with bitter tears stinging her eyes just as a call came through on her internal line.

'What is it?' She knew the answer even before she heard the receptionist's harassed response.

'It's Mr Mason. He's on line one. He's having difficulty getting through to your office.'

'Tell Mr Mason I'm not taking any calls.'

There was a brief hesitation. 'I can't do that.' Grace could almost feel the girl's horror at even being asked to contemplate contradicting their new chief executive.

'Then tell him I'm out,' Grace instructed, her mouth tightening at the sway Seth held over what had been her grandfather's and then her staff.

'I can't do that either.' The disembodied voice sounded even more diffident. 'He already knows you aren't.'

Feeling sorry for the girl and not wanting to put her in an awkward position, Grace grabbed her coat and, imparting a resolute, 'Well, I am now!' she made a hurried exit from the building.

It was wet and murky outside and cold needles of rain stung her face, as she'd left her umbrella in the office. The bare trees around the square she turned into looked like dark shadows of their former selves, and even the houses and shops looked dreary and left-over now that the festive season was gone.

She needed to get out, she told herself in an attempt to justify dropping everything and making her escape from the office, a thing which under normal circumstances she would never even have considered. But these weren't normal circumstances, were they?

The fact of her pregnancy had still scarcely sunk in when Corinne's call had come through, and the woman had made those very personal remarks about her—in front of Seth. Only Grace hadn't known that Seth was with Corinne up until that point. Until then she had simply been wondering how she was going to tell him about her pregnancy.

Anger and jealousy tore at her as she thought about him with Corinne; imagined them lying on the sun deck of that yacht, limbs entwined, pale skin yielding to the sinewy strength of dark bronze.

What would it matter to him that she was carrying his child? She was a woman of the world—or so he thought. Women of the world could handle little set-backs in their lives like unwanted pregnancies, particularly if they weren't in love with the child's father. And she wasn't in love with him, was she? she asked herself fiercely. How could she be with a man who could treat her so badly? Who was determined to make her pay for the way she had treated him when she'd been a spoilt teenager, no matter what the cost?

The blast of a van's horn brought her up sharply as she made to cross the busy road, and she jumped back onto the pavement, berating herself for jeopardising not only her own life but her unborn baby's too.

She wasn't a woman of the world. She would have this baby and she would bear the consequences, she determined grittily. It was just that it was going to be so humiliating, facing Seth.

She hadn't planned to shout it down the phone at him. But she had been so mortified when she'd realised he must have heard the things Corinne had been saying that she hadn't been able to help herself, knowing he must surely think her a wimp—besotted with him! And, if he found out that she had conceived after her rash behaviour with him last time, he'd think her even more of a fool now.

Which she was, she reminded herself with unsparing criticism. Not only for being weak-willed enough to let him break down all her defences, which had led to her winding up in bed with him, but for not even considering that she might not be adequately protected when she had vowed all those years ago that she would never let any man affect her enough for anything like this to happen again. And now here she was, eight years on, older but certainly no wiser. Not only in the same situation, but with the same man!

There were no calls for her when she returned to the office

with her head throbbing, her emotions in turmoil. At least, none from Seth, she was surprised to discover.

Perhaps he had given up trying to get hold of her and had simply gone back to enjoying himself with Corinne, Grace thought bitterly, although it didn't make her feel any better to imagine him stewing over what she had told him. If he had any conscience at all, he had to be! And privately, too, because she couldn't imagine for one moment that he'd discuss it with Corinne.

Or perhaps he would.

Piercingly she remembered the things that he and Corinne had said to make her fling the news of her pregnancy down the phone at him. Perhaps they had continued to discuss her afterwards. Perhaps even now he was taking solace in Corinne's arms.

As she moved around her office, trying to maintain her usual degree of efficiency and failing miserably, she was unable to imagine Corinne not taking exception to her stupendous lover sleeping with another woman. And, not just another woman, her late husband's granddaughter! Although, knowing Corinne, if Seth did tell her he was fathering a child she might even congratulate him on his virility!

Would he make love to the model, put his inconvenient mistake with Grace out of his mind until he returned next week? she wondered torturously. Because wouldn't this unplanned pregnancy be the ultimate revenge as far as he was concerned?

Angry tears stung her eyes as her head continued to pound and it was very late in the day when Simone, aware that her boss was feeling under the weather, came into the office to help Grace find a file that she had misplaced.

When the phone buzzed on the desk and Simone took the call, she said in a dumbfounded whisper to Grace, 'It's Seth. And he's in a hell of a mood.'

'Tough,' Grace responded flatly from the filing cabinet,

still determined not to speak to him. 'I'll talk to him when he gets back.''

'You're damn right you will!'

Both women's heads swivelled round to meet his implacable authority in the doorway. That uncompromising masculinity was only intensified by the white-hot anger in his face as he ordered, 'Simone—out! *Now*!'

The PA didn't stay to be told a second time. Distractedly it registered with Grace that the call that had come through from Reception must have been to warn her that the new CEO had just thundered in.

Her mood, though, matched his as, determined not to be intimidated by him, she snapped, 'Don't you ever come in here and speak to me or my PA like that again!'

'And don't you ever dare to deliver a blow like that closing remark you made this morning and then think you can just put the phone down on me!'

'Why not? Did it cramp your style with Corinne?' His face blanched with fury, but she was angry too. Very angry. 'Well, I'm very sorry to have dragged you back from such adoring company!'

She was near to tears but strove to control them, realising that he could only have used the executive jet to get back here so fast. He'd probably flown it himself, she thought waspishly, remembering his PA telling her once that he was an experienced pilot in his own right.

He moved angrily past her, grabbing her raincoat from the coat stand.

'Here. Take this. We're leaving.'

She only obeyed because her head was throbbing too much to endure a shouting match with him in the office, and because an imperious hand at her elbow was already urging her towards the door.

'Where are you taking me?'

'Somewhere where we can be alone.'

Every cell in her body rebelled against it, although her heart was beating with a wild anticipation that left her despairing with herself.

She caught Simone's discreet glance up at them as Seth marched her past her PA's desk, but she was too keyed up to argue with him or to say anything to Simone.

With his jaw set in stone, Seth summoned the lift, saying nothing as he urged her out of the building to the waiting Mercedes.

'Where are we going?' she demanded to know, as Seth handed her into the back of the car and slid in beside her. 'What makes you think you can just march into my office and start trying to take control of my life?'

The transparent screen closing in front of them obliterated any chance of their being heard by the man who was just pulling the car away.

'I would have thought that was obvious. You're having my child. Much as that must be the last thing that you, or either of us, wanted, I think that gives me some rights.'

He couldn't have made it any plainer than that!

Although, she'd known her pregnancy would be the last thing he'd want or expect, hearing him say it cut as painfully as scaling a wall of broken glass, and she turned away from him to hide the anguish scoring her face.

'I'm sorry,' he said, but coldly, tersely, noticing the pain of rejection in her tight, tense profile. 'I really believed you were on the Pill. It was wrong of me to assume.'

'Yes, it was,' she bit back with her eyes fixed on the head-rest in front of her. If he'd used protection too, then this would never have happened, would it? she reasoned bitterly.

'And you weren't involved?' he challenged thickly before she could go on to explain that she wasn't as irresponsible as he obviously thought she was. 'You weren't the one writhing and sobbing beneath me in that bed?'

With flame colour touching her cheeks, Grace darted a

glance towards the thick neck of the man in front of the glass screen, immensely grateful that he couldn't hear what was being said.

Seth's graphic reminder of the way she had welcomed his love-making until she was begging for him to take her that night, though, shamed her into responding, 'I don't know what *you've* got to be so angry about. Anyway, I *was* on the Pill—or supposed to be.'

'So what happened?' His brows came together over eyes that were interrogative, darkly accusing. 'Did you forget to take it or something?'

'No, I didn't! I'd had a bout of tummy trouble just before we—' She couldn't even bring herself to say it. And because his attitude and his insinuation that it was all her fault was only making her feel worse than she did already, she threw angrily back at him, 'I'm not any happier about this than you are. And I'm sorry if it's messed up whatever you had planned with Corinne, but you needn't worry—I've got no plans to try and trap you!'

'Will you shut up?' It was a soft yet unmistakable command. 'For heaven's sake! Isn't it possible for you to utter one civil word to me unless you're being kissed?'

Turning her head sharply away from him, Grace stared sightlessly through the tinted glass at the surging bodies moving past the endless shops with their 'sale' signs splashed across the windows. She tried not to remember the ecstasy of that firm, male mouth covering hers, the mind-blowing pleasure as it had rediscovered her body like a familiar map, reading it with the deftness of a skilled explorer, recognising every secret curve and dip he had made his own.

'I swore,' she railed at herself. 'I swore I'd never let myself get pregnant—'

Again, she nearly said, but stopped herself in time, cupping her hands over her face with an exasperated sigh.

'It happens.' His voice was low, clipped, matter-of-fact.

'Not to me.' Inhaling deeply, Grace leaned back against the plush cushion of the headrest, closing her eyes against the truth.

Because that was just it—it did happen to her. *Twice.* Twice in her life she had gone the whole way with a man, and only one man. And twice in her life she had conceived, as though something beyond herself was determined that she would be impregnated with his seed. As though her ultimate function in life was to be the mother of his child.

'I expect every woman who finds herself in the same situation without wanting to be probably says the same thing.'

Yes, but they aren't having a baby with a man who doesn't even like them. Whose only reason for making love to them in the first place was just to exact some sort of revenge!

Noticing the increasing tension in the tight line of her jaw, Seth could see that this thing had come as an appalling shock to her, much as it had come as a complete shock to him. She looked now as she had looked the night they had made love and he had queried the possibility of her getting pregnant— like having his child was the last thing she could bear to contemplate. Which it probably was, he thought.

Because of her very high-profile affairs and the way she had treated him originally, he'd believed that to a girl like her men were just things to provide amusement, but in that, at least, he was beginning to realise he'd been wrong. The things Corinne had let slip about her had amazed him, even if he did suspect that they had been disclosed solely to reduce her step-granddaughter's possible appeal to him and boost her own sexual appeal in his eyes.

But in fact it had had the opposite effect. The knowledge that he could turn the haughty little enchantress who dumped men for a pastime, and who was really as cold as a Siberian winter, into a mass of steaming, sultry passion when he got her between the sheets had given him a shameful, chauvinistic satisfaction. Just how pliable did that make her in his hands? he wondered with a rush of masculine hormones raising the level of his libido a few notches. Because there was no doubt that she did things to him that no other woman had ever done.

Just thinking about how she responded to him in bed made him burn with the need to feel her nails digging into his back, to have her crying out his name—and only his—as they drove each other wild until they were sated. It didn't cool his ardour much to tell himself that it was because of his raging hormones where she was concerned that they were in this situation now. But the simple fact was that she *was* pregnant…

'Well, after what I heard Corinne saying on the phone…' he began, with his voice thickened by desire, 'I don't think I need even question whether it's mine, need I?'

As the Mercedes took a sharp left-hand turn that tipped Grace nearly into his lap, shame and humiliation leaped like angry flames to scorch her pride.

'You bastard!' Automatically her hand flew up and was instantly dealt with by a stronger one before it could make contact with his cheek.

Deftly she found herself pressed back against the cream leather upholstery with that long, lean body angled across hers.

'Believe it or not, it was meant as a compliment,' he breathed with menacing softness.

'Some compliment!' It came out on a squeak as excitement ripped through her, her senses leaping into overdrive from the hard, arousing weight of his body. Trying to collect her thoughts, she guessed it would be a major boost to his ego to realise he was the only lover she had ever had. But if he knew that then she would be lost, she thought despairingly, his to do whatever he wanted with, because she would have no defence then against his devastating sexual magnetism.

'Don't believe all Corinne tells you,' she got out tremu- lously, because he hadn't moved. He was still holding her captive as if he didn't trust her not to fly at him the instant he let her go. Or maybe he just liked being in control...

The need to assert command over her own actions had her wriggling against it.

He merely laughed at her ineffectual struggling. 'I won't, if you promise not to,' he said, letting her go.

'Promise not to what?' she quavered, even though he was sitting back on his own side of the car again now.

'Believe everything that Corinne Culverwell says.'

His tone was less than complimentary at the woman with whom he had supposedly shared a recent spell of unfettered passion. So what was he implying? Grace wondered with a leap of hope that made her despair at her own weakness in wanting to believe anything he might chance to tell her. That he really had gone to Madeira just to finalise a deal, as he had assured her he had on the phone that morning?

And if she believed that she would believe anything! she thought, realising that she was in very grave danger of trusting him—at least where his integrity was concerned.

The Mercedes pulled up at the kerbside and Seth handed her out onto the pavement. A young family passed them, a mother pushing a toddler in a buggy, a child of about four riding piggyback on the shoulders of the man beside her. They were all laughing, at ease with one another; happy.

Moments later Seth was guiding Grace through the foyer of one of London's most exclusive apartment-blocks. Chandeliers glittered, silver shone from highly polished surfaces, catching the reflection of a massive floral-display in the centre of the main area, while Grace's pumps sank into a carpet as soft as manicured grass.

This sort of luxury wasn't new to her. She had been born to it and had been accustomed to it until Culverwells' diminishing fortunes had meant everyone having to tighten their belts. But the young man with the motorbike who had had to drag himself out of virtual poverty had to have striven hard for this type of living—the cars, the plane, the power. Unbelievably so. She couldn't help but be impressed and a little overawed by the drive and determination he must have had to bring it about.

Nevertheless, as he brought her up in a lift with mirrored walls and they stepped out into a luxurious suite of rooms on the top floor of the building, she murmured, 'Trying to impress me, Seth? What are you trying to prove? That you've done well for yourself?'

His mouth pulling down on one side, he gestured for her to precede him into a huge room with deep pale sofas and panoramic views of their great city, which at this time of day was a glittering universe of twinkling lights. 'I don't think I need to do that. I leave proving to lawyers and those whose job it is to provide us with our daily bread. But, yes, I have done well.'

'And you're flaunting it for all you're worth.' His droll comment lent a curve to her mouth, though, and she realised that what she had just said wasn't totally true. Though the sumptuous drawing room in which he was inviting her to sit down was well-appointed, it was also uncluttered and exuded an air of understated elegance that was both tasteful and refreshing.

'What did you prefer, Grace—my being poor and totally at your mercy?'

Her eyelids pressed against the dark wells of her eyes as she sank down into the sofa's cushioning softness. Would he flay her with that for ever? It didn't make it any easier that her head felt as though it was splitting in two.

That rough edge to his voice, however, made her wonder if he meant at her mercy *emotionally*, until she realised how dangerous it was to think like that. Seth Mason was hard. He only meant at the mercy of the circumstances that getting involved with her had got him into.

'And you think,' she said feebly, looking painfully up at him, 'That by getting me pregnant you've got me at yours?'

His soft leather shoes made only a light sound over the varnished floor. 'You aren't at my mercy, Grace. Just at the mercy of your inability to resist whatever this thing is between us. Just as I am.' The curl of his mouth was self-mocking. 'And right now, yes, you are carrying my child. But don't worry. The situation can be easily remedied.'

She jumped up, and wished she hadn't when her head felt as though it had just exploded. Even so, that didn't stop her tossing back, 'That's about the sort of reasoning I'd expect from you! If you think I'm going to simply take the easy way out just because you can't bear to think of your *enemy* presenting you with a baby—wasn't that what you said we were the day you took over the company? *Enemies?*—you've got another thing coming! I don't want anything from you beyond a little recognition that you're its father. You can play around with whoever you want to, just so long as you acknowledge that. It makes no difference to me.'

'On the contrary.' His slow stride over the immaculate floor was measured, predatory. 'I find your being pregnant with my child rather satisfying.'

Whatever she had been expecting, it wasn't that.

'Why?' she asked guardedly. 'Because you think it would be one in the eye for the Culverwells to have to acknowledge your offspring as one of theirs?'

She meant because of the desire he'd been nursing all these years to avenge his family for the way they had suffered. Too late, though, she realised how it had sounded, as if he'd be tainting the pedigree blood of her family with the questionable origins of his.

For a moment his eyes blazed, but then his lashes came down and something like self-satisfaction shaped that hard mouth as he said, 'If it pulls you down off that class-conscious cloud you're obviously still clinging to, then, yes, I can't deny that it's a rather ironic twist of fate—don't you think?'

Because he hated snobbery, Grace knew, as much as she did now, although she knew she could never convince him of that in a million years.

'And you will have something from me, Grace. I'm not asking you to take the easy way out. In fact, I strictly forbid you to do anything that would harm our child. No, we're going to assume responsibility for this little one's life—together. And that means a marriage licence.'

'A marriage licence?' She was staring at him, wide-eyed with shock, her heart seeming to stand still. 'You can't be serious?'

There was no humour in his face as he advised, 'Believe me, I've never been more serious about anything in my life. There's no way any child of mine will grow up without the close presence of a father in its life.'

'As you did.'

'And as you did, I believe. After what Corinne told me about your own father deserting you, I'm surprised you'd even consider denying your own child that right.'

She had never talked about her father to Corinne, so the woman had obviously gleaned that information from Lance Culverwell.

'Well, you certainly had a good chin-wag about me, the pair of you, didn't you?' she accused in a wounded voice.

Seth's grimace said it all. Her grandfather's widow was garrulous enough without any help from him.

Amazingly, in spite of everything, some deep-boned intuition told Grace that Seth Mason would never be a party to idle gossip, and once again she found herself coming to believe that his dealings with Corinne were purely professional.

'The fact remains,' he said, 'that you were abandoned by your father, and through whatever circumstances he scarcely figured in your life. Don't let that happen to your own baby.'

Her head was banging so much she was beginning to feel sick; she didn't feel up to having this conversation with him.

Still trying to come to terms with the fact that he had actually proposed, unable to quite believe it, she said quickly, 'A lot of women manage perfectly well as single parents today.'

A shoulder moved beneath the superb tailoring of his jacket. 'It's up to you, but I'd like to think that you wouldn't be that selfish.'

When he was prepared to marry a woman he didn't love for the protection and well-being of his child.

'You make me feel I have no choice,' she uttered, feeling the strands of a silken web being slowly but insidiously woven around her.

'You do have a choice. I'm just asking you to make the right one.' A few lithe steps brought him within heart-stopping distance of her. 'Oh, come on, Grace.' His voice was soft, sultry, deep, like a jungle cat purring. 'It won't be so bad.' The fingers suddenly lifting her chin up, compelling her to look at him, were excruciatingly tender. 'Maybe I'm not the lawyer-doctor-accountant type you've always dreamed you'd be marrying.' *As if!* she thought almost hysterically. 'But we've got something that will ensure that any union between us will never be dull.'

He meant in bed.

A wave of excitement curled along her veins, a silent betrayal by her body of all it wanted—no, *needed*—from him, no matter how strongly her brain tried to deny the fact.

The shock and emotion were too much for her in her present state. As the room seemed to go wavy before her eyes, she dropped her head into her hands with an involuntary little groan, trying to stave off the threatening nausea.

She heard the low invective Seth uttered and could do nothing to resist the arms that were sweeping her effortlessly off her feet. 'Why didn't you tell me you weren't feeling well?' he scolded softly.

Caught against his hard, warm strength, her mind and body reeling with myriad sensations, somehow Grace managed a pained little smile. 'You only seemed concerned with what was going to happen to your baby.'

Those masculine lips curled in self-derision. 'Believe it or not, I do have a vested interest in its mother, too.'

He carried her through into the quiet luxury of the master bedroom. Compared to hers it was a sanctum of modern living, from the sinking carpet that bore his silent, effortless steps, to the monstrous bed with its very masculine but state-of-the-art cushions and covers that he dragged aside before setting her down on the dark-burgundy sheet covering the mattress.

Helping her out of her coat and jacket and then stooping to remove her shoes, he pressed her gently back on the pillow and pulled the duvet up around her.

'If you want anything,' he told her quietly, 'I'll be in the next room.' The degree of solicitude behind that simple statement brought a painful lump to her throat.

'A vested interest', he had said, but only because she was having his baby. He didn't care about her for herself. So why was she letting herself imagine such depth of emotion in his voice?

Nevertheless, no matter how much he had wanted to hurt her and her family, she thought, there was no doubt that he would accept his paternal responsibilities. The hardship and the poverty he had endured as a child and then, thanks to her, as a young man desperate to support the family who had taken him in, had obviously contributed to his determination not to let any child of his suffer in the same way. Although, even without that, there was no question in Grace's mind that he would still have held the same view about being a seriously hands-on parent. But was she prepared to let him help her bring up her child? Marry him? Apprehension coupled with excitement didn't do much to ease the painful banging in her head.

If she didn't, she reflected, and she decided to go it alone, there was no way that her child would go without seeing its father at regular intervals; Seth would demand that, of course, and she wouldn't try and stop him seeing his child—no matter how much it might hurt her to have to face him on a personal level from time to time, because she didn't think she would be able to carry on working with him after this. Her child would never want for anything financially. But was that enough?

She remembered how it had felt growing up. Her grandparents had been wonderful, had given her everything she could have wanted. But, guiltily, sometimes she had missed the fun and activities that her school friends seemed to have with their parents—particularly their fathers—younger, more energetic adults who could get involved in a game of tennis with them, or chase after them before scooping them high into the air shrieking with laughter, as fathers always seemed to be able to do. Fathers who were always there and didn't disappear for months, or even years, on end. She had missed having a birth mother, of course, but she had missed her father more than she could ever put into words, because she had known he was around somewhere. Just not with her. And that had hurt more than she had ever dared to let herself accept.

She thought of the little family she had noticed on the way up here. Two children. Two parents. A happy balance. She owed her child that much, didn't she? And if—*fingers crossed*—this little one growing inside her went to its full term, was born safely…

Fear threatened to rise like a dark spectre, but she fought it back. She couldn't—wouldn't—let herself think about that now, for the same reason she hadn't been able to bring herself to tell Seth what had happened before. It was a part of her life that she wasn't particularly proud of and she had paid for it dearly—then pressed it so far to the back of her mind that it was as though that girl she had been and everything that had happened to her had happened to someone else. It wouldn't help her or him in any way, she reasoned with a kind of muddled logic, to dig it all up now.

So with the muted tones of Seth's voice conducting business over the phone in the other room, and the elusive scent of him surrounding her in his personal bedding, she made her decision, safe in the knowledge that whatever his feelings towards her he would always be there to love and support his child. And that was all that mattered, she told herself resolutely. Wasn't it?

CHAPTER EIGHT

ABSENTLY Grace toyed with the slim gold band on her finger, noticing how brilliantly it shone in the high Mediterranean sun.

'What's the problem Mrs Mason? Still having difficulty digesting it?' Propped up on an elbow on the sun deck of his luxurious yacht, wearing only a pair of dark bathing briefs, his bronzed body slick with oil, Seth was watching her where she lay sunbathing on her back on the soft mattress beside him. His face was alight with teasing. 'Perhaps I'd better give you another dose of something to make it slide down more easily.' His eyes gleamed wickedly as he leant closer to her, his black hair falling forward. 'Or slide up,' he murmured tantalisingly in her ear in a way specifically designed to arouse her, as he had been doing, much to her shaming delight, for the past five days.

She still couldn't quite believe it had taken less than seven weeks from that evening in his apartment, when he had practically demanded they get married, to lying here with him in nothing but the lower half of her shimmering blue bikini. She was unable to get enough of his hands and lips on her body, her deliciously tender nipples already hardening in anticipation of his special therapy, that secret place at the apex of her thighs contracting, burning for him, because he hadn't made love to her for at least two hours.

When she rolled over onto her stomach so that he wouldn't recognise the naked need in her face, the betrayal of her shamelessly aroused body, he laughed knowingly and moved to draw a slow, sensuous line with a finger over the sensitive length of her spine, creating havoc in her as his hand ran caressingly over the smooth, silky mound of her buttocks, temptingly enhanced by the separating blue string at their crease.

'Don't think you can pretend modesty after all that we've done,' he mocked softly against the nape of her neck, causing a pleasurable shudder to shake her still slender body as she thought of the shocking intimacies they had shared since their wedding night—the way he had shown her how to please him, things that she would never have imagined herself doing to any man, but which had only enhanced the pleasure for her too.

'I think from now on you'd better leave these off,' he advised as he peeled her bikini bottom away from her slick, hot body like a sybarite unwrapping an epicurean feast.

Exposed, open to his probing hands and eyes, she squirmed beneath him like a restless filly, groaning into the pillow, a sound both of sensuous delight and defeat. Her excitement was only heightened as he breathed, thrillingly aware, 'I'm sorry. I forgot how reluctant you always are to do this with me,' and pulled her round onto her back to accept her fate.

Much later, lying in the darkness in the big bed in the master cabin, tender in several places after a long evening of making love, Grace marvelled at the iron control that Seth had exercised during the weeks leading up to their marriage—whenever since he had shown himself to be not only a sensational lover, but an insatiable one. too.

After agreeing to be his wife—but only, as she had made clear to him to deflect him from her true feelings, for the sake of their child—she had resolved to refuse to move in with him before the wedding, had he asked her to. But he hadn't. Nor had he even attempted to get her into his bed.

Perhaps he had been busy saying goodbye to his glorious bachelorhood and the women who'd currently figured in his life. *Like Corinne*, she'd thought painfully, although she had refused to dwell on any relationship he might have had with her grandfather's beautiful widow then, and she refused to do so now.

She still wasn't totally sure whether Corinne Culverwell was anything other than a business associate, as Seth had first implied she was, although the reason he had given for being on Corinne's yacht that day in Madeira had been borne out a few days later during a telephone call she'd taken from one of his colleagues. He had unknowingly confirmed what Seth had said, that it had been purely to tie up some loose ends with the takeover, since it was on the way back from the neighbouring Canary Islands where he'd been spending Christmas and New Year with his family. As to any previous intimacies he might have had with the model, Grace had no intention of questioning him further. If she did, she decided, then he might realise the truth—that his new and reluctant bride was already dangerously in love with him. Dangerous to *her*, that was, because she knew full well that he wouldn't have married her if she hadn't been carrying his child.

As for the way he was with her in bed…

Well, he was only behaving the way any healthy, red-blooded male at the peak of his fitness would behave with any reasonably good-looking woman who had given him licence to her body, wasn't he? she reminded herself. Although deep down she was beginning to realise that he was as enslaved by his desire for her as she was by her own for him.

He was attentive in public, too, practically proprietorial—something that Corinne, only recently informed about the baby, had commented on at the wedding.

'Well, you're both a pair of dark horses, aren't you?' she

had remarked in that affectedly polished voice with a smile that left her long green eyes cold, her brightly painted lips stretched falsely wide as she caught Grace momentarily alone. 'You do know how much you'll have to give to please a man like that, don't you?' Jealousy was stamped all over Corinne's beautiful face, though she was battling to hide it and failing miserably. Grace had felt almost sorry for her. 'I really think you might have bitten off more than you can chew this time, sweetheart. He's behaving like he owns you already.'

'Don't I?' Seth had enquired, overhearing, looking dynamic in a pale-grey suit, white shirt and silver tie. He'd turned around from the little group of guests he had been talking to and had slipped an arm around Grace, studying the slender hand he caught in his and which bore his shiny new ring.

Fresh from the register office in her short and simple white sixties-style smock dress, with a sprinkling of white flowers interwoven in her pale, elegantly swept-up hair, Grace had worried that there was more behind his supposedly teasing question than he'd been letting show. A hard arrogance that had said he had her where he wanted her—her master in the office and a soon-to-be-willing plaything in his bed.

It had been a pleasant enough day, in spite of that. At Grace's request, and in view of the relatively short time for arranging everything, it had been a small and very private wedding away from the prying eyes of the press, with only very close friends and family members attending, with Beth and an old friend of Seth's as witnesses. The reception had been a simple affair, too, held in the palm court of one of the West End hotels.

'Grace, I think it's time you met my mother.'

Seeing the grey-haired, tired-looking but straight-backed lady in the moss-green dress and jacket, waiting with a much younger, copper-haired woman as they arrived at the hotel, Grace allowed Seth to lead her across to them, her heart coming up into her mouth.

He hadn't seen fit to take her to meet his foster mother during those few weeks before they were married, and it hadn't taken long for Grace to realise why: this was the woman who had cared for him since he'd been a young teenager until he had been forced to leave home when Lance Culverwell had had him sacked from that boatyard. It was because of her, Grace, and the way she had led Seth on, practically seducing him on that beach and then unknown to him conceiving his child, that her grandfather had made him pay. He had used his influence to crush him, deprive him of his livelihood, splitting the family up and causing them unnecessary hardship when Seth had left town to try to find work elsewhere. But Nadia Purvis, as she was introduced to Grace, couldn't have accepted her son's new bride with a warmer greeting as she kissed Grace on both cheeks and welcomed her into the family circle, putting Grace instantly at ease.

'I apologise for not having been able to meet you before now,' her new mother-in-law said. 'But we've been on a trip to Canada and the Rockies—a present from Seth for my birthday.' The way she looked up at him showed nothing but gratitude and immense pride for the tall dark man to whom she had once given a home—and a lot of love too, Grace knew without being told. 'My special birthday.' Her weary eyes were bright with laughter as she turned back to Grace, making them all laugh with her as she added, 'Although I'm not saying which one. Then we finished up in New England visiting Alvin—'

'My twin,' the long-haired beauty who had been waiting patiently beside her chipped in. 'He's at uni there. We're supposed to be identical but fortunately, I'm happy to say, not in every way.'

Grace laughed again, as the others did, deciding that the girl couldn't have been much older than twenty. 'I'm Alicia, by the way.'

Taking the bangled hand that was being offered, Grace

leant forward and kissed her. 'Hello, Alicia.' And then, as recollections kicked in, she was murmuring before she realised it, 'Aren't you…?' and only managed to stop herself in time.

Of course. That day all those years ago. Hand in hand, sated with love-making, Seth had taken her back to a modest little house on the edge of the woods. She hadn't gone in. He had only taken her there to give her a lift back home on the bike. But as she'd been putting on her helmet a little girl had come running out of the house. A little girl in pyjamas who had begged him to take her for a ride, and whose bright curls he had ruffled before gently but firmly sending her packing back inside.

Amazingly, it seemed that Seth hadn't told his mother just who had been responsible for him losing his job at the boatyard, and secretly she could only thank him for that. But then it only bore out what he had always maintained—that it wasn't his style to kiss and tell. Even when he had been humiliated and demoralised he hadn't stooped to smearing her or her family's name. Instead he had kept it to himself with that private and very personal resolution of one day making them pay…

'You're Seth's sister,' she finished now, amending what she had been going to say, and guessing that the word "foster" would have been dropped from this family's vocabulary a long time ago.

'And the baby of the family,' Seth added, 'as she was born fifteen minutes after her brother. And consequently indulged and spoiled beyond belief.'

'But not by you.' Big hazel eyes twinkled mischievously up at the elder brother whom she obviously adored and who had been around for most of Alicia's young life. Grace calculated that the twins must only have been about two years old when Seth had entered their world. 'Although he *has* said he's going to buy me a BMW convertible if I do well in my exams. I'm doing interior design,' she clarified for Grace's sake.

'He's said nothing of the sort,' Seth denied, though with that charming smile of his, obviously used to Alicia's ploys to try and twist him round her little finger.

'And you better had do well, young lady,' her mother warned. 'After all it's costing him to put you through that college.'

Grace laughed again, liking his sister, liking them all, and wishing with all her heart that this marriage had been one built on love, trust and respect. But an exchange of glances with her new husband showed no more than a fervid desire for her within the closed, inscrutable depths of his eyes.

'I'm sorry my younger son couldn't be with you,' Nadia was saying to Grace. 'But he's in the middle of very important exams, too, although he does send his apologies.'

He had also sent a huge bouquet of mixed roses and a congratulatory telegram that morning which was now displayed, with the simple bouquet of lilies she had carried that morning, on either side of the two-tiered wedding cake. 'Exams are very important,' Grace commented, guessing that Seth was probably funding the best possible education for Alicia's twin brother too, a thing he himself had been deprived of. She had recently learned he had studied long and hard, way into the night, after he had left school.

Simone joined them then with her accountant husband, breaking up the intimate little party, and some time afterwards Alicia came and looped her arm through Grace's, asking her about her gallery. Grace was happy to discover that they shared surprisingly similar tastes in art.

Not long after the cake had been cut and a toast made by Seth's best man, Seth ushered Grace away to the airport, from where they flew out to the Mediterranean island and Seth's private yacht to begin their three-week honeymoon.

'I thought it might be more to your liking than that crude

little boat I made the mistake of thinking I could first woo you on,' he remarked, as he lifted her through the sliding doors on the bough into the vessel's luxurious saloon, where a champagne dinner was waiting for them. But his tone had been cynical and self-derisive, so she responded with a slightly defensive edge to her own voice as he set her down on her feet.

'As a matter of fact, I loved that little dinghy. It was simple and honest. Uncomplicated.' Not like this floating temple to wealth and success that screamed of his power and influence, and was bigger and more luxurious than anything her family had ever owned.

'Uncomplicated?' His laugh expressed something not far short of disdain. 'I suppose something about that day had to be.'

'I meant real. Unpretentious.' She struggled to explain, trying not to let the scorn that still festered inside him get to her, to spoil the day. She wasn't able to keep the regret out of her voice as she said it, though, and realised, with an ache of remorse in her chest, that she had let him know that eight years too late.

They returned to England and moved into Seth's apartment on a sunny spring day that was still rather cool after the kinder climate of the Mediterranean. The place had been cleaned and aired by a discreet staff and there was a 'welcome home' bouquet, professionally arranged in a clear glass vase on the dining room table, from Nadia.

There was a card, too, among their post, sent jointly from the twins, which from the postmark, Grace smilingly noted, had obviously been chosen, signed and posted by Alicia. Even Corinne rang to welcome them home, but not until the following evening, because she had forgotten on which day they were supposed to be coming back.

'And how's my step-granddaughter?' she asked in that

too-perfectly-English voice, then punctuated her question with a very audible shudder. 'Don't you just hate it when people refer to us like that? I do. It makes me sound so...*ancient*,' she announced, and without waiting for Grace to answer any of her questions went on to enquire, 'so how's that gorgeous husband of yours?'

'Fit,' Grace responded, smiling to herself. Corinne was like a runaway train when she got going. 'And disgustingly tanned! He's out at the moment.'

'What, already?'

Grace sighed to herself, wondering why she was always left wishing she hadn't said things that Corinne could pounce on.

'He's at a meeting involving one of his own companies. Some emergency or other.'

'And it's obviously too early in your marriage to ask if you believe him.' Corinne gave an affected little giggle. 'I must admit, I never imagined a man like Seth Mason tying himself down to one woman. Not after what he said to me, not too long ago, when I asked him if he was ever going to settle down with anyone.'

'Don't tell me—he said no?'

'No, he didn't actually. All he said was that if he ever chose to marry anyone it would be because of mutual benefit to them both.'

Mentally, Grace shrugged. 'So, he was cynical about marriage. A lot of people are.'

'Possibly. Who knows what goes on in any man's mind? I do think, though, that you were part of his long-term plan.'

'Plan?' Grace was beginning to feel decidedly uneasy.

'Oh, come on, Grace, you're a prize for any man. You have to see that. Particularly to one who's had to drag himself up from the bottom of the heap. Clever move on his part, getting you pregnant so you'd marry him. He certainly doesn't believe in dilly-dallying, does he?'

'What exactly are you saying, Corinne?' Grace was holding the phone so tensely that her fingers were beginning to hurt. 'Are you accusing Seth of deliberately seducing me just so he could…?' Little doubts were creeping into her mind as to how much truth there was in what Lance Culverwell's widow was saying. Stupid doubts, but doubts nevertheless.

'Not accusing, my little innocent.' Grace cringed at the condescending phrases Corinne was too keen on using whenever she spoke to her. 'I'm applauding him. I'm sure he's madly in love with you, but you must admit that having Grace Tyler beside him won't do him any harm socially, either. What with all your high-flying contacts and upper-crust connections, the man can't fail to get where he's going—and fast.'

Corinne was only saying these things, Grace was sure, because she was jealous of her. After all, Seth Mason had it all—looks, money, power—while Corinne had had to content herself with a man two and a half times her age to give her the type of lifestyle she obviously craved.

'Seth doesn't need anyone to help him get where he's going,' Grace snapped, as much to convince herself as Corinne. 'And he certainly isn't interested in social climbing. He hates that sort of snobbery.'

'That's what we all say, but if the opportunity arises…' Grace could almost see the woman's expressive little gesture. 'And you did accuse him of being an opportunist, before you suddenly surprised us all by announcing you were having his baby and getting hitched to him.' Which wasn't quite how it had happened, Grace thought, but was feeling too unhappy to correct Lance Culverwell's widow.

'Our reason for getting married so soon—and he was as committed to this as I was—was to give our baby the best possible start.'

'That doesn't stop him from being the opportunist you obviously thought he was.'

Only because after we made love he seemed to vanish into

thin air! Because I thought he'd only been using me! Grace wanted to cry out, but realised that that would just endorse the things Corinne was saying.

'And you didn't marry my grandfather for personal gain?' The accusation slipped out before she could stop it.

'Oh, come on! I was very fond of your grandfather. I thought he was a poppet—you know that. But a girl's got to think of her future, too.'

'Well, you certainly succeeded there, Corinne.'

'Which is why I think I know the Seth Masons of this world much better than you do,' the woman persisted, too thick-skinned to be unduly affected by the things her late husband's granddaughter reproached her for. 'I'm not claiming to be a saint. I know I've got my faults. And I really don't want to see you get hurt.' Poor Corinne; she really believed that, Grace thought bitterly. 'But let's face it. You've got a hell of a good deal too, haven't you? I mean, he's got to be *incredible* in bed.' It would dawn on Grace later that for the model to surmise about Seth's mind-blowing prowess as a lover meant that Corinne could have done nothing more than fantasise about sleeping with him. 'And what's wrong with allowing somebody to use you just a little if your reward is mind-blowing sex with a man who looks and sounds like that?'

After Corinne rang off, Grace speculated unhappily on all that the woman had told her. Had Seth really been so keen to propose because of the personal gains he believed he could make by marrying her?

She was sure that first and foremost he had the interests of his baby at heart, but had he also seen her as a way of furthering his brilliant career, as Corinne had so unkindly suggested? Had that supposedly unselfish act to do what was right by her and the baby masked a mercenary streak that allowed him to use his child's mother for his own ends? The mercenary streak that had driven him to take Culverwells from under her nose so humiliatingly? And he'd done it with Corinne's help, because without the model's compliance he'd never have succeeded in exacting revenge in quite the way he had.

The only positive point to come out of that telephone conversation with Corinne, Grace realised, was the confirmation that Seth had been telling the truth—that he and the model weren't, and apparently never had been, lovers. It was small consolation, though, after everything else that her grandfather's widow had said.

Her pregnancy had already begun to show. Grace knew there were whispered comments and wild speculation in the office about the exact timing of her baby's conception, but she deflected the surreptitious glances and casual remarks with her usual air of detachment and calm efficiency.

They had to wonder, though, she thought at the moments when unvoiced curiosity made her feel a little self-conscious, whether their new and dynamic CEO and Lance Culverwell's granddaughter had actually known each other before Seth had seized control of the company in that hostile bid. Or whether, having faced each other on opposite sides of the commercial battlefield, their determined new boss had broken through his pretty opponent's line of defence with guns blazing and had swept her up onto his charging steed and into his bed before she had time to realise what was happening.

Which was about the size of it, Grace couldn't help thinking, still plagued by doubts after that last conversation she had had with Corinne a couple of weeks ago. She wondered if those curious speculators were also silently applauding Seth Mason, as Corinne had, for what must look like a very shrewd move, in view of the antagonism and opposition he had been getting from her.

On the up side, her morning sickness seemed to have all but sorted itself out. Nor did she feel as tired as she had during the first weeks of her pregnancy. But her worries and suspicions about why Seth had actually married her were beginning to make her feel an emotional wreck.

She already knew that he didn't love her, that he had only married her to give her child his name. But, like every woman before her who had found herself in a similar situation, she was troubled by insecurities while nursing a desperate, if not completely vain, hope of making him love her.

That was until the day she found that photograph of herself with Paul.

It was the only snap she had kept of her fiancé because it featured her grandfather standing between them with an arm around them both. It had been taken shortly after they had got engaged.

She didn't realise Seth had come into the bedroom until he said over her shoulder in a voice that was frostily controlled, 'If you still want him, you only have to say.'

Startled, she dropped the photo back into the open drawer she had been sorting through, realising how guilty that must make her look even as she swung round to retort, 'Of course I don't want him. How could you possibly imagine that?' But he did, she realised, because ever since that day she had spoken to Corinne he had clearly sensed a change in her, once or twice even querying if anything was wrong.

His smile didn't warm the steely grey of his eyes, and the fingers that lifted lightly to her cheek were cold too, making her gasp. 'Then why are there tears glistening in your eyes?'

'They're not. I mean…'

Not because of that, she was trying to say. But she couldn't seem to form the words to tell him that it had been the picture of her grandfather looking fit and well that had brought on that spurt of emotion.

'And why, when I touched you, did you flinch?'

Her shoulders sagging, Grace realised that she was in a no-win situation. Seth Mason was a possessive and dominant male and wouldn't take being side-stepped by his wife for another man lightly—even if he didn't love her.

'Perhaps you *want* me to tell you I still want Paul, is that it?' she tossed up at him with disbelieving eyes, barely able to contain the hysterical little laugh that bubbled up in her throat from the absurdity of it all, but even more from the harrowing suspicion that she might just be right. Perhaps he *had* originally married her to suit his own ends but now, realising the enormity of what he had done, just wanted an easy way out.

'Do you?' he challenged again.

'If you believe that, then there's no hope for us, is there?' she murmured dismally. 'I married *you*, didn't I?'

'Yes.' His powerful chest expanded on a sharply drawn breath. 'You married me.' Not a glimmer of emotion moved those harshly sculpted features as he added, exhaling air from his lungs, 'And would you care to tell me why?'

Caught in the trap of her own making, Grace didn't know what to say.

Because I love you!

The admission, even in her own mind, made her go hot and cold. How hopelessly lost she would be if he realised that!

'Well, not for the same reason as you—obviously!' she hurled at him.

'And what would that be?' His narrowing eyes were glinting with anger.

'To open the doors you haven't actually managed to kick down yet.'

There, she had said it, thrown it in his face like a douse of cold water.

Deny it! her heart screamed, only he didn't.

He stood stock-still for a moment, like some cold, unfeeling statue frozen in time. But then a muscle twitched in his jaw, the only indication that there was life pulsing inside him, before he tilted his head in the briefest of acknowledgements.

'So we now know where we both stand, don't we?' he stated grimly, and walked away, his actions only reaffirming what she already knew. That he hadn't a scrap of feeling for her beyond the fact that she was going to be the mother of his child.

After that their marriage seemed to undergo a marked change. What comradeship there was started to ebb out of their relationship. Seth began to stay later at the office, often arranging for his car and driver to bring Grace home.

They seldom made love any more, sleeping back to back like strangers, and when they did it was with an almost antagonised passion, as though each resented the needs that only the other could supply.

Somehow Grace managed to keep up appearances in the office, particularly as Seth was conducting a lot of business outside of it for a lot of the time. When the weekends came she spent most of her Saturdays when he was away working helping Beth at the gallery, feeling lonely and confined in the apartment—for all its spacious luxury—when Seth wasn't there.

'We'll have to find somewhere else to live when the baby comes,' she suggested tentatively to him one morning when they were getting ready to leave for the office. They had made love the night before, a lengthy, wordless exchange of excruciating pleasure; it embarrassed her too much to even look at him as she recalled it, as it only seemed to accentuate his cold detachment this morning, emphasised by his hard executive image in the cold light of day. 'A child needs a garden to play in. Somewhere to run around and make a noise in without upsetting the neighbours.'

'Of course' was Seth's succinct response.

But then two days later he surprised her by coming home and tossing a pile of glossy brochures featuring ultra-superior properties down on the coffee table. Georgian mansions with acres of woodland; huge, modern split-level state-of-the-art glass houses, and one gothic-like stone building with gargoyles and turrets that also boasted its own lake.

'I'm sure you can find something in there to suit you,' he remarked.

'Any limit to the budget?' Grace enquired after a few moments, looking up from a page of homes with hair-raising price tags to see him casually shrugging out of his suit jacket. The sight of his broad shoulders beneath his white silk shirt and that tapering torso, spanned by the dark waistband of his trousers, caused a painful contraction in her throat.

'Let me worry about that,' he advised.

So she kept on browsing, and when she had finished she laid the last of the brochures back on the pile on the coffee table without a word.

'Well?' he enquired over the paper he was reading when she sank back against the creamy cushions of the sofa.

Grace wondered if her disillusionment showed in her face.

She couldn't tell him that looking at those houses had lowered her spirits. That she found them as cold and impersonal as he seemed to be with her the minute she was out of his bed.

Had success and power changed him so much from the home-loving, surprisingly tender young man she had given herself to all those years ago? she couldn't help wondering desolately. Did he just want money to flaunt at the type of people he believed deserved his contempt? Like her grandfather? Like the Paul Harringdales of this world? Like her?

'Perhaps something a little less...obvious,' she suggested, which sounded more gracious than calling the homes 'ostentatious' or 'depressing'. And, to put him more on the right track next time, she added a little coyly, 'If it helps, I prefer... simpler things.'

Surprisingly, to Seth it came as a revelation. But why

should it surprise him? it struck him now. There was the quiet, unfussy wedding she had readily agreed to. He'd thought it was because it had been something she merely wanted to get through for the sake of the baby. But would she still have wanted all that simplicity if they had been a love-struck couple? he wondered, because there were other things, too.

Most of the women he'd met in his life had been shopaholics, and he'd imagined she'd be the greatest, but in that he'd been proven wrong. She didn't particularly like shopping, not for clothes at any rate…and as for those artificial, glitzy parties they were constantly being invited to, amazingly she seemed to spurn them with a passion almost as strong as his own.

'Quite a woman of hidden depths, aren't you?' he commented dryly, joining her on the sofa.

'Does that surprise you?' Her eyes, instantly guarded as he came down beside her, had a rather wounded look about them. 'You thought you were marrying an inveterate snob.'

'Have I ever called you that?' Surely he hadn't? Even if at times, in view of how she had treated him in the past, he might have thought it.

'You didn't have to,' she murmured, adding to his sense of guilt.

'We all make mistakes,' he conceded.

'You?' That familiar scorn heightened the healthy colour in her cheeks. Now that her morning sickness had eased, she was really beginning to blossom. 'Surely not!'

In reply he merely lifted her hand, healthily golden against the darker bronze of his, and pressed it to his lips. Her skin was scented and soft.

Dark-blonde lashes came down as though she couldn't bear it—or what he could do to her, he decided with ruthless satisfaction, aware of her pulse beating frantically against the heel of his hand.

'I thought you were always right.' An edge had crept into

her voice, a tension caused by the sexual undercurrent that dominated everything they said and did. Would it destroy them eventually? he wondered. Because, when it was gone, what would there be left?

'Sometimes it isn't a bad thing to be wrong.'

A question darkened the blue around her dilated pupils, but he glanced down at the hand he still held to avoid a conversation he didn't want to get involved in, studying the simple arrangement of stones that formed her engagement ring.

Not for her the high-carat diamond he'd thought she might pick to cement their hurried betrothal. Or the extortionately priced yellow sapphires that the jeweller had tried to tempt her with in that exclusive goldsmith's in the West End.

Now his thumb brushed lightly over the modest cluster of tiny rubies and emeralds surrounding that single tiny diamond she had selected over all the rest.

Once again, he found himself silently admitting, this lovely girl whom circumstances had virtually forced him into a union with had, without even knowing it, tossed his preconceived ideas about her right back in his face. She was a mixture of simplicity and complexity and he could never tell which one of those facets of her character was going to reveal itself to him each day. The one who stayed reserved and distant from him while they were here like this or alone together in the office, or the one who staved off any suggestion of anything intimate with him for as long as she was able to, then turned into a tigress the instant he took matters into his own hands when they were in bed.

Then no words could deny that what they did together was meant to be—and what both of them wanted. They were from totally different worlds, universes, and yet in bed they spoke the same language, one that consisted only of touch and feel and the most basic of instincts, where only the most exclusively sensual phrases played any part.

He felt the need to speak that language with her now, and

knew that was something he could have fulfilled within seconds if he had taken it upon himself to do so. Because she always responded to him; because she couldn't deny herself the pleasure she craved from him any more than he could resist the scent, taste and feel of her eager body beneath his hands, the hypnotising sweetness of her incredible mouth.

An emotion, more complex and far less primal than the need to have her, stirred inside him, threatening to make him vulnerable to this beautiful woman who had once slain him with just one look. He wasn't prepared to let that happen. Not ever again.

'I'm sure we can find something to please you eventually,' he said dismissively, getting up, his voice sounding strained and distinctly cold from the control he was having to exercise in not tugging off those stuffy office clothes of hers and whisking her off to bed to make love to her until she was sobbing to take him into her. 'Until then we'll just have to manage—if it's not too difficult for you.'

And on that note he turned and strode out of the room.

Everything was going as it should, Grace thought two or three weeks later. At least with her pregnancy. The baby was developing normally, despite her initial fears, and the doctor had said that, although they needed to keep an eye on her because of her mother's and her own medical history, she was a prime example of a healthy mother-to-be.

Everything would be perfect, she decided painfully, if the man she had picked to fall in love with had been in love with her. But he wasn't, and the knowledge that he might never love her, coupled with the strain that that was putting on their marriage, was making her snappy and irritable.

Only this week she had had two migraines and had had to leave the office early. Seth had been away, and as she'd been fine by the time he'd come back she hadn't bothered mentioning it to him.

Now, though, sitting at her desk with another headache coming on, a pain in her lower abdomen and feeling decidedly yucky, Grace wound up the conversation she was having with a customer who was far too chatty and made a merciful escape to the bathroom.

There she made a discovery that left her trembling with shock and fear.

She was bleeding!

She was nearly five months pregnant and she had started a miscarriage!

CHAPTER NINE

SETH'S face was flushed and he was breathing heavily as he burst into Grace's office.

He had been in a board meeting when Simone's call had come through and, too impatient and worried to wait for the lift, he had taken the stairs, flying down them like his life depended upon it.

With a nod at Simone who was just coming out, he crossed over to Grace, who was sitting with her feet up on the couch that stood against the far wall.

There was a deathly pallor to her face that concerned him immensely and her eyes as she looked up at him were dark with something closely akin to desperation. When he took her hand and dropped to his haunches beside her, he could feel how much she was shaking.

'What is it?' It was an anxious whisper as he closed both hands around the cool trembling one he was holding. 'Are you going to be all right for me?'

She looked at him as though she was almost surprised to hear him say that. 'Oh *Seth*…I think I'm losing our baby.' Tears mingled with the desperate emotion in her eyes, an emotion that tugged at him so much that he had to remind himself that it was purely maternal instinct that was making her look like that. They said it kicked in at some point of the pregnancy, however unwanted the child might have been to begin with.

'Hush. Don't upset yourself,' he breathed. He even managed a sort of watery smile. 'You need to conserve all your energy to help that little one hold on. And, anyway, it might not be a miscarriage.'

'It is. It's happening again!'

'Again?' Puzzlement joined the anxious lines scoring his face.

'Just like before.'

'Before when? What are you talking about, Grace? What do you mean? When has this happened before?'

Now she wished she hadn't kept it from him. 'I was pregnant,' she admitted, her shoulders drooping.

'When?' There was so much he didn't know about her, that he had only begun to find out since they were married. But this? When had she been pregnant? Whose child had she been carrying before his? He wanted to know all the answers—but now wasn't the time. Also, Simone was just coming back in.

'Is there anything else I can do for you both, Seth?' Over the weeks, since the brief engagement, Simone Phillips had become as firm a friend and colleague to him as she was to Grace.

Getting to his feet, Seth inhaled heavily. He had already had Simone send for a friend of his, a top gynaecologist with whom he played squash sometimes during the office lunch-breaks.

'Yes, you can put anything that needs handling urgently and which you aren't able to deal with yourself through to my PA's office. She'll know what to do.' Simone had already made Grace a cup of tea, he noticed. 'And perhaps you could see that we aren't disturbed.'

'Of course.'

When she had gone he pulled up a hard chair and sat astride

it, facing Grace. 'Now…' There was a marked hesitancy in his voice. 'Perhaps it's something you didn't want to tell me about, Grace, but in view of the circumstances…' His gaze dropped to the tell-tale mound of her abdomen beneath the overlap of her blouse which she was absently stroking, as though to protect the child she was so afraid of losing.

Their child.

But whose child had she carried and lost before? Had she loved him? Who before him had had such an important claim on her affections?

'It isn't what you think.' As she turned her face to his, he thought he had never seen anyone look more miserable.

His impenetrable gaze caused Grace to lower hers. She could tell what he was thinking and she couldn't bear it. It was enough that she might lose him if she lost the baby, but she couldn't bear to lose what precious little respect he had for her as well.

'It was eight years ago…after I came back to London. Neither of us had taken any precautions.'

'What are you saying?' His voice had dropped to a whisper and all the colour seemed to have seeped out of his olive skin. 'You mean, after we made love down there…?' He was shaking his head sharply as though trying to clear a blinding fog from in front of his eyes—eyes that were dark with disbelief. 'You *conceived*? You were pregnant with *my* child?'

She gave a sort of half-nod.

Now he could see why she had been so livid at finding out she was pregnant for a second time—and by him, a man she couldn't help surrendering to and yet for whom she had never entertained a moment's real feeling.

'We must be one hell of a fertile couple,' he remarked savagely. 'Why didn't you tell me? Why didn't you let me know?'

'At the time?' She sounded and looked sadly cynical. 'What

would you have done, married me? A girl you thought was only out for a good time?'

'Which was why I thought you'd be protected.' He was still shaking his head. 'I never dreamt you wouldn't be.'

'You seem to have made a habit of that.' And, in case he was thinking she'd been totally loose as well as irresponsible, she admitted, laying herself bare, 'It was my first time.'

To say he looked shocked would be an understatement, she thought, as those steely eyes widened and a flush washed up over those strong cheekbones.

He had been her first lover?

While he was still trying to get over one piece of unbelievable news, he was hit smack between the eyes with another.

Grace Tyler, the good-time girl—willing and eager for him without any inhibitions whatsoever—had been a virgin? Beneath the worry, his rampant concern for her, he knew a warming and very misplaced sense of macho pride.

'It wasn't obvious.'

She gave a pained little shrug. 'No. I've read it isn't always, if a girl's athletic or has done a lot of horse riding, which I had.'

'What happened?' he prompted, his eyes searching hers for enlightenment.

'I lost it.'

'How far into…?'

She swallowed. She didn't want to relive it—the pain and the misery, the feelings of isolation. And afterwards the months of depression and self-blame.

'Nearly five months.'

He swore under his breath, while his eyes closed from some inner frustration. With himself? she wondered. With her?

'Why didn't you tell me before? I mean…since?' His deep voice trembled with exasperation. 'We're man and wife, for goodness' sake!'

'I don't know. I treated you badly and I paid for it. It was a bad time in my life. I just wanted to put it behind me.' And, knowing now that it would be wrong to hold anything else back from him, because he was her husband, because he had a right to know and because—heaven help her!—because she loved him, she tagged on reluctantly, 'I was ill for quite some time.'

'Dear…!' He raised his eyes skywards, emitting some unrepeatable oath. 'All the more reason why, in view of your mother losing her life in childbirth, you should have told me,' he rebuked softly. 'And yet, knowing this, you kept it from me. Why?'

'I don't know.' Because it was all in the past. It couldn't happen again. *Dear heaven!* she prayed. *Don't let it happen again.* 'I was shocked and angry when I realised I was pregnant again. I couldn't believe it was happening to me. I'm sorry.' It had been stupid of her; she knew that now.

Turning to him, squeezing the strong hand clasping hers like it was a lifeline, she breathed, 'Oh Seth! What am I going to do?'

There was real fear in her eyes, and for once in his life Seth felt totally helpless. If anything happened to her, or to the baby, or both…

He looked away so she wouldn't guess at the depth of anxiety that was gripping him. He wouldn't let himself think about any of that now.

The consultant arrived then and, after examining his patient, arranged for her to be checked over by the maternity unit, who insisted on keeping her in overnight.

Late the following day, when the initial scare was over, they released her with the firm instruction that in view of her earlier miscarriage she was to take things very carefully for the rest of her pregnancy.

'Which means giving up anything at all stressful,' Seth remarked as he was driving her back to the apartment. 'Like that high-powered job of yours, for a start.'

'But I can't!' Grace wailed in protest. Because then he would have achieved his ultimate objective, wouldn't he? she thought miserably—seeing her give up her position at Culverwells, the thing he had probably most wanted from the beginning. And because she'd let him get her pregnant with his child!

'You can and you will!' There was no arguing against his decision, because, of course, he could take steps to see that she was removed from the board if she didn't comply.

But he was right in any case, she accepted, praying that this pregnancy would go to its full term. If it didn't, she would lose not only this baby, that she craved to hold in her arms, but Seth as well. Because there would be no reason for him to remain in a loveless marriage—loveless where he was concerned, at any rate, she thought wretchedly—if he no longer felt any responsibility towards her and a non-existent child.

'If you haven't the sense to look after yourself while you're in your condition, someone has to,' he told her with strengthening determination. Which was how, the following afternoon, Grace found herself being whizzed along the motorway in the sleek, dark elegance of his Aston Martin.

'Where are we going?' she enquired as he crossed a myriad fast-moving lanes of traffic that would have made her mind boggle to negotiate, bringing the car deftly and safely onto the carriageway headed west.

'Somewhere where I can keep a closer eye on what you're up to until after our baby's been delivered safely,' he informed her, which was the most information she had managed to get out of him ever since he had instructed her last night on what she should pack.

A couple of hours later, and it all became clear.

Oh, no…

Grace sucked in her breath, recognising the all-too-familiar signs for the little seaside retreat, and sat stiff and tense as the car wound its way onto the quieter road that fringed the rugged coast.

She hadn't been here for over seven long years. Not since her grandfather had sold their holiday home up there in the hills the summer after she had met Seth.

'Relax,' he advised, keenly aware of the tension that was gripping her even as he pulled round a slow farm vehicle. 'I know it's the last place you probably imagined—or wanted—me to bring you, but I promise you'll be comfortable. It's the one place in the world where I come when I want to totally unwind.'

Not a lot had changed over the years, Grace noted as he brought the car down through the town and past the same familiar shops. The little cottage library was still there, and the garage with its one petrol pump, although there was a supermarket now, she noticed, where the general store had been.

'It's scarcely changed,' she breathed aloud, thankful that they had taken a route well away from the boatyard as they came onto the outskirts of the town, because she was battling with so many memories and conflicting emotions that she wasn't sure how to deal with them all at that moment.

'Hasn't it?' Scepticism laced Seth's voice as he put his foot down to take the hill road following the coast and brought the car onto a plot of scrubland at its summit, sending dust and gravel spinning beneath the vehicle's powerful wheels.

Now, sitting there with him high above the sea, as he turned off the ignition she understood why he'd sounded amused, and why he had stopped the car at that particular vantage point.

'I don't believe it!' Grace laughed in shocked surprise.

In the distance, eastwards towards the far side of town, where once acres of derelict industrial wasteland had been, luxury high-rise apartments and prestigiously designed houses stood cheek by jowl around the glistening waters of a new marina graced by cabin cruisers, dinghies and shimmering yachts, whose majestic white masts seemed to pierce the sky. 'What an amazing concept... What foresight someone must have had to create all that...'

'I take it you approve?'

'Who wouldn't?' She exhaled, unable to tear her gaze from the spectacular view. 'So often new developments only ever seem to spoil the environment, but it's been done so sympathetically that I can't see—' She broke off suddenly, aware of the way he was looking at her so intently, of the significance of what he had just said. 'You mean...?' Her eyes were wide with incredulity. 'That whole development—it's one of yours?'

His mouth compressed wryly. 'It was the first.' Though there was pride in his voice as he sat there surveying the result of all that had been conceived out of that brilliant brain, Grace could see the genuine satisfaction in him too. 'But I thought I told you what I was intending to do.'

He had, eight years ago. Shamefully now she remembered how she had laughed, even what she had said in response: *Dreams are for people who crave things they haven't a hope of ever attaining.* How naïve she'd been!

As her disconcerted blue eyes clashed uncomfortably with his, she knew that he was remembering it too.

'It wasn't a dream,' he said softly. 'It was a plan.'

And now he would drive her there, she thought, as the Aston Martin fired into life again. Make her eat humble pie by depositing her in one of those luxury penthouses—which would be a close cousin, no doubt, of the one they shared in London. She could look out at that beautiful marina, at all the boats, houses and everything she had made fun of, unaware then of how much she would wish, every day of her life, that she had never said those things, never treated him as she had. And it would just serve her right! she thought.

Only he didn't.

They were following the coast now, travelling westward,

the road ahead wooded and dropping in a steep gradient into deeper countryside. Below them the water reflected a sky that was a very pale, almost icy blue. Rippling waves left the curve of a shingle beach darkened by the receding tide, while across the estuary, on a road running parallel to theirs, the sun bouncing off a car's windscreen was almost dazzling for a second before the road angled away, climbing upward into the distant hills.

'Did you buy your mother one of those houses back there on the marina?' she enquired, remembering that that had all been part of his long-term plan.

Changing gear, because the road was dangerously bendy, he said, 'She didn't want one. She said that modern places down there were for yuppies, and that she definitely isn't young and most certainly not upwardly mobile.'

Grace laughed at the fond indulgence in his voice and wondered if he would ever speak about her in the same way.

'Nowadays she prefers to live farther north—closer to Alicia.'

'So you were right. Not everything works out the way we plan, does it?' she conceded humbly.

'One learns to compromise.'

As he had by marrying her? Or was she all part of the 'plan' he had referred to just now, as Corinne had suggested she was when she had spoken to her on their return from honeymoon? Either way, it wasn't very complimentary.

'Where are we going?' she asked apprehensively when Seth turned the car off the main highway into a narrow lane. In fact, she already knew.

But why would he bring her here? she wondered desolately. A house that his family had had to move out of because they couldn't afford to stay there. Because of her grandfather. Because of her.

'All right. You've made your point,' she breathed, unable to face seeing the little house—already boarded up that summer she'd last come back here—now gone to rack and ruin. 'I think you've handed out enough just deserts for one day without—'

She stopped in mid-sentence as he brought the car to a standstill in front of a small red saloon that was parked outside the old stone building: a homely looking, picture-book property with gleaming paintwork and shiny windows which were open to the May sunshine.

'You bought it back,' she whispered, tears swimming in her eyes. Not only that, but an extension had been added, in keeping with the rest of the property, providing a whole bank of new rooms along one side.

'Come on.' He was already getting out of the car.

A cacophony of deep barks met them as Seth opened the iron gate to the garden, and Grace caught her breath from a startling *déjà vu* as a chocolate-brown Labrador came bounding down the stony path towards them.

'I don't believe this!' she laughed, surprised. It was like stepping back in time to the night he had brought her here and the Labrador had coming rushing out of the house ahead of Alicia. 'Is it the same dog?' she breathed, flabbergasted. Mocha, she remembered him saying it was called. Because of the chocolate connotations.

'No, Mocha went to her happy hunting-ground some years ago.'

'So what's this one called?' she challenged good-humouredly, petting the animal that was bouncing up and down with excitement, undecided which one of them to bestow the most affection on. 'Crème Caramel?'

'This one's called Truffle,' he corrected, his face alight with pleasure as he ruffled the huge, dark head, unperturbed by the massive paws that were almost on his shoulders with little respect for the casual designer shirt he wore with his jeans.

Grace laughed again, feeling the warmth of his personality,

the strength of his potent attraction as he laughed with her.
'Naturally!' She wasn't imagining it; it struck her suddenly:
he seemed more relaxed. Lighter. Different here.

'Seth!'

Grace recognised the pretty copper-haired girl who had
come running down the path and was now launching herself
into her brother's arms.

'You're obviously missed,' Grace observed, still laughing
as she watched him return Alicia's bear-hug, while Truffle
did some sort of doggy dance around them, eager not to miss
out on his share of the attention.

'Missed?' Alicia wrinkled her nose in mock contradiction
as she let her brother go now and treated Grace to a more
or less similar greeting. 'I just know which side my bread's
buttered!'

She shrieked, darting out of the way of that masculine
hand before it could land on her tightly encased, denim-clad
bottom.

'Any more talk like that, and you'll be doing without the
jam as well,' Seth promised playfully.

'Isn't he tyrannical?' Alicia exhaled, rolling her eyes, seeking mock sympathy from Grace as they started along the path
towards the house.

Pulling a face, Grace cast a glance up at Seth and met the
sensual challenge in his eyes that dared her to side with his
mischievous sister.

'Very!' she laughed without taking her eyes off him, and
knew a throb of excitement from the pull of that masculine
mouth, that promised that when they were alone together he
would make her pay.

The cottage garden, ablaze with flowering shrubs, peren-
nials and fruit trees, complemented the interior of the lovely
house. Although retaining many characteristic features in its
stone fireplaces, deep-set windows and the odd, strategically
exposed beam, it managed to exude modern comfort and

convenience in the understated luxury of its furnishings, a blend of the classic and antique.

'So who does Truffle belong to?' Grace asked Alicia a little while later.

The girl had insisted on giving her a tour of the ground floor and showing off the new wing, which comprised a bright and sprawling sitting room and large kitchen which were in total harmony with the rest of the old building.

Apparently, Alicia had only stopped off to stock the fridge on her way to visit her boyfriend in Plymouth, and it was Nadia who had instructed her to leave the dog with her brother.

'I bought him for Seth,' Alicia informed her, ready to leave as they came back into what nowadays served as a dining room in the older part of the house, where they found Seth standing, browsing through an open newspaper on the table. 'I bought him because I thought he needed looking after.'

'Who?' Grace enquired impishly. 'Seth or Truffle?'

'Take your pick.' Alicia giggled, seeming younger suddenly than her twenty years. 'Mum looks after the dog most of the time, though, as Seth doesn't have time to give him all the attention he needs when he's in London. And, apart from that, he's away a lot, so it was a bit of an impulsive move on my part, really.' Something, Grace decided, that Alicia Purvis would be quite prone to.

'You love having him when you're down here, though, don't you, bruv?' she prompted, and was met with a distracted grunt from Seth. With one hand on the back of a chair, one foot on the rung, his dark head bent, idly turning a page, he looked utterly magnificent, Grace thought with her breath catching. 'And having a dog around makes him less of a dynamo and more human like the rest of us,' Alicia was saying. 'Or could it be this house? Again, you'll have to make your own mind up about that. Still, I don't suppose he needs looking after now—now he's got you.'

Propelled into action now, Seth grabbed the soft hat his sister was clutching and with a roguish grin dumped it unceremoniously onto her bright copper head. 'Goodbye, Alicia.'

'Don't let him bully you,' the young woman advised, pulling it straight, darting a glance at Grace from around her brother's lithe and powerful physique. 'If he does, tell Mum. She's the only one he's ever listened to.' And with a shriek, as those keenly honed reflexes made to chase her out the door, his vibrant young sister was gone.

'Is it true?' Grace asked him over the sound of the small saloon starting up.

'Is what true?' He was still wearing that self-satisfied grin.

'That the only person you've ever listened to is Nadia?'

He shrugged, closing the newspaper on the table. 'If I hadn't, I'd have been out of a home—and a good one at that,' he admitted with no pretensions to the contrary. 'At fifteen I was a tearaway with attitude. Someone had to put their foot down or I might well have gone off the rails.'

'She did a very good job,' Grace conceded honestly. 'And your foster father, too.' She remembered him telling her that Nadia had been widowed only a few years after Seth had moved in with them. She guessed, though, that it wasn't only the Purvises' influence that had turned Seth Mason into the self-disciplined, self-sufficient man he was today. He must have wanted to change, or at least to control whatever wild streak he had had. The grit and determination he employed in everything he did and everything he achieved were part of the enduring strength and calibre of his character.

'They knew how to implement just the right balance of understanding, discipline and love,' he told her candidly.

As he would himself with his own child, or children, Grace instinctively decided. With a sudden stab of anguish she prayed that their baby would continue to thrive and grow normally and, when the time came, be delivered safely. She didn't even want to think beyond that.

The upper floor of the house proved to be as full of character and charm as downstairs, although the best room was the master bedroom in the new wing. Spacious and airy, overlooking a private shingle beach, its creamy walls, reflecting the afternoon sun, gave the room a wonderfully golden light.

Behind the king-size bed, dark-rose curtains were tastefully draped from a thick brass pole, blending with the rose-and-cream and brass furnishings in the rest of the room. In the adjoining bathroom a free-standing Victorian bath stood in what seemed like acres of space, surrounded by every modern luxury and amenity for making bath-time pure pleasure.

Seth had gone down for their luggage, but when he returned it wasn't with any of his own.

'Aren't you…?'

'Sharing it with you?' he supplied when she didn't finish her tentatively posed question. His mouth twisted wryly as he set her suitcase down and opened it out for her on the bed. 'I don't think that would be a very good idea, do you?'

Because the doctors had told them that they should be careful?

Just at that moment she didn't care about what the doctors or anyone else had said. *I need you!* she ached to tell him, but kept it to herself.

'If you need me,' he was saying coolly, with no sign of the man who had promised some delightful retribution for teasing him earlier, 'My room's just a stone's throw away.'

Grace nodded, wondering how easy it was for him simply to desert her bed, when inside she craved his love-making more than ever before.

'What else could I need?' she returned with enforced casualness.

CHAPTER TEN

OVER the next few weeks, Grace knew a kind of fragile happiness.

Seth did a lot of work from home, and sometimes when he had to go away he took her with him. She knew, though, from the way she was fussed over by Maisie, the elderly woman who came in to cook and clean on a regular basis, that the woman had been instructed to keep an eye on her whenever he couldn't.

Sometimes he would take whole days off to be with her, and for Grace those were the most precious of all. But there were other times, like now, aching for him, when she would take long walks along the coast with only the sea, the overhead gulls and Truffle at her heels for company.

'It's all right for you,' she told the Labrador as it came running up to her after giving up on a small crab that had disappeared beneath a rock. 'You wouldn't do anything so stupid as falling in love. But I have—and I'm having his baby—and he doesn't even know how much I care about him. You're a dog of the world. Perhaps you could advise me on what I should do?'

Wallowing in all this sudden eye-contact and conversation, the dog jumped up, his big brown nose almost level with her chest, anticipating some exciting treat as well. When a bout of petting was his only reward, he gave a deafening bark and went haring off down the deserted beach, returning soaked to the skin to shake himself violently as soon as he was in drenching distance of Grace.

'Charming!' she laughed, shaking water off her hands. 'What's that supposed to mean? That I drown myself? If that's all the advice you can give, I suggest you keep it to yourself!'

Fondly she stooped to caress the big soggy head before darting out of the way with a little shriek when the dog decided to treat her to another unwelcome shower.

Having just returned from two days of meetings, Seth stopped in his tracks, silencing his barefooted progress across the shingle. It was too evocative a scene to intrude upon, he thought, and stayed there, unnoticed for a few moments, watching Grace with his dog, hoping she wouldn't turn around.

She was wearing a tangerine cotton skirt that floated around her calves like gossamer, and a gypsy-style cream top which she had embellished with a loose string necklace in amber and cream, and a wide matching wrist-band that emphasised her softly golden skin.

With a hand on the burgeoning mound of her midriff that even the loose top couldn't hide now, and her hair—grown long again—blowing softly in the wind, he thought she had never looked so beautiful or so captivatingly maternal as she lifted her other arm to throw a stick for the dog.

Pride was the overriding emotion that rushed over him at the knowledge of this lovely woman being pregnant with his child. But then other emotions rushed in, the least disturbing the surge of hormones that stamped their mark on him as a man, dragging his mind away from those other more complex issues as he strove to bring his body back under control.

She still hadn't seen him; she was still watching Truffle bounding over the shingle. But as the Labrador, stick retrieved, suddenly changed course and raced towards him, she turned around and those precious moments were gone.

Seeing his dark, lean figure advancing along the beach, Grace felt her heart leap like a frisky gazelle.

He had changed before coming out to find her. A white T-shirt hugged the strong contours of his chest, leaving nothing of his magnificent torso to the imagination; his pale-blue denim jeans that encased his powerful legs were frayed at the hems, brushing over feet that were bare and tanned.

'I hadn't seen you as such an animal lover,' he remarked when he was almost level with her, already on his haunches, petting the ecstatic Truffle.

Why was it, Grace wondered, breathless just from the sight of him, that even the sound of his voice should make her heart race?

'You hadn't seen me as a lot of things, including fat and shapeless and undesirable.' Where had that come from? she thought, abashed, adding quickly as grimacing, she tugged at her billowing blouse. 'And unable to get into any of my clothes any more.'

Her words gave him an excuse to visually examine her as he got to his feet.

'There's nothing undesirable about your body being heavy with my child,' he told her dispassionately, with no hint of the need for her that had driven him in the past. 'And your shape will soon come back after it's born. If it doesn't, then I shall take you out and buy you a whole new wardrobe—if it makes you happy. Suits. Dresses. Exotic underwear.'

A fine eyebrow arched dubiously. 'If it makes *me* happy, did you say?'

'All right.' A contorted smile was tugging at his exciting mouth. 'We'll forget the dresses.'

Seeing the mischief twinkling in his eyes, Grace thumped him playfully on the arm. It felt warm and solid, a wall of pure muscle.

'Right!'

She let out a squeal as he made a grab for her, trying to twist away.

'Attack me, would you?'

'No, don't!' she shrieked as she was lifted off her feet, while Truffle, joining in the fun, ran around them, barking hysterically. 'What will the neighbours think?' she protested, clinging to him. Her senses sharpened to the warm softness of his T-shirt, the way his hard body moved beneath it, while his aftershave lotion—still discernible on that darkly shadowed jaw—was sending arrows of want right down through what she thought of as her hippo-proportioned body.

'There aren't any.' Purposefully, Seth carried her over to a small niche between the shallow rocks where he set her on her feet before gently pulling her down beside him on the fine shingle. 'You don't need props to make you excruciatingly desirable to a man. You're too alluring by half—even with the weight of my unborn baby inside you.'

Only not alluring enough for you to love, or make love to, Grace agonised, realising that it had been weeks since he had shown her how much he wanted her—if only sexually, she thought, her pulses suddenly quickening as he leaned over and touched her mouth with his.

It was a mere whisper of a kiss, over too soon when Truffle made his presence felt by clambering all over them.

Grace laughed as a soggy piece of driftwood landed in Seth's lap.

'That dog's going to have to go!' he pretended to threaten. 'I swear the two of you have got some conspiracy going between you.' With enviable strength he hurled the piece of wood farther seawards than Grace ever could have, even from a standing position. 'Go get it, Truffle! See if you can meet the tide!'

'You don't mean that,' Grace chided, laughing again. She

couldn't bring herself to tell him, but she was ecstatic to have him home.

'If it means having my wife to myself for a few minutes, I do,' he said laconically, but the laughter in his face told her he was only teasing. 'Now…where were we?'

'You really think you'll have the chance to find out before he comes back?'

'Is that an evasive answer, Mrs Mason?'

Slipping a hand under her hair, Grace leaned back against the rock with her eyes closed. 'It could be the shortest kiss in the history of the universe.'

'True.'

'It would probably make the Guinness Book of Records.'

'No, that's just the thoughts I've got going through my head right now.'

He hadn't been like this with her since things had started going wrong between them just after their honeymoon: teasing. Tantalising. Playing with her.

'You…!' She couldn't think of an appropriate noun to describe him, and anyway he was leaning over her, his lips tantalisingly close to hers, his breath surprisingly laboured as though he was having some sort of inner battle with himself. One that said he wanted her physically, even while mentally and emotionally she was the last person on earth he would have considered creating a child with, had he but had any choice. 'Ouch!'

'What's wrong?' He drew back sharply on hearing her wince. 'Did I hurt you?'

The concern in his voice made her throat ache, made her realise how lucky the woman would be who he really loved.

'Not you. Your baby,' she admitted, with an inner glow to her face from the beautiful miracle that was unfolding each day inside her. 'It gave one of its stronger than average kicks. It's definitely a boy.'

'You've made up your mind about that, haven't you?' he said, smiling; they had both decided that they would wait until the baby arrived to find out its gender. 'And what's all this unnecessary prejudice I'm sensing against my sex? Can't girl babies do their share of kicking?'

'Of course they can,' she chuckled, her gaze following Truffle who had picked up a scent on the far side of the beach and had happily abandoned his game of throw-and-retrieve. 'But this one's got the boot of a centre forward. Obviously a dominant child who wants to make an impact,' she decided. 'Now, where does he get that from, I… Ouch!'

As another sharp prod had her massaging her swollen middle, the hand that came to rest beside hers was warm and so heart-wrenchingly gentle.

'Can you feel it?' Her mouth was so dry it was difficult getting the words out.

He nodded, those familiar strands of hair moving against his forehead. The pleasure that warmed his features made Grace's heart swell with love for him.

Love me, she ached to say, but she didn't have the nerve.

This wasn't a conventional marriage where they had met and fallen in love, had been desperate to spend the rest of their lives together. This, for Seth, was a partnership he had got himself into out of duty to the mother of his child, and it was just unfortunate that she had been crazy enough to fall in love with him along the way.

'I can't believe how you went through a pregnancy—or halfway through one,' he breathed, 'Before, and I didn't have a clue. Do you know how that makes me feel?'

Grace glanced away, fixing her gaze at some point in the distance where the rocks were turning to gold in the summer-evening sunshine. 'What was the point in letting you know? I scarcely knew you,' she murmured ruefully. 'Anyway, you weren't here.'

'You tried to find me?'

'No.' She sat up quickly, realising she had said too much.

'Then how did you know I wasn't here?'

'My grandfather told me. I didn't know then that the reason he knew about you leaving was that he had got you sacked. But it was the only way I could come back here after my miscarriage.'

'So you did come back?' His face was a contortion of disbelief and something she couldn't quite put her finger on. Horror? she wondered painfully. Was he, in spite of all he had said, wondering what he would have done if she had turned up on his doorstep like a bad penny—not just a stuck-up socialite, as he'd believed she was, but a pregnant one? Putting paid to all his aspirations. His dreams.

'To convalesce,' she enlightened him now. 'My grandparents insisted upon it. I must have been a real pain and a worry to them. I couldn't seem to pick myself up.' She grimaced and, not wanting to sound as though she were courting any sympathy, added with a self-deprecating little laugh, 'Feeling sorry for myself, probably.'

What she didn't tell him, though, was how she had spent those lonely days and nights wandering along the coast, mourning those glorious hours with a man she had found herself wanting more than anything else she had ever wanted in her life, while all the time knowing she had killed all hope of his even liking her—even if she did ever see him again— because of her shameful behaviour.

Caught in the direct line of that steely gaze, she looked quickly away, though not quickly enough not to miss noticing how those thick eyebrows pleated speculatively.

Watching the private emotions that chased across her face, Seth considered what else she wasn't telling him.

'My father sketched me standing next to that rock.' She was pointing to a high ridge where an area of grass clothed the timeless cliffs. She seemed desperate to change the subject.

'Your father?' It came as a surprise to him to hear her mention the man who had deserted her while she'd still been a baby. She seldom did, and he guessed she had only done so now to break the tension between them.

'He came to see me when I was convalescing down here—under sufferance, no doubt, because my grandfather probably demanded it.' She made a cynical little sound down her nostrils. 'It couldn't have been more than a handful of times that he'd been to see me in my life. And you know, he actually asked me to go and live with him that last time. He said he gave me up because he felt it was the right thing to do, but that now I was old enough to make up my own mind. He said he'd come back for me, but then he left and I never saw him again.'

'Did you never think to seek him out? Ask him why?'

The blue eyes that clashed with his were clear and candid. 'Did you, with your mother?'

'Yes. Or at least I tried as soon as I was old enough.'

'What happened?'

'She'd died of a drug overdose the year before.'

Within their frame of gold her flawless features clouded with sympathy. 'I'm sorry.'

There was such intensity of emotion in those two words that he wanted to clasp her to him, bury his lips against her scented hair and lose himself in her tender femininity, in her beautiful body. Not for himself—the man who could scale mountains, remove all obstacles in his path—but for the lost and betrayed young adolescent he had been. But he held back. He wasn't ready to expose himself to such vulnerability.

'Don't be,' he said, getting a grip on himself. 'At least, not on my account. My life turned out well because of Nadia, my foster father, Cory, the twins, and the wonderful family circle I was accepted into. I owe them everything. I couldn't have asked for more. Not for myself.'

'It was pretty much the same for me. It didn't really matter that my father decided to go his own way. My grandparents were great. I didn't need anyone else.' But that wistful note in her voice drew a covert glance from Seth from beneath the heavy fringes of his lashes. She didn't mean that, he was shrewd enough to realise. She might be all bravado up front, but deep down, he suspected, she had felt Matthew Tyler's absence from her life more acutely then she would ever allow anyone to know.

'It's getting late,' he said and catching her hand to pull her to her feet, noticed how cold it was. He gave a shrill whistle that brought Truffle scrambling from somewhere over the rocks towards them. 'We'd best be getting back.'

Her fingers were getting too fat, Grace decided the day she couldn't get her rings on. It didn't make her feel particularly jubilant when the woman who ran the post office referred to her as '*Miss* Mason'.

'One of the drawbacks of being seven months pregnant,' she responded dryly, without really knowing why she felt the need to explain. 'It isn't just the middle bit that swells up!'

It was just that Seth was working such long hours these days, at home and away, that she seemed to be seeing less and less of him, and with the problems they were already facing in their marriage sometimes she felt single as well as unloved. Being forced to discard her wedding band seemed like such an ill-fated thing, she mused now as she sat sketching with Truffle's head resting on her feet under the dining-room table. It was like a curtain closing on a poorly acted scene from a play, a farce, which was what her marriage was. A travesty, she thought torturously, since it would never have taken place had she not been expecting his child.

As her pregnancy progressed, so did her concerns for the baby. Another brief scare when her blood pressure went higher than normal had her constantly worrying that something would go wrong.

Would it come too early? Too late? Would everything be all right?

Her greatest fear was that she would lose the baby altogether, something she couldn't even begin to contemplate.

Nadia came to visit, staying for ten days to be with Grace when Seth had to shoot off to Germany unavoidably on business, and by the time her mother-in-law-left—which, as it turned out, happened to be Grace's birthday—Grace felt considerably better.

'She's done wonders for you,' Seth remarked after they were driving back that day from taking Nadia to the station, a day that couldn't quite make up its mind whether to be blisteringly hot or to cool everyone down with its sudden and unexpected showers. 'It begs the question why you never look that happy and contented when we're on our own.'

'Does it?' Grace murmured, feigning nonchalance. She wasn't going to tell him that she loved him too much to truly let go when he was around for fear of revealing her true feelings for him—not when he didn't love her in the same way—and that sometimes the strain was almost too much for her to bear. 'Perhaps it's because she cooks better than you do,' she added more lightly, although that wasn't strictly true. Nadia was a wizard in the kitchen, but when her son put his mind to it he too could come up with some pretty stupendous dishes.

'In that case,' he said, bringing the Aston Martin through the heavy summer holiday traffic, 'you'll be pleased to know that I'm taking you out for lunch.'

And that turned out to be a four-course meal in her favourite Thai restaurant, which she objected to at first, feeling self-conscious and unattractive in her heavily pregnant state. But Seth had insisted, and she had to admit to having enjoyed it when the lunch was over.

The only down side was having to sit there watching how members of the restaurant's female clientele made no secret of their silent approval of the untamed-looking hunk who was sharing her table, while sparing the odd envious glance at the woman sitting beside him in a sun dress that could have doubled as a tent to see if she measured up.

Now as he was driving her back to the house, sitting there in that silver-grey suit he wore with such mind-blowing style, Grace wondered how she could possibly still be attractive to him when she was waddling around like a lumbering goose. After all, Seth was a sensuous and extremely virile man, yet he hadn't shared a bed with her in weeks.

'You're quiet,' he commented when he was helping her out of the car, the gaze resting on her face softly reflective. 'Are you all right?'

'Of course.' She even managed a little laugh.

The look he gave her as she moved past him told her he wasn't fooled.

'What's the matter?' he pressed when they were inside the house. 'Are you upset because I haven't given you your birthday present yet?'

'Haven't you?' She looked up from petting Truffle, who had nearly knocked her over in his eagerness to welcome her home, her face a picture of mock innocence. 'I hadn't realised.'

He had sent her flowers, though. Red roses, two dozen of them, which had arrived that morning. But what were flowers and presents, she thought achingly, when all she wanted was his love?

'I thought I'd keep something back for later,' he drawled with a flash of something in those incredible steely eyes. 'Something, perhaps, that will show you how beautiful you are. Something you seem to have had difficulty believing lately.'

Unavoidably, her eyes lit up, curiosity breaking through her melancholy mood.

'In the bedroom,' he told her, giving nothing away.

She remembered him coming back inside after he'd handed her into the car earlier with Nadia, and she guessed that that was why.

Frowning, her smile cautious, Grace made her way upstairs.

What did a man like Seth give his wife on her birthday? Something to make her look beautiful, he had said. And in the bedroom.

A sexy nightdress? Enticing underwear?

A leap of reckless excitement was swiftly tempered by unease. He'd said something about that the day he'd come home and found her on the beach with Truffle, but she thought he'd been joking. Would he disappoint her like that?

Gingerly she pushed open the door.

She couldn't see anything unusual at first. There was certainly no exotic clothing spread out on the bed.

A shaft of sunlight slicing through the dark, dramatic clouds broke into the room like a beacon. She followed its path, her head doing a double take as her eyes skimmed over and then returned, shocked and disbelieving, to the figure that graced the top of the bookcase.

Her bronze!

The one she'd always regretted letting go.

She went over to it and ran trembling fingers lightly over the silky-smooth lines of the young woman it depicted, whose blouse hung loosely over her tight-fitting jeans, her long hair blown back by a whipping wind from the sea. Matthew Tyler had captured it all in that lost and lonely look about her. All the turmoil in her face. All the emptiness and lonely longing in her soul.

Hearing the creak of the door, she spun round. Silent tears were trembling on her cheeks.

'Where did you find it?' she whispered.

Seth came in, pushing the door closed behind him. 'You remember the auction?'

How could she forget it? The mixed emotions that had clawed at her that day: the frenetic interest in that sale-room; the escalating bids that had sent the price of her father's work shooting through the roof. The bronze had sold through an agent over the phone on behalf of an anonymous bidder. Someone rich enough and crazy enough to justify spending...

'*You* bought it?' she whispered incredulously.

Beside her now, he ran a hand lovingly over the statuette, just as she had done.

'Why?' Why, when he didn't even like her? she wondered, baffled.

'How could I resist such a work of art?' he said with such a depth of appreciation in his deep voice that she could almost imagine she had heard it tremble.

But why hadn't he resisted it? Because it was a Matthew Tyler sculpture? Or because...?

Her eyelids came down, obliterating the hope that threatened to reveal itself to him, because she didn't think she could really bear to know the answer.

He was a speculator with an eye for an investment. Why else would he have bought it, when his only interest in the girl it represented was to get even with her? While she had gone home, tearing herself apart after the hammer had come down in that auction room for allowing herself to sell it, a decision she had never stopped regretting.

Her eyes clashed with his, her face an open book now. *How had he known?*

'It didn't take much working out to realise how much it had cost you to part with it,' he explained, answering her unspoken question. 'Or why you did.'

'I did it for the money,' she said defensively. 'To pay bills and to save my gallery.' Yet she knew now that, remarkably, it was only Seth's bidding that day that had made it possible. Only *his* money. Nobody else's. So she hadn't been independent from him, even in that.

'Nevertheless...' An arching eyebrow told her that he didn't wholly accept her motives. 'I'm sure if you had had an easier relationship with your father you would have found some other way to raise the money.'

Would she have? Grace bit her lower lip. Possibly. But she had had other grounds for parting with that statue, which were as torturous in their own way as being abandoned by her father.

'Don't be too hard on him for not coming back, Grace. He had his reasons.'

A cloud had crossed the sun again, putting the room in shadow. 'How do you know?'

She saw that broad chest rise then fall after a few moments as he let his breath out slowly.

'Because I made it my business to find out. As big a swine as you think I am, I couldn't stand by and watch you harbouring such hurt and resentment because of the way he deserted you. I found it hard to believe that a man who could create such sensitivity in his work could be so completely without heart. He came from a different background and couldn't fit into your grandparents' world. They didn't want him to marry their daughter, and certainly had no time for him after your mother died. He gave you up, Grace, because they convinced him it was impossible for him to keep you. He believed he was doing the right thing in handing you over and that you'd have a far better life with them than he could ever give you. I had to do some extensive research, but I managed to find out why he didn't contact you again as he promised he would.'

She couldn't believe she was hearing all this. Seth had gone to all this trouble—on her behalf?

'He was a very private person and guarded his privacy jealously, but after a lengthy search I found out from an ex-lady-friend and neighbour of his what happened. He had an accident, Grace, not long after he saw you last. It left him with epilepsy and other problems. She said he didn't want to let you know because he didn't want to ruin your life by making you feel obligated or burdened by him. She said he knew he must have caused you enough pain in your life without causing you any more. Apparently he was banking on the fact that you wouldn't try and contact him, because—as he told his friend and neighbour—he didn't deserve to be contacted.'

And she hadn't, thinking the worst about him.

The tears that had been glistening on her cheeks at having found her most treasured possession now started to flow freely, and suddenly she was sobbing into the warmth of a strong, masculine shoulder.

'I'm sorry, Grace,' he whispered. 'But I couldn't leave you to go through the rest of your life hating him for having broken his promise. His motives were good, even if they kicked in a little too late to do either of you any benefit.'

As her tears subsided he turned her with him to look at her father's work again. 'There's a lot of love in that sculpture,' he observed, running a finger over its fine patina. Because her father had loved her—in his own way. She wasn't in any doubt about that now. 'A lot of love,' Seth reiterated, startling her when he suddenly appended, 'And in more ways than one.'

Could he see it? Had he seen it when he had made that ridiculous bid for it over a year ago? Was it that that had made him buy it?

'I was young. I'd lost my baby.' *And you*, she added silently, but couldn't tell him that.

'Is that all?'

'What else could there be?' she queried, afraid.

He chuckled softly and, reaching out, lifted her chin with a gentle finger. Another shaft of sunlight breaking through the clouds turned his bronzed skin to fiery gold.

'Oh, Grace.' He drew her back to him, his lips against her

hairline so tender that she wanted to weep with the longing for that depth of caring in his voice to mean something. 'You poor, naïve little fool.'

Because, of course, it didn't mean anything—not what she wanted it to mean, anyway. Oh, he would be kind to her. Respect her. Show her all the care and consideration owed to a pregnant wife. But he didn't love her. Wasn't that what he was saying in calling her a naïve fool? Because he must have recognised it on the face of that girl who was immortalised in bronze. One would have had to be blind or stupid not to understand the feelings which her father had captured, the thing which made Matthew Tyler's works stand out over the work of his contemporaries—emotion. And Seth Mason was neither blind nor stupid.

She couldn't resist as his lips moved across her face, her throat, the sensitive hollow at the juncture of her shoulder, and she gave a small murmur of wanting as he slid the thin straps of her dress aside.

Her arms around his neck, she felt his darkly shaded jaw against her cheek, smelled the heaven of his aftershave lotion which, even while it thrilled her, couldn't hide the more potent musk of his own animal scent as he skilfully dispensed with her bra.

Her breasts were heavy in his hands, their large, dark aureoles marking her advanced pregnancy.

Seth groaned as he bent his head to look at her, his hands, his fingers, his touch as reverent as the look of awe that seemed to light his face. Gently then, somehow, they were on the bed, and he was removing the rest of her clothes.

Self-conscious, she uttered a small sound of embarrassment at having him see her naked like this.

'You're so beautiful,' he murmured, and she could see the flush of hard desire, of barely controlled passion, staining his cheeks, a passion that had been stifled and denied them for weeks.

Now it emerged in an urgent fusing of mouths and tongues, and skin against heated skin. He hadn't undressed beyond helping her to remove the shirt she had tugged out of his waistband, so her hands could caress the hair-coarsened contours of his chest and powerful arms, and the velvet-clothed muscles of his back.

Alive and animated with wanting, she could feel the restraint in him, the reined-in passion that he was even now controlling as his lips moved over her face, her neck, her breasts, then down and down, tracing an exquisite path across the most changed and maternal features of her body.

He always had been the most incredible lover, she thought through a drugged and sensuous lethargy, but never more impeccable than this!

Her breath caught sharply at the undeniable pleasure as his lips traced over that most secretive part of her, aware of her need for tenderness, yet aware too of her craving for fulfilment.

Under his consummate mouth, Grace felt a fire starting to build, felt the flames of need leaping and licking upwards through the very core of her femininity until they were too hot to contain, finally exploding in a throbbing inferno that left her sobbing with pleasure, and suddenly gasping with the need for him to stop.

She was so unbelievably sensitive; she couldn't believe how incredibly so as the throes of her orgasm ebbed away. She was too sensitive to be touched any more like that, but she still wanted the one and only thing he could give her—*him*.

Damp, flushed and dishevelled, with a choked murmur of desire she reached for him, but he was already drawing away from her, and a groan of bitter disappointment escaped her when she saw him getting up.

He didn't need her. Not in the way she needed him. Perhaps he had in the beginning, but perhaps he had accepted that that wasn't enough.

'You drive me to distraction,' she heard him whisper, his breathing laboured, but then he left her, and a little later she heard the back door closing downstairs.

Out in the blustery wind, with Truffle at his heels, Seth strode out across the beach, walking off his frustration.

Had it been a mistake, marrying as they had without giving themselves time to get to know each other? He wasn't sure whether, at the time, he'd really known himself whether it was right for the two of them to try to build a life together. He'd only known that he couldn't let any child he'd created suffer in the way that he had.

She'd accused him once, he thought, of marrying her for the doors that she could open for him, and he couldn't deny that in the beginning it had crossed his mind. A sort of added bonus to the knowledge that she was carrying his child. But that was all it had been—a fleeting thought—because he had never needed anything but his own energies and determination to get the things he set his mind on getting. And the one thing he had been determined to get was Grace in his bed on a permanent basis!

But things had backfired on him, things he hadn't envisaged when he had set out to put a wedding ring on her finger. He almost laughed out loud at the way he had thought how smoothly and easily her capitulation to his irresistible charms could be achieved.

She could be in his bed—if he was ruthless enough to forget all that prevented him from exercising that right. But did he want what he had been determined to have—even if he could, without any risk to Grace or the baby—with a whole heap of pride, suspicion and mistrust cooling their bed?

He clicked his tongue for the dog as a squally shower started to blow in off the sea. He only knew that they couldn't go on in the way they were going. Things had changed since the day he had taken her as his bride. Fundamentally changed—for him, at any rate.

After the baby was born, he resolved, gritting his teeth against what he had to do and stepping out against the rain that was already soaking his shirt, he would have to tell her the truth.

CHAPTER ELEVEN

NADIA was fussing around her month-old grandson as if she was the first woman who had ever become a grandmother. The twins, too, had each been to see Grace and Seth at the cottage during the first week of their foster nephew's arrival who, much to their delight had been named Cory—after their father, Seth's foster father—and Matthew, after Grace's father.

'Whatever anyone else does, Seth always has to go one better,' his younger brother, Alvin—who was as every bit as copper-haired and mischievous as his twin sister—had jested, referring to the fact that little Cory Matthew had arrived on the scene weighing nearly ten pounds. 'There should be a law against people like him. You could have killed the girl,' he'd scolded jovially; as everyone had been informed, it hadn't exactly been an easy labour. But then he'd slapped Seth firmly on the shoulder with an unmistakably proud, 'Well done, bro.'

'If ever you need a babysitter, just let me know,' Alicia had begged eagerly, while her mother had wagged a finger in her direction and warned her about getting broody too soon. 'OK, I suppose I won't have much time with my studies,' she'd relented wistfully. 'But while Seth and Grace are looking for a family home nearer London, perhaps now and again I might be able to borrow the dog?'

They had all laughed at that, but Grace had been aware of a distinct unease behind Seth's smile.

Now several weeks on, with the twins having returned to their respective studies, and Cory upstairs in the nursery under the proud supervision of the very capable Nadia, Seth suggested that he and Grace take a drive alone.

'Cory will be fine,' he insisted when she started to express concern over leaving the baby. It was, after all, the first time she had been anywhere without her son. 'Trust me. My mother's an expert at looking after babies,' he said reassuringly and then, his tone turning more sombre, added, 'Grace…we have to talk.'

Something in the way he said that made her stomach muscles clench almost sickeningly. She had known this was coming. She just hadn't realised that it would be so soon.

He didn't say anything as he handed her into the car, not until they were on the tree-flanked road where the turning leaves made a flaming canopy over their heads.

'I think you know why I've brought you out, Grace.'

She glanced at his magnificent figure, casually attired, as she was, in jeans and a light sweater. Looking quickly away again, stalling for time, she said lightly, 'For a drive. Why else?' Her heart, though, was beating wildly and her mouth felt dry.

'Because I think you know as well as I do that things haven't exactly worked out in the way we'd hoped. And that things can't go on in the way they have been.'

'No.' It was a brave attempt to be as practical and realistic as he was.

'Then at least that's half the battle sorted.'

Numbly she uttered, 'I hadn't realised we were fighting a battle.'

He sent her a dubious glance before returning his attention to the road again.

'A cold war—and that's far, far worse.' Deftly he turned the wheel, braking into a bend, before putting his foot down to bring them swiftly yet safely back onto a straight course again. 'I'm sure you'll agree that it isn't a very sound basis on which to build a marriage.'

Achingly she turned away, pulling down the visor to counteract the dappled sunlight that was playing on the windscreen. He'd been different over the past few weeks—no less attentive, yet somehow more distant, preoccupied—although through the long, hard hours when she had been giving birth to his son he hadn't left her side.

'Your family thinks we're very happy. What are you going to tell them?'

'This doesn't concern them.' He brought the car up the steep hill, flicked on the indicator and started slowing down, eventually pulling up on the high area of scrubland where he had parked that day back in the spring when he had first brought her here. 'This is something that only concerns you and me.'

She noticed how the passengers in the car that had been following them glanced back at the Aston Martin as they passed, admiring its low, sleek lines.

'I thought it would be enough,' he stated heavily, turning off the ignition. Something in his voice and the way he sat back on his seat almost with an air of resigned acceptance seemed to squeeze her heart like it was in a vice. 'I thought that expecting and having a child, planning for its future, would be enough to build a relationship on—help us grow together. But it isn't enough, is it, Grace?'

What was he saying? That he wanted out now? It hurt too much even to consider that possibility.

'It doesn't seem to have been, no.' She lifted her chin in defence against the pain, the emotion, that was threatening to overwhelm her. She had to contain it. Stay strong. But how could she when her whole world felt as if it was being torn apart?

'I'm sorry.' His glance took in the rigidity of her pale, tense features, his apology only for the way he was making her feel. 'But I think it's time that one of us, at least, started telling the truth.'

So this was it, the moment she had been dreading, when he explained what it was that had robbed him from her bed. That had taken him away from her—mentally as well as physically—more and more often over the past couple of months, even if he thought she wasn't aware of it. Oh, he had done it discreetly; she had to hand him that. But every woman knew when her husband's attentions were being claimed by something—or someone—else, eventually.

'Who is she?' She couldn't stop herself asking the question, even though she couldn't bear to know the answer and, noticing the line that deepened between the darkening steel of his eyes; she persisted with, 'Who is it, Seth?'

His face was ravaged by some dark emotion she couldn't even begin to comprehend.

'Seth, please…' It was an agonised whisper. 'I've a right to know.'

Seth's breath seemed to shudder through his lungs. 'I suppose you do,' he said in a low voice. Then, surprisingly, he caught her hand, turning it over and studying it intently, as though he were trying to memorise every last detail of its slender, trembling structure.

She didn't trust any man. How could she, he thought, after the experiences she had suffered in the past? She hadn't exactly been ecstatic about getting pregnant and finding herself married to him in the first place, and there had been very little to commend the other men in her life: Paul Harringdale. Lance Culverwell. Her father. So what chance had he imagined there could possibly be for him where the others had failed?

'I suppose,' he said, his voice hesitant, as though he were picking his words carefully. 'I suppose you could say that she's a very special lady.'

Grace closed her eyes. She couldn't, wouldn't, let him see the torture he was putting her through. 'And you're saying you want out of our marriage—is that it?'

His face was slashed with harsh lines. 'Is that what you want me to say? What you've wanted all along?'

She didn't answer. How could he say that?

'I'm well aware that you felt bullied into marrying me. So why did you, Grace?'

'You know why.'

'Tell me. I want to hear you say it.'

She saw his gaze drop to her throat, to the way it worked nervously as she uttered with a painfully disguised version of the truth, 'Because of Cory.'

He nodded, but his face was an inscrutable mask. 'And that's all?'

What did he want her to say? What was he trying to do—wring the truth out of her until there was nothing left? No dignity? No pride? No self-respect?

'No, it isn't, you bastard!' Her chin jerked upwards as she turned away from him. No way was she going to give him the satisfaction of seeing her cry. 'So, now you know.' She was fumbling in her bag for a tissue, but couldn't find one, and when he held out a folded white handkerchief she snatched it from him and blew her nose. 'So, what's she like?' Sightlessly, her eyes were fixed on the boats and waterside apartments way off in the distance. 'This *special* lady.' She couldn't keep the sarcasm out of her voice.

When he didn't answer immediately she sent a guarded look in his direction. Those steely eyes were such dark pools of emotion she felt as though she were drowning in their fathomless depths.

Finally he said, 'Simple. Honest. Uncomplicated.'

It sounded like the echo of something one of them had said a long time ago, but she was too miserable to work out where or when it had been.

'In fact,' he breathed, his tone so velvety-soft that it seemed to brush across her senses, 'I think I can safely say that she's almost as beautiful as you are.'

She couldn't believe he was saying this! Or that she was allowing him to touch her as his fingers strayed across her cheek, tracing the shamefully wet path of her tears.

Even now his touch was unbearably arousing, the scent of his aftershave lotion that still clung to his fingers so achingly dear to her that she could so easily have succumbed to all that he was doing to her, and cried out that she didn't care if he had a thousand mistresses as long as he didn't tear her and their marriage apart like this.

'I really think you should meet her.'

Meet her!

Hurting more than she could believe it was possible to hurt, she pulled back angrily from the dangerous seduction of his touch.

'What the hell are you talking about? What is it you want, Seth—my approval? Or is it my total humiliation you want?'

Quietly, he said, 'It was never my intention to make you this unhappy.' His face was marked with an almost painful intensity. 'I want you to believe that. But I also want you to trust me when I say that what I'm asking of you now is for the best.' His words seemed to tremble from somewhere deep down inside him.

Was that how much he loved her, this woman who was so special to him? At that moment Grace knew a jealousy so fierce that it seemed to consume her.

On a bitter sob, she said, 'Why? To salve your conscience? Haven't you done enough to me already?'

He remained silent for a moment while a nerve started to pulse in that angular jaw.

'I know it might not feel like it to you right at this minute,' he responded at length, taking his keys out of the ignition. 'But anything you think I've done, my love, has all been in your own mind.'

Like expecting her to meet the woman he really loved? Like flaunting his mistress in the way he had flaunted his money, his influence and his power?

A flame of colour surged into her cheeks as bitterly she threw back, 'You set out to destroy me from the beginning. Wasn't that your intention all along?'

His lashes came down as though he were blotting out some truth he didn't want to deal with. But then, exhaling heavily, he admitted, 'In the beginning—yes, I am ashamed to say that I wanted to see you eating humble pie. But then Cory came on the scene—'

'And suddenly your little game of revenge wasn't quite so funny, was it?'

'No,' he murmured, his dark features serious. Contrite, she would have said, if she hadn't felt him incapable of such an emotion. 'It wasn't funny at all.'

Pain corrugated her forehead as she stared out of the passenger window at the red, gold and amber trees that sloped steeply down the hillside, obscuring the tiny bay below.

She'd always known that for him, where she was concerned, all they had going for them was sex. He'd been as driven as she was by the passion that gripped them whenever they came together. But somewhere along the way, while she had fallen deeply and impossibly in love with him, he had met someone else and finally decided that what he had with Grace wasn't enough.

'Come on' she heard him say gently through her darkening despair. 'This isn't doing either of us any good. I think we should take a walk.'

She didn't want to. She didn't have the will or the energy to move, and wouldn't have if he hadn't come round to her side and urged her out of the car.

'Why can't we just go home?' she uttered bleakly, wondering how her legs were going to support her when there was nothing inside her but emptiness.

'Because we both need some fresh air,' he insisted, his hand firm, strong and warm around hers as he tugged her after him down the wooded hillside.

The trees grew thickly in places, and Seth pulled back a branch that encroached over the path so that it wouldn't swing back in her face, his manner caring, at odds with everything that was happening between them. The crisp, dry leaves that had already fallen rustled under their feet, and were still falling—like yesterday's dreams, Grace thought almost unbearably—even as they made their way shorewards.

And suddenly the trees ended and they were stepping out onto the beach, which was protected by a promontory of low rocks immediately to the right of them.

'There,' Seth said softly. 'The lady I want you to meet.' As he spoke it dawned on Grace that they had skirted the headland on their way down through the woods and were standing on the spot where she had come across him on that fateful day all those years before. 'There she is.'

But the beach was deserted, save for a gull that took off with a shriek of protest as their shoes scrunched across the shingle. And the dinghy, on its trailer, just as before.

The sun struck bronze from her gleaming cedar hull and her orange sail was folded neatly against her mast.

It could have been the same sailboat that Seth had been so proud of and which she had practically scoffed at as a spoilt teenager, Grace realised, amazed. Yet she knew it wasn't the same one. This one was new, a replica, lovingly built down to the last detail. But it was the name, painstakingly painted with the same degree of care and loving commitment in gold scripted lettering on the side, that drew the gasp from her lips:

LORELEI

The sea nymph he had likened her to all those years ago!

'She lured me to my fate the day she stumbled upon me on this very beach,' Seth was saying. 'Which was to love her—regardless. Without mercy. Unconditionally. Without any reprieve.'

She couldn't take in what he was saying, nor was she able to speak. Her voice, like her heart, was clogged with so much emotion: shock. Disbelief. Bewilderment.

'I think even you must agree she's a very beautiful lady.'

'Oh, Seth…' As things started to sink in, she found her voice at least. 'Then there isn't…?'

'Isn't what?'

'Anyone else?' She felt as though she was on an emotional rollercoaster, first down, then up, up so high that she felt dizzy from the heights to which she was being driven.

'Why does that surprise you so much, Grace? Haven't you realised yet how much I love you?'

Her heart swelled until she thought it was going to burst, her mind still unable to grasp that he was actually admitting to loving her. 'But I thought…'

'You thought what? That I'd even want to look at another woman after being with you?' Seeing her shake her head with incredulity, that look of amazed incomprehension still etched on her face, he went on, 'What is it going to take, Grace? A full admission—that I fell in love with you so long ago? That

that was what kept me driven and made me so determined to make you pay for shunning me in the way you did?' His grimace was self-deprecating. 'Although I didn't fully realise that that's what it was until I started to get to know the real Grace Tyler for myself.'

She bit her lower lip to try and contain the joy that was oozing through every last part of her, unable to quite believe that she could be the only woman in his heart—this man she adored with her whole being, with her very life.

'But you forced us to stay apart. Sleep in separate rooms. You haven't even wanted to touch me for goodness knows how long,' she added, hurting as she remembered it, and feeling surprisingly shy, in the light of having recently supplied him with a big, beautiful baby son.

'Oh, I wanted to. Believe me, I wanted to!' he stressed fervently, expressing all the torture it had cost him to exercise such restraint and self-denial. 'But it was the only way I could trust myself to keep my hands off you. After what had happened to your mother and all the problems you suffered, first with your miscarriage and then carrying Cory, I didn't want to do anything that would endanger your life or the life of our baby. I wasn't prepared to take any chances, and I knew I'd only wind up making love to you if I shared your bed.

'I also thought that it wouldn't do us any harm to cultivate some other aspects of our relationship—like trust and openness and friendship—without our very pleasurable but uncontrollable need for each other swamping everything else that we should have been sharing. I didn't consider that in doing so I was just pushing you further away from me. But I wanted you—loved you—from the moment that I first laid eyes on you in that boatyard—a haughty little snob who couldn't fight what was happening between us no matter how much she might have wanted to.'

'Was that why you bought my statue?'

'What do you think?' he said. With a wry twist of his mouth, he added, 'Although at the time I felt it gave me some kind of advantage over you to own it. But why did you sell it? It wasn't just because you didn't want to keep anything of your father's, or to get out of a financial fix, was it?'

She shook her head. Now wasn't the time for holding anything back.

'It always made me unhappy to look at it, because of the time in my life that it reminded me of. I'd treated you so badly and I was so sorry for that. When I lost the baby, the one thing that had come about because of that beautiful time we had together—and it was beautiful, no matter what I wanted you to think at the time—I thought I was being punished. And in a way I was, because that miscarriage brought home to me what was valuable in my life and what wasn't—and it certainly wasn't any of the material things I'd thought were so important to me. I knew that what *you* had were the things that really mattered—candidness. Integrity. Being true to yourself. When I thought I'd killed all those things I'd respected about you, I can't tell you how unhappy that made me.'

Lovingly she ran a hand over the gleaming gold name of the siren he had compared her with in the beginning. 'But I hadn't, had I?' she murmured wistfully. He was still the same man she had met what seemed a lifetime ago now: ambitious. Energetic. Driven. But also compassionate and tender. She liked to think, though, that she wasn't the same girl. Or at least she hoped she wasn't.

His eyes followed the slender fingers that were tracing his handiwork before he covered her hand, his fingers interlocking with hers.

'What do you think?' he breathed, pulling a wry face.

'I think I love you,' she whispered, with all the feeling in her heart, and gave a small gasp as he caught her to him.

So much time, so much love, had been wasted because

of her pride—because of his, he thought. But he intended to change all that, starting from now.

'I'll take you out in it some time,' he murmured breathlessly, alluding to the little boat he had built for her, when they finally managed to come up for air, reluctantly breaking from their desperately impassioned kiss. 'But first I need to get home and persuade Nadia that Cory and Truffle could do with some fresh air and exercise, and a bit of human-canine bonding. Because right now, Mrs Mason, I really need to avail myself of the long-awaited delights of my wife's bed.'

Excitement leaped in her as he urged her back towards the car. She hadn't imagined she could be so happy and wondered by what miracle it had all come about.

A couple of hours later, lying in his arms in the beautiful bedroom from which he had once exiled himself, she noticed him looking up at the bookcase and the figurine.

'You called me naïve and a fool that day you gave it to me,' Grace reminded him a little reproachfully, still wondering why he had said it. 'I thought it was because you realised I loved you even then, and that I still did, and that you were feeling sorry for me.'

He laughed indulgently at that. 'I must confess I started to suspect how you felt about me then, but I didn't dare hope for too much. But I called you a fool, my love, for destroying what we could have had from the beginning—and naïve because you let social differences stand in our way. I wanted to tell you how I felt that day—on your birthday—but you didn't trust me enough to talk about your feelings, and I was afraid that I might have been imagining what I wanted to believe. All I hoped was that, if I could do enough to show you how much I cared, you might eventually realise how much I loved you.'

And he had, Grace realised. In so many ways. He'd given

her everything she had ever wanted, that she could ever want: in his child; in a gentler view of her father the day he had surprised her with that figurine; with the boat this afternoon. He'd also saved the company, because shares had rocketed over the past couple of months, and he'd guaranteed her a seat on the board whenever she wanted to return.

'When I discovered I'd been your first lover, I can't begin to tell you how that made me feel. But the thought of another man holding you like this, making love to you—' his deep voice shook with something close to anguish '—when it should have been me...'

'There was only ever you,' she murmured against the dark strength of his throat, desperate that he should know that, and realising how much it would mean to him to be told.

'You mean...?' From the way his voice tailed off and those powerful arms tightened around her, she knew he was totally overwhelmed by her admission. 'You should have let me know,' he breathed at length. 'Opened up to me. Although I knew you'd never admit to loving me, that you didn't trust any man enough to allow your feelings to be exposed so completely.' He paused, then added, 'Which was why I forced you into it in the way I did this afternoon.'

'So it was all a ploy!' She thumped him on his deep bared chest, feeling the thrill of his strength, the solidity of velvet-clad muscle that made her heart race as she remembered how tenderly he used that strength in making love to her. Never had she imagined she could be so happy, or as lucky as to be given a second chance with this wonderful man. But she was, she thought ecstatically, because she knew now how much he loved her, and she also knew that she was worthy of that love. And unlike the other men she had known—Paul, her father, her grandfather—she knew instinctively that this man she cared for more than anything else in the world was never going to let her down.

'I know I should have trusted you.' She brought herself up on an elbow. 'Told you how I felt.' Lovingly she brushed back the familiarly loose strands of hair from his forehead.

'Then tell me now.'

'I love you,' she murmured, lowering her lips to his, and then, rolling on top of him, set out to prove it in the most pleasurable way she knew.

0115_INSHIP

MILLS & BOON®
By Request

RELIVE THE ROMANCE WITH THE BEST OF THE BEST

A sneak peek at next month's titles...

In stores from 20th February 2015:

- **Royal and Ruthless** – Robyn Donald, Annie West and Christina Hollis

- **At the Tycoon's Service** – Maya Banks

In stores from 6th March 2015:

- **He's the One** – Cara Colter, Barbara Hannay and Jackie Braun

- **The Australian's Bride** – Alison Roberts, Meredith Webber and Marion Lennox

---

Available at WHSmith, Tesco, Asda, Eason, Amazon and Apple

Just can't wait?
Buy our books online a month before they hit the shops!
visit www.millsandboon.co.uk

These books are also available in eBook format!

MILLS & BOON®

Why shop at millsandboon.co.uk?

Each year, thousands of romance readers find their perfect read at millsandboon.co.uk. That's because we're passionate about bringing you the very best romantic fiction. Here are some of the advantages of shopping at www.millsandboon.co.uk:

* **Get new books first**—you'll be able to buy your favourite books one month before they hit the shops

* **Get exclusive discounts**—you'll also be able to buy our specially created monthly collections, with up to 50% off the RRP

* **Find your favourite authors**—latest news, interviews and new releases for all your favourite authors and series on our website, plus ideas for what to try next

* **Join in**—once you've bought your favourite books, don't forget to register with us to rate, review and join in the discussions

Visit **www.millsandboon.co.uk**
for all this and more today!